". . . includes MORE OF THE TRUTH
    than conventional minds can bear."
                                        — *New York Post*

Tropic of Cancer was first published in Paris in 1934. Twenty-seven years later, when Henry Miller's famous novel was finally brought out in his own country, readers and critics alike hailed it as a modern American classic, a reputation it has long enjoyed abroad. "The most important book published in the United States this year" . . . "Exploding with life" . . . "Brilliantly written, shamelessly shocking" . . . "the touchstone for a generation" . . . these were some of the leading press comments. Recognition as one of the outstanding writers of our time has come late in Miller's life. Born in New York City in 1891, Miller worked at many jobs before he turned to writing. Since *Tropic of Cancer,* his first published work, he has written many other books, including *The Books in My Life, The Air Conditioned Nightmare,* and *Tropic of Capricorn,* a sequel to *Cancer.* In 1958 Miller was elected to membership in the American Institute of Arts and Letters with a citation acclaiming him as a writer whose "boldness of approach and intense curiosity concerning man and nature are unequalled in the prose literature of our time."

"TROPIC WILL BE DEFENDED BY CRITICS AS AN EXPLOSIVE CORROSIVE WHITMANESQUE MASTERPIECE (WHICH IT IS) AND ATTACKED AS AN UNBRIDLED OBSCENITY (WHICH IT IS)."   — *Life*

These novels will give way, by and by, to diaries or autobiographies—captivating books, if only a man knew how to choose among what he calls his experiences that which is really his experience, and how to record truth truly.

—*Ralph Waldo Emerson*

TROPIC OF CANCER

Henry Miller

BALLANTINE BOOKS • NEW YORK

BALLANTINE BOOKS, INC.
201 E. 50th Street, New York, N. Y. 10022

The Greatest Living Author*

I call Henry Miller the greatest living author because I think he is. I do not call him a poet because he has never written a poem; he even dislikes poetry, I think. But everything he has written is a poem in the best as well as in the broadest sense of the word. Secondly, I do not call him a writer, but an author. The writer is the fly in the ointment of modern letters; Miller has waged ceaseless war against writers. If one had to type him one might call him a Wisdom writer, Wisdom literature being a type of literature which lies between literature and scripture; it is poetry only because it rises above literature and because it sometimes ends up in bibles. I wrote to the British poet and novelist Lawrence Durrell last year and said: Let's put together a bible of Miller's work. (I thought I was being original in calling it a bible.) Let's assemble a bible from his work, I said, and put one in every hotel room in America, after removing the Gideon Bibles and placing them in the laundry chutes. Durrell, however, had been working on this "bible" for years; I was a Johnny-come-lately. In fact, a group of writers all over the world have been working on it, and one version has now come out.

There was a commonplace reason why this volume was very much needed. The author's books have been almost impossible to obtain; the ones that were not banned were stolen from libraries everywhere. Even a copy of one of the nonbanned books was recently stolen from the mails

* Copyright © 1959 by Karl Shapiro; reprinted by permission of the author and Random House. This essay first appeared in *Two Cities*, Paris, France.

en route to me. Whoever got it had better be a book lover, because it was a bibliography.

I will introduce Miller with a quotation from the *Tropic of Cancer:* "I sometimes ask myself how it happens that I attract nothing but crackbrained individuals, neurasthenics, neurotics, psychopaths—and Jews especially. There must be something in a healthy Gentile that excites the Jewish mind, like when he sees sour black bread." The "healthy Gentile" is a good sobriquet for Miller, who usually refers to himself as the Happy Rock, Caliban, "just a Brooklyn boy," "Someone who has gone off the gold standard of Literature" or—the name I like best—the Patagonian. What is a Patagonian? I don't know, but it is certainly something rare and *sui generis*. We can call Miller the greatest living Patagonian.

How is one to talk about Miller? There are authors one cannot write a book or even a good essay about. Arthur Rimbaud is one (and Miller's book on Rimbaud is one of the best books on Rimbaud ever written, although it is mostly about Henry Miller). D. H. Lawrence is another author one cannot encompass in a book "about" (Miller abandoned his book on Lawrence). And Miller himself is one of those Patagonian authors who just won't fit into a book. Every word he has ever written is autobiographical, but only in the way *Leaves of Grass* is autobiographical. There is not a word of "confession" in Miller. His amorous exploits are sometimes read as a kind of Brooklyn Casanova or male Fanny Hill, but there is probably not a word of exaggeration or boasting to speak of—or only as much as the occasion would call for. The reader can and cannot reconstruct the Life of Henry Miller from his books, for Miller never sticks to the subject any more than Lawrence does. The fact is that there isn't any subject and Miller is its poet. But a little information about him might help present him to those who need an introduction. For myself, I do not read him consecutively; I choose one of his books blindly and open it at random. I have just done this; for an example, I find: "Man is not at home in the universe, despite all the efforts of philosophers and metaphysicians to provide a soothing syrup. Thought is still a narcotic. The deepest question is *why*. And it is a forbidden one. The very asking is in the nature of cosmic sabotage. And the penalty is—the afflictions of Job." Not the greatest prose probably, but Miller is not a writer; Henry James is a writer. Miller is a talker, a street corner gabbler, a prophet, and a Patagonian.

What are the facts about Miller? I'm not sure how important they are. He was born in Brooklyn about 1890, of German ancestry, and in certain ways he is quite German. I have often thought that the Germans make the best Americans, though they certainly make the worst Germans. Miller understands the German in himself and in America. He compares Whitman and Goethe: "In Whitman the whole American scene comes to life, her past and her future, her birth and her death. Whatever there is of value in America Whitman has expressed, and there is nothing more to be said. The future belongs to the machine, to the robots. He was the Poet of the Body and the Soul, Whitman. The first and the last poet. He is almost undecipherable today, a monument covered with rude hieroglyphs, for which there is no key. . . . There is no equivalent in the languages of Europe for the spirit which he immortalized. Europe is saturated with art and her soil is full of dead bones and her museums are bursting with plundered treasures, but what Europe has never had is a free, healthy spirit, what you might call a MAN. Goethe was the nearest approach, but Goethe was a stuffed shirt, by comparison. Goethe was a respectable citizen, a pedant, a bore, a universal spirit, but stamped with the German trademark, with the double eagle. The serenity of Goethe, the calm, Olympian attitude, is nothing more than the drowsy stupor of a German bourgeois deity. Goethe is an end of something, Whitman is a beginning."

If anybody can decipher the Whitman key it is Miller. Miller is the twentieth-century reincarnation of Whitman. But to return to the "facts." The Brooklyn Boy went to a Brooklyn high school in a day when most high schools kept higher standards than most American universities today. He started at CCNY but quit almost immediately and went to work for a cement company ("Everlasting Cement"), then for a telegraph company, where he became the personnel manager in the biggest city in the world. The telegraph company is called the Cosmodemonic Telegraph Company in Miller's books, or in moments of gaiety the Cosmococcic Telegraph Company. One day while the vice-president was bawling him out he mentioned to Miller that he would like to see someone write a sort of Horatio Alger book about the messengers.

I thought to myself [said Miller]—you poor old futzer, you, just wait until I get it off my chest. . . . I'll give you an Horatio Alger book. . . . My head was in a whirl to leave his office. I saw the army of men, women and children that had passed through my hands, saw them weeping, begging, beseeching, imploring, cursing, spitting, fuming, threatening. I saw the tracks they left on the highways, lying on the floor of freight trains, the parents in rags, the coal box empty, the sink running over, the walls sweating and between the cold beads of sweat the cockroaches running like mad; I saw them hobbling along like twisted gnomes or falling backwards in the epileptic frenzy. . . . I saw the walls giving way and the pest pouring out like a winged fluid, and the men higher up with their iron-clad logic, waiting for it to blow over, waiting for everything to be patched up, waiting, waiting contentedly . . . saying that things were temporarily out of order. I saw the Horatio Alger hero, the dream of a sick America, mounting higher and higher, first messenger, then operator, then manager, then chief, then superintendent, then vice-president, then president, then trust magnate, then beer baron, then Lord of all the Americas, the money god, the god of gods, the clay of clay, nullity on high, zero with ninety-seven thousand decimals fore and aft. . . . I will give you Horatio Alger as he looks the day after the Apocalypse, when all the stink has cleared away.

And he did. Miller's first book, *Tropic of Cancer,* was published in Paris in 1934 and was immediately famous and immediately banned in all English-speaking countries. It is the Horatio Alger story with a vengeance. Miller had walked out of the Cosmodemonic Telegraph Company one day without a word; ever after he lived on his wits. He had managed to get to Paris on ten dollars, where he lived more than a decade, not during the gay prosperous twenties but during the Great Depression. He starved, made friends by the score, mastered the French language and his own. It was not until the Second World War broke out that he returned to American to live at Big Sur, California. Among his best books several were banned: the two *Tropics* (*Tropic of Cancer,* 1934, and *Tropic of Capricorn,* 1939); *Black Spring,* 1936; and part of the trilogy *The Rosy Crucifixion* (including *Sexus, Plexus,* and *Nexus*).

Unfortunately for Miller he has been a man without honor in his own country and in his own language. When *Tropic of Cancer* was published he was even denied entrance into England, held over in custody by the port authorities and returned to France by the next boat. He made friends with his jailer and wrote a charming essay about him. But Miller has no sense of despair. At the beginning of *Tropic of Cancer* he writes: "I have no money, no resources, no hopes. I am the happiest man alive."

George Orwell was one of the few English critics who saw his worth, though (*mirabile dictu*) T. S. Eliot and even Ezra Pond complimented him. Pound in his usual ungracious manner gave the *Tropic of Cancer* to a friend who later became Miller's publisher, and said: Here is a dirty book worth reading. Pound even went so far as to try to enlist Miller in his economic system to save the world. Miller retaliated by writing a satire called *Money and How It Gets That Way,* dedicated to Ezra Pound. The acquaintanceship halted there, Miller's view of money being something like this (from *Tropic of Capricorn*): "To walk in money through the night crowd, protected by money, lulled by money, dulled by money, the crowd itself a money, the breath money, no least single object anywhere that is not money, money, money everywhere and still not enough, and then no money, or a little money or less money or more money, but money, always money, and if you have money or you don't have money it is the money that counts and money makes money, *but what makes money make money?*" Pound didn't care for that brand of economics.

But all the writers jostled each other to welcome Miller among the elect, for the moment at least: Eliot, Herbert Read, Aldous Huxley, John Dos Passos and among them some who really knew how good Miller was: William Carlos Williams, who called him the Dean, Lawrence Durrell, Paul Rosenfeld, Wallace Fowlie, Osbert Sitwell, Kenneth Patchen, many painters (Miller is a fanatical water colorist). But mostly he is beset by his neurasthenics and psychopaths, as any cosmodemonic poet must be. People of all sexes frequently turn up at Big Spur and announce that they want to join the Sex Cult. Miller gives them bus fare and a good dinner and sends them on their way.

Orwell has written one of the best essays on Miller, although he takes a sociological approach and tries to place Miller as a Depression writer or something of the sort. What astonished Orwell about Miller was the difference between his view and the existential bitterness of a novelist like Céline. Céline's *Voyage au bout de la Nuit* describes the meaninglessness of modern life and is thus a prototype of twentieth-century fiction. Orwell calls Céline's book a cry of unbearable disgust, a voice from the cesspool. And Orwell adds that the *Tropic of Cancer* is almost exactly the opposite! Such a thing as Miller's book "has become so unusual as to seem almost anomalous, [for] it is the book of a man who is happy." Miller also reached the bottom of the pit, as many writers do; but how, Orwell asks, could he have emerged unembittered, whole, laughing with joy? "Exactly the aspects of life that fill Céline with horror are the ones that appeal to him. So far from protesting, he is *accepting*. And the very word 'acceptance' calls up his real affinity, another American, Walt Whitman."

This is, indeed, the crux of the matter and it is unfortunate that Orwell cannot see past the socio-economic situation with Whitman and Miller. Nevertheless, this English critic recognizes Miller's mastery of his material and places him among the great writers of our age; more than that, he predicts that Miller will set the pace and attitude for the novelist of the future. This has not happened yet, but I agree that it must. Miller's influence today is primarily among poets; those poets who follow Whitman must necessarily follow Miller, even to the extent of giving up poetry in its formal sense and writing that personal apocalyptic prose which Miller does. It is the prose of the Bible of Hell that Blake talked about and Arthur Rimbaud wrote a chapter of.

What is this "acceptance" Orwell mentions in regard to Whitman and Henry Miller? On one level it is the poetry of cosmic consciousness, and on the most obvious level it is the poetry of the Romantic nineteenth century. Miller is unknown in this country because he represents the Continental rather than the English influence. He breaks with the English literary tradition just as many of the twentieth-century Americans do, because his ancestry is not British, and not American colonial. He does not read the favored British writers, Milton, Marlowe, Pope, Donne. He reads what his grandparents knew was in the air when Victorianism was the genius of British poetry. He grew up with books by Dostoevski, Knut Hamsun, Strindberg, Nietzsche (especially Nietzsche), Élie Faure, Spengler. Like a true poet he found his way to Rimbaud, Ramakrishna, Blavatsky, Huysmans, Count Keyserling, Prince Kropotkin, Lao-tse, Nostradamus, Petronius, Rabelais, Suzuki, Zen philosophy, Van Gogh. And in English he let himself be influenced not by the solid classics but by *Alice in Wonderland*, Chesterton's *St. Francis*, Conrad, Cooper, Emerson, Rider Haggard, G. A. Henty (the boy's historian—I remember being told when I was a boy that Henty had the facts all wrong), Joyce, Arthur Machen, Mencken, John Cowper Powys, Herbert Spencer's *Autobiography*, Thoreau on Civil Disobedience, Emma Goldman—the great an-

archist (whom he met)—Whitman, of course, and perhaps above all that companion piece to *Leaves of Grass*
called *Huckleberry Finn*. Hardly a Great Books list from
the shores of Lake Michigan—almost a period list. Miller
will introduce his readers to strange masterpieces like
Doughty's *Arabia Deserta* or to the journal of Anaïs Nin
which has never been published but which he (and other
writers) swears is one of the masterpieces of the twentieth
century. I imagine that Miller has read as much as any
man living but he does not have that religious solemnity
about books which we are brought up in. Books, after all,
are only mnemonic devices; and poets are always celebrating the burning of libraries. And as with libraries,
so with monuments, and as with monuments, so with civ-
ilizations. But in Miller's case (*chez* Miller) there is no
vindictiveness, no bitterness. Orwell was bothered when
he met Miller because Miller didn't want to go to the
Spanish Civil War and do battle on one side or the other.
Miller is an anarchist of sorts, and he doesn't especially
care which dog eats which dog. As it happens, the righteous Loyalists were eaten by the Communists and the
righteous Falangists were eaten by the Nazis over the
most decadent hole in Europe; so Miller was right.

Lawrence Durrell has said that the *Tropic* books were
healthy while Céline and D. H. Lawrence were sick.
Lawrence never escaped his puritanism and it is his heroic
try that makes us honor him. Céline is the typical European man of despair—why should he not despair, this
Frenchman of the trenches of World War I? We are
raising up a generation of young American Célines, I'm
afraid, but Miller's generation still had Whitman before
its eyes and was not running back to the potholes and ash
heaps of Europe. Miller is as good an antiquarian as anybody; in the medieval towns of France he goes wild with
happiness; and he has written one of the best "travel
books" on Greece ever done (the critics are unanimous
about the *Colossus of Maroussi*); but to worship the "tradition" is to him the sheerest absurdity. Like most Americans, he shares the view of the first Henry Ford that his-

tory is bunk. He cannot forgive his "Nordic" ancestors
for the doctrines of righteousness and cleanliness. His
people, he says, were painfully clean: "Never once had
they opened the door which leads to the soul; never once
did they dream of taking a blind leap into the dark. After
dinner the dishes were promptly washed and put in the
closet; after the paper was read it was neatly folded and
laid on a shelf; after the clothes were washed they were
ironed and folded and then tucked away in the drawers.
Everything was for tomorrow, but tomorrow never
came. The present was only a bridge and on this bridge
they are still groaning, as the world groans, and not one
idiot ever thinks of blowing up the bridge." As everyone
knows, Cleanliness is the chief American industry. Miller
is the most formidable anticleanliness poet since Walt
Whitman, and his hatred of righteousness is also American, with the Americanism of Thoreau, Whitman, and
Emma Goldman. Miller writes a good deal about cooking
and wine drinking. Americans are the worst cooks in the
world, outside of the British; and Americans are also great
drunkards who know nothing about wine. The Ger-
manic-American Miller reintroduces good food and decent wine into our literature. One of his funniest essays
is about the American loaf of bread, the poisonous loaf
of cleanliness wrapped in cellophane, the manufacture of
which is a heavy industry like steel.

Orwell and other critics tend to regard Miller as a kind
of hedonist and professional do-nothing. And morally,
they tend to regard him as one of that illustrious line of
Americans who undermine the foundations of traditional
morals. Miller quotes Thoreau's statement, which might
almost be the motto of the cosmic writer: "Most of what
my neighbors call good, I am profoundly convinced is
evil, and if I repent anything, it is my good conduct that I
repent." One could hardly call Thoreau a criminal, yet
he had his run-ins with the law, just as Miller has, and for
the same reasons. The strain of anarchism and amorality
is growing stronger in American literature, or that branch
of it that I am talking about, and Miller is one of its chief

carriers. It is not only Emma Goldman, Thoreau, Mark Twain, Whitman, and perhaps Salinger and Mailer, but that whole literature of Detachment from political hysteria and over-organization. I am influenced enough by these people and by Miller to tell my students, the poets at least, to cultivate an ignorance of contemporary political and military events because they do not matter. I tell them not to vote, to join nothing. I try to steer them toward their true leaders and visionaries, men almost unknown in the polite literary world, Reich for instance. Wilhelm Reich furthered a movement in Germany called "Work Democracy"; not machine politics, no politics at all, but democracy within one's immediate orbit; democracy at home. America is still the only country where social idealism and experimentation have elbow room; there are still communities that practice primitive Christianity, such as the Catholic anarchists; and just plain little homemade gardens of Eden such as Miller's cliff at Big Sur. The life he describes in *Big Sur and the Oranges of Hieronymus Bosch* is a far cry from the little fascist dreams of the New Classicists. And it is a far cry from the bitter isolationism of Robinson Jeffers or even of Lawrence. Morally I regard Miller as a holy man, as most of his adherents do—Gandhi with a penis.

Miller says in a little essay on Immorality and Morality: "What is moral and what is immoral? Nobody can ever answer this question satisfactorily. Not because morals ceaselessly evolve, but because the principle on which they depend is factitious. Morality is for slaves, for beings without spirit. And when I say spirit I mean the Holy Spirit." And he ends this little piece with a quotation from ancient Hindu scripture: Evil does not exist.

Whitman, Lawrence, Miller, and even Blake all have the reputation of being sex-obsessed, Miller especially. Whereas Whitman writes "copulation is no more rank to me than death is," Miller writes hundreds of pages describing in the minutest and clearest detail his exploits in bed. Every serious reader of erotica has remarked about Miller that he is probably the only author in history who writes about such things with complete ease and naturalness. Lawrence never quite rid himself of his puritanical salaciousness, nor Joyce; both had too much religion in their veins. It is funny to recollect that Lawrence thought *Ulysses* a smutty book and Joyce thought *Lady Chatterley* a smutty book. Both were right. But at least they *tried* to free themselves from literary morality. Miller's achievement is miraculous: he is screamingly funny without making fun of sex, the way Rabelais does. (Rabelais is, of course, magnificent; so is Boccaccio; but both write against the background of religion, like Joyce and Lawrence.) Miller is accurate and poetic in the highest degree; there is not a smirk anywhere in his writings. Miller undoubtedly profited from the mistakes of his predecessors; his aim was not to write about the erotic but to write the whole truth about the life he knew. This goal demanded the full vocabulary and iconography of sex, and it is possible that he is the first writer outside the Orient who has succeeded in writing as naturally about sex on a large scale as novelists ordinarily write about the dinner table or the battlefield. I think only an American could have performed this feat.

We are dealing with the serious question of banned books, burned books, and fear of books in general. America has the most liberal censorship laws in the West today, but we have done no more than make a start. I have always been amused by the famous decision of Judge Woolsey who lifted the ban on *Ulysses*, although it was certainly a fine thing to do and it is a landmark we can be proud of. Woolsey said various comical things, such as that he could not detect the "leer of the sensualist" in Joyce's book, and that therefore (the logic of it escapes me) it is not pornographic. In excusing the use of old Saxon words he noted that Joyce's "locale was Celtic and his season Spring." And, in order to push his decision through, Judge Woolsey stated that *Ulysses* "did not tend to excite sexual impulses or lustful thoughts," and he closed his argument with the elegant statement that although the book is "somewhat emetic, nowhere does it tend to be an aphrodisiac." Emetic means tending to produce vomiting and I doubt that Joyce savored that description of his masterpiece. The implication, of course, is that vomiting is good for you, and lustful thoughts not. Now everyone who has read *Ulysses* knows that the book is based largely on the lustful thoughts and acts of its characters and that Joyce spared no pains to represent these thoughts and deeds richly and smackingly. *Ulysses* is, since the Judge used the word, a pretty *good* aphrodisiac, partly because of Joyce's own religious tensions. Miller, on the other hand, is no aphrodisiac at all, because religious or so-called moral tension does not exist for him. When one of Miller's characters lusts, he lusts out loud and then proceeds to the business at hand. Joyce actually prevents himself from experiencing the beauty of sex or lust, while Miller is freed at the outset to deal with the overpowering mysteries and glories of love and copulation. Like other Millerites I claim that Miller is one of the few healthy Americans alive today; further, that the circulation of his books would do more to wipe out the obscenities of Broadway, Hollywood, and Madison Avenue than a full-scale social revolution.

Miller has furthered literature for all writers by ignoring the art forms, the novel, the poem, the drama, and by sticking to the autobiographical novel. He says in *The Books in My Life* (one of the available works), "The autobiographical novel, which Emerson predicted would grow in importance with time, has replaced the great confessions. It is not a mixture of truth and fiction, this genre of literature, but an expansion and deepening of truth. It is more authentic, more veridical, than the diary. It is not the flimsy truth of facts which the authors of these autobiographical novels offer but the truth of emotion, reflection and understanding, truth digested and assimilated. The being revealing himself does so on all levels simultaneously." Everything Miller has written is part of this great amorphous autobiographical novel and it must be read not entirely but in large chunks to make sense. Many of the individual works are whole in themselves, one dealing with his life in Paris, one with his life as a New Yorker, and there is, in fact, a definite span of years encompassed in the works. But the volumes of essays are also part of the story and there is no way to make a whole out of the parts. Miller is easy to quote if one quotes carefully; the danger is that one can find massive contradictions, unless there is some awareness of the underlying world and the cosmic attitudes of the author. These views are by no means unique, as they are the same as those of all those poets and mystics I referred to in a previous essay. What makes Miller unique is his time and place; he is the only American of our time who has given us a full-scale interpretation of modern America, other than the kind we find in the cultural journals. Incidentally, we do not find Miller in these journals, which, presuming an interest in letters and art, are really organs of social and political opinion.

Readers of Whitman recall that Whitman was blistering about the materialism of this country a century ago, and its departure from the ideals of the founding fathers. Miller is worse. Now it is a commonplace of modern poetry that the poet dissociates himself from life as it is lived by the average American today. Whitman and Miller heap abuse on the failure of the country to live up to its promise. Miller writes as a poet about the demonic hideousness of New York City, Chicago, the South, or he rhapsodizes when there is anything to be rapturous about. But it is not Art that he cares about; it is man, man's treatment of man in America and man's treatment of nature. What we get in Miller is not a sense of superiority but fury, even the fury of the prophet of doom.

Miller knows America from the bottom up and from coast to coast. In the same way he knows Paris as few Frenchmen do. But when Miller describes slums it is usually with the joyous eye of the artist, not with the self-righteous sneer of the social reformer. Here, too, one might describe his psychology as "Oriental" rather than modern. The cultural situation is a matter of complete indifference to him. Miller frequently immerses himself in such modern Indian mystics as Krishnamurti and Ramakrishna, but without any of the flapdoodle of the cultist. He is himself one of the foremost of the contemporary men of Detachment. His influence (like that of Lawrence) comes as much from his life as from his writings. Here it is better to quote. This is Myrtle Avenue in Brooklyn.

But I saw a street called Myrtle Avenue, which runs from Borough Hall to Fresh Pond Road, and down this street no saint ever walked (else it would have crumbled), down this street no miracle ever passed, nor any poet, nor any species of human genius, nor did any flower ever grow there, nor did the sun strike it squarely, nor did the rain ever wash it. For the genuine Inferno which I had to postpone for twenty years I give you Myrtle Avenue, one of the innumerable bridlepaths ridden by iron monsters which lead to the heart of America's emptiness. If you have only seen Essen or Manchester or Chicago or Levallois-Perret or Glasgow or Hoboken or Canarsie or Bayonne you have seen nothing of the magnificent emptiness of progress and enlightenment. Dear reader, you must see Myrtle Avenue before you die, if only to realize how far into the future Dante saw. You must believe me that on this street, neither in the houses which line it, nor the cobblestones which pave it, nor the elevated structure which cuts it atwain, neither in any creature that bears a name and lives thereon, neither in any animal, bird or insect passing through it to slaughter or already slaughtered, is there hope of "lubet," "sublimate" or "abominate." It is a street not of sorrow, for sorrow would be human and recognizable, but of sheer emptiness: it is emptier than the most extinct volcano, emptier than a vacuum, emptier than the word God in the mouth of an unbeliever.

This is a man describing his own neighborhood, but the street is a type that runs from the Atlantic to the Pacific, with variations:

The whole country is lawless, violent, explosive, demoniacal. It's in the air, in the climate, in the ultra-grandiose landscape, in the stone forests that are lying horizontal, in the torrential rivers that bite through the rock canyons, in the supranormal distances, the supernal arid wastes, the over-lush crops, the monstrous fruits, the mixture of quixotic bloods, the fatras of cults, sects, beliefs, the opposition of laws and languages, the contradictoriness of temperaments, needs, requirements. The continent is full of buried violence, of the bones of antediluvian monsters and of lost races of man, of mysteries which are wrapped in doom. The atmosphere is at times so electrical that the soul is summoned out of its body and runs amok. Like the rain everything comes in bucketsful—or not at all. The whole continent is a huge volcano whose crater is temporarily concealed by a moving panorama which is partly dream, partly fear, partly despair. From Alaska to Yucatan it's the same story. Nature dominates, Nature wins out. Everywhere the same fundamental urge to slay, to ravage, to plunder. Outwardly they seem like a fine, upstanding people—healthy, optimistic, courageous. Inwardly they are filled with worms. A tiny spark and they blow up.

The passages on Times Square repeat and catalogue, like Whitman; they are a little too painful to read out of context. Here is a bit of Chicago; Miller is wandering in the Negro slums with a fellow visitor:

We got into the car, rode a few blocks and got out to visit another shell crater. The street was deserted except for some chickens grubbing for food between the slats of a crumbling piazza. More vacant lots, more gutted houses; fire escapes clinging to the walls with their iron teeth, like drunken acrobats. A Sunday atmosphere here. Everything serene and peaceful. Like Louvain or Rheims between bombardments. Like Phoebus, Virginia, dreaming of bringing her steeds to water, or like modern Eleusis smothered by a wet sock. Then suddenly I saw it chalked up on the side of a house in letters ten feet high:

GOOD NEWS! GOD IS LOVE!

When I saw these words I got down on my knees in the open sewer which had been conveniently placed there for the purpose and I offered up a short prayer, a silent one, which must have registered as far as Mound City, Illinois, where the colored muskrats have built their igloos. It was time for a

good stiff drink of cod-liver oil but as the varnish factories
were all closed we had to repair to the abattoir and quaff a
bucket of blood. Never has blood tasted so wonderful! It was
like taking Vitamins A, B, C, D, E in quick succession and
then chewing a stick of cold dynamite. Good news! Aye,
wonderful news—for Chicago. I ordered the chauffeur to take
us immediately to Mundelein so that I could bless the cardinal and all the real estate operations, but we only got as far
as the Bahai Temple. . . .

Or, again—in explanation:

Oh, Henry, what beautiful golden teeth you have! exclaimed my four-year-old daughter the other morning on
climbing into bed with me. That's how I approach the works
of my confreres. I see how beautiful are their golden teeth,
not how ugly or artificial they are.

Combating the "system" is nonsense. There is only one
aim in life and that is to live it. In America it has become
impossible, except for a few lucky or wise people, to live
one's own life; consequently the poets and artists tend
to move to the fringes of society. Wherever there are individuals, says Miller (like Thoreau), there are new
frontiers. The American way of life has become illusory;
we lead the lives of prisoners while we boast about free
speech, free press, and free religion, none of which we
actually do enjoy in full. The price for security has become too great; abundance has become a travesty. The
only thing for nonenslaved man to do is to move out to
the edge, lose contact with the machines of organization
which are as ubiquitous in this country as in Russia. "Instead of bucking your head against a stone wall, sit quietly
with hands folded and wait for the walls to crumble. . . .
Don't sit and *pray* that it will happen! Just sit and *watch*
it happen!" These sayings the culture *littérateur* con-
demns as irresponsible. Miller follows through with the
complete program of nonparticipation in our machine
society, which is organized from the cradle to the grave.
"Just as Gandhi successfully exploited the doctrine of

nonresistance, these 'saints of the just' practiced non-recognition—nonrecognition of sin, guilt, fear and disease . . . even death." Whitman also believed in nonrecognition of death. His view of death as part of life is one of the many reasons for his unpopularity in America, where death is considered a crime against society. "Why try to solve a problem? *Dissolve* it! [says Miller]. Fear not to be a coward, a traitor, a renegade. In this universe of ours there is room for all, perhaps even need for all. The sun does not inquire about rank and status before shedding its warmth; the cyclone levels the godly and the ungodly; the government takes your tax money even though it be tainted. Nor is the atom bomb a respecter of persons. Perhaps that is why the righteous are squirming so!"

All of this is about modern America and the high cost of security. Do we really have a high standard of living? Miller says not, as most poets do. If living means appreciation of life we have the lowest standard of living in the world, in spite of the fact that it costs more to live in America than in any country in the world. Miller says "the cost is not only in dollars and cents but in sweat and blood, in frustration, ennui, broken homes, smashed ideals, illness and insanity. We have the most wonderful hospitals, the most fabulous prisons, the best equipped and highest paid army and navy, the speediest bombers, the largest stockpile of atom bombs, yet never enough of any of these items to satisfy the demand. Our manual workers are the highest paid in the world; our poets the worst. . . ."

And Miller gives this answer, letting Krishnamurti say it:

The world problem is the individual problem; if the individual is at peace, has happiness, has great tolerance, and an intense desire to help, then the world problem as such ceases to exist. You consider the world problem before you have considered your own problem. Before you have established peace and understanding in your own hearts and in your own minds you desire to establish peace and tranquility in the minds of others, in your nations and in your states;

whereas peace and understanding will only come when there is understanding, certainty and strength in yourselves.

To place the individual before the state, whether the Russian state or the American state, is the first need of modern man. To interpret Miller, man is like the common soldier on the battlefield; he can know nothing of the battle at large or of its causes; he can know only the fifty feet or so in his immediate vicinity; within that radius he is a man responsible for himself and his fellows; beyond that he is powerless. Modern life, having made everyone state conscious, has destroyed the individual. America has as few individuals today as Russia, and as many taboos to keep the individual from coming to life as the USSR. First, we have contaminated the idea of society; second, we have contaminated the idea of community. Miller writing about his little community at Big Sur frowns on the idea of community itself. "To create community— and what is a nation, or a people, without a sense of community—there must be a common purpose. Even here in Big Sur, where the oranges are ready to blossom forth, there is no common purpose, no common effort. There is a remarkable neighborliness, but no community spirit. We have a Grange, as do other rural communities, but what is a 'Grange' in the life of man? The real workers are outside the Grange. Just as the 'real men of God' are outside the Church. And the real leaders outside the world of politics."

"We create our fate," says Miller. And better still: "Forget, forgive, renounce, abdicate." And "scrap the past instantly." Live the good life instantly; it's now or never, and always has been.

Miller is "irresponsible" as far as officials and popular politics go, or as far as common church morality goes, and as far as literary manners go. But he is not a poseur, he has no program, yet he has a deep and pure sense of morality. I would call him a total revolutionary, the man who will settle for nothing less than "Christmas on earth." In his remarkable study of Rimbaud, a prose-poem of one hundred and fifty pages called *The Time of the Assassins*, Miller discourses on the spiritual suicide of modern youth.

I like to think of him as the one who extended the boundaries of that only partially explored domain. Youth ends where manhood begins, it is said. A phrase without meaning, since from the beginning of history man has never enjoyed the full measure of youth or known the limitless possibilities of adulthood. How can one know the splendor and fullness of youth if one's energies are consumed in combating the errors and falsities of parents and ancestors? Is youth to waste its strength unlocking the grip of death? Is youth's only mission on earth to rebel, to destroy, to assassinate? Is youth only to be offered up to sacrifice? What of the *dreams* of youth? Are they always to be regarded as follies? Are they to be populated only with chimeras? . . . Stifle or deform youth's dreams and you destroy the creator. Where there has been no real youth there can be no real manhood. If society has come to resemble a collection of deformities, is it not the work of our educators and preceptors? Today, as yesterday, the youth who would live his own life has no place to turn, no place to live his youth unless, retiring into his chrysalis, he closes all apertures and buries himself alive. The conception of our mother the earth being "an egg which doth contain all good things in it" has undergone a profound change. The cosmic egg contains an addled yolk. This is the present view of mother earth. The psychoanalysts have traced the poison back to the womb, but to what avail? In the light of this profound discovery we are given permission . . . to step from one rotten egg into another. . . . Why breed new monsters of negation and futility? Let society scotch its own rotten corpse! Let us have a new heaven and a new earth!—that was the sense of Rimbaud's obstinate revolt.

Miller calls for an end to revolt once and for all. His message is precisely that of Whitman, of Rimbaud, of Rilke: "Everything we are taught is false"; and "Change your life." As a writer Miller may be second- or third-rate or of no rating at all; as a spiritual example he stands among the great men of our age. Will this ever be recognized? Not in our time probably.

The Rimbaud book ends with a Coda, a little recital of the literature of despair which has surrounded us for a hundred years. Listen to it.

Rimbaud was born in the middle of the nineteenth century, October 20th, 1854, at 6:00 A.M., it is said. A century of unrest, of materialism, and of "progress," as we say. Purgatorial in every sense of the word, and the writers who flourished in that period reflect this ominously. Wars and revolutions were abundant. Russia alone, we are told, waged thirty-three wars (mostly of conquest) during the eighteenth and the nineteenth centuries. Shortly after Rimbaud is born his father is off to the Crimean War. So is Tolstoy. The revolution in 1848, of brief duration but full of consequences, is followed by the bloody Commune of 1871, which Rimbaud as a boy is thought to have participated in. In 1848 we in America are fighting the Mexicans with whom we are now great friends, though the Mexicans are not too sure of it. During this war Thoreau makes his famous speech on Civil Disobedience, a document which will one day be added to the Emancipation Proclamation. . . . Twelve years later the Civil War breaks out, perhaps the bloodiest of all civil wars. . . . From 1874 until his death in 1881 Amiel is writing his *Journal Intime* . . . which . . . gives a thoroughgoing analysis of the moral dilemma in which the creative spirits of the time found themselves. The very titles of the books written by influential writers of the nineteenth century are revelatory. I give just a few . . . *The Sickness unto Death* (Kierkegaard), *Dreams and Life* (Gérard de Nerval), *Les Fleurs du Mal* (Baudelaire), *Les Chants de Maldoror* (Lautréamont), *The Birth of Tragedy* (Nietzsche), *La Bête Humaine* (Zola), *Hunger* (Knut Hamsun), *Les Lauriers Sont Coupés* (Dujardin), *The Conquest of Bread* (Kropotkin), *Looking Backward* (Edward Bellamy), *Alice in Wonderland, The Serpent in Paradise* (Sacher-Masoch), *Les Paradis Artificiels* (Baudelaire), *Dead Souls* (Gogol), *The House of the Dead* (Dostoevski), *The Wild Duck* (Ibsen), *The Inferno* (Strindberg), *The Nether World* (Gissing), *A Rebours* (Huysmans). . . .

Goethe's *Faust* was not so very old when Rimbaud asked a friend for a copy of it. Remember the date of his birth is

October 20th, 1854 (6:00 A.M. Western Standard Diabolical Time). The very next year, 1855, *Leaves of Grass* makes its appearance, followed by condemnation and suppression. Meanwhile *Moby Dick* had come out (1851) and Thoreau's *Walden* (1854). In 1855 Gérard de Nerval commits suicide, having lasted till the remarkable age of 47. In 1854 Kierkegaard is already penning his last words to history in which he gives the parable of "The Sacrificed Ones." Just four or five years before Rimbaud completes *A Season in Hell* (1873), Lautréamont publishes his celebrated piece of blasphemy, another "work of youth," as we say, in order not to take these heartbreaking testaments seriously. . . . By 1888 Nietzsche is explaining to Brandes that he can now boast three readers: Brandes, Taine, and Strindberg. The next year he goes mad and remains that way until his death in 1900. Lucky man! From 1893 to 1897 Strindberg is experiencing a *crise* . . . which he describes with magisterial effects in *The Inferno*. Reminiscent of Rimbaud is the title of another of his works: *The Keys to Paradise*. In 1888 comes Dujardin's curious little book, forgotten until recently. . . . By this time Mark Twain is at his height, *Huckleberry Finn* having appeared in 1884, the same year as *Against the Grain* of Huysmans. . . . By the fall of 1891 Gissing's *New Grub Street* is launched. It is an interesting year in nineteenth-century literature, the year of Rimbaud's death. . . .

What a century of names! . . . Shelley, Blake, Stendhal, Hegel, Fechner, Emerson, Poe, Schopenhauer, Max Stirner, Mallarmé, Chekov, Andreyev, Verlaine, Couperus, Maeterlinck, Madame Blavatsky, Samuel Butler, Claudel, Unamuno, Conrad, Bakunin, Shaw, Rilke, Stefan George, Verhaeren, Gautier, Léon Bloy, Balzac, Yeats. . . .

What revolt, what disillusionment, what longing! Nothing but crises, breakdowns, hallucinations and visions. The foundations of politics, morals, economics, and art tremble. The air is full of warnings and prophecies of the debacle to come —and in the twentieth century it comes! Already two World Wars and a promise of more before the century is out. Have we touched bottom? Not yet. The moral crisis of the nineteenth century has merely given way to the spiritual bankruptcy of the twentieth. It is "the time of the assassins" and no mistaking it. . . .

Rimbaud is indeed the symbol of the death of modern poetry. This seer, this visionary deserts poetry at the age of eighteen to make money, by gunrunning, even by slave-trading, ending with a death-bed conversion. His is a life of slander, beginning with the motto "Death to God" chalked on the church and ending with extreme unction and the money belt under the bed. I think the message of Rimbaud to Miller is the death of poetry, the death of history. The whole romantic agony of the nineteenth century is summed up in this adolescent genius, a curse laid on us. Miller obliterates the curse; he pronounces the benediction over Rimbaud, over the death of poetry, over the death of civilization itself but with a side-splitting laugh without an iota of animosity in it. Miller leads us away from the charnel house of nineteenth-century poetry; he does not even recognize the existence of twentieth-century poetry. For poetry has lost its significance, its relevance, and even its meaning in our time. To begin again it must repair to the wilderness, outside society, outside the city gates, a million miles from books and their keepers. Almost alone of the writers of our time Henry Miller has done this; I would guess that his following is enormous and that it is just beginning to grow. Like Nietzsche, like Lawrence, his word somehow spreads abroad and somehow cleanses the atmosphere of the mind of its age-old detritus of tradition, its habits of despair, its hates.

One word more: at the close of his beautiful clown story, "The Smile at the Foot of the Ladder," Miller talks about the clown, the hero of so much of the best contemporary literature.

Joy is like a river [says Miller], it flows ceaselessly. It seems to me that this is the message which the clown is trying to convey to us, that we should participate through ceaseless flow and movement, that we should not stop to reflect, compare, analyze, possess, but flow on and through, endlessly, like music. This is the gift of surrender, and the clown makes it symbolically. It is for us to make it real.

At no time in the history of man has the world been so full of pain and anguish. Here and there, however, we meet with individuals who are untouched, unsullied, by the common grief. They are not heartless individuals, far from it! They are emancipated beings. For them the world is not what it seems to us. They see with other eyes. We say of them that they have died to the world. They live in the moment, fully, and the radiance which emanates from them is a perpetual song of joy.

And Miller is certainly one of these who have died to the world, like the clown. The ponderous absurdities of modern literature and the world it perpetuates dissolve in the hilarities of this almost unknown American author; this poet who dissociates himself from the so-called modern age and whose one aim is to give literature back to life. There are not many of these emancipated beings left in our world, these clowns and clairvoyants, celebrants of the soul and of the flesh and of the still-remaining promise of America. And of these few great souls the greatest is—the Patagonian.

—Karl Shapiro

Preface

Here is a book which, if such a thing were possible, might restore our appetite for the fundamental realities. The predominant note will seem one of bitterness, and bitterness there is, to the full. But there is also a wild extravagance, a mad gaiety, a verve, a gusto, at times almost a delirium. A continual oscillation between extremes, with bare stretches that taste like brass and leave the full flavor of emptiness. It is beyond optimism or pessimism. The author has given us the last *frisson*. Pain has no more secret recesses.

In a world grown paralyzed with introspection and constipated by delicate mental meals this brutal exposure of the substantial body comes as a vitalizing current of blood. The violence and obscenity are left unadulterated, as manifestation of the mystery and pain which ever accompanies the act of creation.

The restorative value of experience, prime source of wisdom and creation, is reasserted. There remain waste areas of unfinished thought and action, a bundle of shreds and fibers with which the overcritical may strangle themselves. Referring to his *Wilhelm Meister* Goethe once said: "People seek a central point: that is hard, and not even right. I should think a rich, manifold life, brought close to our eyes, would be enough without any express tendency; which, after all, is only for the intellect."

The book is sustained on its own axis by the pure flux and rotation of events. Just as there is no central point, so also there is no question of heroism or of struggle since there is no question of will, but only an obedience to flow.

The gross caricatures are perhaps more vital, "more true to life," than the full portraits of the conventional novel for the reason that the individual today has no centrality and produces not the slightest illusion of wholeness. The characters are integrated to the false, cultural void in which we are drowning; thus is produced the illusion of chaos, to face which requires the ultimate courage.

The humiliations and defeats, given with a primitive honesty, end not in frustration, despair, or futility, but in hunger, an ecstatic, devouring hunger—*for more life.* The poetic is discovered by stripping away the vestiture of art; by descending to what might be styled "a pre-artistic level," the durable skeleton of form which is hidden in the phenomena of disintegration reappears to be transfigured again in the ever-changing flesh of emotion. The scars are burned away—the scars left by the obstetricians of culture. Here is an artist who re-establishes the potency of illusion by gaping at the open wounds, by courting the stern, psychological reality which man seeks to avoid through recourse to the oblique symbolism of art. Here the symbols are laid bare, presented almost as naively and unblushingly by this over-civilized individual as by the well-rooted savage.

It is no false primitivism which gives rise to this savage lyricism. It is not a retrogressive tendency, but a swing forward into unbeaten areas. To regard a naked book such as this with the same critical eye that is turned upon even such diverse types as Lawrence, Breton, Joyce and Céline is a mistake. Rather let us try to look at it with the eyes of a Patagonian for whom all that is sacred and taboo in our world is meaningless. For the adventure which has brought the author to the spiritual ends of the earth is the history of every artist who, in order to express himself, must traverse the intangible gridirons of his imaginary world. The air pockets, the alkali wastes, the crumbling monuments, the putrescent cadavers, the crazy jig and maggot dance, all this forms a grand fresco of our epoch, done with shattering phrases and loud, strident, hammer strokes.

If there is here revealed a capacity to shock, to startle the lifeless ones from their profound slumber, let us congratulate ourselves; for the tragedy of our world is precisely that nothing any longer is capable of rousing it from its lethargy. No more violent dreams, no refreshment, no awakening. In the anaesthesia produced by self-knowledge, life is passing, art is passing, slipping from us: we are drifting with time and our fight is with shadows. We need a blood transfusion.

And it is blood and flesh which are here given us. Drink, food, laughter, desire, passion, curiosity, the simple realities which nourish the roots of our highest and vaguest creations. The superstructure is lopped away. This book brings with it a wind that blows down the dead and hollow trees whose roots are withered and lost in the barren soil of our times. This book goes to the roots and digs under, digs for subterranean springs.

—*Anaïs Nin*
1934

I am living at the Villa Borghese. There is not a crumb of dirt anywhere, nor a chair misplaced. We are all alone here and we are dead.

Last night Boris discovered that he was lousy. I had to shave his armpits and even then the itching did not stop. How can one get lousy in a beautiful place like this? But no matter. We might never have known each other so intimately, Boris and I, had it not been for the lice.

Boris has just given me a summary of his views. He is a weather prophet. The weather will continue bad, he says. There will be more calamities, more death, more despair. Not the slightest indication of a change anywhere. The cancer of time is eating us away. Our heroes have killed themselves, or are killing themselves. The hero, then, is not Time, but Timelessness. We must get in step, a lock step, toward the prison of death. There is no escape. The weather will not change.

It is now the fall of my second year in Paris. I was sent here for a reason I have not yet been able to fathom.

I have no money, no resources, no hopes. I am the happiest man alive. A year ago, six months ago, I thought that I was an artist. I no longer think about it, I *am*. Everything that was literature has fallen from me. There are no more books to be written, thank God.

This then? This is not a book. This is libel, slander, defamation of character. This is not a book, in the ordinary sense of the word. No, this is a prolonged insult, a gob of spit in the face of Art, a kick in the pants to God, Man, Destiny, Time, Love, Beauty . . . what you will. I am going to sing for you, a little off key perhaps, but I will sing. I will sing while you croak, I will dance over your dirty corpse. . . .

To sing you must first open your mouth. You must have a pair of lungs, and a little knowledge of music. It is not necessary to have an accordion, or a guitar. The essential thing is to *want* to sing. This then is a song. I am singing.

It is to you, Tania, that I am singing. I wish that I could sing better, more melodiously, but then perhaps you would never have consented to listen to me. You have heard the others sing and they have left you cold. They sang too beautifully, or not beautifully enough.

It is the twenty-somethingth of October. I no longer keep track of the date. Would you say—my dream of the 14th November last? There are intervals, but they are between dreams, and there is no consciousness of them left. The world around me is dissolving, leaving here and there spots of time. The world is a cancer eating itself away. . . . I am thinking that when the great silence descends upon all and everywhere music will at last triumph. When into the womb of time everything is again withdrawn chaos will be restored and chaos is the score upon which reality is written. You, Tania, are my chaos. It is why I sing. It is not even I, it is the world dying, shedding the skin of time. I am still alive, kicking in your womb, a reality to write upon.

Dozing off. The physiology of love. The whale with his six-foot penis, in repose. The bat—*penis libre*. Animals with a bone in the penis. Hence, *a bone on.* . . . "Happily," says Gourmont, "the bony structure is lost in man." Happily? Yes, happily. Think of the human race walking around with a bone on. The kangaroo has a double penis—one for weekdays and one for holidays. Dozing. A letter from a female asking if I have found a title for my book. Title? To be sure: "Lovely Lesbians."

Your anecdotal life! A phrase of M. Borowski's. It is on Wednesdays that I have lunch with Borowski. His wife, who is a dried-up cow, officiates. She is studying English now—her favorite word is "filthy." You can see immediately what a pain in the ass the Borowskis are. But wait. . . .

Borowski wears corduroy suits and plays the accordion. An invincible combination, especially when you consider that he is not a bad artist. He puts on that he is a Pole, but he is not, of course. He is a Jew, Borowski, and his father was a philatelist. In fact, almost all Montparnasse is Jewish, or half-Jewish, which is worse. There's Carl and Paula, and Cronstadt and Boris, and Tania and Sylvester, and Moldorf and Lucille. All except Fillmore. Henry Jordan Oswald turned out to be a Jew also. Louis Nichols is a Jew. Even Van Norden and Chérie are Jewish. Frances Blake is a Jew, or a Jewess. Titus is a Jew. The Jews then are snowing me under. I am writing this for my friend Carl whose father is a Jew. All this is important to understand.

Of them all the loveliest Jew is Tania, and for her sake I too would become a Jew. Why not? I already speak like a Jew. And I am as ugly as a Jew. Besides, who hates the Jews more than the Jew?

Twilight hour. Indian blue, water of glass, trees glistening and liquescent. The rails fall away into the canal at Jaurès. The long caterpillar with lacquered sides dips like a roller coaster. It is not Paris. It is not Coney Island. It is a crepuscular melange of all the cities of Europe and Central America. The railroad yards below me, the tracks black, webby, not ordered by the engineer but cataclysmic in design, like those gaunt fissures in the polar ice which the camera registers in degrees of black.

Food is one of the things I enjoy tremendously. And in this beautiful Villa Borghese there is scarcely ever any evidence of food. It is positively appalling at times. I have asked Boris time and again to order bread for breakfast, but he always forgets. He goes out for breakfast, it seems. And when he comes back he is picking his teeth and there is a little egg hanging from his goatee. He eats in the restaurant out of consideration for me. He says it hurts to eat a big meal and have me watch him.

I like Van Norden but I do not share his opinion of himself. I do not agree, for instance, that he is a philosopher, or a thinker. He is cunt-struck, that's all. And he will never be a writer. Nor will Sylvester ever be a writer, though his name blaze in 50,000-candle-power red lights. The only writers about me for whom I have any respect, at present, are Carl and Boris. They are possessed. They glow inwardly with a white flame. They are mad and tone deaf. They are sufferers.

Moldorf, on the other hand, who suffers too in his peculiar way, is not mad. Moldorf is word drunk. He has no veins or blood vessels, no heart or kidneys. He is a portable trunk filled with innumerable drawers and in the drawers are labels written out in white ink, brown ink, red ink, blue ink, vermilion, saffron, mauve, sienna, apricot, turquoise, onyx, Anjou, herring, Corona, verdigris, gorgonzola. . . .

I have moved the typewriter into the next room where I can see myself in the mirror as I write.

Tania is like Irène. She expects fat letters. But there is another Tania, a Tania like a big seed, who scatters pollen everywhere—or, let us say, a little bit of Tolstoy, a stable scene in which the fetus is dug up. Tania is a fever, too—*les voies urinaires*, Café de la Liberté, Place des Vosges, bright neckties on the Boulevard Montparnasse, dark bathrooms, Porto Sec, Abdullah cigarettes, the adagio sonata *Pathétique*, aural amplificators, anecdotal seances, burnt sienna breasts, heavy garters, what time is it, golden pheasants stuffed with chestnuts, taffeta fingers, vaporish twilights turning to ilex, acromegaly, cancer and delirium, warm veils, poker chips, carpets of blood and soft thighs. Tania says so that every one may hear: "I love him!" And while Boris scalds himself with whisky she says: "Sit down here! O Boris . . . *Russia* . . . what'll I do? I'm bursting with it!"

At night when I look at Boris' goatee lying on the pillow I get hysterical. O Tania, where now is that warm cunt of yours, those fat, heavy garters, those soft, bulging thighs? There is a bone in my prick six inches long. I will ream out every wrinkle in your cunt, Tania, big with seed. I will send you home to your Sylvester with an ache in your belly and your womb turned inside out. Your Sylvester! Yes, he knows how to build a fire, but I know how to inflame a cunt. I shoot hot bolts into you, Tania, I make your ovaries incandescent. Your Sylvester is a little jealous now? He feels something, does he? He feels the remnants of my big prick. I have set the shores a little wider, I have ironed out the wrinkles. After me you can take on stallions, bulls, rams, drakes, St. Bernards. You can stuff toads, bats, lizards up your rectum. You can shit arpeggios if you like, or string a zither across your navel. I am fucking you, Tania, so that you'll stay fucked. And if you are afraid of being fucked publicly I will fuck you privately. I will tear off a few hairs from your cunt and paste them on Boris' chin. I will bite into your clitoris and spit out two franc pieces. . . .

Indigo sky swept clear of fleecy clouds, gaunt trees infinitely extended, their black boughs gesticulating like a sleepwalker. Somber, spectral trees, their trunks pale as cigar ash. A silence supreme and altogether European. Shutters drawn, shops barred. A red glow here and there to mark a tryst. Brusque the façades, almost forbidding; immaculate except for the splotches of shadow cast by the trees. Passing by the Orangerie I am reminded of another Paris, the Paris of Maugham, of Gauguin, Paris of George Moore. I think of that terrible Spaniard who was then startling the world with his acrobatic leaps from style to style. I think of Spengler and of his terrible pronunciamentos, and I wonder if style, style in the grand manner, is done for. I say that my mind is occupied with these thoughts, but it is not true; it is only later, after I have crossed the Seine, after I have put behind me the carnival of lights, that I allow my mind to play with these ideas. For the moment I can think of nothing—except that I am a sentient being stabbed by the miracle of these waters that reflect a forgotten world. All along the banks the trees lean heavily over the tarnished mirror; when the wind rises and fills them with a rustling murmur they will shed a few tears and shiver as the water swirls by. I am suffocated by it. No one to whom I can communicate even a fraction of my feelings. . . .

The trouble with Irène is that she has a valise instead of a cunt. She wants fat letters to shove in her valise. Immense, *avec des choses inouïes*. Llona now, she had a cunt. I know because she sent us some hairs from down below. Llona—a wild ass snuffing pleasure out of the wind. On every high hill she played the harlot—and sometimes in telephone booths and toilets. She bought a bed for King Carol and a shaving mug with his initials on it. She lay in Tottenham Court Road with her dress pulled up and fingered herself. She used candles, Roman candles, and door knobs. Not a prick in the land big enough for her . . . *not one*. Men went inside her and curled up. She wanted extension pricks, self-exploding rockets, hot boiling oil made of wax and creosote. She would cut off your prick and keep it inside her forever, if you gave her permission. One cunt out of a million, Llona! A laboratory cunt and no litmus paper that could take her color. She was a liar, too, this Llona. She never bought a bed for her King Carol. She crowned him with a whisky bottle and her tongue was full of lice and tomorrows. Poor Carol, he could only curl up inside her and die. She drew a breath and he fell out—like a dead clam.

Enormous, fat letters, *avec des choses inouïes*. A valise without straps. A hole without a key. She had a German mouth, French ears, Russian ass. Cunt international. When the flag waved it was red all the way back to the throat. You entered on the Boulevard Jules-Ferry and came out at the Porte de la Villette. You dropped your sweetbreads into the tumbrils—red tumbrils with two wheels, naturally. At the confluence of the Ourcq and

Marne, where the water sluices through the dikes and lies like glass under the bridges. Llona is lying there now and the canal is full of glass and splinters; the mimosas weep, and there is a wet, foggy fart on the windowpanes. One cunt out of a million Llona! All cunt and a glass ass in which you can read the history of the Middle Ages.

It is the caricature of a man which Moldorf first presents. Thyroid eyes. Michelin lips. Voice like pea soup. Under his vest he carries a little pear. However you look at him it is always the same panorama: netsuke snuffbox, ivory handle, chess piece, fan, temple motif. He has fermented so long now that he is amorphous. Yeast despoiled of its vitamins. Vase without a rubber plant.

The females were sired twice in the ninth century, and again during the Renaissance. He was carried through the great dispersions under yellow bellies and white. Long before the Exodus a Tatar spat in his blood.

His dilemma is that of the dwarf. With his pineal eye he sees his silhouette projected on a screen of incommensurable size. His voice, synchronized to the shadow of a pinhead, intoxicates him. He hears a roar where others hear only a squeak.

There is his mind. It is an amphitheater in which the actor gives a protean performance. Moldorf, multiform and unerring, goes through his roles—clown, juggler, contortionist, priest, lecher, mountebank. The amphitheater is too small. He puts dynamite to it. The audience is drugged. He scotches it.

I am trying ineffectually to approach Moldorf. It is like trying to approach God, for Moldorf *is* God—he has never been anything else. I am merely putting down words. . . .

I have had opinions about him which I have discarded; I have had other opinions which I am revising. I have pinned him down only to find that it was not a dungbeetle I had in my hands, but a dragonfly. He has offended me by his coarseness and then overwhelmed me with his delicacy. He has been voluble to the point of suffocation, then quiet as the Jordan.

When I see him trotting forward to greet me, his little paws outstretched, his eyes perspiring, I feel that I am meeting. . . . No, this is not the way to go about it!

"Comme un œuf dansant sur un jet d'eau."

He has only one cane—a mediocre one. In his pocket scraps of paper containing prescriptions for *Weltschmerz*. He is cured now, and the little German girl who washed his feet is breaking her heart. It is like Mr. Nonentity toting his Gujarati dictionary everywhere. *"Inevitable for everyone"*—meaning, no doubt, *indispensable*. Borowski would find all this incomprehensible. Borowski has a different cane for each day in the week, and one for Easter.

We have so many points in common that it is like looking at myself in a cracked mirror.

I have been looking over my manuscripts, pages scrawled with revisions. Pages of *literature*. This frightens me a little. It is so much like Moldorf. Only I am a Gentile, and Gentiles have a different way of suffering. They suffer without neuroses and, as Sylvester says, a man who has never been afflicted with a neurosis does not know the meaning of suffering.

I recall distinctly how I enjoyed my suffering. It was like taking a cub to bed with you. Once in a while he clawed you—and then you really were frightened. Ordinarily you had no fear—you could always turn him loose, or chop his head off.

There are people who cannot resist the desire to get into a cage with wild beasts and be mangled. They go in even without revolver or whip. Fear makes them fearless. . . . For the Jew the world is a cage filled with wild beasts. The door is locked and he is there without whip or revolver. His courage is so great that he does not even smell the dung in the corner. The spectators applaud but he does not hear. The drama, he thinks, is going on inside the cage. The cage, he thinks, is the world. Standing there alone and helpless, the door locked, he finds that the lions do not understand his language. Not one lion has ever heard of Spinoza. Spinoza? Why they can't even get their teeth into him. "Give us meat!" they roar, while he stands there petrified, his ideas frozen, his *Weltanschauung* a trapeze out of reach. A single blow of the lion's paw and his cosmogony is smashed.

The lions, too, are disappointed. They expected blood, bones, gristle, sinews. They chew and chew, but the words are chicle and chicle is indigestible. Chicle is a base over which you sprinkle sugar, pepsin, thyme, licorice. Chicle, when it is gathered by *chicleros*, is O.K. The *chicleros* came over on the ridge of a sunken continent. They brought with them an algebraic language. In the Arizona desert they met the Mongols of the North, glazed like eggplants. Time shortly after the earth had taken its gyroscopic lean—when the Gulf Stream was parting ways with the Japanese current. In the heart of the soil they found tufa rock. They embroidered the very bowels of the earth with their language. They ate one another's entrails and the forest closed in on them, on their bones and skulls, on their lace tufa. Their language was lost. Here and there one still finds the remnants of a menagerie, a brain plate covered with figures.

What has all this to do with you, Moldorf? The word in your mouth is anarchy. Say it, Moldorf, I am waiting for it. Nobody knows, when we shake hands, the rivers that pour through our sweat. Whilst you are framing your words, your lips half parted, the saliva gurgling in your cheeks, I have jumped halfway across Asia. Were I to take your cane, mediocre as it is, and poke a little hole in your side, I could collect enough material to fill the British Museum. We stand on five minutes and devour centuries. You are the sieve through which my anarchy strains, resolves itself into words. Behind the word is chaos. Each word a stripe, a bar, but there are not and never will be enough bars to make the mesh.

In my absence the window curtains have been hung. They have the appearance of Tyrolean tablecloths dipped in lysol. The room sparkles. I sit on the bed in a daze, thinking about man before his birth. Suddenly bells begin to toll, a weird, unearthly music, as if I had been translated to the steppes of Central Asia. Some ring out with a long, lingering roll, some erupt drunkenly, maudlinly. And now it is quiet again, except for a last note that barely grazes the silence of the night—just a faint, high gong snuffed out like a flame.

I have made a silent compact with myself not to change a line of what I write. I am not interested in perfecting my thoughts, nor my actions. Beside the perfection of Turgenev I put the perfection of Dostoevski. (Is there anything more perfect than *The Eternal Husband*?) Here, then, in one and the same medium, we have two kinds of perfection. But in Van Gogh's letters there is a perfection beyond either of these. It is the triumph of the individual over art.

There is only one thing which interests me vitally now, and that is the recording of all that which is omitted in books. Nobody, so far as I can see, is making use of those elements in the air which give direction and motivation to our lives. Only the killers seem to be extracting from life some satisfactory measure of what they are putting into it. The age demands violence, but we are getting only abortive explosions. Revolutions are nipped in the bud, or else succeed too quickly. Passion is quickly exhausted. Men fall back on ideas, *comme d'habitude*. Nothing is proposed that can last more than twenty-four hours. We are living a million lives in the space of a generation. In the study of entomology, or of deep sea life, or cellular activity, we derive more . . .

The telephone interrupts this thought which I should never have been able to complete. Someone is coming to rent the apartment. . . .

It looks as though it were finished, my life at the Villa

Borghese. Well, I'll take up these pages and move on. Things will happen elsewhere. Things are always happening. It seems wherever I go there is drama. People are like lice—they get under your skin and bury themselves there. You scratch and scratch until the blood comes, but you can't get permanently deloused. Everywhere I go people are making a mess of their lives. Everyone has his private tragedy. It's in the blood now—misfortune, ennui, grief, suicide. The atmosphere is saturated with disaster, frustration, futility. Scratch and scratch—until there's no skin left. However, the effect upon me is exhilarating. Instead of being discouraged, or depressed, I enjoy it. I am crying for more and more disasters, for bigger calamities, for grander failures. I want the whole world to be out of whack, I want everyone to scratch himself to death.

So fast and furiously am I compelled to live now that there is scarcely time to record even these fragmentary notes. After the telephone call, a gentleman and his wife arrived. I went upstairs to lie down during the transaction. Lay there wondering what my next move would be. Surely not to go back to the fairy's bed and toss about all night flicking bread crumbs with my toes. That puking little bastard! If there's anything worse than being a fairy it's being a miser. A timid, quaking little bugger who lived in constant fear of going broke some day—the 18th of March perhaps, or the 25th of May precisely. Coffee without milk or sugar. Bread without butter. Meat without gravy, or no meat at all. Without this and without that! That dirty little miser! Open the bureau drawer one day and find money hidden away in a sock. Over two thousand francs—and checks that he hadn't even cashed. Even that I wouldn't have minded so much if there weren't always coffee grounds in my beret and garbage on the floor, to say nothing of the cold cream jars and the greasy towels and the sink always stopped up. I tell you, the little bastard he smelled bad—except when he doused himself with cologne. His ears were dirty, his eyes were dirty, his ass was dirty. He was double-jointed, asthmatic, lousy, picayune, morbid. I could have forgiven him everything if only he had handed me a decent breakfast! But a man who has two thousand francs hidden away in a dirty sock and refuses to wear a clean shirt or smear a little butter over his bread, such a man is not just a fairy, nor even just a miser—he's an imbecile!

But that's neither here nor there, about the fairy. I'm keeping an ear open as to what's going on downstairs. It's a Mr. Wren and his wife who have called to look at the apartment. They're talking about taking it. Only *talking* about it, thank God. Mrs. Wren has a loose laugh—complications ahead. Now *Mister* Wren is talking. His voice is raucous, scraping, booming, a heavy blunt weapon that wedges its way through flesh and bone and cartilage.

Boris calls me down to be introduced. He is rubbing his hands, like a pawnbroker. They are talking about a story Mr. Wren wrote, a story about a spavined horse.

"But I thought Mr. Wren was a painter?"

"To be sure," says Boris, with a twinkle in his eye, "but in the wintertime he writes. And he writes well . . . remarkably well."

I try to induce Mr. Wren to talk, to say something, anything, to talk about the spavined horse, if necessary. But Mr. Wren is almost inarticulate. When he essays to speak of those dreary months with the pen he becomes unintelligible. Months and months he spends before setting a word to paper. (And there are only three months of winter!) What does he cogitate all those months and months of winter? So help me God, I can't see this guy as a writer. Yet Mrs. Wren says that when he sits down to it the stuff *just pours out*.

The talk drifts. It is difficult to follow Mr. Wren's mind because he says nothing. *He thinks as he goes along* —so Mrs. Wren puts it. Mrs. Wren puts everything about Mr. Wren in the loveliest light. "He thinks as he goes along"—very charming, charming indeed, as Borowski would say, but really very painful, particularly when the thinker is nothing but a spavined horse.

Boris hands me money to buy liquor. Going for the liquor I am already intoxicated. I know just how I'll begin when I get back to the house. Walking down the street it commences, the grand speech inside me that's gurgling like Mrs. Wren's loose laugh. Seems to me she had a slight edge on already. Listens beautifully when she's tight. Coming out of the wine shop I hear the urinal gurgling. Everything is loose and splashy. I want Mrs. Wren to listen. . . .

Boris is rubbing his hands again. Mr. Wren is still stuttering and spluttering. I have a bottle between my legs and I'm shoving the corkscrew in. Mrs. Wren has her mouth parted expectantly. The wine is splashing between my legs, the sun is splashing through the bay window, and inside my veins there is a bubble and splash of a thousand crazy things that commence to gush out of me now pell-mell. I'm telling them everything that comes to mind, everything that was bottled up inside me and which Mrs. Wren's loose laugh has somehow released. With that bottle between my legs and the sun splashing through the window I experience once again the splendor of those miserable days when I first arrived in Paris, a bewildered, poverty-stricken individual who haunted the streets like a ghost at a banquet. Everything comes back to me in a rush—the toilets that wouldn't work, the prince who shined my shoes, the Cinema Splendide where I slept on the patron's overcoat, the bars in the window, the feeling of suffocation, the fat cockroaches, the drinking and carousing that went on between times, Rose Cannaque and Naples dying in the sunlight. Dancing the streets on an empty belly and now and then calling on strange people—Madame Delorme, for instance. How I ever got to Madame Delorme's, I can't imagine any more. But I got there, got inside somehow, past the butler, past the maid with her little white apron, got right inside the palace with my corduroy trousers and my hunting jacket—and not a button on my fly. Even now I can taste again the golden ambiance of that room where Madame Delorme sat upon a throne in her mannish rig, the goldfish in the bowls, the maps of the ancient world, the beautifully bound books; I can feel again her heavy hand resting upon my shoulder, frightening me a little with her heavy Lesbian air. More comfortable down below in that thick stew pouring into the Gare St. Lazare, the whores in the doorways, seltzer bottles on every table; a thick tide of semen flooding the gutters. Nothing better between five and seven than to be pushed around in that throng, to follow a leg or a beautiful bust, to move along with the tide and everything whirling in your brain. A weird sort of contentment in those days. No appointments, no invitations for dinner, no program, no dough. The golden period, when I had not a single friend. Each morning the dreary walk to the American Express, and each morning the inevitable answer from the clerk. Dashing here and there like a bedbug, gathering butts now and then, sometimes furtively, sometimes brazenly; sitting down on a bench and squeezing my guts to stop the gnawing, or walking through the Jardin des Tuileries and getting an erection looking at the dumb statues. Or wandering along the Seine at night, wandering and wandering, and going mad with the beauty of it, the trees leaning to, the broken images in the water, the rush of the current under the bloody lights of the bridges, the women sleeping in doorways, sleeping on newspapers, sleeping in the rain; everywhere the musty porches of the cathedrals and beggars and lice and old hags full of St. Vitus' dance; pushcarts stacked up like wine barrels in the side streets, the smell of berries in the market place and the old church surrounded with vegetables and blue arc lights, the gutters slippery with garbage and women in satin pumps staggering through the filth and vermin at the end of an all-night souse. The Place St. Sulpice, so quiet and deserted, where toward midnight there came every night the woman with the busted umbrella and the crazy veil; every night she slept there on a bench under her torn umbrella, the ribs hanging down, her dress turning green, her bony fingers and the odor of decay oozing from her body; and in the morning I'd be sitting there myself, taking a quiet snooze in the sunshine, cursing the goddamned pigeons gathering up the crumbs everywhere. St. Sulpice! The fat belfries, the garish posters over the door, the candles flaming inside. The Square so beloved of Anatole France, with that drone and buzz from the altar, the splash of the fountain, the pigeons cooing, the crumbs disappearing like magic and only a dull rumbling in the hollow of the guts. Here I would sit day after day thinking of Germaine and that dirty little street near the Bastille where she lived, and that buzz-buzz going on behind the altar, the buses whizzing by, the sun beating down into the asphalt and the asphalt working into me and Germaine, into the asphalt and all Paris in the big fat belfries.

And it was down the Rue Bonaparte that only a year before Mona and I used to walk every night, after we had taken leave of Borowski. St. Sulpice not meaning much to me then, nor anything in Paris. Washed out with talk. Sick of faces. Fed up with cathedrals and squares and menageries and what not. Picking up a book in the red bedroom and the cane chair uncomfortable; tired of sitting on my ass all day long, tired of red wallpaper, tired of seeing so many people jabbering away about nothing. The red bedroom and the trunk always open; her gowns lying about in a delirium of disorder. The red bedrom with my galoshes and canes, the notebooks I never touched, the manuscripts lying cold and dead. Paris! Meaning the Café Select, the Dôme, the Flea Market, the American Express. Paris! Meaning Borowski's canes, Borowski's hats, Borowski's *gouaches*, Borowski's prehistoric fish—and prehistoric jokes. In that Paris of '28 only one night stands out in my memory—the night before sailing for America. A rare night, with Borowski slightly pickled and a little disgusted with me because I'm dancing with every slut in the place. But we're leaving in the morning! That's what I tell every cunt I grab hold of—*leaving in the morning!* That's what I'm telling the blonde with agate-colored eyes. And while I'm telling her she takes my hand and squeezes it between her legs. In the lavatory I stand before the bowl with a tremendous erection; it seems light and heavy at the same time, like a piece of lead with wings on it. And while I'm standing there like that two cunts sail in—Americans. I greet them cordially, prick in hand. They give me a wink and pass on. In the vestibule, as I'm buttoning my fly, I notice one of them waiting for her friend to come out of the can. The music is still playing and maybe Mona'll be coming to fetch me, or Borowski with his gold-knobbed cane, but I'm in her arms now and she has hold of me and I don't care who comes or what happens. We wriggle into the cabinet and there I stand her up, slap up against the wall, and I try to get it into her but it won't work and so we sit down on the seat and try it that way but it won't work either. No matter how we try it it won't work. And all the while she's got hold of my prick, she's clutching it like a lifesaver, but it's no use, we're too hot, too eager. The music is still playing and so we waltz out of the cabinet into the vestibule again and as we're dancing there in the shithouse I come all over her beautiful gown and she's sore as hell about it. I stumble back to the table and there's Borowski with his ruddy face and Mona with her disapproving eye. And Borowski says "Let's all go to Brussels tomorrow," and we agree, and when we get back to the hotel I vomit all over the place, in the bed, in the washbowl, over the suits and gowns and the galoshes and canes and the notebooks I never touched and the manuscripts cold and dead.

A few months later. The same hotel, the same room. We look out on the courtyard where the bicycles are parked, and there is the little room up above, under the attic, where some smart young Alec played the phonograph all day long and repeated clever little things at the top of his voice. I say "we" but I'm getting ahead of myself, because Mona has been away a long time and it's just today that I'm meeting her at the Gare St. Lazare. Toward evening I'm standing there with my face squeezed between the bars, but there's no Mona, and I read the cable over again but it doesn't help any. I go back to the Quarter and just the same I put away a hearty meal. Strolling past the Dôme a little later suddenly I see a pale, heavy face and burning eyes—and the little velvet suit that I always adore because under the soft velvet there were always her warm breasts, the marble legs, cool, firm, muscular. She rises up out of a sea of faces and embraces me, embraces me passionately—a thousand eyes, noses, fingers, legs, bottles, windows, purses, saucers all glaring at us and we in each other's arms oblivious. I sit down beside her and she talks—a flood of talk. Wild consumptive notes of hysteria, perversion, leprosy. I hear not a word because she is beautiful and I love her and now I am happy and willing to die.

We walk down the Rue du Château, looking for Eugene. Walk over the railroad bridge where I used to watch the trains pulling out and feel all sick inside wondering where the hell she could be. Everything soft and enchanting as we walk over the bridge. Smoke coming up between our legs, the tracks creaking, semaphores in our blood. I feel her body close to mine—all mine now—and I stop to rub my hands over the warm velvet. Everything around us is crumbling, crumbling and the warm body under the warm velvet is aching for me. . . .

Back in the very same room and fifty francs to the good, thanks to Eugene. I look out on the court but the phonograph is silent. The trunk is open and her things are lying around everywhere just as before. She lies down on the bed with her clothes on. Once, twice, three times, four times . . . I'm afraid she'll go mad . . . in bed, under the blankets, how good to feel her body again! But for how long? Will it last this time? Already I have a presentiment that it won't.

She talks to me so feverishly—as if there will be no tomorrow. "Be quiet, Mona! Just look at me . . . *don't talk!*" Finally she drops off and I pull my arm from under her. My eyes close. Her body is there beside me . . . it will be there till morning surely. . . . It was in February I pulled out of the harbor in a blinding snowstorm. The last glimpse I had of her was in the window waving good-bye to me. A man standing on the other side of the street, at the corner, his hat pulled down over his eyes, his jowls resting on his lapels. A fetus watching me. A fetus with a cigar in its mouth. Mona at the window waving good-bye. White heavy face, hair streaming wild. And now it is a heavy bedroom, breathing regularly through the gills, sap still oozing from between her legs, a warm feline odor and her hair in my mouth. My eyes are closed. We breathe warmly into each other's mouth. Close together, America three thousand miles away. I never want to see it again. To have her here in bed with me, breathing on me, her hair in my mouth—I count that something of a miracle. Nothing can happen now till morning. . . .

I wake from a deep slumber to look at her. A pale light is trickling in. I look at her beautiful wild hair. I feel something crawling down my neck. I look at her again, closely. Her hair is alive. I pull back the sheet—more of them. They are swarming over the pillow.

It is a little after daybreak. We pack hurriedly and sneak out of the hotel. The cafés are still closed. We walk, and as we walk we scratch ourselves. The day opens in milky whiteness, streaks of salmon-pink sky, snails leaving their shells. Paris. Paris. Everything happens here. Old, crumbling walls and the pleasant sound of water running in the urinals. Men licking their mustaches at the bar. Shutters going up with a bang and little streams purling in the gutters. *Amer Picon* in huge scarlet letters. *Zigzag*. Which way will we go and why or where or what?

Mona is hungry, her dress is thin. Nothing but evening wraps, bottles of perfume, barbaric earrings, bracelets, depilatories. We sit down in a billiard parlor on the Avenue du Maine and order hot coffee. The toilet is out of order. We shall have to sit some time before we can go to another hotel. Meanwhile we pick bedbugs out of each other's hair. Nervous. Mona is losing her temper.

Must have a bath. Must have this. Must have that. Must, must, must. . .

"How much money have you left?"

Money! Forgot all about that.

Hôtel des Etats-Unis. An *ascenseur*. We go to bed in broad daylight. When we get up it is dark and the first thing to do is to raise enough dough to send a cable to America. A cable to the fetus with the long juicy cigar in his mouth. Meanwhile there is the Spanish woman on the Boulevard Raspail—she's always good for a warm meal. By morning something will happen. At least we're going to bed together. No more bedbugs now. The rainy season has commenced. The sheets are immaculate. . . .

A new life opening up for me at the Villa Borghese. Only ten o'clock and we have already had breakfast and been out for a walk. We have an Elsa here with us now. "Step softly for a few days," cautions Boris.

The day begins gloriously: a bright sky, a fresh wind, the houses newly washed. On our way to the Post Office Boris and I discussed the book. *The Last Book*—which is going to be written anonymously.

A new day is beginning. I felt it this morning as we stood before one of Dufresne's glistening canvases, a sort of *déjeuner intime* in the thirteenth century, *sans vin*. A fine, fleshy nude, solid, vibrant, pink as a fingernail, with glistening billows of flesh; all the secondary characteristics, and a few of the primary. A body that stings, that has the moisture of dawn. A still life, only nothing is still, nothing dead here. The table creaks with food; it is so heavy it is sliding out of the frame. A thirteenth century repast—with all the jungle notes that he has memorized so well. A family of gazelles and zebras nipping the fronds of the palms.

And now we have Elsa. She was playing for us this morning while we were in bed. *Step softly for a few days*. . . . Good! Elsa is the maid and I am the guest. And Boris is the big cheese. A new drama is beginning. I'm laughing to myself as I write this. He knows what is going to happen, that lynx, Boris. He has a nose for things too. *Step softly*. . . .

Boris is on pins and needles. At any moment now his

wife may appear on the scene. She weighs well over 180 pounds, that wife of his. And Boris is only a handful. There you have the situation. He tries to explain it to me on our way home at night. It is so tragic and so ridiculous at the same time that I am obliged to stop now and then and laugh in his face. "Why do you laugh so?" he says gently, and then he commences himself, with that whimpering, hysterical note in his voice, like a helpless wretch who realizes suddenly that no matter how many frock coats he puts on he will never make a man. He wants to run away, to take a new name. "She can have everything, that cow, if only she leaves me alone," he whines. But first the apartment has to be rented, and the deeds signed, and a thousand other details for which his frock coat will come in handy. But the size of her!— that's what really worries him. If we were to find her suddenly standing on the doorstep when we arrive he would faint—that's how much he respects her!

And so we've got to go easy with Elsa for a while. Elsa is only there to make breakfast—and to show the apartment.

But Elsa is already undermining me. That German blood. Those melancholy songs. Coming down the stairs this morning, with the fresh coffee in my nostrils, I was humming softly. . . . *"Es wär' so schön gewesen."* For breakfast, that. And in a little while the English boy upstairs with his Bach. As Elsa says—"he needs a woman." And Elsa needs something too. I can feel it. I didn't say anything to Boris about it, but while he was cleaning his teeth this morning Elsa was giving me an earful about Berlin, about the women who look so attractive from behind, and when they turn round—*wow, syphilis!*

It seems to me that Elsa looks at me rather wistfully. Something left over from the breakfast table. This afternoon we were writing, back to back, in the studio. She had begun a letter to her lover who is in Italy. The machine got jammed. Boris had gone to look at a cheap room he will take as soon as the apartment is rented. There was nothing for it but to make love to Elsa. She wanted it. And yet I felt a little sorry for her. She had only written the first line to her lover—I read it out of the corner of my eye as I bent over her. But it couldn't be helped. That damned German music, so melancholy, so sentimental. It undermined me. And then her beady little eyes, so hot and sorrowful at the same time.

After it was over I asked her to play something for me. She's a musician, Elsa, even though it sounded like broken pots and skulls clanking. She was weeping, too, as she played. I don't blame her. Everywhere the same things, she says. Everywhere a man, and then she has to leave, and then there's an abortion and then a new job and then another man and nobody gives a fuck about her except to use her. All this after she's played Schumann for me—Schumann, that slobbery, sentimental German bastard! Somehow I feel sorry as hell for her and yet I don't give a damn. A cunt who can play as she does ought to have better sense than be tripped up by every guy with a big putz who happens to come along. But that Schumann gets into my blood. She's still sniffling, Elsa; but my mind is far away. I'm thinking of Tania and how she claws away at her adagio. I'm thinking of lots of things that are gone and buried. Thinking of a summer afternoon in Greenpoint when the Germans were romping over Belgium and we had not yet lost enough money to be concerned over the rape of a neutral country. A time when we were still innocent enough to listen to poets and to sit around a table in the twilight rapping for departed spirits. All that afternoon and evening the atmosphere is saturated with German music; the whole neighborhood is German, more German even than Germany. We were brought up on Schumann and Hugo Wolf and sauerkraut and kümmel and potato dumplings. Toward evening we're sitting around a big table with the curtains drawn and some fool two-headed wench is rapping for Jesus Christ. We're holding hands under the table and the dame next to me has two fingers in my fly. And finally we lie on the floor, behind the piano, while someone sings a dreary song. The air is stifling and her breath is boozy. The pedal is moving up and down, stiffly, automatically, a crazy, futile movement, like a tower of dung that takes twenty-seven years to build but keeps perfect time. I pull her over me with the sounding board in my ears; the room is dark and the carpet is sticky with the kümmel that has been spilled about. Suddenly it seems as if the dawn were coming: it is like water purling over ice and the ice is blue with a rising mist, glaciers sunk in emerald green, chamois and antelope, golden groupers, sea cows mooching along and the amber jack leaping over the Arctic rim. . . .

Elsa is sitting in my lap. Her eyes are like little belly-buttons. I look at her large mouth, so wet and glistening, and I cover it. She is humming now. . . . *"Es wär' so schön gewesen. . . ."* Ah, Elsa, you don't know yet what that means to me, your *Trompeter von Säckingen*. German Singing Societies, Schwaben Hall, the Turnverein . . . *links um, rechts um* . . . and then a whack over the ass with the end of a rope.

Ah, the Germans! They take you all over like an omnibus. They give you indigestion. In the same night one cannot visit the morgue, the infirmary, the zoo, the signs of the zodiac, the limbos of philosophy, the caves of epistemology, the arcana of Freud and Stekel. . . . On the merry-go-round one doesn't get anywhere, whereas with the Germans one can go from Vega to Lope de Vega, all in one night, and come away as foolish as Parsifal.

As I say, the day began gloriously. It was only this morning that I became conscious again of this physical Paris of which I have been unaware for weeks. Perhaps it is because the book has begun to grow inside me. I am carrying it around with me everywhere. I walk through the streets big with child and the cops escort me across the street. Women get up to offer me their seats. Nobody pushes me rudely any more. I am pregnant. I waddle awkwardly, my big stomach pressed against the weight of the world.

It was this morning, on our way to the Post Office, that we gave the book its final imprimatur. We have evolved a new cosmogony of literature, Boris and I. It is to be a new Bible—*The Last Book*. All those who have anything to say will say it here—*anonymously*. We will exhaust the age. After us not another book—not for a generation, at least. Heretofore we had been digging in the dark, with nothing but instinct to guide us. Now we shall have a vessel in which to pour the vital fluid, a bomb which, when we throw it, will set off the world. We shall put into it enough to give the writers of tomorrow their plots, their dramas, their poems, their myths, their sciences. The world will be able to feed on it for a thousand years to come. It is colossal in its pretentiousness. The thought of it almost shatters us.

For a hundred years or more the world, *our* world, has been dying. And not one man, in these last hundred years or so, has been crazy enough to put a bomb up the asshole of creation and set it off. The world is rotting away, dying piecemeal. But it needs the *coup de grâce*, it needs to be blown to smithereens. Not one of us intact, and yet we have in us all the continents and the seas between the continents and the birds of the air. We are going to put it down—the evolution of this world which has died but which has not been buried. We are swimming on the face of time and all else has drowned, is drowning, or will drown. It will be enormous, the Book. There will be oceans of space in which to move about, to perambulate, to sing, to dance, to climb, to bathe, to leap somersaults, to whine, to rape, to murder. A cathedral, a veritable cathedral, in the building of which everybody will assist who has lost his identity. There will be masses for the dead, prayers, confessions, hymns, a moaning and a chattering, a sort of murderous insouciance; there will be rose windows and gargoyles and acolytes and pallbearers. You can bring your horses in and gallop through the aisles. You can butt your head against the walls—they won't give. You can pray in any language you choose, or you can curl up outside and go to sleep. It will last a thousand years, at least, this cathedral, and there will be no replica, for the builders will be dead and the formula too. We will have postcards made and organize tours. We will build a town around it and set up a free commune. We have no need for genius— genius is dead. We have need for strong hands, for spirits who are willing to give up the ghost and put on flesh. . . .

The day is moving along at a fine tempo. I am up on the balcony at Tania's place. The drama is going on down below in the drawing room. The dramatist is sick and from above his scalp looks more scabrous than ever. His hair is made of straw. His ideas are straw. His wife too is straw, though still a little damp. The whole house is made of straw. Here I am up on the balcony, waiting for Boris to arrive. My last problem—*breakfast*—is gone. I have simplified everything. If there are any new problems I can carry them in my rucksack, along with my dirty wash. I am throwing away all my sous. What need have I for money? I am a writing machine. The last screw has been added. The thing flows. Between me and the machine there is no estrangement. I am the machine. . . .

They have not told me yet what the new drama is about, but I can sense it. They are trying to get rid of me. Yet here I am for my dinner, even a little earlier than they expected. I have informed them where to sit, what to do. I ask them politely if I shall be disturbing them, but what I really mean, and they know it well, is—*will you be disturbing me?* No, you blissful cockroaches, you are not disturbing me. You are *nourishing* me. I see you sitting there close together and I know there is a chasm between you. Your nearness is the nearness of planets. I am the void between you. If I withdraw there will be no void for you to swim in.

Tania is in a hostile mood—I can feel it. She resents me being filled with anything but herself. She knows by the very caliber of my excitement that her value is reduced to zero. She knows that I did not come this evening to fertilize her. She knows there is something germinating inside me which will destroy her. She is slow to realize, but she is realizing it . . .

Sylvester looks more content. He will embrace her this evening at the dinner table. Even now he is reading my manuscript, preparing to inflame my ego, to set my ego against hers.

It will be a strange gathering this evening. The stage is being set. I hear the tinkle of the glasses. The wine is being brought out. There will be bumpers downed and Sylvester who is ill will come out of his illness.

It was only last night, at Cronstadt's, that we projected this setting. It was ordained that the women must suffer, that off-stage there should be more terror and violence, more disasters, more suffering, more woe and misery.

It is not accident that propels people like us to Paris. Paris is simply an artificial stage, a revolving stage that permits the spectator to glimpse all phases of the conflict. Of itself Paris initiates no dramas. They are begun elsewhere. Paris is simply an obstetrical instrument that tears the living embryo from the womb and puts it in the incubator. Paris is the cradle of artificial births. Rocking here in the cradle each one slips back into his soil: one dreams back to Berlin, New York, Chicago, Vienna, Minsk. Vienna is never more Vienna than in Paris. Everything is raised to apotheosis. The cradle gives up its babes and new ones take their places. You can read here on the walls where Zola lived and Balzac and Dante and Strindberg and everbody who ever was anything. Everyone has lived here some time or other. Nobody *dies* here. . . .

They are talking downstairs. Their language is symbolic. The word "struggle" enters into it. Sylvester, the sick dramatist, is saying: "I am just reading the *Manifesto.*" And Tania says—"*Whose?*" Yes, Tania, I heard you. I am up here writing about you and you divine it well. *Speak more,* that I may record you. For when we go to table I shall not be able to make any notes. . . . Suddenly Tania remarks: "There is no prominent hall in this place." Now what does that mean, if anything?

They are putting up pictures now. That, too, is to impress me. See, they wish to say, we are at home here, living the conjugal life. Making the home attractive. We

will even argue a little about the pictures, for *your* benefit. And Tania remarks again: "How the eye deceives
one!" Ah, Tania, what things you say! Go on, carry out
this farce a little longer. I am here to get the dinner you
promised me; I enjoy this comedy tremendously. And
now Sylvester takes the lead. He is trying to explain one
of Borowski's *gouaches*. "Come here, do you see? One of
them is playing the guitar; the other is holding a girl in
his lap." True, Sylvester. Very true. Borowski and his
guitars! The girls in his lap! Only one never quite knows
what it is he holds in his lap, or whether it is really a man
playing the guitar. . . .

Soon Moldorf will be trotting in on all fours and Boris
with that helpless little laugh of his. There will be a
golden pheasant for dinner and Anjou and short fat
cigars. And Cronstadt, when he gets the latest news, will
live a little harder, a little brighter, for five minutes; and
then he will subside again into the humus of his ideology
and perhaps a poem will be born, a big golden bell of a
poem without a tongue.

Had to knock off for an hour or so. Another customer
to look at the apartment. Upstairs the bloody Englishman is practicing his Bach. It is imperative now, when
someone comes to look at the apartment, to run upstairs
and ask the pianist to lay off for a while.

Elsa is telephoning the greengrocer. The plumber is
putting a new seat on the toilet bowl. Whenever the
doorbell rings Boris loses his equilibrium. In the excitement he has dropped his glasses; he is on his hands and
knees, his frock coat is dragging the floor. It is a little like
the Grand Guignol—the starving poet come to give the
butcher's daughter lessons. Every time the phone rings
the poet's mouth waters. Mallarmé sounds like a sirloin
steak, Victor Hugo like *foie de veau*. Elsa is ordering a
delicate little lunch for Boris—"a nice juicy little pork
chop," she says. I see a whole flock of pink hams lying
cold on the marble, wonderful hams cushioned in white
fat. I have a terrific hunger though we've only had break-

fast a few minutes ago—it's the lunch that I'll have to skip. It's only Wednesdays that I eat lunch, thanks to Borowski. Elsa is still telephoning—she forgot to order a piece of bacon. "Yes, a nice little piece of bacon, not too fatty," she says . . . *Zut alors!* Throw in some sweetbreads, throw in some mountain oysters and some psst clams! Throw in some fried liverwurst while you're at it; I could gobble up the fifteen hundred plays of Lope de Vega in one sitting.

It is a beautiful woman who has come to look at the apartment. An American, of course. I stand at the window with my back to her watching a sparrow pecking at a fresh turd. Amazing how easily the sparrow is provided for. It is raining a bit and the drops are very big. I used to think a bird couldn't fly if its wings got wet. Amazing how these rich dames come to Paris and find all the swell studios. A little talent and a big purse. If it rains they have a chance to display their brand new slickers. Food is nothing: sometimes they're so busy gadding about that they haven't time for lunch. Just a little sandwich, a wafer, at the Café de la Paix or the Ritz Bar. "For the daughters of gentlefolk only"—that's what it says at the old studio of Puvis de Chavannes. Happened to pass there the other day. Rich American cunts with paint boxes slung over their shoulders. A little talent and a fat purse.

The sparrow is hopping frantically from one cobblestone to another. Truly herculean efforts, if you stop to examine closely. Everywhere there is food lying about— in the gutter, I mean. The beautiful American woman is inquiring about the toilet. The toilet! Let me show you, you velvet-snooted gazelle! The toilet, you say? *Par ici, Madame. N'oubliez pas que les places numérotées sont réservées aux mutilés de la guerre.*

Boris is rubbing his hands—he is putting the finishing touches to the deal. The dogs are barking in the courtyard; they bark like wolves. Upstairs Mrs. Melverness is moving the furniture around. She had nothing to do all day, she's bored; if she finds a crumb of dirt anywhere she cleans the whole house. There's a bunch of green grapes on the table and a bottle of wine—*vin de choix,* ten degrees. "Yes," says Boris. "I could make a washstand for you, just come here, please. Yes, this is the toilet. There is one upstairs too, of course. Yes, a thousand francs a month. You don't care much for Utrillo, you say? No, this is it. It needs a new washer, that's all. . . ."

She's going in a minute now. Boris hasn't even introduced me this time. The son of a bitch! Whenever it's a rich cunt he forgets to introduce me. In a few minutes I'll be able to sit down again and type. Somehow I don't feel like it any more today. My spirit is dribbling away. She may come back in an hour or so and take the chair from under my ass. How the hell can a man write when he doesn't know where he's going to sit the next half-hour? If this rich bastard takes the place I won't even have a place to sleep. It's hard to know, when you're in such a jam, which is worse—not having a place to sleep or not having a place to work. One can sleep almost anywhere, but one must have a place to work. Even if it's not a masterpiece you're doing. Even a bad novel requires a chair to sit on and a bit of privacy. These rich cunts never think of a thing like that. Whenever they want to lower their soft behinds there's always a chair standing ready for them. . . .

Last night we left Sylvester and his God sitting together before the hearth. Sylvester in his pajamas, Moldorf with a cigar between his lips. Sylvester is peeling an orange. He puts the peel on the couch cover. Moldorf draws closer to him. He asks permission to read again that brilliant parody, *The Gates of Heaven.* We are getting ready to go, Boris and I. We are too gay for this sickroom atmosphere. Tania is going with us. She is gay because she is going to escape. Boris is gay because the God in Moldorf is dead. I am gay because it is another act we are going to put on.

Moldorf's voice is reverent. "Can I stay with you, Sylvester, until you go to bed?" He has been staying with him for the last six days, buying medicine, running errands for Tania, comforting, consoling, guarding the portals against malevolent intruders like Boris and his scalawags. He is like a savage who has discovered that his idol was mutilated during the night. There he sits, at the idol's feet, with breadfruit and grease and jabberwocky prayers. His voice goes out unctuously. His limbs are already paralyzed.

To Tania he speaks as if she were a priestess who had broken her vows. "You must make yourself worthy. Sylvester is your God." And while Sylvester is upstairs suffering (he has a little wheeze in the chest) the priest and the priestess devour the food. "You are polluting yourself," he says, the gravy dripping from his lips. He has the capacity for eating and suffering at the same time. While he fends off the dangerous ones he puts out his fat little paw and strokes Tania's hair. "I'm beginning to fall in love with you. You are like my Fanny."

In other respects it has been a fine day for Moldorf. A letter arrived from America. Moe is getting A's in everything. Murray is learning to ride the bicycle. The victrola was repaired. You can see from the expression on his face that there were other things in the letter besides report cards and velocipedes. You can be sure of it because this afternoon he bought 325 francs worth of jewelry for his Fanny. In addition he wrote her a twenty-page letter. The *garçon* brought him page after page, filled his fountain pen, served his coffee and cigars, fanned him a little when he perspired, brushed the crumbs from the table, lit his cigar when it went out, bought stamps for him, danced on him, pirouetted, salaamed . . . broke his spine damned near. The tip was fat. Bigger and fatter than a Corona Corona. Moldorf probably mentioned it in his diary. It was for Fanny's sake. The bracelet and the earrings, they were worth every sou he spent. Better to spend it on Fanny than waste it on little strumpets like Germaine and Odette. Yes, he told Tania so. He showed her his trunk. It is crammed with gifts—for Fanny, and for Moe and Murray.

"My Fanny is the most intelligent woman in the world. I have been searching and searching to find a flaw in her—but there's not one.

"She's perfect. I'll tell you what Fanny can do. She plays bridge like a shark; she's interested in Zionism; you give her an old hat, for instance, and see what she can do with it. A little twist here, a ribbon there, and *voilà quelque chose de beau!* Do you know what is perfect bliss? To sit beside Fanny, when Moe and Murray have gone to bed, and listen to the radio. She sits there so peacefully. I am rewarded for all my struggles and heartaches in just watching her. She listens intelligently. When I think of your stinking Montparnasse and then of my evening in Bay Ridge with Fanny after a big meal, I tell you there is no comparison. A simple thing like food, the children, the soft lamps, and Fanny sitting there, a little tired, but cheerful, contented, heavy with bread . . . We just sit there for hours without saying a word. That's bliss!

"Today she writes me a letter—not one of those dull stock-report letters. She writes me from the heart, in language that even my little Murray could understand. She's delicate about everything, Fanny. She says that the children must continue their education but the expense worries her. It will cost a thousand bucks to send little Murray to school. Moe, of corse, will get a scholarship. But little Murray, that little genius, Murray, what are we going to do about him? I wrote Fanny not to worry. Send Murray to school, I said. What's another thousand dollars? I'll make more money this year than ever before. I'll do it for little Murray—because he's a genius, that kid."

I should like to be there when Fanny opens the trunk. "See, Fanny, this is what I bought in Budapest from an old Jew. . . . This is what they wear in Bulgaria—it's pure wool. . . . This belonged to the Duke of something or other—no, you don't wind it, you put it in the sun. . . . This I want you to wear, Fanny, when we go to the Opera . . . wear it with that comb I showed you. . . . And this, Fanny, is something Tania picked up for me . . . she's a little bit on your type. . . ."

And Fanny is sitting there on the settee, just as she was in the oleograph, with Moe on one side of her and little Murray, Murray the genius, on the other. Her fat legs are a little too short to reach the floor. Her eyes have a dull permanganate glow. Breasts like ripe red cabbage; they bobble a little when she leans forward. But the sad thing about her is that the juice has been cut off. She sits there like a dead storage battery; her face is out of plumb —it needs a little animation, a sudden spurt of juice to bring it back into focus. Moldorf is jumping around in front of her like a fat toad. His flesh quivers. He slips and it is difficult for him to roll over again on his belly. She prods him with her thick toes. His eyes protrude a little further. "Kick me again, Fanny, that was good." She gives him a good prod this time—it leaves a permanent dent in his paunch. His face is close to the carpet; the wattles are joggling in the nap of the rug. He livens up a bit, flips around, springs from furniture to furniture. "Fanny, you are marvelous!" He is sitting now on her shoulder. He bites a little piece from her ear, just a little tip from the lobe where it doesn't hurt. But she's still dead—all storage battery and no juice. He falls on her lap and lies there quivering like a toothache. He is all warm now and helpless. His belly glistens like a patent-leather shoe. In the sockets of his eyes a pair of fancy vest buttons. "Unbutton my eyes, Fanny, I want to see you better!" Fanny carries him to bed and drops a little hot wax over his eyes. She puts rings around his navel and a thermometer up his ass. She places him and he quivers again. Suddenly he's dwindled, shrunk completely out of sight. She searches all over for him, in her intestines, everywhere. Something is tickling her—she doesn't know where exactly. The bed is full of toads and fancy vest buttons. "Fanny, where are you?" Something is tickling her—she can't say where. The buttons are dropping off the bed. The toads are climbing the walls. A tickling and a tickling. "Fanny, take the wax out of my eyes!

I want to look at you!" But Fanny is laughing, squirming with laughter. There is something inside her, tickling and tickling. She'll die laughing if she doesn't find it. "Fanny, the trunk is full of beautiful things. Fanny, do you hear me?" Fanny is laughing, laughing like a fat worm. Her belly is swollen with laughter. Her legs are getting blue. "O God, Morris, there is something tickling me. . . I can't help it!"

Sunday! Left the Villa Borghese a little before noon, just as Boris was getting ready to sit down to lunch. I left out of a sense of delicacy, because it really pains Boris to see me sitting there in the studio with an empty belly. Why he doesn't invite me to lunch with him I don't know. He says he can't afford it, but that's no excuse. Anyway, I'm delicate about it. If it pains him to eat alone in my presence it would probably pain him more to share his meal with me. It's not my place to pry into his secret affairs.

Dropped in at the Cronstadts' and they were eating too. A young chicken with wild rice. Pretended that I had eaten already, but I could have torn the chicken from the baby's hands. This is not just false modesty—it's a kind of perversion, I'm thinking. Twice they asked me if I wouldn't join them. No! No! Wouldn't even accept a cup of coffee after the meal. I'm *delicat*, I am! On the way out I cast a lingering glance at the bones lying on the baby's plate—there was still meat on them.

Prowling around aimlessly. A beautiful day—so far. The Rue de Buci is alive, crawling. The bars wide open and the curbs lined with bicycles. All the meat and vegetable markets are in full swing. Arms loaded with truck bandaged in newspapers. A fine Catholic Sunday—in the morning, at least.

High noon and here I am standing on an empty belly at the confluence of all these crooked lanes that reek with the odor of food. Opposite me is the Hôtel de Louisiane.

34

A grim old hostelry known to the bad boys of the Rue de Buci in the good old days. Hotels and food, and I'm walking about like a leper with crabs gnawing at my entrails. On Sunday mornings there's a fever in the streets. Nothing like it anywhere, except perhaps on the East Side, or down around Chatham Square. The Rue de l'Echaudé is seething. The streets twist and turn, at every angle a fresh hive of activity. Long queues of people with vegetables under their arms, turning in here and there with crisp, sparkling appetites. Nothing but food, food, food. Makes one delirious.

Pass the Square de Furstenberg. Looks different now, at high noon. The other night when I passed by it was deserted, bleak, spectral. In the middle of the square four black trees that have not yet begun to blossom. Intellectual trees, nourished by the paving stones. Like T. S. Eliot's verse. Here, by God, if Marie Laurencin ever brought her Lesbians out into the open, would be the place for them to commune. *Très lesbienne ici.* Sterile, hybrid, dry as Boris' heart.

In the little garden adjoining the Eglise St. Germain are a few dismounted gargoyles. Monsters that jut forward with a terrifying plunge. On the benches other monsters—old people, idiots, cripples, epileptics. Snoozing there quietly, waiting for the dinner bell to ring. At the Galerie Zak across the way some imbecile has made a picture of the cosmos—*on the flat.* A painter's cosmos! Full of odds and ends, bric-a-brac. In the lower left-hand corner, however, there's an anchor—and a dinner bell. Salute! Salute! O Cosmos!

Still prowling around. Mid afternoon. Guts rattling. Beginning to rain now. Notre-Dame rises tomblike from the water. The gargoyles lean far out over the lace façade. They hang there like an *idée fixe* in the mind of a monomaniac. An old man with yellow whiskers approaches me. Has some Jaworski nonsense in his hand. Comes up to me with his head thrown back and the rain splashing in his face turns the golden sands to mud. Bookstore with some of Raoul Dufy's drawings in the window. Drawings of charwomen with rosebushes between their legs. A treatise on the philosophy of Joan Miró. The *philosophy*, mind you!

In the same window: *A Man Cut In Slices!* Chapter one: the man in the eyes of his family. Chapter two: the same in the eyes of his mistress. Chapter three:—No chapter three. Have to come back tomorrow for chapters three and four. Every day the window trimmer turns a fresh page. *A man cut in slices*. . . . You can't imagine how furious I am not to have thought of a title like that! Where is this bloke who writes "the same in the eyes of his mistress . . . the same in the eyes of . . . the same . . .?" Where is this guy? Who is he? I want to hug him. I wish to Christ I had had brains enough to think of a title like that—instead of *Crazy Cock* and the other fool things I invented. Well, fuck a duck! I congratulate him just the same.

I wish him luck with his fine title. Here's another slice for you—for your next book! Ring me up some day. I'm living at the Villa Borghese. We're all dead, or dying, or about to die. We need good titles. We need meat—slices and slices of meat—juicy tenderloins, porterhouse steaks, kidneys, mountain oysters, sweetbreads. Some day, when I'm standing at the corner of 42nd Street and Broadway, I'm going to remember this title and I'm going to put down everything that goes on in my noodle—caviar, rain drops, axle grease, vermicelli, liverwurst—slices and slices of it. And I'll tell no one why, after I had put everything down, I suddenly went home and chopped the baby to pieces. *Un acte gratuit pour vous, cher monsieur si bien coupé en tranches!*

How a man can wander about all day on an empty belly, and even get an erection once in a while, is one of those mysteries which are too easily explained by the "anatomists of the soul." On a Sunday afternoon, when the shutters are down and the proletariat possesses the street in a kind of dumb torpor, there are certain thoroughfares which remind one of nothing less than a big chancrous cock laid open longitudinally. And it is just these highways, the Rue St. Denis, for instance, or the Faubourg du Temple—which attract one irresistibly, much as in the old days, around Union Square or the upper reaches of the Bowery, one was drawn to the dime museums where in the show windows there were displayed wax reproductions of various organs of the body eaten away by syphilis and other venereal diseases. The city sprouts out like a huge organism diseased in every part, the beautiful thoroughfares only a little less repulsive because they have been drained of their pus.

At the Cité Nortier, somewhere near the Place du Combat, I pause a few minutes to drink in the full squalor of the scene. It is a rectangular court like many another which one glimpses through the low passageways that flank the old arteries of Paris. In the middle of the court is a clump of decrepit buildings which have so rotted away that they have collapsed on one another and formed a sort of intestinal embrace. The ground is uneven, the flagging slippery with slime. A sort of human dump heap which has been filled in with cinders and dry garbage. The sun is setting fast. The colors die. They shift from purple to dried blood, from nacre to bister, from cool dead grays to pigeon shit. Here and there a lopsided monster stands in the window blinking like an owl. There is the shrill squawk of children with pale faces and bony limbs, rickety little urchins marked with the forceps. A fetid odor seeps from the walls, the odor of a mildewed mattress. Europe—medieval, grotesque, monstrous: a symphony in B-mol. Directly across the street the Ciné Combat offers its distinguished clientele *Metropolis*.

Coming away my mind reverts to a book that I was reading only the other day. "The town was a shambles; corpses, mangled by butchers and stripped by plunderers, lay thick in the streets; wolves sneaked from the suburbs to eat them; the black death and other plagues crept in to keep them company, and the English came marching on; the while the *danse macabre* whirled about the tombs in all the cemeteries. . . ." Paris during the days of Charles the Silly! A lovely book! Refreshing, appetizing. I'm still enchanted by it. About the patrons and prodromes of the Renaissance I know little, but Madam Pimpernel, *la belle boulangère*, and Maître Jehan Crapotte, *l'orfèvre*, these occupy my spare thoughts still. Not forgetting Rodin, the evil genius of *The Wandering Jew*, who practiced his nefarious ways "until the day when he was enflamed and outwitted by the octoroon Cecily." Sitting in the Square du Temple, musing over the doings of the horse knackers led by Jean Caboche, I have thought long and ruefully over the sad fate of Charles the Silly. A half-wit, who prowled about the halls of his Hôtel St. Paul, garbed in the filthiest rags, eaten away by ulcers and vermin, gnawing a bone, when they flung him one, like a mangy dog. At the Rue des Lions I looked for the stones of the old menagerie where he once fed his pets. His only diversion, poor dolt, aside from those card games with his "low-born companion," Odette de Champdivers.

It was a Sunday afternoon, much like this, when I first met Germaine. I was strolling along the Boulevard Beaumarchais, rich by a hundred francs or so which my wife had frantically cabled from America. There was a touch of spring in the air, a poisonous, malefic spring that seemed to burst from the manholes. Night after night I had been coming back to this quarter, attracted by certain leprous streets which only revealed their sinister splendor when the light of day had oozed away and the whores commenced to take up their posts. The Rue du Pasteur-Wagner is one I recall in particular, corner of the Rue Amelot which hides behind the boulevard like a slumbering lizard. Here, at the neck of the bottle, so to speak, there was always a cluster of vultures who croaked and flapped their dirty wings, who reached out with sharp talons and plucked you into a doorway. Jolly, rapacious devils who didn't even give you time to button your pants when it was over. Led you into a little room off the street, a room without a window usually, and, sitting on the edge of the bed with skirts tucked up gave you a quick inspection, spat on your cock, and placed it for you. While you washed yourself another one stood at the door and, holding her victim by the hand, watched nonchalantly as you gave the finishing touches to your toilet.

Germaine was different. There was nothing to tell me so from her appearance. Nothing to distinguish her from the other trollops who met each afternoon and evening at the Café de l'Eléphant. As I say, it was a spring day and the few francs my wife had scraped up to cable me were jingling in my pocket. I had a sort of vague premonition that I would not reach the Bastille without being taken in tow by one of these buzzards. Sauntering along the boulevard I had noticed her verging toward me with that curious trot-about air of a whore and the run-down heels and cheap jewelry and the pasty look of their kind which the rouge only accentuates. It was not difficult to come to terms with her. We sat in the back of the little *tabac* called L'Eléphant and talked it over quickly. In a few minutes we were in a five franc room on the Rue Amelot, the curtains drawn and the covers thrown back. She didn't rush things, Germaine. She sat on the *bidet* soaping herself and talked to me pleasantly about this and that; she liked the knickerbockers I was wearing. *Très chic!* she thought. They were once, but I had worn the seat out of them; fortunately the jacket covered my ass. As she stood up to dry herself, still talking to me pleasantly, suddenly she dropped the towel and, advancing toward me leisurely, she commenced rubbing her pussy affectionately, stroking it with her two hands, caressing it, patting it, patting it. There was something about her eloquence at that moment and the way she thrust that rosebush under my nose which remains unforgettable; she spoke of it as if it were some extraneous object which she had acquired at great cost, an object whose value had increased with time and which now she prized above everything in the world. Her words imbued it with a peculiar fragrance; it was no longer just her private organ, but a treasure, a magic, potent treasure, a God-given thing—and none the less so because she traded it day in and day out for a few pieces of silver. As she flung herself on the bed, with legs spread wide apart, she cupped it with her hands and stroked it some more, murmuring all the while in that hoarse, cracked voice of hers that it was good, beautiful, a treasure, a little treasure. And it *was* good, that little pussy of hers! That Sunday afternoon, with its poisonous breath of spring in the air, everything clicked again. As we stepped out of the hotel I looked her over again in the harsh light of day and I saw clearly what a whore she was—the gold teeth, the geranium in her hat, the run-down heels, etc., etc. Even the fact that she had wormed a dinner out of me and cigarettes and taxi hadn't the least disturbing effect upon me. I encouraged it, in fact. I liked her so well that after dinner we went back to the hotel again and took another shot at it. "For love," this time. And again that big, bushy thing of hers worked its bloom and magic. It began to have an independent existence—for me too. There was Germaine and there was that rose-bush of hers. I liked them separately and I liked them together.

As I say, she was different, Germaine. Later, when she discovered my true circumstances, she treated me nobly —blew me to drinks, gave me credit, pawned my things, introduced me to her friends, and so on. She even apologized for not lending me money, which I understood quite well after her *maquereau* had been pointed out to me. Night after night I walked down the Boulevard Beaumarchais to the little *tabac* where they all congregated and I waited for her to stroll in and give me a few minutes of her precious time.

When some time later I came to write about Claude, it was not Claude that I was thinking of but Germaine. . . . "All the men she's been with and now you, just you, and barges going by, masts and hulls, the whole damned current of life flowing through you, through her, through all the guys behind you and after you, the flowers and the birds and the sun streaming in and the fragrance of it choking you, annihilating you." That was for Germaine! Claude was not the same, though I admired her tremendously—I even thought for a while that I loved her. Claude had a soul and a conscience; she had refinement, too, which is bad—in a whore. Claude always imparted a feeling of sadness; she left the impression, unwittingly, of course, that you were just one more added to the stream which fate had ordained to destroy her. *Unwittingly*, I say, because Claude was the last person in the world who would consciously create such an image in one's mind. She was too delicate, too sensitive for that. At bottom, Claude was just a good French girl of average breed and intelligence whom life had tricked somehow; something in her there was which was not tough enough to withstand the shock of daily experience. For her were meant those terrible words of Louis-Philippe, "and a night comes when all is over, when so many jaws have closed upon us that we no longer have the strength to stand, and our meat hangs upon our bodies, as though it had been masticated by every mouth." Germaine, on the other hand, was a whore from the cradle; she was thoroughly satisfied with her role, enjoyed it in fact, except when her stomach pinched or her shoes gave out, little surface things of no account, nothing that ate into her soul, nothing that created torment. *Ennui!* That was the worst she ever felt. Days there were, no doubt, when she had a bellyful, as we say—but no more than that! Most of the time she enjoyed it—or gave the illusion of enjoying it. It made a difference of course, whom she went with—or *came* with. But the principal thing was *a man*. A man! That was what she craved. A man with something between his legs that could tickle her, that could make her writhe in ecstasy, make her grab that bushy twat of hers with both hands and rub it joyfully, boastfully, proudly, with a sense of connection, a sense of life. That was the only place where she experienced any life—down there where she clutched herself with both hands.

Germaine was a whore all the way through, even down to her good heart, her whore's heart which is not really a good heart but a lazy one, an indifferent, flaccid heart that can be touched for a moment, a heart without reference to any fixed point within, a big, flaccid whore's heart that can detach itself for a moment from its true center. However vile and circumscribed was that world which she had created for herself, nevertheless she functioned in it superbly. And that in itself is a tonic thing. When, after we had become well acquainted, her companions would twit me, saying that I was in love with Germaine (a situation almost inconceivable to them), I would say: "Sure! Sure, I'm in love with her! And what's more, I'm going to be faithful to her!" A lie, of course, because I could no more think of loving Germaine than I could think of loving a spider; and if I *was* faithful, it was not to Germaine but to that bushy thing she carried between her legs. Whenever I looked at another woman I thought immediately of Germaine, of that flaming bush which she had left in my mind and which seemed imperishable. It gave me pleasure to sit on the *terrasse* of the little *tabac* and observe her as she plied her trade, observe her as she resorted to the same grimaces, the same tricks, with others as she had with me. "She's doing her job!"—that's how I felt about it, and it was with approbation that I regarded her transactions. Later, when I had taken up with Claude, and I saw her night after night sitting in her acustomed place, her round little buttocks chubbily ensconced in the plush settee, I felt a sort of inexpressible rebellion toward her; a whore, it seemed to me, had no right to be sitting there like a lady, waiting timidly for someone to approach and all the while abstemiously sipping her *chocolat*. Germaine was a hustler. She didn't wait for you to come to her—she went out and grabbed you. I remember so well the holes in her stockings, and the torn ragged shoes; I remember too how she stood at the bar and with blind, courageous defiance threw a strong drink down her stomach and marched out again. A hustler! Perhaps it wasn't so pleasant to smell that boozy breath of hers, that breath compounded of weak coffee, cognac, *apéritifs*, Pernods and all the other stuff she guzzled between times, what to warm herself and what to summon up strength and courage, but the fire of it penetrated her, it glowed down there between her legs where women ought to glow, and there was established that circuit which makes one feel the earth under his legs again. When she lay there with her legs apart and moaning, even if she did moan that way for any and everybody, it was good, it was a proper show of feeling. She didn't stare up at the ceiling with a vacant look or count the bedbugs on the wallpaper; she kept her mind on her business, she talked about the things a man wants to hear when he's climbing over a woman. Whereas Claude—well, with Claude there was always a certain delicacy, even when she got under the sheets with you. And her delicacy offended. Who wants a *delicate* whore! Claude would even ask you to turn your face away when she squatted over the *bidet*. All wrong! A man, when he's burning up with passion, wants to see things; he wants to see *everything*, even how they make water. And while it's all very nice to know that a woman has a mind, literature coming from the cold corpse of a whore is the last thing to be served in bed. Germaine had the right idea: she was ignorant and lusty, she put her heart and soul into her work. She was a whore all the way through—and that was her virtue!

Easter came in like a frozen hare—but it was fairly warm in bed. Today it is lovely again and along the Champs-Elysées at twilight it is like an outdoor seraglio choked with dark-eyed houris. The trees are in full foliage and of a verdure so pure, so rich, that it seems as though they were still wet and glistening with dew. From the Palais du Louvre to the Etoile it is like a piece of music for the pianoforte. For five days I have not touched the typewriter nor looked at a book; nor have I had a single idea in my head except to go to the American Express. At nine this morning I was there, just as the doors were being opened, and again at one o'clock. No news. At four-thirty I dash out of the hotel, resolved to make a last-minute stab at it. Just as I turn the corner I brush against Walter Pach. Since he doesn't recognize me, and since I have nothing to say to him, I make no attempt to arrest him. Later, when I am stretching my legs in the Tuileries his figure reverts to mind. He was a little stooped, pensive, with a sort of serene yet reserved smile on his face. I wonder, as I look up at this softly enameled sky, so faintly tinted, which does not bulge today with heavy rain clouds but smiles like a piece of old china, I wonder what goes on in the mind of this man who translated the four thick volumes of the *History of Art* when he takes in this blissful cosmos with his drooping eye.

Along the Champs-Elysées, ideas pouring from me like sweat. I ought to be rich enough to have a secretary to whom I could dictate as I walk, because my best thoughts always come when I am away from the machine.

Walking along the Champs-Elysées I keep thinking of my really superb health. When I say "health" I mean optimism, to be truthful. Incurably optimistic! Still have one foot in the nineteenth century. I'm a bit retarded, like most Americans. Carl finds it disgusting, this optimism. "I have only to talk about a meal," he says, "and you're radiant!" It's a fact. The mere thought of a meal—*another* meal—rejuvenates me. A meal! That means something to go on—a few solid hours of work, an erection possibly. I don't deny it. I have health, good solid, animal health. The only thing that stands between me and a future is a meal, *another* meal.

As for Carl, he's not himself these days. He's upset, his nerves are jangled. He says he's ill, and I believe him, but I don't feel badly about it.

I *can't*. In fact, it makes me laugh. And that offends him, of course. Everything wounds him—my laughter, my hunger, my persistence, my insouciance, *everything*. One day he wants to blow his brains out because he can't stand this lousy hole of a Europe any more; the next day he talks of going to Arizona "where they look you square in the eye."

"Do it!" I say. "Do one thing or the other, you bastard, but don't try to cloud my healthy eye with your melancholy breath!"

But that's just it! In Europe one gets used to doing nothing. You sit on your ass and whine all day. You get contaminated. You rot.

Fundamentally Carl is a snob, an aristocratic little prick who lives in a dementia praecox kingdom all his own. "I hate Paris!" he whines. "All these stupid people playing cards all day . . . look at them! And the writing! What's the use of putting words together? I can be a writer without writing, can't I? What does it prove if I write a book? What do we want with books anyway? There are too many books already. . . ."

My eye, but I've been all over that ground—years and

years ago. I've lived out my melancholy youth. I don't
give a fuck any more what's behind me, or what's ahead
of me. I'm healthy. Incurably healthy. No sorrows, no
regrets. No past, no future. The present is enough for
me. Day by day. Today! *Le bel aujourd'hui!*

He has one day a week off, Carl, and on that day he's
more miserable, if you can imagine it, than on any other
day of the week. Though he professes to despise food,
the only way he seems to enjoy himself on his day off is
to order a big spread. Perhaps he does it for my benefit—
I don't know, and I don't ask. If he chooses to add martyr-
dom to his list of vices, let him—it's O.K. with me. Anyway, last Tuesday, after squandering what he had on a
big spread, he steers me to the Dôme, the last place in the
world I would seek on my day off. But one not only gets
acquiescent here—one gets supine.

Standing at the Dôme bar is Marlowe, soused to the
ears. He's been on a bender, as he calls it, for the last
five days. That means a continuous drunk, a peregrina-
tion from one bar to another, day and night without in-
terruption, and finally a layoff at the American Hospital. Marlowe's bony emaciated face is nothing but a skull
perforated by two deep sockets in which there are buried
a pair of dead clams. His back is covered with sawdust—
he has just had a little snooze in the water closet. In his
coat pocket are the proofs for the next issue of his review,
he was on his way to the printer with the proofs, it seems,
when some one inveigled him to have a drink. He talks
about it as though it happened months ago. He takes out
the proofs and spreads them over the bar; they are full of
coffee stains and dried spittle. He tries to read a poem
which he had written in Greek, but the proofs are undecipherable. Then he decides to deliver a speech, in
French, but the *gérant* puts a stop to it. Marlowe is
piqued: his one ambition is to talk a French which even
the *garçon* will understand. Of Old French he is a master;
of the surrealists he has made excellent translations; but
to say a simple thing like "get the hell out of here, you
old prick!"—that is beyond him. Nobody understands

Marlowe's French, not even the whores. For that matter, it's difficult enough to understand his English when he's under the weather. He blabbers and spits like a confirmed stutterer . . . no sequence to his phrases. *"You pay!"* that's one thing he manages to get out clearly.

Even if he is fried to the hat some fine preservative instinct always warns Marlowe when it is time to act. If there is any doubt in his mind as to how the drinks are going to be paid he will be sure to put on a stunt. The usual one is to pretend that he is going blind. Carl knows all his tricks by now, and so when Marlowe suddenly claps his hands to his temples and begins to act it out Carl gives him a boot in the ass and says: "Come out of it, you sap! You don't have to do that with me!"

Whether it is a cunning piece of revenge or not, I don't know, but at any rate Marlowe is paying Carl back in good coin. Leaning over us confidentially he relates in a hoarse, croaking voice a piece of gossip which he picked up in the course of his peregrinations from bar to bar. Carl looks up in amazement. He's pale under the gills. Marlowe repeats the story with variations. Each time Carl wilts a little more. "But that's impossible!" he finally blurts out. "No it ain't!" croaks Marlowe. "You're gonna lose your job . . . I got it straight." Carl looks at me in despair. "Is he shitting me, that bastard?" he murmurs in my ear. And then aloud—"What am I going to do now? I'll never find another job. It took me a year to land this one."

This, apparently, is all that Marlowe has been waiting to hear. At last he has found someone worse off than himself. "They be hard times!" he croaks, and his bony skull glows with a cold, electric fire.

Leaving the Dôme Marlowe explains between hiccups that he's got to return to San Francisco. He seems genuinely touched now by Carl's helplessness. He proposes that Carl and I take over the review during his absence. "I can trust you, Carl," he says. And then suddenly he gets an attack, a real one this time. He almost collapses in the gutter. We haul him to a *bistro* at the Boulevard

Edgar-Quinet and sit him down. This time he's really got
It—a blinding headache that makes him squeal and grunt
and rock himself to and fro like a dumb brute that's been
struck by a sledge hammer. We spill a couple of Fernet-
Brancas down his throat, lay him out on the bench and
cover his eyes with his muffler. He lies there groaning. In
a little while we hear him snoring.

"What about his proposition?" says Carl. "Should we
take it up? He says he'll give me a thousand francs when
he comes back. I know he won't, but what about it?" He
looks at Marlowe sprawled out on the bench, lifts the
muffler from his eyes, and puts it back again. Suddenly
a mischievous grin lights up his face. "Listen, Joe," he
says, beckoning me to move closer, "we'll take him up
on it. We'll take his lousy review and we'll fuck him
good and proper."

"What do you mean by that?"

"Why we'll throw out all the other contributors and
we'll fill it with our own shit—that's what!"

"Yeah, but what kind of shit?"

"Any kind . . . he won't be able to do anything about it.
We'll fuck him good and proper. One good number and
after that the magazine'll be finished. Are you game,
Joe?"

Grinning and chuckling we lift Marlowe to his feet and
haul him to Carl's room. When we turn on the lights
there's a woman in the bed waiting for Carl. "I forgot all
about her," says Carl. We turn the cunt loose and shove
Marlowe into bed. In a minute or so there's a knock at the
door. It's Van Norden. He's all aflutter. Lost a plate of
false teeth—at the Bal Nègre, he thinks. Anyway, we
get to bed, the four of us. Marlowe stinks like a smoked
fish.

In the morning Marlowe and Van Norden leave to
search for the false teeth. Marlowe is blubbering. He
imagines they are *his* teeth.

It is my last dinner at the dramatist's home. They have just rented a new piano, a concert grand. I meet Sylvester coming out of the florist's with a rubber plant in his arms. He asks me if I would carry it for him while he goes for the cigars. One by one I've fucked myself out of all these free meals which I had planned so carefully. One by one the husbands turn against me, or the wives. As I walk along with the rubber plant in my arms I think of that night a few months back when the idea first occurred to me. I was sitting on a bench near the Coupole, fingering the wedding ring which I had tried to pawn off on a *garçon* at the Dôme. He had offered me six francs for it and I was in a rage about it. But the belly was getting the upper hand. Ever since I left Mona I had worn the ring on my pinkie. It was so much a part of me that it had never occurred to me to sell it. It was one of those orange-blossom affairs in white gold. Worth a dollar and a half once, maybe more. For three years we went along without a wedding ring and then one day when I was going to the pier to meet Mona I happened to pass a jewelry window on Maiden Lane and the whole window was stuffed with wedding rings. When I got to the pier Mona was not to be seen. I waited for the last passenger to descend the gangplank, but no Mona. Finally I asked to be shown the passenger list. Her name was not on it. I slipped the wedding ring on my pinkie and there it stayed. Once I left it in a public bath, but then I got it back again. One of the orange blossoms had fallen off.

Anyway, I was sitting there on the bench with my head down, twiddling the ring, when suddenly someone clapped me on the back. To make it brief, I got a meal and a few francs besides. And then it occurred to me, like a flash, that no one would refuse a man a meal if only he had the courage to demand it. I went immediately to a café and wrote a dozen letters. "Would you let me have dinner with you once a week? Tell me what day is most convenient for you." It worked like a charm. I was not only fed . . . I was feasted. Every night I went home drunk. They couldn't do enough for me, these generous once-a-week souls. What happened to me between times was none of their affair. Now and then the thoughtful ones presented me with cigarettes, or a little pin money. They were all obviously relieved when they realized that they would see me only once a week. And they were still more relieved when I said—"it won't be necessary any more." They never asked why. They congratulated me, and that was all. Often the reason was I had found a better host; I could afford to scratch off the ones who were a pain in the ass. But that thought never occurred to them. Finally I had a steady, solid program—a fixed schedule. On Tuesdays I knew it would be this kind of a meal and on Fridays that kind. Cronstadt, I knew, would have champagne for me and homemade apple pie. And Carl would invite me out, take me to a different restaurant each time, order rare wines, invite me to the theater afterward or take me to the Cirque Médrano. They were curious about one another, my hosts. Would ask me which place I liked best, who was the best cook, etc. I think I liked Cronstadt's joint best of all, perhaps because he chalked the meal up on the wall each time. Not that it eased my conscience to see what I owed him, because I had no intention of paying him back nor had he any illusions about being requited. No, it was the odd numbers which intrigued me. He used to figure it out to the last centime. If I was to pay in full I would have had to break a sou. His wife was a marvelous cook and she didn't give a fuck about those centimes Cronstadt added up. She took it out of me in carbon copies. A fact! If I hadn't any fresh carbons for her when I showed up, she was crestfallen. And for that I would have to take the little girl to the Luxembourg next day, play with her for two or three hours, a task which drove me wild because she spoke nothing but Hungarian and French. They were a queer lot on the whole, my hosts. . . .

At Tania's I look down on the spread from the balcony. Moldorf is there, sitting beside his idol. He is warming his feet at the hearth, a monstrous look of gratitude in his watery eyes. Tania is running over the adagio. The adagio says very distinctly: no more words of love! I am at the fountain again, watching the turtles pissing green milk. Sylvester has just come back from Broadway with a heart full of love. All night I was lying on a bench outside the mall while the globe was sprayed with warm turtle piss and the horses stiffened with priapic fury galloped like mad without ever touching the ground. All night long I smell the lilacs in the little dark room where she is taking down her hair, the lilacs that I bought for her as she went to meet Sylvester. He came back with a heart full of love, she said, and the lilacs are in her hair, her mouth, they are choking her armpits. The room is swimming with love and turtle piss and warm lilacs and the horses are galloping like mad. In the morning dirty teeth and scum on the windowpanes; the little gate that leads to the mall is locked. People are going to work and the shutters are rattling like coats of mail. In the bookstore opposite the fountain is the story of Lake Chad, the silent lizards, the gorgeous gamboge tints. All the letters I wrote her, drunken ones with a blunt stub, crazy ones with bits of charcoal, little pieces from bench to bench, firecrackers, doilies, tutti-frutti; they will be going over them now, together, and he will compliment me one day. He will say, as he flicks his cigar ash: "Really, you write quite well. Let's see, you're a surrealist, aren't you?" Dry, brittle voice, teeth full of dandruff, solo for solar plexus, g for gaga.

Upon the balcony with the rubber plant and the adagio

going on down below. The keys are black and white,
then black, then white, then white and black. And you
want to know if you can play something for me. Yes, play
something with those big thumbs of yours. Play the adagio since that's the only goddamned thing you know.
Play it, and then cut off your big thumbs.

That adagio! I don't know why she insists on playing
it all the time. The old piano wasn't good enough for her;
she had to rent a concert grand—for the adagio! When
I see her big thumbs pressing the keyboard and that silly
rubber plant beside me I feel like that madman of the
North who threw his clothes away and, sitting naked in
the wintry boughs, threw nuts down into the herring-
frozen sea. There is something exasperating about this
movement, something abortively melancholy about it, as
if it had been written in lava, as if it had the color of lead
and milk mixed. And Sylvester, with his head cocked to
one side like an auctioneer, Sylvester says: "Play that
other one you were practicing today." It's beautiful to
have a smoking jacket, a good cigar and a wife who plays
the piano. So relaxing. So lenitive. Between the acts you
go out for a smoke and a breath of fresh air. Yes, her fingers are very supple, extraordinarily supple. She does
batik work too. Would you like to try a Bulgarian cigarette? I say, pigeon breast, what's that other movement
I like so well? The scherzo! Ah, yes, the scherzo! Excellent, the scherzo! Count Waldemar von Schwisseneinzug
speaking. Cool, dandruff eyes. Halitosis. Gaudy socks.
And croutons in the pea soup, if you please. We always
have pea soup Friday nights. Won't you try a little red
wine? The red wine goes with the meat, you know. A
dry, crisp voice. Have a cigar, won't you? Yes, I like my
work, but I don't attach any importance to it. My next
play will involve a pluralistic conception of the universe.
Revolving drums with calcium lights. O'Neill is dead. I
think, dear, you should lift your foot from the pedal
more frequently. Yes, that part is very nice . . . *very* nice,
don't you think? Yes, the characters go around with
microphones in their trousers. The locale is in Asia, be-

cause the atmospheric conditions are more conducive. Would you like to try a little Anjou? We bought it especially for you. . . .

All through the meal this patter continues. It feels exactly as if he had taken out that circumcised dick of his and was peeing on us. Tania is bursting with the strain. Ever since he came back with a heart full of love this monologue has been going on. He talks while he's undressing, she tells me—a steady stream of warm piss, as though his bladder had been punctured. When I think of Tania crawling into bed with this busted bladder I get enraged. To think that a poor, withered bastard with those cheap Broadway plays up his sleeve should be pissing on the woman I love. Calling for red wine and revolving drums and croutons in his pea soup. The cheek of him! To think that he can lie beside that furnace I stoked for him and do nothing but make water! My God, man, you ought to get down on your knees and thank me. Don't you see that you have a *woman* in your house now? Can't you see she's bursting? You telling me with those strangulated adenoids of yours—" well now, I'll tell you . . . there's two ways of looking at that. . . ." Fuck your two ways of looking at things! Fuck your pluralistic universe, and your Asiatic acoustics! Don't hand me your red wine or your Anjou . . . hand *her* over . . . she belongs to me! *You* go sit by the fountain, and let *me* smell the lilacs! Pick the dandruff out of your eyes . . . and take that damned adagio and wrap it in a pair of flannel pants! And the other little movement too . . . all the little movements that you make with your weak bladder. You smile at me so confidently, so calculatingly. I'm flattering the ass off you, can't you tell? While I listen to your crap she's got her hand on me—but you don't see that. You think I like to suffer—that's my role, you say. O.K. Ask her about it! She'll tell you how I suffer. "You're cancer and delirium," she said over the phone the other day. She's got it now, the cancer and delirium, and soon you'll have to pick the scabs. Her veins are bursting, I tell you, and your talk is all sawdust. No matter how much you piss away you'll never plug up the holes. What did Mr. Wren say? *Words are loneliness.* I left a couple of words for you on the tablecloth last night—you covered them with your elbows.

He's put a fence around her as if she were a dirty, stinking bone of a saint. If he only had the courage to say "Take her!" perhaps a miracle would occur. Just that. *Take her!* and I swear everything would come out all right. Besides, maybe I wouldn't take her—did that ever occur to him, I wonder? Or I might take her for a while and hand her back, *improved.* But putting up a fence around her, that won't work. You can't put a fence around a human being. It ain't done any more. . . . You think, you poor, withered bastard, that I'm no good for her, that I might pollute her, desecrate her. You don't know how palatable is a polluted woman, how a change of semen can make a woman bloom! You think a heart full of love is enough, and perhaps it is, for the right woman, but you haven't got a heart any more . . . you are nothing but a big, empty bladder. You are sharpening your teeth and cultivating your growl. You run at her heels like a watchdog and you piddle everywhere. She didn't take you for a watchdog . . . she took you for a poet. You were a poet once, she said. And now what are you? Courage, Sylvester, courage! Take the microphone out of your pants. Put your hind leg down and stop making water everywhere. Courage, I say, because she's ditched you already. She's contaminated, I tell you, and you might as well take down the fence. No use asking me politely if the coffee doesn't taste like carbolic acid: that won't scare me away. Put rat poison in the coffee, and a little ground glass. Make some boiling hot urine and drop a few nutmegs in it. . . .

It is a communal life I have been living for the last few weeks. I have had to share myself with others, principally with some crazy Russians, a drunken Dutchman, and a big Bulgarian woman named Olga. Of the Russians there are chiefly Eugene and Anatole.

It was just a few days ago that Olga got out of the hospital where she had her tubes burned out and lost a little excess weight. However she doesn't look as if she had gone through much suffering. She weighs almost as much as a camel-backed locomotive; she drips with perspiration, has halitosis, and still wears her Circassian wig that looks like excelsior. She has two big warts on her chin from which there sprouts a clump of little hairs; she is growing a mustache.

The day after Olga was released from the hospital she commenced making shoes again. At six in the morning she is at her bench; she knocks out two pairs of shoes a day. Eugene complains that Olga is a burden, but the truth is that Olga is supporting Eugene and his wife with her two pairs of shoes a day. If Olga doesn't work there is no food. So everyone endeavors to pull Olga to bed on time, to give her enough food to keep going, etc.

Every meal starts off with soup. Whether it be onion soup, tomato soup, vegetable soup, or what not, the soup always tastes the same. Mostly it tastes as if a dish rag had been stewed in it—slightly sour, mildewed, scummy. I see Eugene hiding it away in the commode after the meal. It stays there, rotting away, until the next meal. The butter, too, is hidden away in the commode; after three days it tastes like the big toe of a cadaver.

The smell of rancid butter frying is not particularly appetizing, especially when the cooking is done in a room in which there is not the slightest form of ventilation. No sooner than I open the door I feel ill. But Eugene, as soon as he hears me coming, usually opens the shutters and pulls back the bedsheet which is strung up like a fishnet to keep out the sunlight. Poor Eugene! He looks about the room at the few sticks of furniture, at the dirty bedsheets and the wash basin with the dirty water still in it, and he says: "I am a slave!" Every day he says it, not once, but a dozen times. And then he takes his guitar from the wall and sings.

But about the smell of rancid butter. . . . There are good associations too. When I think of this rancid butter

I see myself standing in a little, old-world courtyard, a very smelly, very dreary courtyard. Through the cracks in the shutters strange figures peer out at me . . . old women with shawls, dwarfs, rat-faced pimps, bent Jews, *midinettes*, bearded idots. They totter out into the courtyard to draw water or to rinse the slop pails. One day Eugene asked me if I would empty the pail for him. I took it to the corner of the yard. There was a hole in the ground and some dirty paper lying around the hole. The little well was slimy with excrement, which in English is *shit*. I tipped the pail and there was a foul, gurgling splash followed by another and unexpected splash. When I returned the soup was dished out. All through the meal I thought of my toothbrush—it is getting old and the bristles get caught in my teeth.

When I sit down to eat I always sit near the window. I am afraid to sit on the other side of the table—it is too close to the bed and the bed is crawling. I can see bloodstains on the gray sheets if I look that way, but I try not to look that way. I look out on the courtyard where they are rinsing the slop pails.

The meal is never complete without music. As soon as the cheese is passed around Eugene jumps up and reaches for the guitar which hangs over the bed. It is always the same song. He says he has fifteen or sixteen songs in his repertoire, but I have never heard more than three. His favorite is *Charmant poème d'amour*. It is full of *angoisse* and *tristesse*.

In the afternoon we go to the cinema which is cool and dark. Eugene sits at the piano in the big pit and I sit on a bench up front. The house is empty, but Eugene sings as if he had for audience all the crowned heads of Europe. The garden door is open and the odor of wet leaves sops in and the rain blends with Eugene's *angoisse* and *tristesse*. At midnight, after the spectators have saturated the hall with perspiration and foul breaths, I return to sleep on a bench. The exit light, swimming in a halo of tobacco smoke, sheds a faint light on the lower corner of the asbestos curtain; I close my eyes every night on an artificial eye. . . .

Standing in the courtyard with a glass eye; only half the world is intelligible. The stones are wet and mossy and in the crevices are black toads. A big door bars the entrance to the cellar; the steps are slippery and soiled with bat dung. The door bulges and sags, the hinges are falling off, but there is an enameled sign on it, in perfect condition, which says: "Be sure to close the door." Why close the door? I can't make it out. I look again at the sign but it is removed; in its place there is a pane of colored glass. I take out my artificial eye, spit on it and polish it with my handkerchief. A woman is sitting on a dais above an immense carven desk; she has a snake around her neck. The entire room is lined with books and strange fish swimming in colored globes; there are maps and charts on the wall, maps of Paris before the plague, maps of the antique world, of Knossos and Carthage, of Carthage before and after the salting. In the corner of the room I see an iron bedstead and on it a corpse is lying; the woman gets up wearily, removes the corpse from the bed and absent-mindedly throws it out the window. She returns to the huge carven desk, takes a goldfish from the bowl and swallows it. Slowly the room begins to revolve and one by one the continents slide into the sea; only the woman is left, but her body is a mass of geography. I lean out the window and the Eiffel Tower is fizzing champagne; it is built entirely of numbers and shrouded in black lace. The sewers are gurgling furiously. There are nothing but roofs everywhere, laid out with execrable geometric cunning.

I have been ejected from the world like a cartridge. A deep fog has settled down, the earth is smeared with frozen grease. I can feel the city palpitating, as if it were a heart just removed from a warm body. The windows of my hotel are festering and there is a thick, acrid stench as of chemicals burning. Looking into the Seine I see mud and desolation, street lamps drowning, men and women choking to death, the bridges covered with houses,

slaughterhouses of love. A man is standing against a wall
with an accordion strapped to his belly; his hands are cut
off at the wrists, but the accordion writhes between his
stumps like a sack of snakes. The universe has dwindled;
it is only a block long and there are no stars, no trees, no
rivers. The people who live here are dead; they make
chairs which other people sit on in their dreams. In the
middle of the street is a wheel and in the hub of the
wheel a gallows is fixed. People already dead are trying
frantically to mount the gallows, but the wheel is turning
too fast. . . .

Something was needed to put me right with myself.
Last night I discovered it: *Papini*. It doesn't matter to me
whether he's a chauvinist, a little Christer, or a near-
sighted pedant. As a failure he's marvelous. . . .

The books he read—at eighteen! Not only Homer,
Dante, Goethe, not only Aristotle, Plato, Epictetus, not
only Rabelais, Cervantes, Swift, not only Walt Whitman, Edgar Allan Poe, Baudelaire, Villon, Carducci,
Manzoni, Lope de Vega, not only Nietzsche, Schopenhauer, Kant, Hegel, Darwin, Spencer, Huxley—not only
these but all the small fry in between. This on page 18.
Alors, on page 232 he breaks down and confesses. I know
nothing, he admits. I know the titles, I have compiled
bibliographies, I have written critical essays, I have ma-
ligned and defamed. . . . I can talk for five minutes or for
five days, but then I give out, I am squeezed dry.

Follows this: "Everybody wants to see me. Everybody insists on talking to me. People pester me and they
pester others with inquiries about what I am doing. How
am I? Am I quite well again? Do I still go for my walks
in the country? Am I working? Have I finished my
book? Will I begin another soon?

"A skinny monkey of a German wants me to translate
his works. A wild-eyed Russian girl wants me to write
an account of my life for her. An American lady wants
the *very latest* news about me. An American gentleman
will send his carriage to take me to dinner—just an inti-

mate, confidential talk, you know. An old schoolmate and chum of mine, of ten years ago, wants me to read him all that I write as fast as I write it. A painter friend I know expects me to pose for him by the hour. A newspaperman wants my present address. An acquaintance, a mystic, inquires about the state of my soul; another, more practical, about the state of my pocketbook. The president of my club wonders if I will make a speech for the boys! A lady, spiritually inclined, hopes I will come to her house for tea as often as possible. She wants to have my opinion of Jesus Christ, and—what do I think of that new medium? . . .

"Great God! what have I turned into? What right have you people to clutter up my life, steal my time, probe my soul, suckle my thoughts, have me for your companion, confidant, and information bureau? What do you take me for? Am I an entertainer on salary, required every evening to play an intellectual farce under your stupid noses? Am I a slave, bought and paid for, to crawl on my belly in front of you idlers and lay at your feet all that I do and all that I know? Am I a wench in a brothel who is called upon to lift her skirts or take off her chemise at the bidding of the first man in a tailored suit who comes along?

"I am a man who would live an heroic life and make the world more endurable in his own sight. If, in some moment of weakness, of relaxation, of need, I blow off steam—a bit of red-hot rage cooled off in words—a passionate dream, wrapped and tied in imagery—well, take it or leave it . . . *but don't bother me!*

"I am a free man—and I need my feedom. I need to be alone. I need to ponder my shame and my despair in seclusion; I need the sunshine and the paving stones of the streets without companions, without conversation, face to face with myself, with only the music of my heart for company. What do you want of me? When I have something to say, I put it in print. When I have something to give, I give it. Your prying curiosity turns my stomach! Your compliments humiliate me! Your tea poisons me!

I owe nothing to any one. I would be responsible to God alone—if He existed!"

It seems to me that Papini misses something by a hair's breadth when he talks of the need to be alone. It is not difficult to be alone if you are poor and a failure. An artist is always alone—if he *is* an artist. No, what the artist needs is *loneliness*.

The artist, I call myself. So be it. A beautiful nap this afternoon that put velvet between my vertebrae. Generated enough ideas to last me three days. Chock-full of energy and nothing to do about it. Decide to go for a walk. In the street I change my mind. Decide to go to the movies. Can't go to the movies—short a few sous. A walk then. At every movie house I stop and look at the billboards, then at the price list. Cheap enough, these opium joints, but I'm short just a few sous. If it weren't so late I might go back and cash an empty bottle.

By the time I get to the Rue Amélie I've forgotten all about the movies. The Rue Amélie is one of my favorite streets. It is one of those streets which by good fortune the municipality has forgotten to pave. Huge cobblestones spreading convexly from one side of the street to the other. Only one block long and narrow. The Hôtel Pretty is on this street. There is a little church, too, on the Rue Amélie. It looks as though it were made especially for the President of the Republic and his private family. It's good occasionally to see a modest little church. Paris is full of pompous cathedrals.

Pont Alexandre III. A great windswept space approaching the bridge. Gaunt, bare trees mathematically fixed in their iron gates; the gloom of the Invalides welling out of the dome and overflowing the dark streets adjacent to the Square. The morgue of poetry. They have him where they want him now, the great warrior, the last big man of Europe. He sleeps soundly in his granite bed. No fear of him turning over in his grave. The doors are well bolted, the lid is on tight. Sleep, Napoleon! It was not your ideas they wanted, it was only your corpse!

The river is still swollen, muddy, streaked with lights.

I don't know what it is rushes up in me at the sight of this dark, swift-moving current, but a great exultation lifts me up, affirms the deep wish that is in me never to leave this land. I remember passing this way the other morning on my way to the American Express, knowing in advance that there would be no mail for me, no check, no cable, nothing, nothing. A wagon from the Galeries Lafayette was rumbling over the bridge. The rain had stopped and the sun breaking through the soapy clouds touched the glistening rubble of roofs with a cold fire. I recall now how the driver leaned out and looked up the river toward Passy way. Such a healthy, simple approving glance, as if he were saying to himself: "Ah, spring is coming!" And God knows, when spring comes to Paris the humblest mortal alive must feel that he dwells in paradise. But it was not only this—it was the intimacy with which his eyes rested upon the scene. It was *his* Paris. A man does not need to be rich, nor even a citizen, to feel this way about Paris. Paris is filled with poor people—the proudest and filthiest lot of beggars that ever walked the earth, it seems to me. And yet they give the illusion of being at home. It is that which distinguishes the Parisian from all other metropolitan souls.

When I think of New York I have a very different feeling. New York makes even a rich man feel his unimportance. New York is cold, glittering, malign. The buildings dominate. There is a sort of atomic frenzy to the activity going on; the more furious the pace, the more diminished the spirit. A constant ferment, but it might just as well be going on in a test tube. Nobody knows what it's all about. Nobody directs the energy. Stupendous. Bizarre. Baffling. A tremendous reactive urge, but absolutely uncoordinated.

When I think of this city where I was born and raised, this Manhattan that Whitman sang of, a blind, white rage licks my guts. New York! The white prisons, the sidewalks swarming with maggots, the breadlines, the opium joints that are built like palaces, the kikes that are there, the lepers, the thugs, and above all, the *ennui*, the monotony of faces, streets, legs, houses, skyscrapers, meals, posters, jobs, crimes, loves. . . . A whole city erected over a hollow pit of nothingness. Meaningless. Absolutely meaningless. And Forty-second Street! The top of the world, they call it. Where's the bottom then? You can walk along with your hands out and they'll put cinders in your cap. Rich or poor, they walk along with head thrown back and they almost break their necks looking up at their beautiful white prisons. They walk along like blind geese and the searchlights spray their empty faces with flecks of ecstasy.

Life," said Emerson, "consists in what a man is thinking all day." If that be so, then my life is nothing but a big intestine. I not only think about food all day, but I dream about it at night.

But I don't ask to go back to America, to be put in double harness again, to work the treadmill. No, I prefer to be a poor man of Europe. God knows, I am poor enough; it only remains to be a man. Last week I thought the problem of living was about to be solved, thought I was on the way to becoming self-supporting. It happened that I ran across another Russian—Serge is his name. He lives in Suresnes where there is a little colony of *émigrés* and run-down artists. Before the revolution Serge was a captain in the Imperial Guard; he stands six foot three in his stockinged feet and drinks vodka like a fish. His father was an admiral, or something like that, on the battleship "Potemkin."

I met Serge under rather peculiar circumstances. Sniffing about for food I found myself toward noon the other day in the neighborhood of the Folies-Bergère—the back entrance, that is to say, in the narrow little lane with an iron gate at one end. I was dawdling about the stage entrance, hoping vaguely for a casual brush with one of the butterflies, when an open truck pulls up to the sidewalk. Seeing me standing there with my hands in my pockets the driver, who was Serge, asks me if I would give him a hand unloading the iron barrels. When he learns that I am an American and that I'm broke he almost weeps with joy. He has been looking high and low for an English teacher, it seems. I help him roll the barrels of insecticide inside and I look my fill at the butterflies fluttering about the wings. The incident takes on strange proportions to me—the empty house, the sawdust dolls bouncing in the wings, the barrels of germicide, the battleship "Potemkin"—above all, Serge's gentleness. He is big and tender, a man every inch of him, but with a woman's heart.

In the café nearby—Café des Artistes—he proposes immediately to put me up; says he will put a mattress on the floor in the hallway. For the lessons he says he will give me a meal every day, a big Russian meal, or if for any reason the meal is lacking then five francs. It sounds wonderful to me—*wonderful*. The only question is, how will I get from Suresnes to the American Express every day?

Serge insists that we begin at once—he gives me the carfare to get out to Suresnes in the evening. I arrive a little before dinner, with my knapsack, in order to give Serge a lesson. There are some guests on hand already—seems as though they always eat in a crowd, everybody chipping in.

There are eight of us at the table—and three dogs. The dogs eat first. They eat oatmeal. Then we commence. We eat oatmeal too—as an hors d'œuvre. "*Chez nous,*" says Serge, with a twinkle in his eye, "*c'est pour les chiens, les Quaker Oats. Ici pour le gentleman. Ca va.*" After the oatmeal, mushroom soup and vegetables; after that bacon omelet, fruit, red wine, vodka, coffee, cigarettes. Not bad, the Russian meal. Everyone talks with his mouth full. Toward the end of the meal Serge's wife, who is a lazy slut of an Armenian, flops on the couch and begins to nibble bonbons. She fishes around in the box with her fat fingers, nibbles a tiny piece to see if there is any juice inside, and then throws it on the floor for the dogs.

The meal over, the guests rush away. They rush away precipitously, as if they feared a plague. Serge and I are left with the dogs—his wife has fallen asleep on the couch. Serge moves about unconcernedly, scraping the garbage for the dogs. "Dogs like very much," he says. "Very good for dogs. Little dog he has worms . . . he is too young yet." He bends down to examine some white worms lying on the carpet between the dog's paws. Tries to explain about the worms in English, but his vocabulary is lacking. Finally he consults the dictionary. "Ah," he says, looking at me exultantly, "*tapeworms!*" My response is evidently not very intelligent. Serge is confused. He gets down on his hands and knees to examine them better. He picks one up and lays it on the table beside the fruit. "Huh, him not very beeg," he grunts. "Next lesson you learn me worms, no? You are gude teacher. I make progress with you. . . ."

Lying on the mattress in the hallway the odor of the germicide stifles me. A pungent, acrid odor that seems to invade every pore of my body. The food begins to repeat on me—the Quaker Oats, the mushrooms, the bacon, the fried apples. I see the little tapeworm lying beside the fruit and all the varieties of worms that Serge drew on the tablecloth to explain what was the matter with the dog. I see the empty pit of the Folies-Bergère and in every crevice there are cockroaches and lice and bedbugs; I see people scratching themselves frantically, scratching and scratching until the blood comes. I see the worms crawling over the scenery like an army of red ants, devouring everything in sight. I see the chorus girls throwing away their gauze tunics and running through the aisles naked; I see the spectators in the pit throwing off their clothes also and scratching each other like monkeys.

I try to quiet myself. After all, this is a home I've found, and there's a meal waiting for me every day. And Serge is a brick, there's no doubt about that. But I can't sleep. It's like going to sleep in a morgue. The mattress is saturated with embalming fluid. It's a morgue for lice, bedbugs, cockroaches, tapeworms. I can't stand it. I *won't* stand it! After all I'm a man, not a louse.

In the morning I wait for Serge to load the truck. I ask him to take me in to Paris. I haven't the heart to tell him

I'm leaving. I leave the knapsack behind, with a few things that were left me. When we get to the Place Péreire I jump out. No particular reason for getting off here. No particular reason for anything. *I'm free*—that's the main thing. . . .

Light as a bird I flit about from one quarter to another. It's as though I had been released from prison. I look at the world with new eyes. Everything interests me profoundly. Even trifles. On the Rue du Faubourg Poissonnière I stop before the window of a physical culture establishment. There are photographs showing specimens of manhood "before and after." All frogs. Some of them are nude, except for a pince-nez or a beard. Can't understand how these birds fall for parallel bars and dumbbells. A frog should have just a wee bit of a paunch, like the Baron de Charlus. He should wear a beard and a pince-nez, but he should never be photographed in the nude. He should wear twinkling patent-leather boots and in the breast pocket of his sack coat there should be a white handkerchief protruding about three-quarters of an inch above the vent. If possible, he should have a red ribbon in his lapel, through the buttonhole. He should wear pajamas on going to bed.

Approaching the Place Clichy toward evening I pass the little whore with the wooden stump who stands opposite the Gaumont Palace day in and day out. She doesn't look a day over eighteen. Has her regular customers, I suppose. After midnight she stands there in her black rig rooted to the spot. Back of her is the little alleyway that blazes like an inferno. Passing her now with a light heart she reminds me somehow of a goose tied to a stake, a goose with a diseased liver, so that the world may have its *pâté de foie gras*. Must be strange taking that wooden stump to bed with you. One imagines all sorts of things—splinters, etc. However, every man to his taste!

Going down the Rue des Dames I bump into Peckover, another poor devil who works on the paper. He complains of getting only three or four hours' sleep a night—has to get up at eight in the morning to work at

a dentist's office. It isn't for the money he's doing it, so
he explains—it's for to buy himself a set of false teeth.
"It's hard to read proof when you're dropping with
sleep," he says. "The wife, she thinks I've got a cinch of
it. What would we do if you lost your job? she says." But
Peckover doesn't give a damn about the job; it doesn't
even allow him spending money. He has to save his cigarette butts and use them for pipe tobacco. His coat is
held together with pins. He has halitosis and his hands
sweat. And only three hours' sleep a night. "It's no way
to treat a man," he says. "And that boss of mine, he bawls
the piss out of me if I miss a semicolon." Speaking of his
wife he adds: "That woman of mine, she's got no fucking
gratitude, I tell you!"

In parting I manage to worm a franc fifty out of him.
I try to squeeze another fifty centimes out of him but
it's impossible. Anyway I've got enough for a coffee and
croissants. Near the Gare St. Lazare there's a bar with
reduced prices.

As luck would have it I find a ticket in the *lavabo* for
a concert. Light as a feather now I go there to the Salle
Gaveau. The usher looks ravaged because I overlook
giving him his little tip. Every time he passes me he looks
at me inquiringly, as if perhaps I will suddenly remember.

It's so long since I've sat in the company of well-
dressed people that I feel a bit panic-stricken. I can still
smell the formaldehyde. Perhaps Serge makes deliveries
here too. But nobody is scratching himself, thank God.
A faint odor of perfume . . . very faint. Even before the
music begins there is that bored look on people's faces. A
polite form of self-imposed torture, the concert. For a
moment, when the conductor raps with his little wand,
there is a tense spasm of concentration followed almost
immediately by a general slump, a quiet vegetable sort of
repose induced by the steady, uninterrupted drizzle from
the orchestra. My mind is curiously alert; it's as though
my skull had a thousand mirrors inside it. My nerves are
taut, vibrant! The notes are like glass balls dancing on a
million jets of water. I've never been to a concert before

on such an empty belly. Nothing escapes me, not even the tiniest pin falling. It's as though I had no clothes on and every pore of my body was a window and all the windows open and the light flooding my gizzards. I can feel the light curving under the vault of my ribs and my ribs hang there over a hollow nave trembling with reverberations. How long this lasts I have no idea; I have lost all sense of time and place. After what seems like an eternity there follows an interval of semiconsciousness balanced by such a calm that I feel a great lake inside me, a lake of iridescent sheen, cool as jelly; and over this lake, rising in great swooping spirals, there emerge flocks of birds of passage with long slim legs and brilliant plumage. Flock after flock surge up from the cool, still surface of the lake and, passing under my clavicles, lose themselves in the white sea of space. And then slowly, very slowly, as if an old woman in a white cap were going the rounds of my body, slowly the windows are closed and my organs drop back into place. Suddenly the lights flare up and the man in the white box whom I had taken for a Turkish officer turns out to be a woman with a flowerpot on her head.

There is a buzz now and all those who want to cough, cough to their heart's content. There is the noise of feet shuffling and seats slamming, the steady, frittering noise of people moving about aimlessly, of people fluttering their programs and pretending to read and then dropping their programs and scuffling under their seats, thankful for even the slightest accident which will prevent them from asking themselves what they were thinking about because if they knew they were thinking about nothing they would go mad. In the harsh glare of the lights they look at each other vacuously and there is a strange tenseness with which they stare at one another. And the moment the conductor raps again they fall back into a cataleptic state—they scratch themselves unconsciously or they remember suddenly a show window in which there was displayed a scarf or a hat; they remember every detail of that window with amazing clarity, but where it was exactly, that they can't recall; and that bothers them, keeps them wide awake, restless, and they listen now with redoubled attention because they are wide awake and no matter how wonderful the music is they will not lose consciousness of that show window and that scarf that was hanging there, or the hat.

And this fierce attentiveness communicates itself; even the orchestra seems galvanized into an extraordinary alertness. The second number goes off like a top—so fast indeed that when suddenly the music ceases and the lights go up some are stuck in their seats like carrots, their jaws working convulsively, and if you suddenly shouted in their ear *Brahms, Beethoven, Mendeleev, Herzegovina,* they would answer without thinking—4, 967, 289.

By the time we get to the Debussy number the atmosphere is completely poisoned. I find myself wondering what it feels like, during intercourse, to be a woman—whether the pleasure is keener, etc. Try to imagine something penetrating my groin, but have only a vague sensation of pain. I try to focus, but the music is too slippery. I can think of nothing but a vase slowly turning and the figures dropping off into space. Finally there is only light turning, and how does light turn, I ask myself. The man next to me is sleeping soundly. He looks like a broker, with his big paunch and his waxed mustache. I like him thus. I like especially that big paunch and all that went into the making of it. Why shouldn't he sleep soundly? If he wants to listen he can always rustle up the price of a ticket. I notice that the better dressed they are the more soundly they sleep. They have an easy conscience, the rich. If a poor man dozes off, even for a few seconds, he feels mortified; he imagines that he has committed a crime against the composer.

In the Spanish number the house was electrified. Everybody sat on the edge of his seat—the drums woke them up. I thought when the drums started it would keep up forever. I expected to see people fall out of the boxes or throw their hats away. There was something heroic about it and he could have driven us stark mad, Ravel, if he had wanted to. But that's not Ravel. Suddenly it all died down. It was as if he remembered, in the midst of his antics, that he had on a cutaway suit. He arrested himself. A great mistake, in my humble opinion. Art consists in going the full length. If you start with the drums you have to end with dynamite, or TNT. Ravel sacrificed something for form, for a vegetable that people must digest before going to bed.

My thoughts are spreading. The music is slipping away from me, now that the drums have ceased. People everywhere are composed to order. Under the exit light is a Werther sunk in despair; he is leaning on his two elbows, his eyes are glazed. Near the door, huddled in a big cape, stands a Spaniard with a sombrero in his hand. He looks as if he were posing for the "Balzac" of Rodin. From the neck up he suggests Buffalo Bill. In the gallery opposite me, in the front row, sits a woman with her legs spread wide apart; she looks as though she had lockjaw, with her neck thrown back and dislocated. The woman with the red hat who is dozing over the rail—marvelous if she were to have a hemorrhage! if suddenly she spilled a bucketful on those stiff shirts below. Imagine these bloody no-accounts going home from the concert with blood on their dickies!

Sleep is the keynote. No one is listening any more. Impossible to think and listen. Impossible to dream even when the music itself is nothing but a dream. A woman with white gloves holds a swan in her lap. The legend is that when Leda was fecundated she gave birth to twins. Everybody is giving birth to something—everybody but the Lesbian in the upper tier. Her head is uptilted, her throat wide open; she is all alert and tingling with the shower of sparks that burst from the radium symphony. Jupiter is piercing her ears. Little phrases from California, whales with big fins, Zanzibar, the Alcazar. *When along the Guadalquivir there were a thousand mosques ashimmer.* Deep in the icebergs and the days all lilac. The Money Street with two white hitching posts. The gargoyles . . . the man with the Jaworski nonsense . . . the river lights . . . the . . .

In America I had a number of Hindu friends, some good, some bad, some indifferent. Circumstances had placed me in a position where fortunately I could be of aid to them; I secured jobs for them, I harbored them, and I fed them when necessary. They were very grateful, I must say; so much so, in fact that they made my life miserable with their attentions. Two of them were saints, if I know what a saint is; particularly Gupte who was found one morning with his throat cut from ear to ear. In a little boarding house in Greenwich Village he was found one morning stretched out stark naked on the bed, his flute beside him, and his throat gashed, as I say, from ear to ear. It was never discovered whether he had been murdered or whether he had committed suicide. But that's neither here nor there. . . .

I'm thinking back to the chain of circumstances which has brought me finally to Nanantatee's place. Thinking how strange it is that I should have forgotten all about Nanantatee until the other day when lying in a shabby hotel room on the Rue Cels. I'm lying there on the iron bed thinking what a zero I have become, what a cipher, what a nullity, when bango! out pops the word: NONENTITY! That's what we called him in New York—Nonentity. *Mister* Nonentity.

I'm lying on the floor now in that gorgeous suite of rooms he boasted of when he was in New York. Nanantatee is playing the good Samaritan; he has given me a pair of itchy blankets, horse blankets they are, in which

I curl up on the dusty floor. There are little jobs to do every hour of the day—that is, if I am foolish enough to remain indoors. In the morning he wakes me rudely in order to have me prepare the vegetables for his lunch: onions, garlic, beans, etc. His friend, Kepi, warns me not to eat the food—he says it's bad. Bad or good what difference? *Food!* That's all that matters. For a little food I am quite willing to sweep his carpets with a broken broom, to wash his clothes and to scrape the crumbs off the floor as soon as he has finished eating. He's become absolutely immaculate since my arrival: everything has to be dusted now, the chairs must be arranged a certain way, the clock must ring, the toilet must flush properly. . . . A crazy Hindu if ever there was one! And parsimonious as a string bean. I'll have a great laugh over it when I get out of his clutches, but just now I'm a prisoner, a man without caste, an untouchable. . . .

If I fail to come back at night and roll up in the horse blankets he says to me on arriving: "Oh, so you didn't die then? I thought you had died." And though he knows I'm absolutely penniless he tells me every day about some cheap room he has just discovered in the neighborhood. "But I can't take a room yet, you know that," I say. And then, blinking his eyes like a Chink, he answers smoothly: "Oh, yes, I forgot that you had no money. I am always forgetting, Endree. . . . But when the cable comes . . . when Miss Mona sends you the money, then you will come with me to look for a room, eh?" And in the next breath he urges me to stay as long as I wish—"six months . . . seven months, Endree . . . you are very good for me here."

Nanantatee is one of the Hindus I never did anything for in America. He represented himself to me as a wealthy merchant, a pearl merchant, with a luxurious suite of rooms on the Rue Lafayette, Paris, a villa in Bombay, a bungalow in Darjeeling. I could see from first glance that he was a half-wit, but then half-wits sometimes have the genius to amass a fortune. I didn't know that he paid his hotel bill in New York by leaving a couple of fat pearls in the proprietor's hands. It seems amusing to me now that this little duck once swaggered about the lobby of that hotel in New York with an ebony cane, bossing the bellhops around, ordering luncheons for his guests, calling up the porter for theater tickets, renting a taxi by the day, etc., etc., all without a sou in his pocket. Just a string of fat pearls around his neck which he cashed one by one as time wore on. And the fatuous way he used to pat me on the back, thank me for being so good to the Hindu boys—"they are all very intelligent boys, Endree . . . very intelligent!" Telling me that the good lord so-and-so would repay me for my kindness. That explains now why they used to giggle so, these intelligent Hindu boys, when I suggested that they touch Nanantatee for a five-spot.

Curious now how the good lord so-and-so is requiting me for my benevolence. I'm nothing but a slave to this fat little duck. I'm at his beck and call continually. He needs me here—he tells me so to my face. When he goes to the crap-can he shouts: "Endree, bring me a pitcher of water, please. I must wipe myself." He wouldn't think of using toilet paper, Nanantatee. Must be against his religion. No, he calls for a pitcher of water and a rag. He's *delicate*, the fat little duck. Sometimes when I'm drinking a cup of pale tea in which he has dropped a rose leaf he comes alongside of me and lets a loud fart, right in my face. He never says "Excuse me!" The word must be missing from his Gujarati dictionary.

The day I arrived at Nanantatee's apartment he was in the act of performing his ablutions, that is to say, he was standing over a dirty bowl trying to work his crooked arm around toward the back of his neck. Beside the bowl was a brass goblet which he used to change the water. He requested me to be silent during the ceremony. I sat there silently, as I was bidden, and watched him as he sang and prayed and spat now and then into the wash-bowl. So this is the wonderful suite of rooms he talked about in New York! The Rue Lafayette! It sounded like an important street to me back there in New York. I thought only millionaires and pearl merchants inhabited the street. It sounds wonderful, the Rue Lafayette, when you're on the other side of the water. So does Fifth Avenue, when you're over here. One can't imagine what dumps there are on these swell streets. Anyway, here I am at last, sitting in the gorgeous suite of rooms on the Rue Lafayette. And this crazy duck with his crooked arm is going through the ritual of washing himself. The chair on which I'm sitting is broken, the bedstead is falling apart, the wallpaper is in tatters, there is an open valise under the bed crammed with dirty wash. From where I sit I can glance at the miserable courtyard down below where the aristocracy of the Rue Lafayette sit and smoke their clay pipes. I wonder now, as he chants the doxology, what that bungalow in Darjeeling looks like. It's interminable, his chanting and praying.

He explains to me that he is obliged to wash in a certain prescribed way—his religion demands it. But on Sundays he takes a bath in the tin tub—the Great I AM will wink at that, he says. When he's dressed he goes to the cupboard, kneels before a little idol on the third shelf, and repeats the mumbo jumbo. If you pray like that every day, he says, nothing will happen to you. The good lord what's his name never forgets an obedient servant. And then he shows me the crooked arm which he got in a taxi accident on a day doubtless when he had neglected to rehearse the complete song and dance. His arm looks like a broken compass; it's not an arm any more, but a knucklebone with a shank attached. Since the arm has been repaired he has developed a pair of swollen glands in the armpit—fat little glands, exactly like a dog's testicles. While bemoaning his plight he remembers suddenly that the doctor had recommended a more liberal diet. He begs me at once to sit down and make up a menu with plenty of fish and meat. "And what about oysters, Endree—for *le petit frère*?" But all this is only to make an impression on me. He hasn't the slightest intention of buying himself oysters, or meat, or fish. Not as long as I am there, at least. For the time being we are going to nourish ourselves on lentils and rice and all the dry foods he has stored away in the attic. And the butter he bought last week, that won't go to waste either. When he commences to cure the butter the smell is unbearable. I used to run out at first, when he started frying the butter, but now I stick it out. He'd be only too delighted if he could make me vomit up my meal—that would be something else to put away in the cupboard along with the dry bread and the moldy cheese and the little grease cakes that he makes himself out of the stale milk and the rancid butter.

For the last five years, so it seems, he hasn't done a stroke of work, hasn't turned over a penny. Business has gone to smash. He talks to me about pearls in the Indian Ocean—big fat ones on which you can live for a lifetime. The Arabs are ruining the business, he says. But meanwhile he prays to the lord so-and-so every day, and that sustains him. He's on a marvelous footing with the deity: knows just how to cajole him, how to wheedle a few sous out of him. It's a pure commercial relationship. In exchange for the flummery before the cabinet every day he gets his ration of beans and garlic, to say nothing of the swollen testicles under his arm. He is confident that everything will turn out well in the end. The pearls will sell again some day, maybe five years hence, maybe twenty—when the Lord Boomaroom wishes it. "And when the business goes, Endree, you will get ten per cent—for writing the letters. But first, Endree, you must write the letter to find out if we can get credit from India. It will take about six months for an answer, maybe seven months . . . the boats are not fast in India." He has no conception of time at all, the little duck. When I ask him if he has slept well he will say: "Ah, yes, Endree, I sleep very well . . . I sleep sometimes ninety-two hours in three days."

Mornings he is usually too weak to do any work. His arm! That poor broken crutch of an arm! I wonder sometimes when I see him twisting it around the back of his neck how he will ever get it into place again. If it weren't for that little paunch he carries he'd remind me of one of those contortionists at the Cirque Médrano. All he needs is to break a leg. When he sees me sweeping the carpet, when he sees what a cloud of dust I raise, he begins to cluck like a pygmy. "Good! Very good, Endree. And now I will pick up the knots." That means that there are a few crumbs of dust which I have overlooked; it is a polite way he has of being sarcastic.

Afternoons there are always a few cronies from the pearl market dropping in to pay him a visit. They're all very suave, butter-tongued bastards with soft, doelike eyes; they sit around the table drinking the perfumed tea with a loud hissing noise while Nanantatee jumps up and down like a jack-in-the box or points to a crumb on the floor and says in this smooth slippery voice—"Will you please to pick that up, Endree." When the guests arrive he goes unctuously to the cupboard and gets out the dry crusts of bread which he toasted maybe a week ago and which taste strongly now of the moldy wood. Not a crumb is thrown away. If the bread gets too sour he takes it downstairs to the concierge who, so he says, has been very kind to him. According to him, the concierge is delighted to get the stale bread—he makes bread pudding with it.

One day my friend Anatole came to see me. Nanantatee was delighted. Insisted that Anatole stay for tea. Insisted that he try little grease cakes and the stale bread. "You must come every day," he says, "and teach me Russian. Fine language, Russian . . . I want to speak it. How do you say that again, Endree—*borsht?* You will write that down for me, please, Endree. . . ." And I must write it on the typewriter, no less, so that he can observe my technique. He bought the typewriter, after he had collected on the bad arm, because the doctor recommended it as a good exercise. But he got tired of the typewriter shortly—it was an *English* typewriter.

When he learned that Anatole played the mandolin

he said: "Very good! You must come every day and teach me the music. I will buy a mandolin as soon as business is better. It is good for my arm." The next day he borrows a phonograph from the concierge. "You will please teach me to dance, Endree. My stomach is too big." I am hoping that he will buy a porterhouse steak some day so that I can say to him: "You will please bite it for me, *Mister* Nonentity. My teeth are not strong!"

As I said a moment ago, ever since my arrival he has become extraordinarily meticulous. "Yesterday," he says, "you made three mistakes, Endree. First, you forgot to close the toilet door and so all night it makes boom-boom; second, you left the kitchen window open and so the window is cracked this morning. And you forgot to put out the milk bottle! Always you will put out the milk bottle please, before you go to bed, and in the morning you will please bring in the bread."

Every day his friend Kepi drops in to see if any visitors have arrived from India. He waits for Nanantatee to go out and then he scurries to the cupboard and devours the sticks of bread that are hidden away in a glass jar. The food is no good, he insists, but he puts it away like a rat. Kepi is a scrounger, a sort of human tick who fastens himself to the hide of even the poorest compatriot. From Kepi's standpoint they are all nabobs. For a Manila cheroot and the price of a drink he will suck any Hindu's ass. A Hindu's, mind you, but not an Englishman's. He has the address of every whorehouse in Paris, and the rates. Even from the ten franc joints he gets his little commission. And he knows the shortest way to any place you want to go. He will ask you first if you want to go by taxi; if you say no, he will suggest the bus, and if that is too high then the streetcar or the metro. Or he will offer to walk you there and save a franc or two, knowing very well that it will be necessary to pass a *tabac* on the way and that you will please be so good as to buy me a little cheroot.

Kepi is interesting, in a way, because he has absolutely no ambition except to get a fuck every night. Every penny he makes, and they are damned few, he squanders in the dance halls. He has a wife and eight children in Bombay, but that does not prevent him from proposing marriage to any little *femme de chambre* who is stupid and credulous enough to be taken in by him. He has a little room on the Rue Condorcet for which he pays sixty francs a month. He papered it all himself. Very proud of it, too. He uses violet-colored ink in his fountain pen because it lasts longer. He shines his own shoes, presses his own pants, does his own laundry. For a little cigar, a cheroot, if you pleae, he will escort you all over Paris. If you stop to look at a shirt or a collar button his eyes flash. "Don't buy it here," he will say. "They ask too much. I will show you a cheaper place." And before you have time to think about it he will whisk you away and deposit you before another show window where there are the same ties and shirts and collar buttons— maybe it's the very same store! but you don't know the difference. When Kepi hears that you want to buy something his soul becomes animated. He will ask you so many questions and drag you to so many places that you are bound to get thirsty and ask him to have a drink, whereupon you will discover to your amazement that you are again standing in a *tabac*—maybe the same *tabac!* —and Kepi is saying again in that small unctuous voice: "Will you please be so good as to buy me a little cheroot?" No matter what you propose doing, even if it's only to walk around the corner, Kepi will economize for you. Kepi will show you the shortest way, the cheapest place, the biggest dish, because whatever you have to do you *must* pass a *tabac*, and whether there is a revolution or a lockout or a quarantine Kepi must be at the Moulin Rouge or the Olympia or the Ange Rouge when the music strikes up.

The other day he brought a book for me to read. It was about a famous suit between a holy man and the editor of an Indian paper. The editor, it seems had openly accused the holy man of leading a scandalous life; he went further, and accused the holy man of being diseased. Kepi says it must have been the great French pox, but Nanantatee avers that it was the Japanese clap. For Nanantatee everything has to be a little exaggerated. At any rate, says Nanantatee cheerily: "You will please tell me what it says, Endree. I can't read the book—it hurts my arm." Then, by way of encouraging me—"it is a fine book about the fucking, Endree. Kepi has brought it for you. He thinks about nothing but the girls. So many girls he fucks—just like Krishna. We don't believe in that business, Endree. . . ."

A little later he takes me upstairs to the attic which is loaded down with tin cans and crap from India wrapped in burlap and firecracker paper. "Here is where I bring the girls," he says. And then rather wistfully: "I am not a very good fucker, Endree. I don't screw the girls any more. I hold them in my arms and I say the words. I like only to say the words now." It isn't necessary to listen any further: I know that he is going to tell me about his arm. I can see him lying there with that broken hinge dangling from the side of the bed. But to my surprise he adds: "I am no good for the fucking, Endree. I never was a very good fucker. My brother, he is good! Three times a day, every day! And Kepi, he is good—just like Krishna."

His mind is fixed now on the "fucking business." Downstairs, in the little room where he kneels before the open cabinet, he explains to me how it was when he was rich and his wife and the children were here. On holidays he would take his wife to the House of All Nations and hire a room for the night. Every room was appointed in a different style. His wife liked it there very much. "A wonderful place for the fucking, Endree. I know all the rooms. . . ."

The walls of the little room in which we are sitting are crammed with photographs. Every branch of the family is represented, it is like a cross section of the Indian empire. For the most part the members of this genealogical tree look like withered leaves: the women are frail and they have a startled, frightened look in their

eyes: the men have a keen, intelligent look, like edu-
cated chimpanzees. They are all there, about ninety of
them, with their white bullocks, their dung cakes, their
skinny legs, their old-fashioned spectacles; in the background, now and then, one catches a glimpse of the
parched soil, of a crumbling pediment, of an idol with
crooked arms, a sort of human centipede. There is something so fantastic, so incongruous about this gallery that
one is reminded inevitably of the great spawn of temples which stretch from the Himalayas to the tip of Cey-
lon, a vast jumble of architecture, staggering in beauty
and at the same time monstrous, hideously monstrous
because the fecundity which seethes and ferments in the
myriad ramifications of design seems to have exhausted
the very soil of India itself. Looking at the seething hive
of figures which swarm the façades of the temples one
is overwhelmed by the potency of these dark, handsome
peoples who mingled their mysterious streams in a sexual
embrace that has lasted thirty centuries or more. These
frail men and women with piercing eyes who stare out
of the photographs seem like the emaciated shadows of
those virile, massive figures who incarnated themselves
in stone and fresco from one end of India to the other
in order that the heroic myths of the races who here
intermingled should remain forever entwined in the
hearts of their countrymen. When I look at only a frag-
ment of these spacious dreams of stone, these toppling,
sluggish edifices studded with gems, coagulated with
human sperm, I am overwhelmed by the dazzling splendor of those imaginative flights which enabled half a
billion people of diverse origins to thus incarnate the
most fugitive expressions of their longing.

It is a strange, inexplicable medley of feelings which
assails me now as Nanantatee prattles on about the sister who died in childbirth. There she is on the wall, a
frail, timid thing of twelve or thirteen clinging to the
arm of a dotard. At ten years of age she was given in
wedlock to this old roué who had already buried five
wives. She had seven children, only one of whom sur-

vived her. She was given to the aged gorilla in order to keep the pearls in the family. As she was passing away, so Nanantatee puts it, she whispered to the doctor: "I am tired of this fucking. . . . I don't want to fuck any more, doctor." As he relates this to me he scratches his head solemnly with his withered arm. "The fucking business is bad, Endree," he says. "But I will give you a word that will always make you lucky; you must say it every day, over and over, a million times you must say it. It is the best word there is, Endree . . . say it now . . . OOMAHARUMOOMA!"

"OOMARABOO. . . ."

"No, Endree . . . like this . . . OOMAHARUMOOMA!"

"OOMAMABOOMBA. . . ."

"No, Endree . . . like this. . . ."

. . . But what with the murky light, the botchy print, the tattered cover, the jigjagged page, the fumbling fingers, the fox-trotting fleas, the lie-a-bed lice, the scum on his tongue, the drop in his eye, the lump in his throat, the drink in his pottle, the itch in his palm, the wail of his wind, the grief from his breath, the fog of his brain-fag, the tic of his conscience, the height of his rage, the gush of his fundament, the fire in his gorge, the tickle of his tail, the rats in his garret, the hullabaloo and the dust in his ears, since it took him a month to steal a march, he was hard-set to memorize more than a word a week.

I suppose I would never have gotten out of Nanantatee's clutches if fate hadn't intervened. One night, as luck would have it, Kepi asked me if I wouldn't take one of his clients to a whorehouse nearby. The young man had just come from India and he had not very much money to spend. He was one of Gandhi's men, one of that little band who made the historic march to the sea during the salt trouble. A very gay disciple of Gandhi's I must say, despite the vows of abstinence he had taken. Evidently he hadn't looked at a woman for ages. It was all I could do to get him as far as the Rue Laferrière; he was like a dog with his tongue hanging out. And a pompous, vain little devil to boot! He had decked himself out in a corduroy suit, a beret, a cane, a Windsor tie; he had bought himself two fountain pens, a kodak, and some fancy underwear. The money he was spending was a gift from the merchants of Bombay; they were sending him to England to spread the gospel of Gandhi.

Once inside Miss Hamilton's joint he began to lose his *sang-froid*. When suddenly he found himself surrounded by a bevy of naked women he looked at me in consternation. "Pick one out," I said. "You can have your choice." He had become so rattled that he could scarcely look at them. "You do it for me," he murmured, blushing violently. I looked them over coolly and picked out a plump young wench who seemed full of feathers. We sat down in the reception room and waited for the drinks. The madam wanted to know why I didn't take a girl also. "Yes, you take one too," said the young Hindu. "I don't want to be alone with her." So the girls were brought in again and I chose one for myself, a rather tall, thin one with melancholy eyes. We were left alone, the four of us, in the reception room. After a few moments my young Gandhi leans over and whispers something in my ear. "Sure, if you like her better, take her," I said, and so, rather awkwardly and considerably embarrassed, I explained to the girls that we would like to switch. I saw at once that we had made a *faux pas*, but by now my young friend had became gay and lecherous and nothing would do but to get upstairs quickly and have it over with.

We took adjoining rooms with a connecting door between. I think my companion had in mind to make another switch once he had satisfied his sharp, gnawing hunger. At any rate, no sooner had the girls left the room to prepare themselves than I hear him knocking on the door. "Where is the toilet, please?" he asks. Not thinking that it was anything serious I urge him to do in the *bidet*. The girls return with towels in their hands. I hear him giggling in the next room.

As I'm putting on my pants suddenly I hear a commotion in the next room. The girl is bawling him out, calling him a pig, a dirty little pig. I can't imagine what he has done to warrant such an outburst. I'm standing there with one foot in my trousers listening attentively. He's trying to explain to her in English, raising his voice louder and louder until it becomes a shriek.

I hear a door slam and in another moment the madam bursts into my room, her face as red as a beet, her arms gesticulating wildly. "You ought to be ashamed of yourself," she screams, "bringing a man like that to my place! He's a barbarian . . . he's a pig . . . he's a . . . !" My companion is standing behind her, in the doorway, a look of utmost discomfiture on his face. "What did you do?" I ask.

"What did he do?" yells the madam. "I'll show you. . . . Come here!" And grabbing me by the arm she drags me into the next room. "There! There!" she screams, pointing to the *bidet*.

"Come on, let's get out," says the Hindu boy.

"Wait a minute, you can't get out as easily as all that."

The madam is standing by the *bidet*, fuming and spitting. The girls are standing there too, with towels in their hands. The five of us are standing there looking at the *bidet*. There are two enormous turds floating in the water. The madam bends down and puts a towel over it. "Frightful! Frightful!" she wails. "Never have I seen anything like this! A pig! A dirty little pig!"

The Hindu boy looks at me reproachfully. "You should have told me!" he says. "I didn't know it wouldn't go down. I asked you where to go and you told me to use that." He is almost in tears.

Finally the madam takes me to one side. She has become a little more reasonable now. After all, it was a mistake. Perhaps the gentlemen would like to come downstairs and order another drink—for the girls. It was a great shock to the girls. They are not used to such things. And if the good gentlemen will be so kind as to remember the *femme de chambre*. . . . It is not so pretty for the *femme de chambre*—that mess, that ugly mess.

She shrugs her shoulders and winks her eye. A lamentable incident. But an accident. If the gentlemen will wait here a few moments the maid will bring the drinks. Would the gentlemen like to have some champagne? Yes?

"I'd like to get out of here," says the Hindu boy weakly.

"Don't feel so badly about it," says the madam. "It is all over now. Mistakes will happen sometimes. Next time you will ask for the toilet." She goes on about the toilet—one on every floor, it seems. And a bathroom too. "I have lots of English clients," she says. "They are all gentlemen. The gentleman is a Hindu? Charming people, the Hindus. So intelligent. So handsome."

When we get into the street the charming young gentleman is almost weeping. He is sorry now that he bought a corduroy suit and the cane and the fountain pens. He talks about the eight vows that he took, the control of the palate, etc. On the march to Dandi even a plate of ice cream it was forbidden to take. He tells me about the spinning wheel—how the little band of Satyagrahists imitated the devotion of their master. He relates with pride how he walked beside the master and conversed with him. I have the illusion of being in the presence of one of the twelve disciples.

During the next few days we see a good deal of each other; there are interviews to be arranged with the newspaper men and lectures to be given to the Hindus of Paris. It is amazing to see how these spineless devils order one another about; amazing also to see how ineffectual they are in all that concerns practical affairs. And the jealousy and the intrigues, the petty, sordid rivalries. Wherever there are ten Hindus together there is India with her sects and schisms, her racial, lingual, religious, political antagonisms. In the person of Gandhi they are experiencing for a brief moment the miracle of unity, but when he goes there will be a crash, an utter relapse into that strife and chaos so characteristic of the Indian people.

The young Hindu, of course, is optimistic. He has been to America and he has been contaminated by the cheap idealism of the Americans, contaminated by the ubiquitous bathtub, the five-and-ten-cent store bric-a-brac, the bustle, the efficiency, the machinery, the high wages, the free libraries, etc., etc. His ideal would be to Americanize India. He is not at all pleased with Gandhi's retrogressive mania. *Forward*, he says, just like a YMCA man. As I listen to his tales of America I see how absurd it is to expect of Gandhi that miracle which will deroute the trend of destiny. India's enemy is not England, but America. India's enemy is the time spirit, the hand which cannot be turned back. Nothing will avail to offset this virus which is poisoning the whole world. America is the very incarnation of doom. She will drag the whole world down to the bottomless pit.

He thinks the Americans are a very gullible people. He tells me about the credulous souls who succored him there—the Quakers, the Unitarians, the Theosophists, the New Thoughters, the Seventh-day Adventists, etc. He knew where to sail his boat, this bright young man. He knew how to make the tears come to his eyes at the right moment; he knew how to take up a collection, how to appeal to the minister's wife, how to make love to the mother and daughter at the same time. To look at him you would think him a saint. And he is a saint, in the modern fashion; a contaminated saint who talks in one breath of love, brotherhood, bathtubs, sanitation, efficiency, etc.

The last night of his sojourn in Paris is given up to "the fucking business." He has had a full program all day—conferences, cablegrams, interviews, photographs for the newspapers, affectionate farewells, advice to the faithful, etc., etc. At dinner time he decides to lay aside his troubles. He orders champagne with the meal, he snaps his fingers at the *garçon* and behaves in general like the boorish little peasant that he is. And since he has had a bellyful of all the good places he suggests now that I show him something more primitive. He would like to go to a very cheap place, order two or three girls at once. I steer him along the Boulevard de la Chapelle, warning him all the while to be careful of his pocketbook. Around Aubervilliers we duck into a cheap dive and immediately we've got a flock of them on our hands. In a few minutes he's dancing with a naked wench, a huge blonde with creases in her jowls. I can see her ass reflected a dozen times in the mirrors that line the room—and those dark, bony fingers of his clutching her tenaciously. The table is full of beer glasses, the mechanical piano is wheezing and gasping. The girls who are unoccupied are sitting placidly on the leather benches, scratching themselves peacefully just like a family of chimpanzees. There is a sort of subdued pandemonium in the air, a note of repressed violence, as if the awaited explosion required the advent of some utterly minute detail, something microscopic but thoroughly unpremeditated, completely unexpected. In that sort of half-reverie which permits one to participate in an event and yet remain quite aloof, the little detail which was lacking began obscurely but insistently to coagulate, to assume a freakish, crystalline form, like the frost which gathers on the windowpane. And like those frost patterns which seem so bizarre, so utterly free and fantastic in design, but which are nevertheless determined by the most rigid laws, so this sensation which commenced to take form inside me seemed also to be giving obedience to ineluctable laws. My whole being was responding to the dictates of an ambiance which it had never before experienced, that which I could call myself seemed to be contracting, condensing, shrinking from the stale, customary boundaries of the flesh whose perimeter knew only the modulations of the nerve ends.

And the more substantial, the more solid the core of me became, the more delicate and extravagant appeared the close, palpable reality out of which I was being squeezed. In the measure that I became more and more metallic, in the same measure the scene before my eyes became inflated. The state of tension was so finely drawn now that the introduction of a single foreign particle, even a microscopic particle, as I say, would have shattered everything. For the fraction of a second perhaps I experienced that utter clarity which the epileptic, it is said, is given to know. In that moment I lost completely the illusion of time and space: the world unfurled its drama simultaneously along a meridian which had no axis. In this sort of hair-trigger eternity I felt that everything was justified, supremely justified; I felt the wars inside me that had left behind this pulp and wrack; I felt the crimes that were seething here to emerge tomorrow in blatant screamers; I felt the misery that was grinding itself out with pestle and mortar, the long dull misery that dribbles away in dirty handkerchiefs. On the meridian of time there is no injustice: there is only the poetry of motion creating the illusion of truth and drama. If at any moment anywhere one comes face to face with the absolute, that great sympathy which makes men like Gautama and Jesus seem divine freezes away; the monstrous thing is not that men have created roses out of this dung heap, but that, for some reason or other, they should *want* roses. For some reason or other man looks for the miracle, and to accomplish it he will wade through blood. He will debauch himself with ideas, he will reduce himself to a shadow if for only one second of his life he can close his eyes to the hideousness of reality. Everything is endured—disgrace, humiliation, poverty, war, crime, *ennui*—in the belief that overnight something will occur, a miracle, which will render life tolerable. And all the while a meter is running inside and there is no hand that can reach in there and shut it off. All the while someone is eating the bread of life and drinking the wine, some dirty fat cockroach of a priest who hides away in the cellar guzzling it, while up above in the light of the street a phantom host touches the lips and the blood is pale as water. And out of the endless torment and misery no miracle comes forth, no microscopic vestige even of relief. Only ideas, pale, attenuated ideas which have to be fattened by slaughter;

ideas which come forth like bile, like the guts of a pig when the carcass is ripped open.

And so I think what a miracle it would be if this miracle which man attends eternally should turn out to be nothing more than these two enormous turds which the faithful disciple dropped in the *bidet*. What if at the last moment, when the banquet table is set and the cymbals clash, there should appear suddenly, and wholly without warning, a silver platter on which even the blind could see that there is nothing more, and nothing less, than two enormous lumps of shit. That, I believe would be more miraculous than anything which man has looked forward to. It would be miraculous because it would be undreamed of. It would be more miraculous than even the wildest dream because *anybody* could imagine the possibility but nobody ever has, and probably nobody ever again will.

Somehow the realization that nothing was to be hoped for had a salutary effect upon me. For weeks and months, for years, in fact, all my life I had been looking forward to something happening, some extrinsic event that would alter my life, and now suddenly, inspired by the absolute hopelessness of everything, I felt relieved, felt as though a great burden had been lifted from my shoulders. At dawn I parted company with the young Hindu, after touching him for a few francs, enough for a room. Walking toward Montparnasse I decided to let myself drift with the tide, to make not the least resistance to fate, no matter in what form it presented itself. Nothing that had happened to me thus far had been sufficient to destroy me; nothing had been destroyed except my illusions. I myself was intact. The world was intact. Tomorrow there might be a revolution, a plague, an earthquake; tomorrow there might not be left a single soul to whom one could turn for sympathy, for aid, for faith. It seemed to me that the great calamity had already manifested itself, that I could be no more truly alone than at this very moment. I made up my mind that I would hold on to nothing, that I would expect nothing, that henceforth I would live as an animal, a beast of prey, a rover, a plunderer. Even if war were declared, and it were my lot to go, I would grab the bayonet and plunge it, plunge it up to the hilt. And if rape were the order of the day then rape I would, and with a vengeance. At this very moment, in the quiet dawn of a new day, was not the earth giddy with crime and distress? Had one single element of man's nature been altered, vitally, fundamentally altered, by the incessant march of history? By what he calls the better part of his nature, man has been betrayed, that is all. At the extreme limits of his spiritual being man finds himself again naked as a savage. When he finds God, as it were, he has been picked clean: he is a skeleton. One must burrow into life again in order to put on flesh. The word must become flesh; the soul thirsts. On whatever crumb my eye fastens, I will pounce and devour. If to live is the paramount thing, then I will live, even if I must become a cannibal. Heretofore I have been trying to save my precious hide, trying to preserve the few pieces of meat that hid my bones. I am done with that. I have reached the limits of endurance. My back is to the wall; I can retreat no further. As far as history goes I am dead. If there is something beyond I shall have to bounce back. I have found God, but he is insufficient. I am only spiritually dead. Physically I am alive. Morally I am free. The world which I have departed is a menagerie. The dawn is breaking on a new world, a jungle world in which the lean spirits roam with sharp claws. If I am a hyena I am a lean and hungry one: I go forth to fatten myself.

At one-thirty I called on Van Norden, as per agreement. He had warned me that if he didn't answer it would mean that he was sleeping with someone, probably his Georgia cunt.

Anyway, there he was, tucked away comfortably, but with an air of weariness as usual. He wakes up cursing himself, or cursing the job, or cursing life. He wakes up utterly bored and discomfited, chagrined to think that he did not die overnight.

I sit down by the window and give him what encouragement I can. It is tedious work. One has to actually coax him out of bed. Mornings—he means by mornings anywhere between one and five p.m.—mornings, as I say, he gives himself up to reveries. Mostly it is about the past he dreams. About his "cunts." He endeavors to recall how they felt, what they said to him at certain critical moments, where he laid them, and so on. And as he lies there, grinning and cursing, he manipulates his fingers in that curious, bored way of his, as though to convey the impression that his disgust is too great for words. Over the bedstead hangs a douche bag which he keeps for emergencies—for the *virgins* whom he tracks down like a sleuth. Even after he has slept with one of these mythical cratures he will still refer to her as a virgin, and almost never by name. "My virgin," he will say, just as he says "my Georgia cunt." When he goes to the toilet he says: "If my Georgia cunt calls tell her to wait.

Say I said so. And listen, you can have her if you like. I'm tired of her."

He takes a squint at the weather and heaves a deep sigh. If it's rainy he says: "Goddamn this fucking climate, it makes one morbid." And if the sun is shining brightly he says: "Goddamn that fucking sun, it makes you blind!" As he starts to shave he suddenly remembers that there is no clean towel. "Goddamn this fucking hotel, they're too stingy to give you a clean towel every day!" No matter what he does or where he goes things are out of joint. Either it's the fucking country or the fucking job, or else it's some fucking cunt who's put him on the blink.

"My teeth are all rotten," he says, gargling his throat. "It's the fucking bread they give you to eat here." He opens his mouth wide and pulls his lower lip down. "See that? Pulled out six teeth yesterday. Soon I'll have to get another plate. That's what you get working for a living. When I was on the bum I had all my teeth, my eyes were bright and clear. Look at me now! It's a wonder I can make a cunt any more. Jesus, what I'd like is to find some rich cunt—like that cute little prick, Carl. Did he ever show you the letters she sends him? Who is she, do you know? He wouldn't tell me her name, the bastard . . . he's afraid I might take her away from him." He gargles his throat again and then takes a long look at the cavities. "You're lucky," he says ruefully. "You've got friends, at least. I haven't anybody, except that cute little prick who drives me bats about his rich cunt."

"Listen," he says, "do you happen to know a cunt by the name of Norma? She hangs around the Dôme all day. I think she's queer. I had her up here yesterday, tickling her ass. She wouldn't let me do a thing. I had her on the bed. . . . I even had her drawers off . . . and then I got disgusted. Jesus, I can't bother struggling that way any more. It isn't worth it. Either they do or they don't—it's foolish to waste time wrestling with them. While you're struggling with a little bitch like that there may be a dozen cunts on the *terrasse* just dying to be laid. It's a fact. They all come over here to get laid. They think it's sinful here . . . *the poor boobs!* Some of these schoolteachers from out West, they're honestly virgins . . . I mean it! They sit around on their can all day thinking about it. You don't have to work over them very much. They're dying for it. I had a married woman the other day who told me she hadn't had a lay for six months. Can you imagine that? Jesus, she was hot! I thought she'd tear the cock off me. And groaning all the time. "*Do you? Do you?*" She kept saying that all the time, like she was nuts. And do you know what that bitch wanted to do? She wanted to move in here. Imagine that! Asking me if I loved her. I didn't even know her name. I never know their names . . . I don't want to. The married ones! Christ, if you saw all the married cunts I bring up here you'd never have any more illusions. They're worse than the virgins, the married ones. They don't wait for you to start things—they fish it out for you themselves. And then they talk about love afterwards. It's disgusting. I tell you, I'm actually beginning to hate cunt!"

He looks out the window again. It's drizzling. It's been drizzling this way for the last five days.

"Are we going to the Dôme, Joe?" I call him Joe because he calls me Joe. When Carl is with us he is Joe too. Everybody is Joe because it's easier that way. It's also a pleasant reminder not to take yourself too seriously. Anyway, Joe doesn't want to go to the Dôme—he owes too much money there. He wants to go to the Coupole. Wants to take a little walk first around the block.

"But it's raining, Joe."

"I know, but what the hell! I've got to have my constitutional. I've got to wash the dirt out of my belly." When he says this I have the impression that the whole world is wrapped up there inside his belly, and that it's rotting there.

As he's putting on his things he falls back again into a semi-comatose state. He stands there with one arm in his coat sleeve and his hat on assways and he begins to

dream aloud—about the Riviera, about the sun, about
lazing one's life away. "All I ask of life," he says, "is a
bunch of books, a bunch of dreams, and a bunch of
cunt." As he mumbles this meditatively he looks at me
with the softest, the most insidious smile. "Do you like
that smile?" he says. And then disgustedly—"Jesus, if I
could only find some rich cunt to smile at that way!"

"Only a rich cunt can save me now," he says with an
air of utmost weariness. "One gets tired of chasing after
new cunts all he time. It gets mechanical. The trouble is,
you see, I can't fall in love. I'm too much of an egoist.
Women only help me to dream, that's all. It's a vice, like
drink or opium. I've got to have a new one every day; if
I don't I get morbid. I think too much. Sometimes I'm
amazed at myself, how quick I pull it off—and how little
it really means. I do it automatically like. Sometimes I'm
not thinking about a woman at all, but suddenly I notice a woman looking at me and then, bangol it starts all
over again. Before I know what I'm doing I've got her up
to the room. I don't even remember what I say to them.
I bring them up to the room, give them a pat on the ass,
and before I know what it's all about it's over. It's like a
dream. . . . Do you know what I mean?"

He hasn't much use for the French girls. Can't stand
them. "Either they want money or they want you to
marry them. At bottom they're all whores. I'd rather
wrestle with a virgin," he says. "They give you a little
illusion. They put up a fight at least." Just the same, as
we glance over the *terrasse* there is hardly a whore in
sight whom he hasn't fucked at some time or other.
Standing at the bar he points them out to me, one by
one, goes over them anatomically, describes their good
points and their bad. "They're all frigid," he says. And
then begins to mold his hands, thinking of the nice, juicy
virgins who are just dying for it.

In the midst of his reveries he suddenly arrests himself, and grabbing my arm excitedly, he points to a whale
of a woman who is just lowering herself into a seat.
"There's my Danish cunt," he grunts. "See that ass?

Danish. How that woman loves it! She just begs me for it. Come over here . . . look at her now, from the side! Look at that ass, will you? It's enormous. I tell you, when she climbs over me I can hardly get my arms around it. It blots out the whole world. She makes me feel like a little bug crawling inside her. I don't know why I fall for her—I suppose it's that ass. It's so incongruous like. And the creases in it! You can't forget an ass like that. It's a fact . . . a solid fact. The others, they may bore you, or they may give you a moment's illusion, but this one—with her ass!—zowie, you can't obliterate her . . . it's like going to bed with a monument on top of you."

The Danish cunt seems to have electrified him. He's lost all his sluggishness now. His eyes are popping out of his head. And of course one thing reminds him of another. He wants to get out of the fucking hotel because the noise bothers him. He wants to write a book too so as to have something to occupy his mind. But then the goddamned job stands in the way. "It takes it out of you, that fucking job! I don't want to write about Montparnasse. . . . I want to write my life, my thoughts. I want to get the dirt out of my belly . . . Listen, get that one over there! I had her a long time ago. She used to be down near Les Halles. A funny bitch. She lay on the edge of the bed and pulled her dress up. Ever try it that way? Not bad. She didn't hurry me either. She just lay back and played with her hat while I slugged away at her. And when I come she says sort of bored like—'Are you through?' Like it didn't make any difference at all. Of course, it doesn't make any difference, I know that goddamn well . . . but the cold-blooded way she had . . . I sort of like it . . . it was fascinating, you know? When she goes to wipe herself she begins to sing. Going out of the hotel she was still singing. Didn't even say *Au revoir!* Walks off swinging her hat and humming to herself like. That's a whore for you! A good lay though. I think I liked her better than my virgin. There's something depraved about screwing a woman who doesn't give a fuck about it. It heats your blood. . . ." And then, after a moment's meditation—"Can you imagine what she'd be like if she had any feelings?"

"Listen," he says, "I want you to come to the Club with me tomorrow afternoon . . . there's a dance on."

"I can't tomorrow, Joe. I promised to help Carl out. . . ."

"Listen, forget that prick! I want you to do me a favor. It's like this"—he commences to mold his hands again. "I've got a cunt lined up . . . she promised to stay with me on my night off. But I'm not positive about her yet. She's got a mother, you see . . . some shit of a painter, she chews my ear off every time I see her. I think the truth is, the mother's jealous. I don't think she'd mind so much if I gave her a lay first. You know how it is. . . . Anyway, I thought maybe you wouldn't mind taking the mother . . . she's not so bad . . . if I hadn't seen the daughter I might have considered her myself. The daughter's nice and young, fresh like, you know what I mean? There's a clean smell to her. . . ."

"Listen, Joe, you'd better find somebody else. . . ."

"Aw, don't take it like that! I know how you feel about it. It's only a little favor I'm asking you to do for me. I don't know how to get rid of the old hen. I thought first I'd get drunk and ditch her—but I don't think the young one'd like that. They're sentimental like. They come from Minnesota or somewhere. Anyway, come around tomorrow and wake me up, will you? Otherwise I'll oversleep. And besides, I want you to help me find a room. You know I'm helpless. Find me a room in a quiet street, somewhere near here. I've got to stay around here . . . I've got credit here. Listen, promise me you'll do that for me. I'll buy you a meal now and then. Come around anyway, because I go nuts talking to these foolish cunts. I want to talk to you about Havelock Ellis. Jesus, I've had the book out for three weeks now and I haven't looked at it. You sort of rot here. Would you believe it, I've never been to the Louvre—nor the Comédie-Française. Is it worth going to those joints? Still, it sort of takes your mind off things, I suppose. What do you do with yourself all day? Don't you get bored? What do you do for a lay? Listen . . . come here! Don't run away yet . . . I'm lonely. Do you know something—if this keeps up another year I'll go nuts. I've got to get out of this fucking country. There's nothing for me here. I know it's lousy now, in America, but just the same. . . . You go queer over here . . . all these cheap shits sitting on their ass all day bragging about their work and none of them is worth a stinking damn. They're all failures—that's why they come over here. Listen, Joe, don't you ever get homesick? You're a funny guy . . . you seem to like it over here. What do you see in it? . . . I wish you'd tell me. I wish to Christ I could stop thinking about myself. I'm all twisted up inside . . . it's like a knot in there. . . . Listen, I know I'm boring the shit out of you, but I've got to talk to someone. I can't talk to those guys upstairs . . . you know what those bastards are like . . . they all take a byline. And Carl, the little prick, he's so goddamned selfish. I'm an egotist, but I'm not selfish. There's a difference. I'm a neurotic, I guess. I can't stop thinking about myself. It isn't that I think myself so important. . . . I simply can't think about anything else, that's all. If I could fall in love with a woman that might help some. But I can't find a woman who interests me. I'm in a mess, you can see that can't you? What do you advise me to do? What would you do in my place? Listen, I don't want to hold you back any longer, but wake me up tomorrow—at one-thirty—will you? I'll give you something extra if you'll shine my shoes. And listen, if you've got an extra shirt, a clean one, bring it along, will you? Shit, I'm grinding my balls off on that job, and it doesn't even give me a clean shirt. They've got us over here like a bunch of niggers. Ah, well, shit! I'm going to take a walk . . . wash the dirt out of my belly. Don't forget, *tomorrow!*"

For six months or more it's been going on, this correspondence with the rich cunt, Irene. Recently I've been reporting to Carl every day in order to bring the affair to a head, because as far as Irene is concerned this thing could go on indefinitely. In the last few days there's been a perfect avalanche of letters exchanged; the last letter we dispatched was almost forty pages long, and written in three languages. It was a potpourri, the last letter—tag ends of old novels, slices from the Sunday supplement, reconstructed versions of old letters to Llona and Tania, garbled transliterations of Rabelais and Petronius—in short, we exhausted ourselves. Finally Irene decides to come out of her shell. Finally a letter arrives giving a rendezvous at her hotel. Carl is pissing in his pants. It's one thing to write letters to a woman you don't know; it's another thing entirely to call on her and make love-to her. At the last moment he's quaking so that I almost fear I'll have to substitute for him. When we get out of the taxi in front of her hotel he's trembling so much that I have to walk him around the block first. He's already had two Pernods, but they haven't made the slightest impression on him. The sight of the hotel itself is enough to crush him: it's a pretentious place with one of those huge empty lobbies in which Englishwomen sit for hours with a blank look. In order to make sure that he wouldn't run away I stood by while the porter telephoned to announce him. Irene was there, and she was waiting for him. As he got into the lift he threw me a last despairing glance, one of those mute appeals which a dog makes when you put a noose around its neck. Going through the revolving door I thought of Van Norden. . . .

I go back to the hotel and wait for a telephone call. He's only got an hour's time and he's promised to let me know the results before going to work. I look over the carbons of the letters we sent her. I try to imagine the situation as it actually is, but it's beyond me. Her letters are much better than ours—they're sincere, that's plain. By now they've sized each other up. I wonder if he's still pissing in his pants.

The telephone rings. His voice sounds queer, squeaky,

as though he were frightened and jubilant at the same
time. He asks me to substitute for him at the office. "Tell
the bastard anything! Tell him I'm dying. . . ."

"Listen, Carl . . . can you tell me . . .?"

"Hello! Are you Henry Miller?" It's a woman's voice.
It's Irene. She's saying hello to me. Her voice sounds
beautiful over the phone . . . beautiful. For a moment
I'm in a perfect panic. I don't know what to say to her.
I'd like to say: "Listen, Irene, I think you are beautiful . . . I think you're *wonderful*." I'd like to say one true
thing to her, no matter how silly it would sound, because now that I hear her voice everything is changed.
But before I can gather my wits Carl is on the phone
again and he's saying in that queer squeaky voice: "She
likes you, Joe. I told her all about you. . . ."

At the office I have to hold copy for Van Norden.
When it comes time for the break he pulls me aside. He
looks glum and ravaged.

"So he's dying, is he, the little prick? Listen, what's the
lowdown on this?"

"I think he went to see his rich cunt," I answer calmly.

"*What!* You mean he called on her?" He seems beside
himself. "Listen, where does she live? What's her name?"
I pretend ignorance. "Listen," he says, "you're a decent
guy. Why the hell don't you let me in on this racket?"

In order to appease him I promise finally that I'll tell
him everything as soon as I get the details from Carl. I
can hardly wait myself until I see Carl.

Around noon next day I knock at his door. He's up
already and lathering his beard. Can't tell a thing from
the expression on his face. Can't even tell whether he's
going to tell me the truth. The sun is streaming in
through the open window, the birds are chirping, and
yet somehow, why it is I don't know, the room seems
more barren and poverty-stricken than ever. The floor
is slathered with lather, and on the rack there are the
two dirty towels which are never changed. And somehow Carl isn't changed either, and that puzzles me more

than anything. This morning the whole world ought to be changed, for bad or good, but changed, radically changed. And yet Carl is standing there lathering his face and not a single detail is altered.

"Sit down . . . sit down there on the bed," he says. "You're going to hear everything . . . but wait first . . . wait a little." He commences to lather his face again, and then to hone his razor. He even remarks about the water . . . no hot water again.

"Listen, Carl, I'm on tenterhooks. You can torture me afterward, if you like, but tell me now, tell me one thing . . . was it good or bad?"

He turns away from the mirror with brush in hand and gives me a strange smile. "Wait! I'm going to tell you everything. . . ."

"That means it was a failure."

"No," he says, drawing out his words. "It wasn't a failure, and it wasn't a success either. . . . By the way, did you fix it up for me at the office? What did you tell them?"

I see it's no use trying to pull it out of him. When he gets good and ready he'll tell me. Not before. I lie back on the bed, silent as a clam. He goes on shaving.

Suddenly, apropos of nothing at all, he begins to talk—disconnectedly at first, and then more and more clearly, emphatically, resolutely. It's a struggle to get it out, but he seems determined to relate everything; he acts as if he were getting something off his conscience. He even reminds me of the look he gave me as he was going up the elevator shaft. He dwells on that lingeringly, as though to imply that everything were contained in that last moment, as though, if he had the power to alter things, he would never have put foot outside the elevator.

She was in her dressing sack when he called. There was a bucket of champagne on the dresser. The room was rather dark and her voice was lovely. He gives me all the details about the room, the champagne, how the *garçon* opened it, the noise it made, the way her dress-

ing sack rustled when she came forward to greet him—
he tells me everything but what I want to hear.

It was about eight when he called on her. At eight-
thirty he was nervous, thinking about the job. "It was
about nine when I called you, wasn't it?" he says.

"Yes, about that."

"I was nervous, see. . . ."

"I know that. Go on. . . ."

I don't know whether to believe him or not, especially
after those letters we concocted. I don't even know
whether I've heard him accurately, because what he's
telling me sounds utterly fantastic. And yet it sounds
true too, knowing the sort of guy he is. And then I remember his voice over the telephone, that strange mixture of fright and jubilation. But why isn't he more jubilant now? He keeps smiling all the time, smiling like a
rosy little bedbug that has had its fill. "It was nine
o'clock," he says once again, "when I called you up,
wasn't it?" I nod my head wearily. Yes, it was nine
o'clock. He is certain now that it was nine o'clock because he remembers having taken out his watch. Anyway, when he looked at his watch again it was ten
o'clock. At ten o'clock she was lying on the divan with
her boobies in her hands. That's the way he gives it to
me—in driblets. At eleven o'clock it was all settled; they
were going to run away, to Borneo. Fuck the husband!
She never loved him anyway. She would never have
written the first letter if the husband wasn't old and
passionless. "And then she says to me: 'But listen, dear,
how do you know you won't get tired of me?'"

At this I burst out laughing. This sounds preposterous
to me, I can't help it.

"And you said?"

"What did you expect me to say? I said: 'How could
anyone ever grow tired of *you?*'"

And then he describes to me what happened after that,
how he bent down and kissed her breasts, and how, after
he had kissed them fervidly, he stuffed them back into

her corsage, or whatever it is they call these things. And
after that another *coupe* of champagne.

Around midnight the *garçon* arrives with beer and
sandwiches—caviar sandwiches. And all the while, so he
says, he has been dying to take a leak. He had one hard
on, but it faded out. All the while his bladder is fit to
burst, but he imagines, the cute little prick that he is, that
the situation calls for delicacy.

At one-thirty she's for hiring a carriage and driving
through the Bois. He has only one thought in his head—
how to take a leak? "I love you . . . I adore you," he says.
"I'll go anywhere you say—Istanbul, Singapore, Hono-
lulu. Only I must go now. . . . It's getting late."

He tells me all this in his dirty little room, with the sun
pouring in and the birds chirping away like mad. I don't
yet know whether she was beautiful or not. He doesn't
know whether she was beautiful or not. He doesn't
know himself, the imbecile. He rather thinks she wasn't.
The room was dark and then there was the champagne
and his nerves all frazzled.

"But you ought to know something about her—if this
isn't all a goddamned lie!"

"Wait a minute," he says. "Wait . . . let me think! No,
she wasn't beautiful. I'm sure of that now. She had a
streak of gray hair over her forehead . . . I remember that.
But that wouldn't be so bad—I had almost forgotten it
you see. No, it was her arms—they were thin . . . they
were thin and brittle." He begins to pace back and
forth.—Suddenly he stops dead. "If she were only ten
years younger!" he exclaims. "If she were ten years younger I might overlook the streak of gray hair . . . and even
the brittle arms. But she's too old. You see, with a cunt
like that every year counts now. She won't be just one
year older next year—she'll be ten years older. Another
year hence and she'll be twenty years older. And I'll be
getting younger looking all the time—at least for another
five years. . . ."

"But how did it end?" I interrupt.

"That's just it . . . it didn't end. I promised to see her

Tuesday around five o'clock. That's bad, you know! There were lines in her face which will look much worse in daylight. I suppose she wants me to fuck her Tuesday. Fucking in the daytime—you don't do it with a cunt like that. Especially in a hotel like that. I'd rather do it on my night off . . . but Tuesday's not my night off. And that's not all. I promised her a letter in the meantime. How am I going to write her a letter now? I haven't anything to say. . . . Shit! If only she were ten years younger. Do you think I should go with her . . . to Borneo or wherever it is she wants to take me? What would I do with a rich cunt like that on my hands? I don't know how to shoot. I am afraid of guns and all that sort of thing. Besides, she'll be wanting me to fuck her night and day . . . nothing but hunting and fucking all the time . . . I can't do it!"

"Maybe it won't be so bad as you think. She'll buy you ties and all sorts of things. . . ."

"Maybe you'll come along with us, eh? I told her all about you. . . ."

"Did you tell her I was poor? Did you tell her I needed things?"

"I told her everything. Shit, everything would be fine, if she were just a few years younger. She said she was turning forty. That means fifty or sixty. It's like fucking your own mother . . . you can't do it . . . it's impossible."

"But she must have had some attractiveness . . . you were kissing her breasts, you said."

"Kissing her breasts—what's that? Besides it was dark, I'm telling you."

Putting on his pants a button falls off. "Look at that, will you. It's falling apart, the goddamned suit. I've worn it for seven years now. . . . I never paid for it either. It was a good suit once, but it stinks now. And that cunt would buy me suits too, all I wanted most likely. But that's what I don't like, having a woman shell out for me. I never did that in my life. That's *your* idea. I'd rather live alone. Shit, this is a good room isn't it? What's wrong with it? It's a damned sight better than her room, isn't it? I don't like her fine hotel. I'm against hotels like that. I told her so. She said she didn't care where she lived . . . said she'd come and live with me if I wanted her to. Can you picture her moving in here with her big trunks and her hatboxes and all that crap she drags around with her? She has too many things—too many dresses and bottles and all that. It's like a clinic, her room. If she gets a little scratch on her finger it's serious. And then she has to be massaged and her hair has to be waved and she mustn't eat this and she mustn't eat that. Listen, Joe, she'd be all right if she were just a little younger. You can forgive a young cunt anything. A young cunt doesn't have to have any brains. They're better without brains. But an old cunt, even if she's brilliant, even if she's the most charming woman in the world, nothing makes any difference. A young cunt is an investment; an old cunt is a dead loss. All they can do for you is buy you things. But that doesn't put meat on their arms or juice between the legs. She isn't bad, Irene. In fact, I think you'd like her. With you it's different. You don't have to fuck her. You can afford to like her. Maybe you wouldn't like all those dresses and the bottles and what not, but you could be tolerant. She wouldn't bore you, that I can tell you. She's even interesting, I might say. But she's withered. Her breasts are all right yet—but her arms! I told her I'd bring you around some day. . . . I didn't know what to say to her. Maybe you'd like her, especially when she's dressed. I don't know. . . ."

"Listen, she's rich, you say? I'll like her! I don't care how old she is, so long as she's not a hag. . . ."

"She's not a hag! What are you talking about? She's charming, I tell you. She talks well. She looks well too . . . only her arms. . . ."

"All right, if that's how it is, *I'll* fuck her—if you don't want to. Tell her that. Be subtle about it, though. With a woman like that you've got to do things slowly. You bring me around and let things work out for themselves. Praise the shit out of me. Act jealous like. . . . Shit, maybe we'll fuck her together . . . and we'll go places and we'll eat together . . . and we'll drive and hunt and wear nice

things. If she wants to go to Borneo let her take us along.
I don't know how to shoot either, but that doesn't matter. She doesn't care about that either. She just wants to
be fucked that's all. You're talking about her arms all the
time. You don't have to look at her arms all the time, do
you? Look at this bedspread! Look at the mirror! Do you
call this living? Do you want to go on being delicate and
live like a louse all your life? You can't even pay your
hotel bill . . . and you've got a job too. This is no way to
live. I don't care if she's seventy years old—it's better
than this. . . ."

"Listen, Joe, you fuck her for me . . . then everything'll be fine. Maybe I'll fuck her once in a while too . . .
on my night off. It's four days now since I've had a good
shit. There's something sticking to me, like grapes. . . ."

"You've got the piles, that's what."

"My hair's falling out too . . . and I ought to see the
dentist. I feel as though I were falling apart. I told her
what a good guy you are. . . . You'll do things for me, eh?
You're not too delicate, eh? If we go to Borneo I won't
have hemorrhoids any more. Maybe I'll develop something else . . . something worse . . . fever perhaps . . . or
cholera. Shit, it's better to die of a good disease like that
than to piss your life away on a newspaper with grapes
up your ass and buttons falling off your pants. I'd like to
be rich, even if it were only for a week, and then go to a
hospital with a good disease, a fatal one, and have flowers
in the room and nurses dancing around and telegrams
coming. They take good care of you if you're rich. They
wash you with cotton batting and they comb your hair
for you. Shit, I know all that. Maybe I'd be lucky and not
die at all. Maybe I'd be a cripple all my life . . . maybe I'd
be paralyzed and have to sit in a wheelchair. But then
I'd be taken care of just the same . . . even if I had no
more money. If you're an invalid—a *real* one—they don't
let you starve. And you get a clean bed to lie in . . . and
they change the towels every day. This way nobody gives
a fuck about you, especially if you have a job. They think
a man should be happy if he's got a job. What would you

rather do—be a cripple all your life, or have a job . . . or marry a rich cunt? You'd rather marry a rich cunt, I can see that. You only think about food. But supposing you married her and then you couldn't get a hard on any more—that happens sometimes—what would you do then? You'd be at her mercy. You'd have to eat out of her hand, like a little poodle dog. You'd like that, would you? Or maybe you don't think of those things? *I think of everything.* I think of the suits I'd pick out and the places I'd like to go to, but I also think of the other thing. That's the important thing. What good are the fancy ties and the fine suits if you can't get a hard on any more? You couldn't even betray her—because she'd be on your heels all the time. No, the best thing would be to marry her and then get a disease right away. Only not syphilis. Cholera, let's say, or yellow fever. So that if a miracle did happen and your life was spared you'd be a cripple for the rest of your days. Then you wouldn't have to worry about fucking her any more, and you wouldn't have to worry about the rent either. She'd probably buy you a fine wheelchair with rubber tires and all sorts of levers and what not. You might even be able to use your hands—I mean enough to be able to write. Or you could have a secretary, for that matter. That's it—that's the best solution for a writer. What does a guy want with his arms and legs? He doesn't need arms and legs to write with. He needs security . . . peace . . . protection. All those heroes who parade in wheelchairs—it's too bad they're not writers. If you could only be sure, when you go to war, that you'd have only your legs blown off . . . if you could be sure of that I'd say let's have a war tomorrow. I wouldn't give a fuck about the medals—they could keep the medals. All I'd want is a good wheelchair and three meals a day. Then I'd give them something to read, those pricks."

The following day, at one-thirty, I call on Van Norden. It's his day off, or rather his night off. He has left word with Carl that I am to help him move today.

I find him in a state of unusual depression. He hasn't

slept a wink all night, he tells me. There's something on his mind, something that's eating him up. It isn't long before I discover what it is; he's been waiting impatiently for me to arrive in order to spill it.

"That guy," he begins, meaning Carl, "that guy's an artist. He described every detail minutely. He told it to me with such accuracy that I know it's all a goddamned lie . . . but I can't dismiss it from my mind. You know how my mind works!"

He interrupts himself to inquire if Carl has told me the whole story. There isn't the least suspicion in his mind that Carl may have told me one thing and him another. He seems to think that the story was invented expressly to torture him. He doesn't seem to mind so much that it's a fabrication. It's the "images" as he says, which Carl left in his mind, that get him. The images are real, even if the whole story is false. And besides, the fact that there actually is a rich cunt on the scene and that Carl actually paid her a visit, that's undeniable. What actually happened is secondary; he takes it for granted that Carl put the boots to her. But what drives him desperate is the thought that what Carl has described to him might have been *possible*.

It's just like that guy," he says, "to tell me he put it to her six or seven times. I know that's a lot of shit and I don't mind that so much, but when he tells me that she hired a carriage and drove him out to the Bois and that they used the husband's fur coat for a blanket, that's too much. I supose he told you about the chauffeur waiting respectfully . . . and listen, did he tell you how the engine purred all the time? Jesus, he built that up wonderfully. It's just like him to think of a detail like that . . . it's one of those little details which makes a thing psychologically real . . . you can't get it out of your head afterward. And he tells it to me so smoothly, so naturally. . . . I wonder, did he think it up in advance or did it just pop out of his head like that, spontaneously? He's such a cute little liar you can't walk away from him . . . it's like he's writing you a letter, one of those flowerpots that he makes overnight.

I don't understand how a guy can write such letters . . . I don't get the mentality behind it . . . it's a form of masturbation . . . what do you think?"

But before I have an opportunity to venture an opinion, or even to laugh in his face, Van Norden goes on with his monologue.

"Listen, I suppose he told you everything . . . did he tell you how he stood on the balcony in the moonlight and kissed her? That sounds banal when you repeat it, but the way that guy describes it . . . I can just see the little prick standing there with the woman in his arms and already he's writing another letter to her, another flowerpot about the roof tops and all that crap he steals from his French authors. That guy never says a thing that's original, I found that out. You have to get a clue like . . . find out whom he's been reading lately . . . and it's hard to do that because he's so damned secretive. Listen, if I didn't know that you went there with him, I wouldn't believe that the woman existed. A guy like that could write letters to himself. And yet he's lucky . . . he's so damned tiny, so frail, so romantic looking, that women fall for him now and then . . . they sort of adopt him . . . they feel sorry for him, I guess. And some cunts like to receive flowerpots . . . it makes them feel important. . . . But this woman's an intelligent woman, so he says. You ought to know . . . you've seen her letters. What do you suppose a woman like that saw in him? I can understand her falling for the letters . . . but how do you suppose she felt when she *saw* him?

"But listen, all that's beside the point. What I'm getting at is the way he tells it to me. You know how he embroiders things . . . well, after that scene on the balcony— he gives me that like an hors d'œuvre, you know— after that, so he says, they went inside and he unbuttoned her pajamas. What are you smiling for? Was he shitting me about that?"

"No, no! You're giving it to me exactly as he told me. Go ahead. . . ."

"After that"—here Van Norden has to smile himself—"after that, mind you, he tells me how she sat in the chair with her legs up . . . not a stitch on . . . and he's sitting on the floor looking up at her, telling her how beautiful she looks . . . did he tell you that she looked like a Matisse? . . . Wait a minute . . . I'd like to remember exactly what he said. He had some cute little phrase there about an odalisque . . . what the hell's an odalisque anyway? He said it in French, that's why it's hard to remember the fucking thing . . . but it sounded good. It sounded just like the sort of thing he might say. And she probably thought it was original with him . . . I suppose she thinks he's a poet or something. But listen, all this is nothing . . . I make allowance for his imagination. It's what happened after that that drives me crazy. All night long I've been tossing about, playing with these images he left in my mind. I can't get it out of my head. It sounds so real to me that if it didn't happen I could strangle the bastard. A guy has no right to invent things like that. Or else he's diseased. . . .

"What I'm getting at is that moment when, he says, he got down on his knees and with those two skinny fingers of his he spread her cunt open. You remember that? He says she was sitting there with her legs dangling over the arms of the chair and suddenly, he says, he got an inspiration. This was after he had given her a couple of lays already . . . after he had made that little spiel about Matisse. He gets down on his knees—*get this!*—and with his two fingers . . . just the tips of them, mind you . . . he opens the little petals . . . *squish-squish* . . . just like that. A sticky little sound . . . almost inaudible. *Squish-squish!* Jesus, I've been hearing it all night long! And then he says—as if that weren't enough for me—then he tells me he buried his head in her muff. And when he did that, so help me Christ, if she didn't swing her legs around his neck and lock him there. *That finished me!* Imagine it! Imagine a fine, sensitive woman like that swinging her legs around *his neck!* There's something poisonous about it. It's so fantastic that it sounds convincing. If he had only told me about the champagne and the ride in the

Bois and even that scene on the balcony I could have dismissed it. But this thing is so incredible that it doesn't sound like a lie any more. I can't believe that he ever read anything like that anywhere, and I can't see what could have put the idea into his head unless there was some truth in it. With a little prick like that, you know, anything can happen. He may not have fucked her at all, but she may have let him diddle her . . . you never know with these rich cunts what they might expect you to do. . . ."

When he finally pulls himself out of bed and starts to shave the afternoon is already well advanced. I've finally succeeded in switching his mind to other things, to the moving principally. The maid comes in to see if he's ready—he's supposed to have vacated the room by noon. He's just in the act of slipping into his trousers. I'm a little surprised that he doesn't excuse himself, or turn away. Seeing him standing there nonchalantly buttoning his fly as he gives her orders I begin to titter. "Don't mind her," he says, throwing her a look of supreme contempt, "she's just a big sow. Give her a pinch in the ass, if you like. She won't say anything." And then addressing her, in English, he says. "Come here, you bitch, put your hand on this!" At this I can't restrain myself any longer. I burst out laughing, a fit of hysterical laughter which infects the maid also, though she doesn't know what it's all about. The maid commences to take down the pictures and the photographs, mostly of himself, which line the walls. "*You*," he says, jerking his thumb, "come here! Here's something to remember me by"—ripping a photograph off the wall—"when I go you can wipe your ass with it. See," he says, turning to me, "she's a dumb bitch. She wouldn't look any more intelligent if I said it in French." The maid stands there with her mouth open; she is evidently convinced that he is cracked. "Hey!" he yells at her as if she were hard of hearing. "Hey, *you!* Yes, *you!* Like this . . . !" and he takes the photograph, his own photograph, and wipes his ass with it. "*Comme ça!* Savvy? You've got to draw pictures for her," he says, thrusting his lower lip forward in absolute disgust.

He watches her helplessly as she throws his things into the big valises. "Here, put these in too," he says handing her a toothbrush and the douche bag. Half of his belongings are lying on the floor. The valises are crammed full and there is nowhere to put the paintings and the books and the bottles that are half empty. "Sit down a minute," he says. "We've got plenty of time. We've got to think this thing out. If you hadn't come around I'd never have gotten out of here. You see how helpless I am. Don't let me forget to take the bulbs out . . . they belong to me. That wastebasket belongs to me too. They expect you to live like pigs, these bastards." The maid has gone downstairs to get some twine. . . . "Wait till you see . . . she'll charge me for the twine even if it's only three sous. They wouldn't sew a button on your pants here without charging for it. The lousy, dirty scroungers!" He takes a bottle of Calvados from the mantelpiece and nods to me to grab the other. "No use carrying these to the new place. Let's finish them off now. But don't give *her* a drink! That bastard, I wouldn't leave her a piece of toilet paper. I'd like to ruin the joint before I go. Listen . . . piss on the floor, if you like. I wish I could take a crap in the bureau drawer." He feels so utterly disgusted with himself and everything else that he doesn't know what to do by way of venting his feelings. He walks over to the bed with the bottle in his hand and pulling back the covers he sprinkles Calvados over the mattress. Not content with that he digs his heel into the mattress. Unfortunately there's no mud on his heels. Finally he takes the sheet and cleans his shoes with it. "That'll give them something to do," he mutters vengefully. Then, taking a good swig, he throws his head back and gargles his throat, and after he's gargled it good and proper he spits it out on the mirror. "There, you cheap bastards! Wipe that off when I go!" He walks back and forth mumbling to himself. Seeing his torn socks lying on the floor he picks them up and tears them to bits. The paintings enrage him too.

He picks one up—a portrait of himself done by some Lesbian he knew and he puts his foot through it. "That bitch! You know what she had the nerve to ask me? She asked me to turn over my cunts to her after I was through with them. She never gave me a sou for writing her up. She thought I honestly admired her work. I wouldn't have gotten that painting out of her if I hadn't promised to fix her up with that cunt from Minnesota. She was nuts about her . . . used to follow us around like a dog in heat . . . we couldn't get rid of the bitch! She bothered the life out of me. I got so that I was almost afraid to bring a cunt up here for fear that she'd bust in on me. I used to creep up here like a burglar and lock the door behind me as soon as I got inside. . . . She and that Georgia cunt—they drive me nuts. The one is always in heat and the other is always hungry. I hate fucking a woman who's hungry. It's like you push a feed inside her and then you push it out again. . . . Jesus, that reminds me of something . . . where did I put that blue ointment? That's important. Did you ever have those things? It's worse than having a dose. And I don't know where I got them from either. I've had so many women up here in the last week or so I've lost track of them. Funny too, because they all smelled so fresh. But you know how it is. . . ."

The maid has piled his things up on the sidewalk. The *patron* looks on with a surly air. When everything has been loaded into the taxi there is only room for one of us inside. As soon as we commence to roll Van Norden gets out a newspaper and starts bundling up his pots and pans; in the new place all cooking is strictly forbidden. By the time we reach our destination all his luggage has come undone; it wouldn't be quite so embarrassing if the madam had not stuck her head out of the doorway just as we rolled up. "My God!" she exclaims, "what in the devil is all this? What does it mean?" Van Norden is so intimidated that he can think of nothing more to say than "*C'est moi . . . c'est moi, madame!*" And turning to me he mumbles savagely: "That cluck! Did you notice her face? She's going to make it hard for me."

The hotel lies back of a dingy passage and forms a rectangle very much on the order of a modern penitentiary. The *bureau* is large and gloomy, despite the brilliant reflections from the tile walls. There are bird cages hanging in the windows and little enamel signs everywhere begging the guests in an obsolete language not to do this and not to forget that. It is almost immaculately clean but absolutely poverty-stricken, threadbare, woebegone. The upholstered chairs are held together with wired thongs; they remind one unpleasantly of the electric chair. The room he is going to occupy is on the fifth floor. As we climb the stairs Van Norden informs me that Maupassant once lived here. And in the same breath remarks that there is a peculiar odor in the hall. On the fifth floor a few windowpanes are missing; we stand a moment gazing at the tenants across the court. It is getting toward dinner time and people are straggling back to their rooms with that weary, dejected air which comes from earning a living honestly. Most of the windows are wide open: the dingy rooms have the appearance of so many yawning mouths. The occupants of the rooms are yawning too, or else scratching themselves. They move about listlessly and apparently without much purpose; they might just as well be lunatics.

As we turn down the corridor toward room 57, a door suddenly opens in front of us and an old hag with matted hair and the eyes of a maniac peers out. She startles us so that we stand transfixed. For a full minute the three of us stand there powerless to move or even to make an intelligent gesture. Back of the old hag I can see a kitchen table and on it lies a baby all undressed, a puny little brat no bigger than a plucked chicken. Finally the old one picks up a slop pail by her side and makes a move forward. We stand aside to let her pass and as the door closes behind her the baby lets out a piercing scream. It is room 56, and between 56 and 57 is the toilet where the old hag is emptying her slops.

Ever since we have mounted the stairs Van Norden has kept silence. But his looks are eloquent. When he opens the door of 57 I have for a fleeting moment the sensation of going mad. A huge mirror covered with green gauze and tipped at an angle of 45 degrees hangs directly opposite the entrance over a baby carriage which is filled with books. Van Norden doesn't even crack a smile; instead he walks nonchalantly over to the baby carriage and picking up a book begins to skim it through, much as a man would enter the public library and go unthinkingly to the rack nearest to hand. And perhaps this would not seem so ludicrous to me if I had not espied at the same time a pair of handle bars resting in the corner. They look so absolutely peaceful and contented, as if they had been dozing there for years, that suddenly it seems to me as if we had been standing in this room, in exactly this position, for an incalculably long time, that it was a pose we had struck in a dream from which we never emerged, a dream which the least gesture, the wink of an eye even, will shatter. But more remarkable still is the remembrance that suddenly floats up of an actual dream which occurred only the other night, a dream in which I saw Van Norden in just such a corner as is occupied now by the handle bars, only instead of the handle bars there was a woman crouching with her legs drawn up. I see him standing over the woman with that alert, eager look in his eye which comes when he wants something badly. The street in which this is going on is blurred—only the angle made by the two walls is clear, and the cowering figure of the woman. I can see him going at her in that quick, animal way of his, reckless of what's going on about him, determined only to have his way. And a look in his eyes as though to say—"you can kill me afterwards, but just let me get it in . . . I've got to get it in!" And there he is, bent over her, their heads knocking against the wall, he has such a tremendous erection that it's simply impossible to get it in her. Suddenly, with that disgusted air which he knows so well how to summon, he picks himself up and adjusts his clothes. He is about to walk away when suddenly he notices that his penis is lying on the sidewalk. It is about the size of a sawed-off broomstick. He picks it up nonchalantly and slings it under his arm. As he walks off I notice two huge bulbs, like tulip bulbs, dangling from the end of the broomstick, and I can hear him muttering to himself "flowerpots . . . flowerpots."

The *garçon* arrives panting and sweating. Van Norden looks at him uncomprehendingly. The madam now marches in and, walking straight up to Van Norden, she takes the book out of his hand, thrusts it in the baby carriage, and, without saying a word, wheels the baby carriage into the hallway.

"This is a bughouse," says Van Norden, smiling distressedly. It is such a faint, indescribable smile that for a moment the dream feeling comes back and it seems to me that we are standing at the end of a long corridor at the end of which is a corrugated mirror. And down this corridor, swinging his distress like a dingy lantern, Van Norden staggers, staggers in and out as here and there a door opens and a hand yanks him in or a hoof pushes him out. And the further off he wanders the more lugubrious is his distress; he wears it like a lantern which the cyclists hold between their teeth on a night when the pavement is wet and slippery. In and out of the dingy rooms he wanders, and when he sits down the chair collapses, when he opens his valise there is only a toothbrush inside. In every room there is a mirror before which he stands attentively and chews his rage, and from the constant chewing, from the grumbling and mumbling and the muttering and cursing his jaws have gotten unhinged and they sag badly and, when he rubs his beard, pieces of his jaw crumble away and he's so disgusted with himself that he stamps on his own jaw, grinds it to bits with his big heels.

Mean while the luggage is being hauled in. And things begin to look crazier even then before—particularly when he attaches his exerciser to the bedstead and begins his Sandow exercises. "I like this place," he says, smiling at the *garçon*. He takes his coat and vest off. The *garçon* is watching him with a puzzled air; he has a valise in one hand and the douche bag in the other. I'm standing apart in the antechamber holding the mirror with the green gauze. Not a single object seems to possess a practical use. The antechamber itself seems useless, a sort of vestibule to a barn. It is exactly the same sort of sensation which I get when I enter the Comédie-Française or the Palais-Royal Theatre; it is a world of bric-a-brac, of trap doors, of arms and busts and waxed floors, of candelabras and men in armor, of statues without eyes and love letters lying in glass cases. Something is going on, but it makes no sense; it's like finishing the half-etmpty bottle of Calvados because there's no room in the valise.

Climbing up the stairs, as I said a moment ago, he had mentioned the fact that Maupassant used to live here. The coincidence seems to have made an impression upon him. He would like to believe that it was in this very room that Maupassant gave birth to some of those gruesome tales on which his reputation rests. "They lived like pigs, those poor bastards," he says. We are sitting at the round table in a pair of comfortable old armchairs that have been trussed up with thongs and braces; the bed is right beside us, so close indeed that we can put our feet on it. The *armoire* stands in a corner behind us, also conveniently within reach. Van Norden has emptied his dirty wash on the table; we sit there with our feet buried in his dirty socks and shirts and smoke contentedly. The sordidness of the place seems to have worked a spell on him: he is content here. When I get up to switch on the light he suggests that we play a game of cards before going out to eat. And so we sit there by the window, with the dirty wash strewn over the floor and the Sandow exerciser hanging from the chandelier, and we play a few rounds of two-handed pinochle. Van Norden has put away his pipe and packed a wad of snuff on the underside of his lower lip. Now and then he spits out of the window, big healthy gobs of brown juice which resound with a smack on the pavement below. He seems content now.

"In America," he says, "you wouldn't dream of living in a joint like this. Even when I was on the bum I slept in better rooms than this. But here is seems natural—it's like the books you read. If I ever go back there I'll forget all about this life, just like you forget a bad dream. I'll probably take up the old life again just where I left off . . . if I ever get back. Sometimes I lie in bed dreaming about the past and it's so vivid to me that I have to shake myself in order to realize where I am. Especially when I have a woman beside me; a woman can set me off better than anything. That's all I want of them—to forget myself. Sometimes I get so lost in my reveries that I can't remember the name of the cunt or where I picked her up. That's funny, eh? It's good to have a fresh warm body beside you when you wake up in the morning. It gives you a clean feeling. You get spiritual like . . . until they start pulling that mushy crap about love et cetera. Why do all these cunts talk about love so much, can you tell me that? A good lay isn't enough for them apparently . . . they want your soul too. . . ."

Now this word soul, which pops up frequently in Van Norden's soliloquies, used to have a droll effect upon me at first. Whenever I heard the word soul from his lips I would get hysterical; somehow it seemed like a false coin, more particularly because it was usually accompanied by a gob of brown juice which left a trickle down the corner of his mouth. And as I never hesitated to laugh in his face it happened invariably that when this little word bobbed up Van Norden would pause just long enough for me to burst into a cackle and then, as if nothing had happened, he would resume his monologue, repeating the word more and more frequently and each time with a more caressing emphasis. It was the soul of him that women were trying to possess—that he made clear to me. He has explained it over and over again, but he comes back to it afresh each time like a paranoiac to his obsession. In a sense Van Norden is mad, of that I'm convinced. His one fear is to be left alone, and this fear is so deep and so persistent that even when he is on top of a woman, even when he has welded himself to her, he cannot escape the prison which he has created for himself. "I try all sorts of things," he explains to me. "I even count sometimes, or I begin to think of a problem in philosophy, but is doesn't work. It's like I'm two people, and one of them is watching me all the time. I get so goddamned mad at myself that I could kill myself . . . and in a way, that's what I do every time I have an orgasm. For one second like I obliterate myself. There's not even one me then . . . there's nothing . . . not even the cunt. It's like receiving communion. Honest, I mean that. For a few seconds afterward I have a fine spiritual glow . . . and maybe it would continue that way indefinitely—how can you tell?—if it weren't for the fact that there's a woman beside you and then the douche bag and the water running . . . all those little details that make you desperately self-conscious, desperately lonely. And for that one moment of freedom you have to listen to all that love crap . . . it drives me nuts sometimes . . . I want to kick them out immediately . . . I do now and then. But that doesn't keep them away. They like it, in fact. The less you notice them the more they chase after you. There's something perverse about women . . . they're all masochists at heart."

"But what is it you want of a woman, then?" I demand.

He begins to mold his hands; his lower lip droops. He looks completely frustrated. When eventually he succeeds in stammering out a few broken phrases it's with the conviction that behind his words lies an overwhelming futility. "I want to be able to surrender myself to a woman," he blurts out. "I want her to take me out of myself. But to do that, she's got to be better than I am; she's got to have a mind, not just a cunt. She's got to make me believe that I need her, that I can't live without her. Find me a cunt like that, will you? If you could do that I'd give you my job. I wouldn't care then what happened to me: I wouldn't need a job or friends or books or anything. If she could only make me believe that there was something more important on earth than myself. Jesus, I

hate myself! But I hate these bastardly cunts even
more—because they're none of them any good.

"You think I like myself," he continues. "That shows
how little you know me. I know I'm a great guy. . . .
I wouldn't have these problems if there weren't something to me. But what eats me up is that I can't express
myself. People think I'm a cunt-chaser. That's how
shallow they are, these high-brows who sit on the *terrasse*
all day chewing the psychologic cud. . . . That's not so
bad, eh—psychologic cud? Write it down for me. I'll use
it in my column next week. . . . By the way, did you ever
read Stekel? Is he any good? It looks like nothing but
case histories to me. I wish to Christ I could get up
enough nerve to visit an analyst . . . a good one, I mean.
I don't want to see these little shysters with goatees
and frock coats, like your friend Boris. How do you manage to tolerate those guys? Don't they bore you stiff?
You talk to anybody, I notice. You don't give a goddamn. Maybe you're right. I wish I weren't so damned
critical. But these dirty little Jews who hang around the
Dôme, Jesus, they give me the creeps. They sound just
like textbooks. If I could talk to you every day maybe I
could get things off my chest. You're a good listener. I
know you don't give a damn about me, but you're
patient. And you don't have any theories to exploit. I
suppose you put it all down afterward in that notebook
of yours. Listen, I don't mind what you say about me, but
don't make me out to be a cunt-chaser—it's too simple.
Some day I'll write a book about myself, about my
thoughts. I don't mean just a piece of introspective analysis . . . I mean that I'll lay myself down on the operating
table and I'll expose my whole guts . . . every goddamned
thing. Has anybody ever done that before?—What the
hell are you smiling at? Does it sound naïf?"

I'm smiling because whenever we touch on the subject
of this book which he is going to write some day things
assume an incongruous aspect. He has only to say "my
book" and immediately the world shrinks to the private
dimensions of Van Norden and Co. The book must be

absolutely original, absolutely perfect. That is why, among other things, it is impossible for him to get started on it. As soon as he gets an idea he begins to question it. He remembers that Dostoevski used it, or Hamsun, or somebody else. "I'm not saying that I want to be better than them, but I want to be different," he explains. And so, instead of tackling his book, he reads one author after another in order to make absolutely certain that he is not going to tread on their private property. And the more he reads the more disdainful he becomes. None of them are satisfying; none of them arrive at that degree of perfection which he has imposed on himself. And forgetting completely that he has not written as much as a chapter he talks about them condescendingly, quite as though there existed a shelf of books bearing his name, books which everyone is familiar with and the titles of which it is therefore superfluous to mention. Though he has never overtly lied about this fact, nevertheless it is obvious that the people whom he buttonholes in order to air his private philosophy, his criticism, and his grievances, take it for granted that behind his loose remarks there stands a solid body of work. Especially the young and foolish virgins whom he lures to his room on the pretext of reading to them his poems, or on the still better pretext of asking their advice. Without the least feeling of guilt or self-consciousness he will hand them a piece of soiled paper on which he has scribbled a few lines—the basis of a new poem, as he puts it—and with absolute seriousness demand of then an honest expression of opinion. As they usually have nothing to give by way of comment, wholly bewildered as they are by the utter senselessness of the lines, Van Norden seizes the occasion to expound to them his view of art, a view, needless to say, which is spontaneously created to suit the event. So expert has he become in this role that the transition from Ezra Pound's cantos to the bed is made as simply and naturally as a modulation from one key to another; in fact, if it were not made there would be a discord, which is what happens now and then when he makes a mistake as regards those nitwits whom he refers to as "push-overs." Naturally, constituted as he is, it is with reluctance that he refers to these fatal errors of judgment. But when he does bring himself to confess to an error of this kind it is with absolute frankness; in fact, he seems to derive a perverse pleasure in dwelling upon his inaptitude. There is one woman, for example, whom he has been trying to make for almost ten years now—first in America, and finally here in Paris. It is the only person of the opposite sex with whom he has a cordial, friendly relationship. They seem not only to like each other, but to understand each other. At first it seemed to me that if he could really make this creature his problem might be solved. All the elements for a successful union were there—except the fundamental one. Bessie was almost as unusual in her way as himself. She had as little concern about giving herself to a man as she had about the dessert which follows the meal. Usually she singled out the object of her choice and made the proposition herself. She was not bad-looking, nor could one say that she was good-looking either. She had a fine body, that was the chief thing—and she liked it, as they say.

They were so chummy, these two, that sometimes, in order to gratify her curiosity (and also in the vain hope of inspiring her by his prowess), Van Norden would arrange to hide her in his closet during one of his seances. After it was over Bessie would emerge from her hiding place and they would discuss the matter casually, that is to say, with an almost total indifference to everything except "technique." Technique was one of her favorite terms, at least in those discussions which I was privileged to enjoy. "What's wrong with my technique?" he would say. And Bessie would answer: "You're too crude. If you ever expect to make me you've got to become more subtle."

There was such a perfect understanding between them, as I say, that often when I called for Van Norden at one-thirty, I would find Bessie sitting on the bed, the covers thrown back and Van Norden inviting her to stroke his penis . . . "just a few silken strokes," he would say, "so as I'll have the courage to get up." Or else he would urge her to blow on it, or failing that, he would grab hold of himself and shake it like a dinner bell, the two of them laughing fit to die. "I'll never make this bitch," he would say. "She has no respect for me. That's what I get for taking her into my confidence." And then abruptly he might add: "What do you make of that blonde I showed you yesterday?" Talking to Bessie, of course. And Bessie would jeer at him, telling him he had no taste. "Aw, don't give me that line," he would say. And then playfully, perhaps for the thousandth time, because by now it had become a standing joke between them—"Listen, Bessie, what about a quick lay? Just one little lay . . . no." And when this had passed off in the usual manner he would add, in the same tone: "Well, what about *him?* Why don't you give *him* a lay?"

The whole point about Bessie was that she couldn't, or just wouldn't, regard herself as a lay. She talked about passion, as if it were a brand new word. She was passionate about things, even a little thing like a lay. She had to put her soul into it.

"I get passionate too sometimes," Van Norden would say.

"Oh, *you*," says Bessie. "You're just a worn-out satyr. You don't know the meaning of passion. When you get an erection you think you're passionate."

"All right, maybe it's not passion . . . but you can't get passionate without having an erection, that's true isn't it?"

All this about Bessie, and the other women whom he drags to his room day in and out, occupies my thoughts as we walk to the restaurant. I have adjusted myself so well to his monologues that without interrupting my own reveries I make whatever comment is required automatically, the moment I hear his voice die out. It is a duet, and like most duets moreover in that one listens attentively only for the signal which announces the advent of one's own voice. As it is his night off, and as I have promised to keep him company, I have already dulled myself to his queries. I know that before the evening is over I shall be thoroughly exhausted; if I am lucky, that is, if I can worm a few francs out of him on some pretext or other, I will duck him the moment he goes to the toilet. But he knows my propensity for slipping away, and, instead of being insulted, he simply provides against the possibility by guarding his sous. If I ask him for money to buy cigarettes he insists on going with me to purchase them. He will not be left alone, not for a second. Even when he has succeeded in grabbing off a woman, even then he is terrified to be left alone with her. If it were possible he would have me sit in the room while he puts on the performance. It would be like asking me to wait while he took a shave.

On his night off Van Norden generally manages to have at least fifty francs in his pocket, a circumstance which does not prevent him from making a touch whenever he encounters a prospect. "Hello," he says, "give me twenty francs . . . I need it." He has a way of looking panic-stricken at the same time. And if he meets with a rebuff he becomes insulting. "Well, you can buy a drink at least." And when he gets his drink he says more graciously—"Listen give me five francs then . . . give me *two* francs. . . ." We go from bar to bar looking for a little excitement and always accumulating a few more francs.

At the Coupole we stumble into a drunk from the newspaper. One of the upstairs guys. There's just been an accident at the office, he informs us. One of the proof-readers fell down the elevator shaft. Not expected to live.

At first Van Norden is shocked, deeply shocked. But when he learns that it was Peckover, the Englishman, he looks relieved. "The poor bastard," he says, "he's better off dead than alive. He just got his false teeth the other day too. . . ."

The allusion to the false teeth moves the man upstairs to tears. He relates in a slobbery way a little incident connected with the accident. He is upset about it, more upset about this little incident than about the catastrophe itself.

It seems that Peckover, when he hit the bottom of the shaft, regained consciousness before anyone could reach him. Despite the fact that his legs were broken and his ribs busted, he had managed to rise to all fours and grope about for his false teeth. In the ambulance he was crying out in his delirium for the teeth he had lost. The incident was pathetic and ludicrous at the same time. The guy from upstairs hardly knew whether to laugh or to weep as he related it. It was a delicate moment because with a drunk like that, one false move and he'd crash a bottle over your skull. He had never been particularly friendly with Peckover—as a matter of fact, he had scarely ever set foot in the proofreading department: there was an invisible wall like between the guys upstairs and the guys down below. But now, since he had felt the touch of death, he wanted to display his comradeship. He wanted to weep, if possible, to show that he was a regular guy. And Joe and I, who new Peckover well and who knew also that he wasn't worth a good goddamn, even a few tears, we felt annoyed with this drunken sentimentality. We wanted to tell him so too, but with a guy like that you can't afford to be honest; you have to buy a wreath and go to the funeral and pretend that you're miserable. And you have to congratulate him too for the delicate obituary he's written. He'll be carrying his delicate little obituary around with him for months, praising the shit out of himself for the way he handled the situation. We felt all that, Joe and I, without saying a word to each other. We just stood there and listened with a murderous, silent contempt. And as soon as we could break away we did so; we left him there at the bar blubbering to himself over his Pernod.

Once out of his sight we began to laugh hysterically. The false teeth! No matter what we said about the poor devil, and we said some good things about him too, we always came back to the false teeth. There are people in this world who cut such a grotesque figure that even death renders them ridiculous. And the more horrible the death the more ridiculous they seem. It's no use trying to invest

the end with a little dignity—you have to be a liar and a
hypocrite to discover anything tragic in their going. And
since we didn't have to put on a false front we could laugh
about the incident to our heart's content. We laughed all
night about it, and in between times we vented our scorn
and disgust for the guys upstairs, the fatheads who were
trying to persuade themselves, no doubt, that Peckover
was a fine fellow and that his death was a catastrophe. All
sorts of funny recollections came to our minds—the semicolons that he overlooked and for which they bawled the
piss out of him. They made his life miserable with their
fucking little semicolons and the fractions which he always got wrong. They were even going to fire him once
because he came to work with a boozy breath. They despised him because he always looked so miserable and because he had eczema and dandruff. He was just a nobody,
as far as they were concerned, but, now that he was dead,
they would all chip in lustily and buy him a huge wreath
and they'd put his name in big type in the obituary column. Anything to throw a little reflection on themselves;
they'd make him out to be a *big* shit if they could. But
unfortunately, with Peckover, there was little they could
invent about him. He was a zero, and even the fact that he
was dead wouldn't add a cipher to his name.

"There's only one good aspect to it," says Joe. "You
may get his job. And if you have any luck, maybe you'll
fall down the elevator shaft and break your neck too.
We'l buy you a nice wreath, I promise you that."

Toward dawn we're sitting on the *terrasse* of the
Dôme. We've forgotten about poor Peckover long ago.
We've had a little excitement at the Bal Nègre and Joe's
mind has slipped back to the eternal preoccupation: cunt.
It's at this hour, when his night off is almost concluded,
that his restlessness mounts to a fever pitch. He thinks of
the women he passed up earlier in the evening and of the
steady ones he might have had for the asking, if it weren't
that he was fed up with them. He is reminded inevitably
of his Georgia cunt—she's been hounding him lately, beg-

ging him to take her in, at least until she can find herself a job. "I don't mind giving her a feed once in a while," he says, "but I couldn't take her on as a steady thing . . . she'd ruin it for my other cunts." What gripes him most about her is that she doesn't put on any flesh. "It's like taking a skeleton to bed with you," he says. "The other night I took her on—out of pity—and what do you think the crazy bitch had done to herself? She had shaved it clean . . . not a speck of hair on it. Did you ever have a woman who shaved her twat? It's repulsive, ain't it? And it's funny, too. Sort of mad like. It doesn't look like a twat any more: it's like a dead clam or something." He describes to me how, his curiosity aroused, he got out of bed and searched for his flashlight. "I made her hold it open and I trained the flashlight on it. You should have seen me . . . it was comical. I got so worked up about it that I forgot all about her. I never in my life looked at a cunt so seriously. You'd imagine I'd never seen one before. And the more I looked at it the less interesting it became. It only goes to show you there's nothing to it after all, especially when it's shaved. It's the hair that makes it mysterious. That's why a statue leaves you cold. Only once I saw a real cunt on a statue—that was by Rodin. You ought to see it some time . . . she has her legs spread wide apart. . . . I don't think there was any head on it. Just a cunt you might say. Jesus, it looked ghastly. The thing is this—they all look alike. When you look at them with their clothes on you imagine all sorts of things; you give them an individuality like, which they haven't got, of course. There's just a crack there between the legs and you get all steamed up about it—you don't even look at it half the time. You know it's there and all you think about is getting your ramrod inside: it's as though your penis did the thinking for you. It's an illusion. You get all burned up about nothing . . . about a crack with hair on it, or without hair. It's so absolutely meaningless that it fascinated me to look at it. I must have studied it for ten minutes or more. When you look at it that way, sort of detached like, you get funny notions in your head. All that mystery about sex and then you discover that it's nothing—just a blank. Wouldn't it be funny if you found a harmonica inside . . . or a calendar? But there's nothing there . . . nothing at all. It's disgusting. It almost drove me mad. . . . Listen, do you know what I did afterwards? I gave her a quick lay and then I turned my back on her. Yeah, I picked up a book and I read. You can get something out of a book, even a bad book . . . but a cunt, it's just sheer loss of time. . . ."

It just so happened that as he was concluding his speech a whore gave us the eye. Without the slightest transition he says to me abruptly: "Would you like to give her a tumble? It won't cost much . . . she'll take the two of us on." And without waiting for a reply he staggers to his feet and goes over to her. In a few minutes he comes back. "It's all fixed," he says. "Finish your beer. She's hungry. There's nothing doing any more at this hour . . . she'll take the both of us for fifteen francs. We'll go to my room . . . it'll be cheaper."

On the way to the hotel the girl is shivering so that we have to stop and buy her a coffee. She's a rather gentle sort of creature and not at all bad to look at. She evidently knows Van Norden, knows there's nothing to expect from him but the fifteen francs. "You haven't got any dough," he says, mumbling to me under his breath. As I haven't a centime in my pocket I don't quite see the point of this, until he bursts out: "For Christ's sake, remember that we're broke. Don't get tenderhearted when we get upstairs. She's going to ask you for a little extra—I know this cunt! I could get her for ten francs, if I wanted to. There's no use spoiling them. . . ."

"*Il est méchant, celui-là,*" she says to me, gathering the drift of his remarks in her dull way.

"*Non, il n'est pas méchant, il est très gentil.*"

She shakes her head laughingly. "*Je le connais bien, ce type.*" And then she commences a hard luck story, about the hospital and the back rent and the baby in the country. But she doesn't overdo it. She knows that our ears are stopped; but the misery is there inside her, like a stone, and there's no room for any other thoughts. She isn't trying to make an appeal for our sympathies—she's just shifting this big weight inside her from one place to another. I rather like her. I hope to Christ she hasn't got a disease. . . .

In the room she goes about her preparations mechanically. "There isn't a crust of bread about by any chance?" she inquires, as she squats over the *bidet*. Van Norden laughs at this. "Here, take a drink," he says, shoving a bottle at her. She doesn't want anything to drink; her stomach's already on the bum, she complains.

"That's just a line with her," says Van Norden. "Don't let her work on your sympathies. Just the same, I wish she'd talk about something else. How the hell can you get up any passion when you've got a starving cunt on your hands?"

Precisely! We haven't any passion either of us. And as for her, one might as well expect her to produce a diamond necklace as to show a spark of passion. But there's the fifteen francs and something has to be done about it. It's like a state of war: the moment the condition is precipated nobody thinks about anything but peace, about getting it over with. And yet nobody has the courage to lay down his arms, to say, "I'm fed up with it . . . I'm through." No, there's fifteen francs somewhere, which nobody gives a damn about any more and which nobody is going to get in the end anyhow, but the fifteen francs is like the primal cause of things and rather than listen to one's own voice, rather than walk out on the primal cause, one surrenders to the situation, one goes on butchering and butchering and the more cowardly one feels the more heroically does he behave, until a day when the bottom drops out and suddenly all the guns are silenced and the stretcher-bearers pick up the maimed and bleeding heroes and pin medals on their chest. Then one has the rest of his life to think about the fifteen francs. One hasn't any eyes or arms or legs, but he has the consolation of dreaming for the rest of his days about the fifteen francs which everybody has forgotten.

It's exactly like a state of war—I can't get it out of my head. The way she works over me, to blow a spark of passion into me, makes me think what a damned poor soldier I'd be if I was ever silly enough to be trapped like this and dragged to the front. I know for my part that I'd surrender everything, honor included, in order to get out of the mess. I haven't any stomach for it, and that's all there is to it. But she's got her mind set on the fifteen francs and if I don't want to fight about it she's going to make me fight. But you can't put fight into a man's guts if he hasn't any fight in him. There are some of us so cowardly that you can't ever make heroes of us, not even if you frighten us to death. We know too much, maybe. There are some of us who don't live in the moment, who live a little ahead, or a little behind. My mind is on the peace treaty all the time. I can't forget that it was the fifteen francs which started all the trouble. Fifteen francs! What does fifteen francs mean to me, particularly since it's not my fifteen francs?

Van Norden seems to have a more normal attitude about it. He doesn't care a rap about the fifteen francs either now; it's the situation itself which intrigues him. It seems to call for a show of mettle—his manhood is involved. The fifteen francs are lost, whether we succeed or not. There's something more involved—not just manhood perhaps, but will. It's like a man in the trenches again: he doesn't know any more why he should go on living, because if he escapes now he'll only be caught later, but he goes on just the same, and even though he has the soul of a cockroach and has admitted as much to himself, give him a gun or a knife or even just his bare nails, and he'll go on slaughtering and slaughtering, he'd slaughter a million men rather than stop and ask himself why.

As I watch Van Norden tackle her, it seems to me that I'm looking at a machine whose cogs have slipped. Left to themselves, they could go on this way forever, grind-

ing and slipping, without ever anything happening. Until
a hand shuts the motor off. The sight of them coupled like
a pair of goats without the least spark of passion, grinding
and grinding away for no reason except the fifteen francs,
washes away every bit of feeling I have except the inhuman one of satisfying my curiosity. The girl is lying
on the edge of the bed and Van Norden is bent over her
like a satyr with his two feet solidly planted on the floor.
I am sitting on a chair behind him, watching their movements with a cool, scientific detachment; it doesn't matter to me if it should last forever. It's like watching one
of those crazy machines which throw the newspaper out,
millions and billions and trillions of them with their meaningless headlines. The machine seems more sensible, crazy
as it is, and more fascinating to watch, than the human
beings and the events which produced it. My interest in
Van Norden and the girl is nil; if I could sit like this and
watch every single performance going on at this minute
all over the world my interest would be even less than
nil. I wouldn't be able to differentiate between this phe-
nomenon and the rain falling or a volcano erupting. As
long as that spark of passion is missing there is no human
significance in the performance. The machine is better to
watch. And these two are like a machine which has
slipped its cogs. It needs the touch of a human hand to
set it right. It needs a mechanic.

I get down on my knees behind Van Norden and I examine the machine more attentively. The girl throws her
head on one side and gives me a despairing look. "It's no
use," she says. "It's impossible." Upon which Van Norden sets to work with renewed energy, just like an old
billy goat. He's such an obstinate cuss that he'll break his
horns rather than give up. And he's getting sore now because I'm tickling him in the rump.

"For God's sake, Joe, give it up! You'll kill the poor
girl."

"Leave me alone," he grunts. "I almost got it in that
time."

The posture and the determined way in which he blurts

this out suddenly bring to my mind, for the second time, the remembrance of my dream. Only now it seems as though that broomstick, which he had so nonchalantly slung under his arm, as he walked away, is lost forever. It is like the sequel to the dream—the same Van Norden, but minus the primal cause. He's like a hero come back from the war, a poor maimed bastard living out the reality of his dreams. Wherever he sits himself the chair collapses; whatever door he enters the room is empty; whatever he put in his mouth leaves a bad taste. Everything is just the same as it was before; the elements are unchanged, the dream is no different than the reality. Only, between the time he went to sleep and the time he woke up, his body was stolen. He's like a machine throwing out newspapers, millions and billions of them every day, and the front page is loaded with catastrophes, with riots, murders, explosions, collisions, but he doesn't feel anything. If somebody doesn't turn the switch off he'll never know what it means to die; you can't die if your own proper body has been stolen. You can get over a cunt and work away like a billy goat until eternity; you can go to the trenches and be blown to bits; nothing will create that spark of passion if there isn't the intervention of a human hand. Somebody has to put his hand into the machine and let it be wrenched off if the cogs are to mesh again. Somebody has to do this without hope of reward, without concern over the fifteen francs; somebody whose chest is so thin that a medal would make him hunchbacked. And somebody has to throw a feed into a starving cunt without fear of pushing it out again. Otherwise this show'll go on forever. There's no way out of the mess. . . .

After sucking the boss's ass for a whole week—it's the thing to do here—I managed to land Peckover's job. He died all right, the poor devil, a few hours after he hit the bottom of the shaft. And just as I predicted, they gave him a fine funeral, with solemn mass, huge wreaths, and everything. *Tout compris.* And after the ceremonies they regaled themselves, the upstairs guys, at a *bistro.* It was too bad Peckover couldn't have had just a little snack—he would have appreciated it so much to sit with the men upstairs and hear his own name mentioned so frequently.

I must say, right at the start, that I haven't a thing to complain about. It's like being in a lunatic asylum, with permission to masturbate for the rest of your life. The world is brought right under my nose and all that is requested of me is to punctuate the calamities. There is nothing in which these slick guys upstairs do not put their fingers: no joy, no misery passes unnoticed. They live among the hard facts of life, reality, as it is called. It is the reality of a swamp and they are the frogs who have nothing better to do than to croak. The more they croak the more real life becomes. Lawyer, priest, doctor, politician, newspaperman—these are the quacks who have their fingers on the pulse of the world. A constant atmosphere of calamity. It's marvelous. It's as if the barometer never changed, as if the flag were always at half-mast. One can see now how the idea of heaven takes hold of men's consciousness, how it gains ground even when all the props have been knocked from under it. There must be another world beside this swamp in which everything is dumped pell-mell. It's hard to imagine what it can be like, this heaven that men dream about. A frog's heaven, no doubt. Miasma, scum, pond lilies, stagnant water. Sit on a lily pad unmolested and croak all day. Something like that, I imagine.

They have a wonderful therapeutic effect upon me, these catastrophes which I proofread. Imagine a state of perfect immunity, a charmed existence, a life of absolute security in the midst of poison bacilli. Nothing touches me, neither earthquakes nor explosions nor riots nor famine nor collisions nor wars nor revolutions. I am inoculated against every disease, every calamity, every sorrow and misery. It's the culmination of a life of fortitude. Seated at my little niche all the poisons which the world gives off each day pass through my hands. Not even a fingernail gets stained. I am absolutely immune. I am even better off than a laboratory attendant, because there are no bad odors here, just the smell of lead burning. The world can blow up—I'll be here just the same to put in a comma or a semicolon. I may even touch a little overtime, for with an event like that there's bound to be a final extra. When the world blows up and the final edition has gone to press the proofreaders will quietly gather up all commas, semicolons, hyphens, asterisks, brackets, parentheses, periods, exclamation marks, etc. and put them in a little box over the editorial chair. *Comme ça tout est réglé.* . . .

None of my companions seem to understand why I appear so contented. They grumble all the time, they have ambitions, they want to show their pride and spleen. A good proofreader has no ambitions, no pride, no spleen. A good proofreader is a little like God Almighty, he's in the world but not of it. He's for Sundays only. Sunday is his night off. On Sundays he steps down from his pedestal and shows his ass to the faithful. Once a week he listens in on all the private grief and misery of the world; it's enough to last him for the rest of the week. The rest of the week he remains in the frozen winter marshes, an absolute, an impeccable absolute, with only a vaccination mark to distinguish him from the immense void.

The greatest calamity for a proofreader is the threat of losing his job. When we get together in the break the question that sends a shiver down our spines is: what'll you do if you lose your job? For the man in the paddock, whose duty it is to sweep up manure, the supreme terror is the possibility of a world without horses. To tell him that it is disgusting to spend one's life shoveling up hot turds is a piece of imbecility. A man can get to love shit if his livelihood depends on it, if his happiness is involved.

This life which, if I were still a man with pride, honor, ambition and so forth, would seem like the bottom rung of degradation, I welcome now, as an invalid welcomes death. It's a negative reality, just like death—a sort of heaven without the pain and terror of dying. In this chthonian world the only thing of importance is orthography and punctuation. It doesn't matter what the nature of the calamity is, only whether it is spelled right. Everything is on one level, whether it be the latest fashion for evening gowns, a new battleship, a plague, a high explosive, an astronomic discovery, a bank run, a railroad wreck, a bull market, a hundred-to-one shot, an execution, a stick-up, an assassination, or what. Nothing escapes the proofreader's eye, but nothing penetrates his bulletproof vest. To the Hindoo Agha Mir, Madam Scheer (formerly Miss Esteve) writes saying she is quite satisfied with his work. "I was married June 6th and I thank you. We are very happy and I hope that thanks to your power it will be so forever. I am sending you by telegraph money order the sum of . . . to reward you. . . ." The Hindoo Agha Mir foretells your future and reads all your thoughts in a precise and inexplicable way. He will advise you, will help you rid yourself of all your worries and troubles of all kinds, etc. *Call or write 20 Avenue Mac-Mahon, Paris.*

He reads all your thoughts in a marvelous way! I take it that means without exception, from the most trivial thoughts to the most shameless. He must have a lot of time on his hands, this Agha Mir. Or does he only concentrate on the thoughts of those who send money by telegraph money order? In the same edition I notice a headline announcing that "the universe is expanding so fast it may burst" and underneath it is the photograph of a splitting headache. And then there is a spiel about the pearl, signed Tecla. The oyster produces both, he informs all and sundry. Both the "wild" or Oriental pearl, and the "cultured" pearl. On the same day, at the Cathedral of Trier, the Germans are exhibiting the Coat of Christ; it's the first time it's been taken out of the moth balls in forty-two years. Nothing said about the pants and vest. In Salzburg, also the same day, two mice were born in a man's stomach, believe it or not. A famous movie actress is shown with her legs crossed: she is taking a rest in Hyde Park, and underneath a well-known painter remarks "I'll admit that Mrs. Coolidge has such charm and personality that she would have been one of the 12 famous Americans, even had her husband not been President." From an interview with Mr. Humhal, of Vienna, I glean the following . . . "Before I stop," said Mr. Humhal, "I'd like to say that faultless cut and fit does not suffice; the proof of good tailoring is seen in the wearing. A suit must bend to the body, yet keep its line when the wearer is walking or sitting." And whenever there is an explosion in a coal mine—a *British* coal mine—notice please that the King and Queen always send their condolences promptly, *by telegraph.* And they always attend the important races, though the other day, according to the copy, it was at the Derby, I believe, "heavy rains began to fall, much to the surprise of the King and Queen." More heart-rending, however, is an item like this. "It is claimed in Italy that the persecutions are not against the Church, but nevertheless they are conducted against the most exquisite parts of the Church. It is claimed that they are not against the Pope, but they are against the very heart and eyes of the Pope."

I had to travel precisely all around the world to find just such a comfortable, agreeable niche as this. It seems incredible almost. How could I have foreseen, in America, with all those firecrackers they put up your ass to give you pep and courage, that the ideal position for a man of my temperament was to look for orthographic mistakes? Over there you think of nothing but becoming President of the United States some day. Potentially every man is Presidential timber. Here it's different. Here every man is potentially a zero. If you become something or somebody it is an accident, a miracle. The chances are a thousand to one that you will never leave your native village. The chances are a thousand to one that you'll have your legs shot off or your eyes blown out. Unless the miracle happens and you find yourself a general or a rear admiral.

But it's just because the chances are all against you, just because there is so little hope, that life is sweet over here. Day by day. No yesterdays and no tomorrows. The barometer never changes, the flag is always at half-mast.

You wear a piece of black crepe on your arm, you have a little ribbon in your buttonhole, and, if you are lucky enough to afford it, you buy yourself a pair of artificial lightweight limbs, aluminum preferably. Which does not prevent you from enjoying an *apéritif* or looking at the animals in the zoo or flirting with the vultures who sail up and down the boulevards always on the alert for fresh carrion. Time passes. If you're a stranger and your papers are in order you can expose yourself to infection without fear of being contaminated. It is better, if possible, to have a proofreader's job. *Comme ça, tout s'arrange.* That means, that if you happen to be strolling home at three in the morning and you are intercepted by the bicycle cops, you can snap your fingers at them. In the morning, when the market is in swing, you can buy Belgian eggs, at fifty centimes apiece. A proofreader doesn't get up usually until noon, or a little after. It's well to choose a hotel near a cinema, because if you have a tendency to oversleep the bells will wake you up in time for the matinee. Or if you can't find a hotel near a cinema, choose one near a cemetery, it comes to the same thing. Above all, never despair. *Il ne faut jamais désespérer.*

Which is what I try to din into Carl and Van Norden every night. A world without hope, but no despair. It's as though I had been converted to a new religion, as though I were making an annual novena every night to Our Lady of Solace. I can't imagine what there would be to gain if I were made editor of the paper, or even President of the United States. I'm up a blind alley, and it's cosy and comfortable. With a piece of copy in my hand I listen to the music around me, the hum and drone of voices, the tinkle of the linotype machines, as if there were a thousand silver bracelets passing through a wringer; now and then a rat scurries past our feet or a cockroach descends the wall in front of us, moving nimbly and gingerly on his delicate legs. The events of the day are slid under your nose, quietly, unostentatiously, with, now and then, a by-line to mark the presence of a human hand, an ego, a touch of vanity. The procession passes serenely, like a cortege entering the cemetery gates. The paper under the copy desk is so thick that it almost feels like a carpet with a soft nap. Under Van Norden's desk it is stained with brown juice. Around eleven o'clock the peanut vendor arrives, a half-wit of an Armenian who is also content with his lot in life.

Now and then I get a cablegram from Mona saying that she's arriving on the next boat. "Letter following," it always says. It's been going on like this for nine months, but I never see her name in the list of boat arrivals, nor does the *garçon* ever bring me a letter on a silver platter. I haven't any more expectations in that direction either. If she ever does arrive she can look for me downstairs, just behind the lavatory. She'll probably tell me right away that it's unsanitary. That's the first thing that strikes an American woman about Europe—that it's unsanitary. Impossible for them to conceive of a paradise without modern plumbing. If they find a bedbug they want to write a letter immediately to the chamber of commerce. How am I ever going to explain to her that I'm contented here? She'll say I've become a degenerate. I know her line from beginning to end. She'll want to look for a studio with a garden attached—and a bathtub to be sure. She wants to be poor in a romantic way. I know her. But I'm prepared for her this time.

There are days, nevertheless, when the sun is out and I get off the beaten path and think about her hungrily. Now and then, despite my grim satisfaction, I get to thinking about another way of life, get to wondering if it would make a difference having a young, restless creature by my side. The trouble is I can hardly remember what she looks like, nor even how it feels to have my arms around her. Everything that belongs to the past seems to have fallen into the sea; I have memories, but the images have lost their vividness, they seem dead and desultory, like time-bitten mummies stuck in a quagmire. If I try to recall my life in New York I get a few splintered fragments, nightmarish and covered with verdigris. It seems as if my own proper existence had come to an end somewhere, just where exactly I can't make out. I'm not an American any more, nor a New Yorker, and even less a European, or a Parisian. I haven't any allegiance, any responsibilities, any hatreds, any worries, any prejudices, any passion. I'm neither for nor against. I'm a neutral.

When we walk home of a night, the three of us, it often happens after the first spasms of disgust that we get to talking about the condition of things with that enthusiasm which only those who bear no active part in life can muster. What seems strange to me sometimes, when I crawl into bed, is that all this enthusiasm is engendered just to kill time, just to annihilate the three-quarters of an hour which it requires to walk from the office to Montparnasse. We might have the most brilliant, the most feasible ideas for the amelioration of this or that, but there is no vehicle to hitch them to. And what is more strange is that the absence of any relationship between ideas and living causes us no anguish, no discomfort. We have become so adjusted that, if tomorrow we were ordered to walk on our hands, we would do so without the slightest protest. Provided, of course, that the paper came out as usual. And that we touched our pay regularly. Otherwise nothing matters. Nothing. We have become Orientalized. We have become coolies, white-collar coolies, silenced by a handful of rice each day. A special feature in American skulls, I was reading the other day, is the presence of the epactal bone, or *os Incae*, in the occiput. The presence of this bone, so the savant went on to say, is due to a persistence of the transverse occipital suture which is usually closed in fetal life. Hence it is a sign of arrested development and indicative of an inferior race. "The average cubical capacity of the American skull," so he went on to say, "falls below that of the white, and rises above that of the black race. Taking both sexes, the Parisians of today have a cranial capacity of 1,448 cubic centimeters; the Negroes 1,344 centimeters; the American Indians 1,376." From all of which I deduce nothing because I am an American and not an Indian. But it's cute to explain things that way, by a bone, an *os Incae*, for example. It doesn't disturb his theory at all to admit that single examples of Indian skulls have yielded the extraordinary capacity of 1,920 cubic centimeters, a cranial capacity not exceeded in any other race. What I note with satisfaction is that the Parisians, of both sexes, seem to have a normal cranial capacity. The transverse occipital suture is evidently not so persistent with them. They know how to enjoy an *apéritif* and they don't worry if the houses are unpainted. There's nothing extraordinary about their skulls, so far as cranial indices go. There must be some other explanation for the art of living which they have brought to such a degree of perfection.

At Monsieur Paul's, the *bistro* across the way, there is a back room reserved for the newspapermen where we can eat on credit. It is a pleasant little room with sawdust on the floor and flies in season and out. When I say that it is reserved for the newspapermen I don't mean to imply that we eat in privacy; on the contrary, it means that we have the privilege of associating with the whores and pimps who form the more substantial element of Monsieur Paul's clientle. The arrangement suits the guys upstairs to a T, because they're always on the lookout for tail, and even those who have a steady little French girl are not averse to making a switch now and then. The principal thing is not to get a dose; at times it would seem as if an epidemic had swept the office, or perhaps it might be explained by the fact that they all sleep with the same woman. Anyhow, it's gratifying to observe how miserable they can look when they are obliged to sit beside a pimp who, despite the little hardships of his profession, lives a life of luxury by comparison.

I'm thinking particularly now of one tall, blond fellow who delivers the Havas messages by bicycle. He is always a little late for his meal, always perspiring profusely and his face covered with grime. He has a fine, awkward way of strolling in, saluting everybody with two fingers and making a beeline for the sink which is just between the toilet and the kitchen. As he wipes his face he gives the edibles a quick inspection; if he sees a nice steak lying on the slab he picks it up and sniffs it, or he will dip the ladle into the big pot and try a mouthful of soup. He's like a fine bloodhound, his nose to the ground all the time. The preliminaries over, having made peepee and blown his nose vigorously, he walks nonchalantly over to his wench and gives her a big, smacking kiss together with an affectionate pat on the rump. Her, the wench, I've never seen look anything but immaculate—even at three a.m., after an evening's work. She looks exactly as if she had just stepped out of a Turkish bath. It's a pleasure to look at such healthy brutes, to see such repose, such affection, such appetite as they display. It's the evening meal I'm speaking of now, the little snack that she takes before entering upon her duties. In a little while she will be obliged to take leave of her big blond brute, to flop somewhere on the boulevard and sip her *digestif*. If the job is irksome or wearing or exhaustive, she certainly doesn't show it. When the big fellow arrives, hungry as a wolf, she puts her arms around him and kisses him hungrily—his eyes, nose, cheeks, hair, the back of his neck . . . she'd kiss his ass if it could be done publicly. She's grateful to him, that's evident. She's no wage slave. All through the meal she laughs convulsively. You wouldn't think she had a care in the world. And now and then, by way of affection, she gives him a resounding slap in the face, such a whack as would knock a proofreader spinning.

They don't seem to be aware of anything but themselves and the food that they pack away in shovelsful. Such perfect contentment, such harmony, such mutual understanding, it drives Van Norden crazy to watch them. Especially when she slips her hand in the big fellow's fly and caresses it, to which he generally responds by grabbing her teat and squeezing it playfully.

There is another couple who arrive usually about the same time and they behave just like two married people. They have their spats, they wash their linen in public and after they've made things disagreeable for themselves and everybody else, after threats and curses and reproaches and recriminations, they make up for it by bill-ing and cooing, just like a pair of turtle doves. Lucienne, as he calls her, is a heavy platinum blonde with a cruel, saturnine air. She has a full underlip which she chews venomously when her temper runs away with her. And a cold, beady eye, a sort of faded china blue, which makes him sweat when she fixes him with it. But she's a good sort, Lucienne, despite the condor-like profile which she presents to us when the squabbling begins. Her bag is always full of dough, and if she deals it out cautiously, it is only because she doesn't want to encourage him in his bad habits. He has a weak character; that is, if one takes Lucienne's tirades seriously. He will spend fifty francs of an evening while waiting for her to get through. When the waitress comes to take his order he has no appetite. "Ah, you're not hungry again!" growls Lucienne. "Humpf! You were waiting for me, I suppose, on the Faubourg Montmartre. You had a good time, I hope, while I slaved for you. *Speak, imbecile, where were you?*"

When she flares up like that, when she gets enraged, he looks up at her timidly and then, as if he had decided that silence was the best course, he lets his head drop and he fiddles with his napkin. But this little gesture, which she knows so well and which of course is secretly pleasing to her because she is convinced now that he is guilty, only increases Lucienne's anger. "*Speak, imbecile!*" she shrieks. And with a squeaky, timid little voice he explains to her woefully that while waiting for her he got so hungry that he was obliged to stop off for a sandwich and a glass of beer. It was just enough to ruin his appetite—he says it dolefully, though it's apparent that food just now is the least of his worries. "But"—and he tries to make his voice sound more convincing—"I was waiting for you all the time," he blurts out.

"Liar!" she screams. "Liar! Ah, fortunately, I too am a liar . . . a *good liar*. You make me ill with your petty little lies. Why don't you tell me a big lie?"

He hangs his head again and absent-mindedly he gathers a few crumbs and puts them to his mouth. Where-upon she slaps his hand. "Don't do that! You make me tired. You're such an imbecile. Liar! Just you wait! I have more to say. I am a liar too, but I am not an imbecile."

In a little while, however, they are sitting close together, their hands locked, and she is murmuring softly: "Ah, my little rabbit, it is hard to leave you now. Come here, kiss me! What are you going to do this evening? Tell me the truth, my little one. . . . I am sorry that I have such an ugly temper." He kisses her timidly, just like a little bunny with long pink ears; gives her a little peck on the lips as if he were nibbling a cabbage leaf. And at the same time his bright round eyes fall caressingly on her purse which is lying open beside her on the bench. He is only waiting for the moment when he can graciously give her the slip; he is itching to get away, to sit down in some quiet café on the Rue du Faubourg Montmartre.

I know him, the innocent little devil, with his round, frightened eyes of a rabbit. And I know what a devil's street is the Faubourg Montmartre with its brass plates and rubber goods, the lights twinkling all night and sex running through the street like a sewer. To walk from the Rue Lafayette to the boulevard is like running the gauntlet; they attach themselves to you like barnacles, they eat into you like ants, they coax, wheedle, cajole, implore, beseech, they try it out in German, English, Spanish, they show you their torn hearts and their busted shoes, and long after you've chopped the tentacles away, long after the fizz and sizzle has died out, the fragrance of the *lavabo* clings to your nostrils—it is the odor of the *Parfum de Danse* whose effectiveness is guaranteed only for a distance of twenty centimeters. One could piss away a whole lifetime in that little stretch between the boulevard and the Rue Lafayette. Every bar is alive, throbbing, the dice loaded; the cashiers are perched like vultures on their high stools and the money they handle has a human stink to it. There is no equivalent in the Banque de France for the blood money that passes currency here, the money that glistens with human sweat, that passes like a forest fire from hand to hand and leaves behind it a smoke and stench. A man who can walk through the Faubourg

Montmartre at night without panting or sweating, without a prayer or a curse on his lips, a man like that has no balls, and if he has, then he ought to be castrated.

Supposing the timid little rabbit does spend fifty francs of an evening while waiting for his Lucienne? Supposing he does get hungry and buy a sandwich and a glass of beer, or stop and chat with somebody else's trollop? You think he ought to be weary of that round night after night? You think it ought to weigh on him, oppress him, bore him to death? You don't think that a pimp is inhuman, I hope? A pimp has his private grief and misery too, don't you forget. Perhaps he would like nothing better than to stand on the corner every night with a pair of white dogs and watch them piddle. Perhaps he would like it if, when he opened the door, he would see her there reading the *Paris-Soir*, her eyes already a little heavy with sleep. Perhaps it isn't so wonderful, when he bends over his Lucienne, to taste another man's breath. Better maybe to have only three francs in your pocket and a pair of white dogs that piddle on the corner than to taste those bruised lips. Bet you, when she squeezes him tight, when she begs for that little package of love which only he knows how to deliver, bet you he fights like a thousand devils to pump it up, to wipe out that regiment that has marched between her legs. Maybe when he takes her body and practices a new tune, maybe it isn't all passion and curiosity with him, but a fight in the dark, a fight single-handed against the army that rushed the gates. the army that walked over her, trampled her, that left her with such a devouring hunger that not even a Rudolph Valentino could appease. When I listen to the reproaches that are leveled against a girl like Lucienne, when I hear her being denigrated or despised because she is cold and mercenary, because she is too mechanical, or because she's in too great a hurry, or because this or because that, I say to myself, hold on there bozo, not so fast! Remember that you're far back in the procession; remember that a whole army corps has laid siege to her, that she's been laid waste, plundered and pillaged. I say to myself, listen, bozo, don't begrudge the fifty francs you hand her because you know her pimp is pissing it away in the Faubourg Montmartre. It's *her* money and *her* pimp. It's blood money. It's money that'll never be taken out of circulation because there's nothing in the Banque de France to redeem it with.

That's how I think about it often when I'm seated in my little niche juggling the Havas reports or untangling the cables from Chicago, London and Montreal. In between the rubber and silk markets and the Winnipeg grains there oozes a little of the fizz and sizzle of the Faubourg Montmartre. When the bonds go weak and spongy and the pivotals balk and the volatiles effervesce, when the grain market slips and slides and the bulls commence to roar, when every fucking calamity, every ad, every sport item and fashion article, every boat arrival, every travelogue, every tag of gossip has been punctuated, checked, revised, pegged and wrung through the silver bracelets, when I hear the front page being hammered into whack and see the frogs dancing around like drunken squibs, I think of Lucienne sailing down the boulevard with her wings outstretched, a huge silver condor suspended over the sluggish tide of traffic, a strange bird from the tips of the Andes with a rose-white belly and a tenacious little knob. Sometimes I walk home alone and I follow her through the dark streets, follow her through the court of the Louvre, over the Pont des Arts, through the arcade, through the fents and slits, the somnolence, the drugged whiteness, the quill of the Luxembourg, the tangled boughs, the snores and groans, the green slats, the strum and tinkle, the points of the stars, the spangles, the jetties, the blue and white striped awnings that she brushed with the tips of her wings.

In the blue of an electric dawn the peanut shells look wan and crumpled; along the beach at Montparnasse the water lilies bend and break. When the tide is on the ebb and only a few syphilitic mermaids are left stranded in the muck, the Dôme looks like a shooting gallery that's been struck by a cyclone. Everything is slowly dribbling back to the sewer. For about an hour there is a deathlike calm during which the vomit is mopped up. Suddenly the trees begin to screech. From one end of the boulevard to the other a demented song rises up. It is like the signal that announces the close of the exchange. What hopes there were are swept up. The moment has come to void the last bagful of urine. The day is sneaking in like a leper. . . .

One of the things to guard against when you work nights is not to break your schedule; if you don't get to bed before the birds begin to screech it's useless to go to bed at all. This morning, having nothing better to do, I visited the *Jardin des Plantes*. Marvelous pelicans here from Chapultepec and peacocks with studded fans that look at you with silly eyes. Suddenly it began to rain.

Returning to Montparnasse in the bus I noticed a little French woman opposite me who sat stiff and erect as if she were getting ready to preen herself. She sat on the edge of the seat as if she feared to crush her gorgeous tail. Marvelous, I thought, if suddenly she shook herself and from her *derrière* there sprung open a huge studded fan with long silken plumes.

At the Café de l'Avenue, where I stop for a bite, a woman with a swollen stomach tries to interest me in her condition. She would like me to go to a room with her and while away an hour or two. It is the first time I have ever been propositioned by a pregnant woman: I am almost tempted to try it. As soon as the baby is born and handed over to the authorities she will go back to her trade, she says. She makes hats. Observing that my interest is waning she takes my hand and puts it on her abdomen. I feel something stirring inside. It takes my appetite away.

I have never seen a place like Paris for varieties of sexual provender. As soon as a woman loses a front tooth or an eye or a leg she goes on the loose. In America she'd starve to death if she had nothing to recommend her but a mutilation. Here it is different. A missing tooth or a nose eaten away or a fallen womb, any misfortune that aggravates the natural homeliness of the female, seems to be regarded as an added spice, a stimulant for the jaded appetites of the male.

I am speaking naturally of that world which is peculiar to the big cities, the world of men and women whose last drop of juice has been squeezed out by the machine—the martyrs of modern progress. It is this mass of bones and collar buttons which the painter finds so difficult to put flesh on.

It is only later, in the afternoon, when I find myself in an art gallery on the Rue de Sèze, surrounded by the men and women of Matisse, that I am drawn back again to the proper precincts of the human world. On the threshold of that big hall whose walls are now ablaze, I pause a moment to recover from the shock which one experiences when the habitual gray of the world is rent asunder and the color of life splashes forth in song and poem. I find myself in a world so natural, so complete, that I am lost. I have the sensation of being immersed in the very plexus of life, focal from whatever place, position or attitude I take my stance. Lost as when once I sank into the quick of a budding grove and seated in the dining room of that enormous world of Balbec, I caught for the first time the profound meaning of those interior stills which manifest their presence through the exorcism of sight and touch. Standing on the threshold of that world which Matisse has created I re-experienced the power of that revelation which had permitted Proust to so deform the picture of life that only those who, like himself, are sensible to the alchemy of sound and sense, are capable of transforming the negative reality of life into the substantial and significant outlines of art. Only those who can admit the light into their gizzards can translate what is there in the heart. Vividly now I recall how the glint and sparkle of light caroming from the massive chandeliers splintered and ran blood, flecking the tips of the waves that beat monotonously on the dull gold outside the windows. On the beach, masts and chimneys interlaced, and like a fuliginous shadow the figure of Albertine gliding through the surf, fusing into the mysterious quick and prism of a protoplasmic realm, uniting her shadow to the dream and harbinger of death. With the close of day, pain rising like a mist from the earth, sorrow closing in, shuttering the endless vista of sea and sky. Two waxen hands lying listlessly on the bedspread and along the pale veins the fluted murmur of a shell repeating the legend of its birth.

In every poem by Matisse there is the history of a particle of human flesh which refused the consummation of death. The whole run of flesh, from hair to nails, expresses the miracle of breathing, as if the inner eye, in its thirst for a greater reality, had converted the pores of the flesh into hungry seeing mouths. By whatever vision one passes there is the odor and the sound of voyage. It is impossible to gaze at even a corner of his dreams without feeling the lift of the wave and the cool of flying spray. He stands at the helm peering with steady blue eyes into the portfolio of time. Into what distant corners has he not thrown his long, slanting gaze? Looking down the vast promontory of his nose he has beheld everything—the Cordilleras falling away into the Pacific, the history of the Diaspora done in vellum, shutters fluting the froufrou of the beach, the piano curving like a conch, corollas giving out diapasons of light, chameleons squirming under the book press, seraglios expiring in oceans of dust, music issuing like fire from the hidden chromosphere of pain, spore and madrepore fructifying the earth, navels vomiting their bright spawn of anguish. . . . He is a bright sage, a dancing seer who, with a sweep of the brush, removes the ugly scaffold to which the body of man is chained by the incontrovertible facts of life. He it is, if any man today possesses the gift, who knows where to dissolve the human figure, who has the courage to sacrifice an harmonious line in order to detect the rhythm and murmur of the blood, who takes the light that has been refracted inside him and lets it flood the keyboard of color. Behind the minutiae, the chaos, the mockery of life, he detects the invisible pattern; he announces his discoveries in the metaphysical pigment of space. No searching for formulae, no crucifixion of ideas, no compulsion other than to create. Even as the world goes to smash there is one man who remains at the core, who becomes more solidly fixed and anchored, more centrifugal as the process of dissolution quickens.

More and more the world resembles an entomologist's dream. The earth is moving out of its orbit, the axis has shifted; from the north the snow blows down in huge knife-blue drifts. A new ice age is setting in, the transverse sutures are closing up and everywhere throughout the corn belt the fetal world is dying, turning to dead mastoid. Inch by inch the deltas are drying out and the river beds are smooth as glass. A new day is dawning, a metallurgical day, when the earth shall clink with showers of bright yellow ore. As the thermometer drops, the form of the world grows blurred; osmosis there still is, and here and there articulation, but at the periphery the veins are all varicose, at the periphery the light waves bend and the sun bleeds like a broken rectum.

At the very hub of this wheel which is falling apart, is Matisse. And he will keep on rolling until everything that has gone to make up the wheel has disintegrated. He has already rolled over a goodly portion of the globe, over Persia and India and China, and like a magnet he has attached to himself microscopic particles from Kurd, Baluchistan, Timbuktu, Somaliland, Angkor, Tierra del Fuego. The odalisques he has studded with malachite and jasper, their flesh veiled with a thousand eyes, perfumed eyes dipped in the sperm of whales. Wherever a breeze stirs there are breasts as cool as jelly, white pigeons come to flutter and rut in the ice-blue veins of the Himalayas.

The wallpaper with which the men of science have covered the world of reality is falling to tatters. The grand whorehouse which they have made of life requires no decoration; it is essential only that the drains function adequately. Beauty, that feline beauty which has us by the balls in America, is finished. To fathom the new reality it is first necessary to dismantle the drains, to lay open the gangrened ducts which compose the genito-urinary system that supplies the excreta of art. The odor of the day is permanganate and formaldehyde. The drains are clogged with strangled embryos.

The world of Matisse is still beautiful in an old-fashioned bedroom way. There is not a ball bearing in evidence, nor a boiler plate, nor a piston, nor a monkey wrench. It is the same old world that went gaily to the Bois in the pastoral days of wine and fornication. I find it soothing and refreshing to move amongst these creatures with live, breathing pores whose background is stable and solid as light itself. I feel it poignantly when I walk along the Boulevard de la Madeleine and the whores rustle beside me, when just to glance at them causes me to tremble. Is it because they are exotic or well-nourished? No, it is rare to find a beautiful woman along the Boulevard de la Madeleine. But in Matisse, in the exploration of his brush, there is the trembling glitter of a world which demands only the presence of the female to crystallize the most fugitive aspirations. To come upon a woman offering herself outside a urinal, where there are advertised cigarette papers, rum, acrobats, horse races, where the heavy foliage of the trees breaks the heavy mass of walls and roofs, is an experience that begins where the boundaries of the known world leave off. In the evening now and then, skirting the cemetery walls, I stumble upon the phantom odalisques of Matisse fastened to the trees, their tangled manes drenched with sap. A few feet away, removed by incalculable eons of time, lies the prone and mummy-swathed ghost of Baudelaire, of a whole world that will belch no more. In the dusky corners of cafés are men and women with hands locked, their loins slather-flecked; nearby stands the *garçon* with his apron full of sous, waiting patiently for the entr'acte in order to fall upon his wife and gouge her. Even as the world falls apart the Paris that belongs to Matisse shudders with bright, gasping orgasms, the air itself is steady with a stagnant sperm, the trees tangled like hair. On its wobbly axle the wheel rolls steadily downhill; there are no brakes, no ball bearings, no balloon tires. The wheel is falling apart, but the revolution is intact. . . .

Out of a clear sky there comes one day a letter from Boris whom I have not seen for months and months. It is a strange document and I don't pretend to understand it all clearly. "What happened between us—at any rate, as far as I go—is that you touched me, touched my life, that is, at the one point where I am still alive: my death. By the emotional flow I went through another immersion. I lived again, alive. No longer by reminiscence, as I do with others, but alive."

That's how it began. Not a word of greeting, no date, no address. Written in a thin, pompous scrawl on ruled paper torn out of a blank book. "That is why, whether you like me or not—deep down I rather think you hate me—you are very close to me. By you I know how I died: I see myself dying again: I *am* dying. That is something. More than to be dead simply. That may be the reason why I am so afraid to see you: you may have played the trick on me, and died. Things happen so fast nowadays."

I'm reading it over, line by line, standing by the stones. It sounds nutty to me, all this palaver about life and death and things happening so fast. Nothing is happening that I can see, except the usual calamities on the front page. He's been living all by himself for the last six months, tucked away in a cheap little room—probably holding telepathic communication with Cronstadt. He talks about the line falling back, the sector evacuated, and so on and so forth, as though he were dug into a trench and writing a report to headquarters. He probably had his frock coat

151

on when he sat down to pen this missive, and he probably rubbed his hands a few times as he used to do when a customer was calling to rent the apartment. "The reason I wanted you to commit suicide . . ." he begins again. At that I burst out laughing. He used to walk up and down with one hand stuck in the tail flap of his frock coat at the Villa Borghese, or at Cronstadt's—wherever there was deck space, as it were—and reel off this nonsense about living and dying to his heart's content. I never understood a word of it, I must confess, but it was a good show and, being a Gentile, I was naturally interested in what went on in that menagerie of a brainpan. Sometimes he would lie on his couch full length, exhausted by the surge of ideas that swept through his noodle. His feet just grazed the bookrack where he kept his Plato and Spinoza—he couldn't understand why I had no use for them. I must say he made them sound interesting, though what it was all about I hadn't the least idea. Sometimes I would glance at a volume furtively, to check up on these wild ideas which he imputed to them—but the connection was frail, tenuous. He had a language all his own, Boris, that is, when I had him alone; but when I listened to Cronstadt it seemed to me that Boris had plagiarized his wonderful ideas. They talked a sort of higher mathematics, these two. Nothing of flesh and blood ever crept in; it was weird, ghostly, ghoulishly abstract. When they got on to the dying business it sounded a little more concrete; after all, a cleaver or a meat ax has to have a handle. I enjoyed those sessions immensely. It was the first time in my life that death had ever seemed fascinating to me—all these abstract deaths which involved a bloodless sort of agony. Now and then they would compliment me on being alive, but in such a way that I felt embarrassed. They made me feel that I was alive in the nineteenth century, a sort of atavistic remnant, a romantic shred, a soulful Pithecanthropus erectus. Boris especially seemed to get a great kick out of touching me; he wanted me to be alive so that he could die to his heart's content. You would think that all those millions in the street were nothing but dead cows the way he looked at me and touched me. But the letter . . . I'm forgetting the letter. . . .

"The reason why I wanted you to commit suicide that evening at the Cronstadts', when Moldorf became God, was that I was very close to you then. Perhaps closer than I shall ever be. And I was afraid, terribly afraid, that some day you'd go back on me, die on my hands. And I would be left high and dry with my idea of you simply, and nothing to sustain it. I should never forgive you for that."

Perhaps you can visualize him saying a thing like that! Myself it's not clear what his idea of me was, or at any rate, it's clear that I was just pure idea, an idea that kept itself alive without food. He never attached much importance, Boris, to the food problem. He tried to nourish me with ideas. Everything was idea. Just the same, when he had his heart set on renting the apartment, he wouldn't forget to put a new washer in the toilet. Anyway, he didn't want me to die on his hands. "You must be life for me to the very end," so he writes. "That is the only way in which you can sustain my idea of you. Because you have gotten, as you see, tied up with something so vital to me, I do not think I shall ever shake you off. Nor do I wish to. I want you to live more vitally every day, as I am dead. That is why, when I speak of you to others, I am just a bit ashamed. It's hard to talk of one's self so intimately."

You would imagine perhaps that he was anxious to see me, or that he would like to know what I was doing—but no, not a line about the concrete or the personal, except in this living-dying language, nothing but this little message from the trenches, this whiff of poison gas to apprise all and sundry that the war was still on. I sometimes ask myself how it happens that I attract nothing but crackbrained individuals, neurasthenics, neurotics, psychopaths—and Jews especially. There must be something in a healthy Gentile that excites the Jewish mind, like when he sees sour black bread. There was Moldorf, for example, who had made himself God, according to Boris and Cronstadt. He positively hated me, the little viper—yet he couldn't stay away from me. He came round regularly for his little dose of insults—it was like a tonic to him. In the beginning, it's true, I was lenient with him; after all, he was paying me to listen to him. And though I never displayed much sympathy I knew how to be silent when it involved a meal and a little pin money. After a while, however, seeing what a masochist he was, I permitted myself to laugh in his face now and then; that was like a whip for him, it made the grief and agony gush forth with renewed vigor. And perhaps everything would have gone smoothly between us if he had not felt it his duty to protect Tania. But Tania being a Jewess, that brought up a moral question. He wanted me to stick to Mlle. Claude for whom, I must admit, I had a genuine affection. He even gave me money occasionally to sleep with her. Until he realized that I was a hopeless lecher.

I mention Tania now because she's just got back from Russia—just a few days ago. Sylvester remained behind to worm his way into a job. He's given up literature entirely. He's dedicated himself to the new Utopia. Tania wants me to go back there with her, to the Crimea preferably, and start a new life. We had a fine drinking bout up in Carl's room the other day discussing the possibilities. I wanted to know what I could do for a living back there—if I could be a proofreader, for example. She said I didn't need to worry about what I would do—they would find a job for me as long as I was earnest and sincere. I tried to look earnest, but I only succeeded in looking pathetic. They don't want to see sad faces in Russia; they want you to be cheerful, enthusiastic, light-hearted, optimistic. It sounded very much like America to me. I wasn't born with this kind of enthusiasm. I didn't let on to her, of course, but secretly I was praying to be left alone, to go back to my little niche, and to stay there until the war breaks. All this hocus-pocus about Russia disturbed me a little. She got so excited about it, Tania, that we finished almost a half dozen bottles of *vin ordinaire*. Carl was jumping about like a cockroach. He has just enough Jew in him to lose his head over an idea like Russia. Nothing would do but to marry us off—immedi ately. "Hitch up!" he says, "you have nothing to lose!" And then he pretends to run a little errand so that we can pull off a fast one. And while she wanted it all right, Tania, still that Russia business had gotten so solidly planted in her skull that she pissed the interval away chewing my ear off, which made me somewhat grumpy and ill at ease. Anyway, we had to think about eating and getting to the office, so we piled into a taxi on the Boulevard Edgar-Quinet, just a stone's throw away from the cemetery, and off we whizzed. It was just a nice hour to spin through Paris in an open cab, and the wine rolling around in our tanks made it seem even more lovely than usual. Carl was sitting opposite us, on the *strapontin*, his face as red as a beet. He was happy, the poor bastard, thinking what a glorious new life he would lead on the other side of Europe. And at the same time he felt a bit wistful, too—I could see that. He didn't really want to leave Paris, any more than I did. Paris hadn't been good to him, any more than it had to me, or to anybody, for that matter, but when you've suffered and endured things here it's then that Paris takes hold of you, grabs you by the balls, you might say, like some lovesick bitch who'd rather die than let you get out of her hands. That's how it looked to him, I could see that. Rolling over the Seine he had a big foolish grin on his face and he looked around at the buildings and the statues as though he were seeing them in a dream. To me it was like a dream too: I had my hand in Tania's bosom and I was squeezing her titties with all my might and I noticed the water under the bridges and the barges and Notre-Dame down below, just like the post cards show it, and I was thinking drunkenly to myself that's how one gets fucked, but I was sly about it too and I knew I wouldn't ever trade all this whirling about my head for Russia or heaven or anything on earth. It was a fine afternoon, I was thinking to myself, and soon we'd be pushing a feed down our bellies and what could we order as a special treat, some good heavy wine that would drown out all this Russia business. With a woman like Tania, full of sap and everything, they don't give a damn what happens to you once they get an idea in their heads. Let them go far enough and they'll pull the pants off you, right in the taxi. It was grand though, milling through the traffic, our faces all smudged with rouge and the wine gurgling like a sewer inside us, especially when we swung into the Rue Laffitte which is just wide enough to frame the little temple at the end of the street and above it the Sacré-Cœur, a kind of exotic jumble of architecture, a lucid French idea that gouges right through your drunkenness and leaves you swimming helplessly in the past, in a fluid dream that makes you wide awake and yet doesn't jar your nerves.

With Tania back on the scene, a steady job, the drunken talk about Russia, the walks home at night, and Paris in full summer, life seems to lift its head a little higher. That's why perhaps, a letter such as Boris sent me seems absolutely cockeyed. Most every day I meet Tania around five o'clock, to have a Porto with her, as she calls it. I let her take me to places I've never seen before, the swell bars around the Champs-Elysées where the sound of jazz and baby voices crooning seems to soak right through the mahogany woodwork. Even when you go to the *lavabo* these pulpy, sappy strains pursue you, come floating into the cabinet through the ventilators and make life all soap and iridescent bubbles. And whether it's because Sylvester is away and she feels free now, or whatever it is, Tania certainly tries to behave like an angel. "You treated me lousy just before I went away," she says to me one day. "Why did you want to act that way? I never did anything to hurt you, did I?" We were getting sentimental, what with the soft lights and that creamy, mahogany music seeping through the place. It was getting near time to go to work and we hadn't eaten yet. The stubs were lying there in front of us—six francs, four-fifty, seven francs, two-fifty—I was counting them up mechanically and wondering too at the same time if I would like it better being a bartender. Often like that, when she was talking to me, gushing about Russia, the future, love, and all that crap, I'd get to thinking about the most irrelevant things, about shining shoes or being a lavatory attendant, particularly I suppose because it was so cosy in these joints that she dragged me to and it never occurred to me that I'd be stone sober and perhaps old and bent . . . no, I imagined always that the future, however modest, would be in just this sort of ambiance, with the same tunes playing through my head and the glasses clinking and behind every shapely ass a trail of perfume a yard wide that would take the stink out of life, even downstairs in the *lavabo*.

The strange thing is it never spoiled me trotting around to the swell bars with her like that. It was hard to leave her, certainly. I used to lead her around to the porch of a church near the office and standing there in the dark we'd take a last embrace, she whispering to me "Jesus, what am I going to do now?" She wanted me to quit the job so as I could make love night and day; she didn't even care about Russia any more, just so long as we were together. But the moment I left her my head cleared. It was another kind of music, not so croony but good just the same, which greeted my ears when I pushed through the swinging door. And another kind of perfume, not just a yard wide, but omnipresent, a sort of sweat and patchouli that seemed to come from the machines. Coming in with a skinful, as I usually did, it was like dropping suddenly to a low altitude. Generally I made a beeline for the toilet —that braced me up rather. It was a little cooler there, or else the sound of water running made it seem so. It was always a cold douche, the toilet. It was real. Before you got inside you had to pass a line of Frenchmen peeling off their clothes. Ugh! but they stank, those devils! And they were well paid for it, too. But there they were, stripped down, some in long underwear, some with beards, most of them pale, skinny rats with lead in their veins. Inside the toilet you could take an inventory of their idle thoughts. The walls were crowded with sketches and epithets, all of them jocosely obscene, easy to understand, and on the whole rather jolly and sympathetic. It must have required a ladder to reach certain

spots, but I suppose it was worth while doing it even
looking at it from just the psychological viewpoint. Sometimes, as I stood there taking a leak, I wondered what an
impression it would make on those swell dames whom I
observed passing in and out of the beautiful lavatories on
the Champs-Elysées. I wondered if they would carry
their tails so high if they could see what was thought of
an ass here. In their world, no doubt, everything was
gauze and velvet—or they made you think so with the
fine scents they gave out, swishing past you. Some of
them hadn't always been such fine ladies either; some of
them swished up and down like that just to advertise their
trade. And maybe, when they were left alone with themselves, when they talked out loud in the privacy of their
boudoirs, maybe some strange things fell out of their
mouths too; because in that world, just as in every world,
the greater part of what happens is just muck and filth,
sordid as any garbage can, only they are lucky enough to
be able to put covers over the can.

As I say, that afternoon life with Tania never had any
bad effect upon me. Once in a while I'd get too much of a
skinful and I'd have to stick my finger down my throat—
because it's hard to read proof when you're not all there.
It requires more concentration to detect a missing comma
than to epitomize Nietzsche's philosophy. You can be
brilliant sometimes, when you're drunk, but brilliance is
out of place in the proofreading department. Dates, fractions, semicolons—these are the things that count. And
these are the things that are most difficult to track down
when your mind is all ablaze. Now and then I made some
bad blunders, and if it weren't that I had learned how to
kiss the boss's ass, I would have been fired, that's certain.
I even got a letter one day from the big mogul upstairs, a
guy I never even met, so high up he was, and between a
few sarcastic phrases about my more than ordinary intelligence, he hinted pretty plainly that I'd better learn my
place and toe the mark or there'd be what's what to pay.
Frankly, that scared the shit out of me. After that I never
used a polysyllabic word in conversation; in fact, I hardly

ever opened my trap all night. I played the high-grade
moron, which is what they wanted of us. Now and then,
to sort of flatter the boss, I'd go up to him and ask politely
what such and such a word might mean. He liked that. He
was a sort of dictionary and timetable, that guy. No
matter how much beer he guzzled during the break—and
he made his own private breaks too, seeing as how he was
running the show—you could never trip him up on a date
or a definition. He was born to the job. My only regret
was that I knew too much. It leaked out now and then,
despite all the precautions I took. If I happened to come to
work with a book under my arm this boss of ours would
notice it, and if it were a good book it made him venomous. But I never did anything intentionally to displease
him; I liked the job too well to put a noose around my
neck. Just the same it's hard to talk to a man when you
have nothing in common with him; you betray yourself,
even if you use only monosyllabic words. He knew goddamn well, the boss, that I didn't take the least bit of interest in his yarns; and yet, explain it how you will, it
gave him pleasure to wean me away from my dreams and
fill me full of dates and historical events. It was his way
of taking revenge, I suppose.

The result was that I developed a bit of a neurosis. As
soon as I hit the air I became extravagant. It wouldn't
matter what the subject of conversation happened to be,
as we started back to Montparnasse in the early morning,
I'd soon turn the fire hose on it, squelch it, in order to trot
out my perverted dreams. I liked best talking about those
things which none of us knew anything about. I had cultivated a mild sort of insanity, echolalia, I think it's called.
All the tag ends of a night's proofing danced on the tip
of my tongue. *Dalmatia*—I had held copy on an ad for
that beautiful jeweled resort. All right, *Dalmatia*. You
take a train and in the morning your pores are perspiring
and the grapes are bursting their skins. I could reel it off
about Dalmatia from the grand boulevard to Cardinal
Mazarin's palace, further, if I chose to. I don't even know
where it is on the map, and I don't want to know ever,

but at three in the morning with all that lead in your veins and your clothes saturated with sweat and patchouli and the clink of bracelets passing through the wringer and those beer yarns that I was braced for, little things like geography, costume, speech, architecture don't mean a goddamn thing. Dalmatia belongs to a certain hour of the night when those high gongs are snuffed out and the court of the Louvre seems so wonderfully ridiculous that you feel like weeping for no reason at all, just because it's so beautifully silent, so empty, so totally unlike the front page and the guys upstairs rolling the dice. With that little piece of Dalmatia resting on my throbbing nerves like a cold knife blade I could experience the most wonderful sensations of voyage. And the funny thing is again that I could travel all around the globe but America would never enter my mind; it was even further lost than a lost continent, because with the lost continents I felt some mysterious attachment, whereas with America I felt nothing at all. Now and then, it's true, I did think of Mona, not as of a person in a definite aura of time and space, but separately, detached, as though she had blown up into a great cloudlike form that blotted out the past. I couldn't allow myself to think about her very long; if I had I would have jumped off the bridge. It's strange. I had become so reconciled to this life without her, and yet if I thought about her only for a minute it was enough to pierce the bone and marrow of my contentment and shove me back again into the agonizing gutter of my wretched past.

For seven years I went about, day and night, with only one thing on my mind—*her*. Were there a Christian so faithful to his God as I was to her we would all be Jesus Christs today. Day and night I thought of her, even when I was deceiving her. And now sometimes, in the very midst of things, sometimes when I feel that I am absolutely free of it all, suddenly, in rounding a corner perhaps, there will bob up a little square, a few trees and a bench, a deserted spot where we stood and had it out, where we drove each other crazy with bitter, jealous scenes. Always some deserted spot, like the Place de l'Estrapade, for example, or those dingy, mournful streets off the Mosque or along that open tomb of an Avenue de Breteuil which at ten o'clock in the evening is so silent, so dead, that it makes one think of murder or suicide, anything that might create a vestige of human drama. When I realize that she is gone, perhaps gone forever, a great void opens up and I feel that I am falling, falling, falling into deep, black space. And this is worse than tears, deeper than regret or pain or sorrow; it is the abyss into which Satan was plunged. There is no climbing back, no ray of light, no sound of human voice or human touch of hand.

How many thousand times, in walking through the streets at night, have I wondered if the day would ever come again when she would be at my side: all those yearning looks I bestowed on the buildings and statues, I had looked at them so hungrily, so desperately, that by now my thoughts must have become a part of the very buildings and statues, they must be saturated with my anguish. I could not help but reflect also that when we had walked side by side through these mournful, dingy streets now so saturated with my dream and longing, she had observed nothing, felt nothing: they were like any other streets to her, a little more sordid perhaps, and that is all. She wouldn't remember that at a certain corner I had stopped to pick up her hairpin, or that, when I bent down to tie her laces, I remarked the spot on which her foot had rested and that it would remain there forever, even after the cathedrals had been demolished and the whole Latin civilization wiped out forever and ever.

Walking down the Rue Lhomond one night in a fit of unusual anguish and desolation, certain things were revealed to me with poignant clarity. Whether it was that I had so often walked this street in bitterness and despair or whether it was the remembrance of a phrase which she had dropped one night as we stood at the Place Lucien-Herr I do not know. "Why don't you show me that Paris," she said, "that you have written about?" One thing I know, that at the recollection of these words I suddenly realized the impossibility of ever revealing to her that Paris which I had gotten to know, the Paris whose *arrondissements* are undefined, a Paris that has never existed except by virtue of my loneliness, my hunger for her. Such a huge Paris! It would take a lifetime to explore it again. This Paris, to which I alone had the key, hardly lends itself to a tour, even with the best of intentions; it is a Paris that has to be lived, that has to be experienced each day in a thousand different forms of torture, a Paris that grows inside you like a cancer, and grows and grows until you are eaten away by it.

Stumbling down the Rue Mouffetard, with these reflections stirring in my brain, I recalled another strange item out of the past, out of that guidebook whose leaves she had asked me to turn but which, because the covers were so heavy, I then found impossible to pry open. For no reason at all—because at the moment my thoughts were occupied with Salavin in whose sacred precincts I was now meandering—for no reason at all, I say, there came to mind the recollection of a day when, inspired by the plaque which I passed day in and day out, I impulsively entered the Pension Orfila and asked to see the room Strindberg had occupied. Up to that time nothing very terrible had befallen me, though I had already lost all my worldly possessions and had known what it was to walk the streets in hunger and in fear of the police. Up to then I had not found a single friend in Paris, a circumstance which was not so much depressing as bewildering, for wherever I have roamed in this world the easiest thing for me to discover has been a friend. But in reality, nothing very terrible had happened to me yet. One can live without friends, as one can live without love, or even without money, that supposed *sine qua non*. One can live in Paris—I discovered that!—on just grief and anguish. A bitter nourishment—perhaps the best there is for certain people. At any rate, I had not yet come to the end of my rope. I was only flirting with disaster. I had time and sentiment enough to spare to peep into other people's lives, to dally with the dead stuff of romance which, however morbid it may be, when it is wrapped between the covers of a book, seems deliciously remote and anonymous. As I was leaving the place I was conscious of an ironic smile hovering over my lips, as though I were saying to myself "Not yet, the Pension Orfila!"

Since then, of course, I have learned what every madman in Paris discovers sooner or later; that there are no ready-made infernos for the tormented.

It seems to me I understand a little better now why she took such huge delight in reading Strindberg. I can see her looking up from her book after reading a *delicious* passage, and, with tears of laughter in her eyes, saying to me: "You're just as mad as he was . . . you *want* to be punished!" What a delight that must be to the sadist when she discovers her own proper masochist! When she bites herself, as it were, to test the sharpness of her teeth. In those days, when I first knew her, she was saturated with Strindberg. That wild carnival of maggots which he reveled in, that eternal duel of the sexes, that spiderish ferocity which had endeared him to the sodden oafs of the northland, it was that which had brought us together. We came together in a dance of death and so quickly was I sucked down into the vortex that when I came to the surface again I could not recognize the world. When I found myself loose the music had ceased; the carnival was over and I had been picked clean. . . .

After leaving the Pension Orfila that afternoon I went to the library and there, after bathing in the Ganges and pondering over the signs of the zodiac, I began to reflect on the meaning of that inferno which Strindberg had so mercilessly depicted. And, as I ruminated, it began to grow clear to me, the mystery of his pilgrimage, the flight which the poet makes over the face of the earth and then, as if he had been ordained to re-enact a lost drama, the heroic descent to the very bowels of the earth, the dark and fearsome sojourn in the belly of the whale, the bloody struggle to liberate himself, to emerge clean of the past, a bright, gory sun god cast up on an alien shore. It was no mystery to me any longer why he and others (Dante, Rabelais, Van Gogh, etc., etc.) had made their pilgrimage to Paris. I understood then why it is that Paris attracts the tortured, the hallucinated, the great maniacs of love. I understood why it is that here, at the very hub of the wheel, one can embrace the most fantastic, the most impossible theories, without finding them in the least strange; it is here that one reads again the books of his youth and the enigmas take on new meanings, one for every white hair. One walks the streets knowing that he is mad, possessed, because it is only too obvious that these cold, indifferent faces are the visages of one's keepers. Here all boundaries fade away and the world reveals itself for the mad slaughterhouse that it is. The treadmill stretches away to infinitude, the hatches are closed down tight, logic runs rampant, with bloody cleaver flashing. The air is chill and stagnant, the language apocalyptic. Not an exit sign anywhere; no issue save death. A blind alley at the end of which is a scaffold.

An eternal city, Paris! More eternal than Rome, more splendorous than Nineveh. The very navel of the world to which, like a blind and faltering idiot, one crawls back on hands and knees. And like a cork that has drifted to the dead center of the ocean, one floats here in the scum and wrack of the seas, listless, hopeless, heedless even of a passing Columbus. The cradles of civilization are the putrid sinks of the world, the charnel house to which the stinking wombs confide their bloody packages of flesh and bone.

The streets were my refuge. And no man can understand the glamor of the streets until he is obliged to take refuge in them, until he has become a straw that is tossed here and there by every zephyr that blows. One passes along a street on a wintry day and, seeing a dog for sale, one is moved to tears. While across the way, cheerful as a cemetery, stands a miserable hut that calls itself "Hôtel du Tombeau des Lapins." That makes one laugh, laugh fit to die. Until one notices that there are hotels everywhere, for rabbits, dogs, lice, emperors, cabinet ministers, pawnbrokers, horse knackers, and so on. And almost every other one is an "Hôtel de l'Avenir." Which makes one more hysterical still. So many hotels of the future! No hotels in the past participle, no subjunctive modes, no conjunctivitis. Everything is hoary, grisly, bristling with merriment, swollen with the future, like a gumboil. Drunk with this lecherous eczema of the future, I stagger over to the Place Violet, the colors all mauve and slate, the doorways so low that only dwarfs and goblins could hobble in; over the dull cranium of Zola the chimneys are belching pure coke, while the Madonna of Sandwiches listens with cabbage ears to the bubbling of the gas tanks, those beautiful bloated toads which squat by the roadside.

Why do I suddenly recollect the Passage des Thermopyles? Because that day a woman addressed her puppy in the apocalyptic language of the slaughterhouse, and the little bitch, she understood what this greasy slut of a midwife was saying. How that depressed me! More even than the sight of those whimpering curs that were being sold on the Rue Brancion, because it was not the dogs which filled me so with pity, but the huge iron railing, those rusty spikes which seemed to stand between me and my rightful life. In the pleasant little lane near the Abattoir de Vaugirard (Abattoir Hippophagique), which is called the Rue des Périchaux, I had noticed here and there signs of blood. Just as Strindberg in his madness had recognized omens and portents in the very flagging of the Pension Orfila, so, as I wandered aimlessly through this muddy lane bespattered with blood, fragments of the past detached themselves and floated listlessly before my eyes, taunting me with the direst forebodings. I saw my own blood being spilled, the muddy road stained with it, as far back as I could remember, from the very beginning doubtless. One is ejected into the world like a dirty little mummy; the roads are slippery with blood and no one knows why it should be so. Each one is traveling his own way and, though the earth be rotting with good things, there is no time to pluck the fruits; the procession scrambles toward the exit sign, and such a panic is there, such a sweat to escape, that the weak and the helpless are trampled into the mud and their cries are unheard.

My world of human beings had perished; I was utterly alone in the world and for friends I had the streets, and the streets spoke to me in that sad, bitter language compounded of human misery, yearning, regret, failure, wasted effort. Passing under the viaduct along the Rue Broca, one night after I had been informed that Mona was ill and starving, I suddenly recalled that it was here in the squalor and gloom of this sunken street, terrorized perhaps by a premonition of the future, that Mona clung to me and with a quivering voice begged me to promise that I would never leave her, never, no matter what happened. And, only a few days later, I stood on the platform of the Gare St. Lazare and I watched the train pull out, the train that was bearing her away; she was leaning out of the window, just as she had leaned out of the window when I left her in New York, and there was that same, sad, inscrutable smile on her face, that last-minute look which is intended to convey so much, but which is only a mask that is twisted by a vacant smile. Only a few days before, she had clung to me desperately and then something happened, something which is not even clear to me now, and of her own volition she boarded the train and she was looking at me again with that sad, enigmatic smile which baffles me, which is unjust, unnatural, which I distrust with all my soul. And now it is I, standing in the shadow of the viaduct, who reach out for her, who cling to her desperately and there is that same inexplicable smile on my lips, the mask that I have clamped down over my grief. I can stand here and smile vacantly, and no matter how fervid my prayers, no matter how desperate my longing, there is an ocean between us; there she will stay and starve, and here I shall walk from one street to the next, the hot tears scalding my face.

It is that sort of cruelty which is embedded in the

streets; it is *that* which stares out from the walls and terrifies us when suddenly we respond to a nameless fear, when suddenly our souls are invaded by a sickening panic. It is *that* which gives the lampposts their ghoulish twists, which makes them beckon to us and lure us to their strangling grip; it is *that* which makes certain houses appear like the guardians of secret crimes and their blind windows like the empty sockets of eyes that have seen too much. It is that sort of thing, written into the human physiognomy of the streets which makes me flee when overhead I suddenly see inscribed "Impasse Satan." That which makes me shudder when at the very entrance to the Mosque I observe that it is written: "Mondays and Thursdays *tuberculosis;* Wednesdays and Fridays *syphilis.*" In every Metro station there are grinning skulls that greet you with *"Défendez-vous contre la syphilis!"* Wherever there are walls, there are posters with bright venomous crabs heralding the approach of cancer. No matter where you go, no matter what you touch, there is cancer and syphilis. It is written in the sky; it flames and dances, like an evil portent. It has eaten into our souls and we are nothing but a dead thing, like the moon.

I think it was the Fourth of July when they took the chair from under my ass again. Not a word of warning. One of the big muck-a-mucks from the other side of the water had decided to make economies; cutting down on proofreaders and helpless little *dactylos* enabled him to pay the expenses of his trips back and forth and the palatial quarters he occupied at the Ritz. After paying what little debts I had accumulated among the linotype operators and a goodwill token at the *bistro* across the way, in order to preserve my credit, there was scarcely anything left out of my final pay. I had to notify the *patron* of the hotel that I would be leaving; I didn't tell him why because he'd have worried about his measly two hundred francs.

"What'll you do if you lose your job?" That was the phrase that rang in my ears continually. *Ça y est maintenant! Ausgespielt!* Nothing to do but to get down into the street again, walk, hang around, sit on benches, kill time. By now, of course, my face was familiar in Montparnasse; for a while I could pretend that I was still working on the paper. That would make it a little easier to bum a breakfast or a dinner. It was summertime and the tourists were pouring in. I had schemes up my sleeve for mulcting them. "What'll you do. . . .?" Well, I wouldn't starve, that's one thing. If I should do nothing else but concentrate on food that would prevent me from falling to pieces. For a week or two I could still go to Monsieur Paul's and have a square meal every evening;

168

he wouldn't know whether I was working or not. The main thing is to eat. Trust to Providence for the rest!

Naturally, I kept my ears open for anything that sounded like a little dough. And I cultivated a whole new set of acquaintances—bores whom I had sedulously avoided heretofore, drunks whom I loathed, artists who had a little money, Guggenheim-prize men, etc. It's not hard to make friends when you squat on a *terrasse* twelve hours a day. You get to know every sot in Montparnasse. They cling to you like lice, even if you have nothing to offer them but your ears.

Now that I had lost my job Carl and Van Norden had a new phrase for me: "What if your wife should arrive now?" Well, what of it? Two mouths to feed, instead of one. I'd have a companion in misery. And, if she hadn't lost her good looks, I'd probably do better in double harness than alone: the world never permits a good-looking woman to starve. Tania I couldn't depend on to do much for me; she was sending money to Sylvester. I had thought at first that she might let me share her room, but she was afraid of compromising herself; besides, she had to be nice to her boss.

The first people to turn to when you're down and out are the Jews. I had three of them on my hands almost at once. Sympathetic souls. One of them was a retired fur merchant who had an itch to see his name in the papers; he proposed that I write a series of articles under his name for a Jewish daily in New York. I had to scout around the Dôme and the Coupole searching for prominent Jews. The first man I picked on was a celebrated mathematician; he couldn't speak a word of English. I had to write about the theory of shock from the diagrams he left on the paper napkins; I had to describe the movements of the astral bodies and demolish the Einsteinian conception at the same time. All for twenty-five francs. When I saw my articles in the newspaper I couldn't read them; but they looked impressive, just the same, especially with the pseudonym of the fur merchant attached. I did a lot of pseudonymous writing during this period.

When the big new whorehouse opened up on the Boulevard Edgar-Quinet, I got a little rake-off, for writing the pamphlets. That is to say, a bottle of champagne and a free fuck in one of the Egyptian rooms. If I succeeded in bringing a client I was to get my commission, just like Kepi got his in the old days. One night I brought Van Norden; he was going to let me earn a little money by enjoying himself upstairs. But when the *madame* learned that he was a newspaperman she wouldn't hear of taking money from him; it was a bottle of champagne again and a free fuck. I got nothing out of it. As a matter of fact, I had to write the story for him because he couldn't think how to get round the subject without mentioning the kind of place it was. One thing after another like that. I was getting fucked good and proper.

The worst job of all was a thesis I undertook to write for a deaf and dumb psychologist. A treatise on the care of crippled children. My head was full of diseases and braces and workbenches and fresh air theories; it took about six weeks off and on, and then, to rub it in, I had to proofread the goddamned thing. It was in French, such a French as I've never in my life seen or heard. But it brought me in a good breakfast every day, an American breakfast, with orange juice, oatmeal, cream, coffee, now and then ham and eggs for a change. It was the only period of my Paris days that I ever indulged in a decent breakfast, thanks to the crippled children of Rockaway Beach, the East Side, and all the coves and inlets bordering on these sore points.

Then one day I fell in with a photographer; he was making a collection of the slimy joints of Paris for some degenerate in Munich. He wanted to know if I would pose for him with my pants down, and in other ways. I thought of those skinny little runts, who look like bellhops and messenger boys, that one sees on pornographic post cards in little bookshop windows occasionally, the mysterious phantoms who inhabit the Rue de la Lune and other malodorous quarters of the city. I didn't like very much the idea of advertising my physiog in the company of these élite. But, since I was assured that the photographs were for a strictly private collection, and since it was destined for Munich, I gave my consent. When you're not in your home town you can permit yourself little liberties, particularly for such a worthy motive as earning your daily bread. After all, I hadn't been so squeamish, come to think of it, even in New York. There were nights when I was so damned desperate, back there, that I had to go out right in my own neighborhood and panhandle.

We didn't go to the show places familiar to the tourists, but to the little joints where the atmosphere was more congenial, where we could play a game of cards in the afternoon before getting down to work. He was a good companion, the photographer. He knew the city inside out, the walls particularly; he talked to me about Goethe often, and the days of the Hohenstaufen, and the massacre of the Jews during the reign of the Black Death. Interesting subjects, and always related in some obscure way to the things he was doing. He had ideas for scenarios too, astounding ideas, but nobody had the courage to execute them. The sight of a horse, split open like a saloon door, would inspire him to talk of Dante or Leonardo da Vinci or Rembrandt; from the slaughterhouse at Villette he would jump into a cab and rush me to the Trocadéro Museum, in order to point out a skull or a mummy that had fascinated him. We explored the 5th, the 13th, the 19th and the 20th *arrondissements* thoroughly. Our favorite resting places were lugubrious little spots such as the Place Nationale, Place des Peupliers, Place de la Contrescarpe, Place Paul-Verlaine. Many of these places were already familiar to me, but all of them I now saw in a different light owing to the rare flavor of his conversation. If today I should happen to stroll down the Rue du Château-des-Rentiers, for example, inhaling the fetid stench of the hospital beds with which the 13th *arrondissement* reeks, my nostrils would undoubtedly expand with pleasure, because, compounded with that odor of stale piss and formaldehyde, there would be the odors of our imaginative voyages through the charnel house of Europe which the Black Death had created.

Through him I got to know a spiritual-minded individual named Kruger, who was a sculptor and painter. Kruger took a shine to me for some reason or other; it was impossible to get away from him once he discovered that I was willing to listen to his "esoteric" ideas. There are people in this world for whom the word "esoteric" seems to act as a divine ichor. Like "settled" for Herr Peeperkorn of the *Magic Mountain*. Kruger was one of those saints who have gone wrong, a masochist, an anal type whose law is scrupulousness, rectitude and conscientiousness, who on an off day would knock a man's teeth down his throat without a qualm. He seemed to think I was ripe to move on to another plane, "a *higher* plane," as he put it. I was ready to move on to any plane he designated, provided that one didn't eat less or drink less. He chewed my head off about the "threadsoul," the "causal body," "ablation," the Upanishads, Plotinus, Krishnamurti, "the Karmic vestiture of the soul," "the nirvanic consciousness," all that flapdoodle which blows out of the East like a breath from the plague. Sometimes he would go into a trance and talk about his previous incarnations, how he imagined them to be, at least. Or he would relate his dreams which, so far as I could see, were thoroughly insipid, prosaic, hardly worth even the attention of a Freudian, but, for him, there were vast esoteric marvels hidden in their depths which I had to aid him to decipher. He had turned himself inside out, like a coat whose nap is worn off.

Little by little, as I gained his confidence, I wormed my way into his heart. I had him at such a point that he would come running after me, in the street, to inquire if he could lend me a few francs. He wanted to hold me together in order to survive the transition to a higher plane. I acted like a pear that is ripening on the tree. Now and then I had relapses and I would confess my need for more earthly nourishment—a visit to the Sphinx

or the Rue St. Apolline where I knew he repaired in
weak moments when the demands of the flesh had become too vehement.

As a painter he was nil; as a sculptor less than nil. He
was a good housekeeper, that I'll say for him. And an
economical one to boot. Nothing went to waste, not even
the paper that the meat was wrapped in. Friday nights
he threw open his studio to his fellow artists; there was
always plenty to drink and good sandwiches, and if by
chance there was anything left over I would come round
the next day to polish it off.

Back of the Bal Bullier was another studio I got into
the habit of frequenting—the studio of Mark Swift. If he
was not a genius he was certainly an eccentric, this caus-
tic Irishman. He had for a model a Jewess whom he had
been living with for years; he was now tired of her and
was searching for a pretext to get rid of her. But as he
had eaten up the dowry which she had originally brought
with her, he was puzzled as to how to disembarrass himself of her without making restitution. The simplest
thing was to so antagonize her that she would choose
starvation rather than support his cruelties.

She was rather a fine person, his mistress; the worst
that one could say against her was that she had lost her
shape, *and* her ability to support him any longer. She was
a painter herself and, among those who professed to
know, it was said that she had far more talent than he.
But no matter how miserable he made life for her she
was just; she would never allow anyone to say that he
was not a great painter. It was because he really has
genius, she said, that he was such a rotten individual.
One never saw her canvases on the wall—only his. Her
things were stuck away in the kitchen. Once it happened,
in my presence, that someone insisted on seeing her
work. The result was painful. "You see this figure," said
Swift, pointing to one of her canvases with his big foot.
"The man standing in the doorway there is just about to
go out for a leak. He won't be able to find his way back
because his head is on wrong. . . . Now take that nude

over there. . . . It was all right until she started to paint the cunt. I don't know what she was thinking about, but she made it so big that her brush slipped and she couldn't get it out again."

By way of showing us what a nude ought to be like he hauls out a huge canvas which he had recently completed. It was a picture of *her*, a splendid piece of vengeance inspired by a guilty conscience. The work of a madman—vicious, petty, malign, brilliant. You had the feeling that he had spied on her through the keyhole, that he had caught her in an off moment, when she was picking her nose absent-mindedly, or scratching her ass. She sat there on the horsehair sofa, in a room without ventilation, an enormous room without a window; it might as well have been the anterior lobe of the pineal gland. Back of her ran the zigzag stairs leading to the balcony; they were covered with a bilious-green carpet, such a green as could only emanate from a universe that had been pooped out. The most prominent thing was her buttocks, which were lopsided and full of scabs; she seemed to have slightly raised her ass from the sofa, as if to let a loud fart. Her face he had idealized: it looked sweet and virginal, pure as a cough drop. But her bosom was distended, swollen with sewer gas; she seemed to be swimming in a menstrual sea, an enlarged fetus with the dull, syrupy look of an angel.

Nevertheless one couldn't help but like him. He was an indefatigable worker, a man who hadn't a single thought in his head but paint. And cunning as a lynx withal. It was he who put it into my head to cultivate the friendship of Fillmore, a young man in the diplomatic service who had found his way into the little group that surrounded Kruger and Swift. "Let him help you," he said. "He doesn't know what to do with his money."

When one spends what he has on himself, when one has a thoroughly good time with his own money, people are apt to say "he doesn't know what to do with his money." For my part, I don't see any better use to which one can put money. About such individuals one can't say that they're generous or stingy. They put money into circulation—that's the principal thing. Fillmore knew that his days in France were limited; he was determined to enjoy them. And as one always enjoys himself better in the company of a friend it was only natural that he should turn to one like myself, who had plenty of time on his hands, for that companionship which he needed. People said he was a bore, and so he was, I suppose, but when you're in need of food you can put up with worse things than being bored. After all, despite the fact that he talked incessantly, and usually about himself or the authors whom he admired slavishly—such birds as Anatole France and Joseph Conrad—he nevertheless made my nights interesting in other ways. He liked to dance, he liked good wines, and he liked women. That he liked Byron also, and Victor Hugo, one could forgive; he was only a few years out of college and he had plenty of time ahead of him to be cured of such tastes. What he had that I liked was a sense of adventure.

We got even better acquainted, more intimate, I might say, due to a peculiar incident that occurred during my brief sojourn with Kruger. It happened just after the arrival of Collins, a sailor whom Fillmore had got to know on the way over from America. The three of us used to meet regularly on the *terrasse* of the Rotonde before going to dinner. It was always Pernod, a drink which put Collins in good humor and provided a base, as it were, for the wine and beer and *fines*, etc., which had to be guzzled afterward. All during Collins's stay in Paris I lived like a duke; nothing but fowl and good vintages and desserts that I hadn't even heard of before. A month of this regimen and I should have been obliged to go to Baden-Baden or Vichy or Aix-les-Bains. Meanwhile Kruger was putting me up at his studio. I was getting to be a nuisance because I never showed up before three a.m. and it was difficult to rout me out of bed before noon. Overtly Kruger never uttered a word of reproach but his manner indicated plainly enough that I was becoming a bum.

One day I was taken ill. The rich diet was taking effect upon me. I don't know what ailed me, but I couldn't get out of bed. I had lost all my stamina, and with it whatever courage I possessed. Kruger had to look after me, had to make broths for me, and so on. It was a trying period for him, more particularly because he was just on the verge of giving an important exhibition at his studio, a private showing to some wealthy connoisseurs from whom he was expecting aid. The cot on which I lay was in the studio; there was no other room to put me in.

The morning of the day he was to give his exhibition, Kruger awoke thoroughly disgruntled. If I had been able to stand on my feet I know he would have given me a clout in the jaw and kicked me out. But I was prostrate, and weak as a cat. He tried to coax me out of bed, with the idea of locking me up in the kitchen upon the arrival of his visitors. I realized that I was making a mess of it for him. People can't look at pictures and statues with enthusiasm when a man is dying before their eyes. Kruger honestly thought I was dying. So did I. That's why, despite my feelings of guilt, I couldn't muster any enthusiasm when he proposed calling for the ambulance and having me shipped to the American Hospital. I wanted to die there, comfortably, right in the studio; I didn't want to be urged to get up and find a better place to die in. I didn't care where I died, really, so long as it wasn't necessary to get up.

When he heard me talk this way Kruger became alarmed. Worse than having a sick man in his studio should the visitors arrive, was to have a dead man. That would completely ruin his prospects, slim as they were. He didn't put it that way to me, of course, but I could see from his agitation that that was what worried him. And that made me stubborn. I refused to let him call the hospital. I refused to let him call a doctor. I refused everything.

He got so angry with me finally that, despite my protestations, he began to dress me. I was too weak to resist. All I could do was to murmur weakly—"you bastard

you!" Though it was warm outdoors I was shivering like
a dog. After he had completely dressed me he flung an
overcoat over me and slipped outside to telephone. "I
won't go! I won't go!" I kept saying but he simply
slammed the door on me. He came back in a few minutes
and, without addressing a word to me, busied himself
about the studio. Last minute preparations. In a little
while there was a knock on the door. It was Fillmore.
Collins was waiting downstairs, he informed me.

The two of them, Fillmore and Kruger, slipped their
arms under me and hoisted me to my feet. As they
dragged me to the elevator Kruger softened up. "It's for
your own good," he said. "And besides, it wouldn't be
fair to me. You know what a struggle I've had all these
years. You ought to think about me too." He was actually
on the point of tears.

Wretched and miserable as I felt, his words almost
made me smile. He was considerably older than I, and
even though he was a rotten painter, a rotten artist all
the way through, he deserved a break—at least once in a
lifetime.

"I don't hold it against you," I muttered. "I understand
how it is."

"You know I always liked you," he responded. "When
you get better you can come back here again . . . you can
stay as long as you like."

"Sure, I know. . . . I'm not going to croak yet,"I managed to get out.

Somehow, when I saw Collins down below my spirits
revived. If ever any one seemed to be thoroughly alive,
healthy, joyous, magnanimous, it was he. He picked me
up as if I were a doll and laid me out on the seat of the
cab—gently too, which I appreciated after the way Kruger had manhandled me.

When we drove up to the hotel—the hotel that Collins
was stopping at—there was a bit of a discussion with the
proprietor, during which I lay stretched out on the sofa
in the *bureau*. I could hear Collins saying to the *patron*
that it was nothing . . . just a little breakdown . . . be all

right in a few days. I saw him put a crisp bill in the man's hands and then, turning swiftly and lithely, he came back to where I was and said: "Come on, buck up! Don't let him think you're croaking." And with that, he yanked me to my feet and, bracing me with one arm, escorted me to the elevator.

Don't let him think you're croaking! Obviously it was bad taste to die on people's hands. One should die in the bosom of his family, in private, as it were. His words were encouraging. I began to see it all as a bad joke. Upstairs, with the door closed, they undressed me and put me between the sheets. "You can't die now, goddamn it!" said Collins warmly. "You'll put me in a hole. . . . Besides, what the hell's the matter with you? Can't stand good living? Keep your chin up! You'll be eating a porterhouse steak in a day or two. You think you're ill! Wait, by Jesus until you get a dose of syphilis! That's something to make you worry. . . ." And he began to relate, in a humorous way, his trip down the Yangtze Kiang, with hair falling out and teeth rotting away. In the feeble state that I was in, the yarn that he spun had an extraordinary soothing effect upon me. It took me completely out of myself. He had guts, this guy. Perhaps he put it on a bit thick, for my benefit, but I wasn't listening to him critically at the moment. I was all ears and eyes. I saw the dirty yellow mouth of the river, the lights going up at Hankow, the sea of yellow faces, the sampans shooting down through the gorges and the rapids flaming with the sulfurous breath of the dragon. What a story! The coolies swarming around the boat each day, dredging for the garbage that was flung overboard, Tom Slattery rising up on his deathbed to take a last look at the lights of Hankow, the beautiful Eurasian who lay in a dark room and filled his veins with poison, the monotony of blue jackets and yellow faces, millions and millions of them hollowed out by famine, ravaged by disease, subsisting on rats and dogs and roots, chewing the grass off the earth, devouring their own children. It was hard to imagine that this man's body had once been a mass of

sores, that he had been shunned like a leper; his voice
was so quiet and gentle, it was as though his spirit had
been cleansed by all the suffering he had endured. As he
reached for his drink his face grew more and more soft
and his words actually seemed to caress me. And all the
while China hanging over us like Fate itself. A China
rotting away, crumbling to dust like a huge dinosaur, yet
preserving to the very end the glamor, the enchantment,
the mystery, the cruelty of her hoary legends.

I could no longer follow his story; my mind had
slipped back to a Fourth of July when I bought my first
package of firecrackers and with it the long pieces of
punk which break so easily, the punk that you blow on
to get a good red glow, the punk whose smell sticks to
your fingers for days and makes you dream of strange
things. The Fourth of July the streets are littered with
bright red paper stamped with black and gold figures
and everywhere there are tiny firecrackers which have
the most curious intestines; packages and packages of
them, all strung together by their thin, flat, little gut-
strings, the color of human brains. All day long there
is the smell of powder and punk and the gold from the
bright red wrappers sticks to your fingers. One never
thinks of China, but it is there all the time on the tips
of your fingers and it makes your nose itchy; and long
afterward, when you have forgotten almost what a firecracker smells like, you wake up one day with gold leaf
choking you and the broken pieces of punk waft back
their pungent odor and the bright red wrappers give
you a nostalgia for a people and a soil you have never
known, but which is in your blood, mysteriously there
in your blood, like the sense of time or space, a fugitive,
constant value to which you turn more and more as you
get old, which you try to seize with your mind, but ineffectually, because in everything Chinese there is wisdom and mystery and you can never grasp it with two
hands or with your mind but you must let it rub off, let
it stick to your fingers, let it slowly infiltrate your veins.

A few weeks later, upon receipt of a pressing invitation from Collins who had returned to Le Havre, Fillmore and I boarded the train one morning, prepared to spend the weekend with him. It was the first time I had been outside of Paris since my arrival here. We were in fine fettle, drinking Anjou all the way to the coast. Collins had given us the address of a bar where we were to meet; it was a place called Jimmie's Bar, which everyone in Le Havre was supposed to know.

We got into an open barouche at the station and started on a brisk trot for the rendezvous; there was still a half bottle of Anjou left which we polished off as we rode along. Le Havre looked gay, sunny; the air was bracing, with that strong salty tang which almost made me homesick for New York. There were masts and hulls cropping up everywhere, bright bits of bunting, big open squares and high-ceilinged cafés such as one only sees in the provinces. A fine impression immediately; the city was welcoming us with open arms.

Before we ever reached the bar we saw Collins coming down the street on a trot, heading for the station, no doubt, and a little late as usual. Fillmore immediately suggested a Pernod; we were all slapping each other on the back, laughing and spitting, drunk already from the sunshine and the salt sea air. Collins seemed undecided about the Pernod at first. He had a little dose of clap, he informed us. Nothing very serious—"a strain" most likely. He showed us a bottle he had in his pocket—"Vénétienne" it was called, if I remember rightly. The sailors' remedy for clap.

We stopped off at a restaurant to have a little snack before repairing to Jimmie's place. It was a huge tavern with big, smoky rafters and tables creaking with food. We drank copiously of the wines that Collins recommended. Then we sat down on a *terrasse* and had coffee and liqueurs. Collins was talking about the Baron de Charlus, a man after his own heart, he said. For almost a year now he had been staying at Le Havre, going through the money that he had accumulated during his bootlegging days. His tastes were simple—food, drink, women and books. And a private bath! That he insisted on.

We were still talking about the Baron de Charlus when we arrived at Jimmie's Bar. It was late in the afternoon and the place was just beginning to fill up. Jimmie was there, his face red as a beet, and beside him was his spouse, a fine buxom Frenchwoman with glittering eyes. We were given a marvelous reception all around. There were Pernods in front of us again, the gramophone was shrieking, people were jabbering away in English and French and Dutch and Norwegian and Spanish, and Jimmie and his wife, both of them looking very brisk and dapper, were slapping and kissing each other heartily and raising their glasses and clinking them—altogether such a bubble and blabber of merriment that you felt like pulling off your clothes and doing a war dance. The women at the bar had gathered around like flies. If we were friends of Collins that meant we were rich. It didn't matter that we had come in our old clothes; all *Anglais* dressed like that. I hadn't a sou in my pocket, which didn't matter, of course, since I was the guest of honor. Nevertheless I felt somewhat embarrassed with two stunning-looking whores hanging on my arms waiting for me to order something. I decided to take the bull by the horns. You couldn't tell any more which drinks were on the house and which were to be paid for. I had to be a *gentleman*, even if I didn't have a sou in my pocket.

Yvette—that was Jimmie's wife—was extraordinarily gracious and friendly with us. She was preparing a little spread in our honor. It would take a little while yet. We were not to get too drunk—she wanted us to enjoy the meal. The gramophone was going like wild and Fillmore had begun to dance with a beautiful mulatto who had on a tight velvet dress that revealed all her charms. Collins slipped over to my side and whispered a few words about the girl at my side. "The *madame* will invite her to dinner," he said, "if you'd like to have her." She was an ex-whore who owned a beautiful home on the outskirts of the city. The mistress of a sea captain now. He was away and there was nothing to fear. "If she likes you she'll invite you to stay with her," he added.

That was enough for me. I turned at once to Marcelle and began to flatter the ass off her. We stood at the corner of the bar, pretending to dance, and mauled each other ferociously. Jimmie gave me a big horse-wink and nodded his head approvingly. She was a lascivious bitch, this Marcelle, and pleasant at the same time. She soon got rid of the other girl, I noticed, and then we settled down for a long and intimate conversation which was interrupted unfortunately by the announcement that dinner was ready.

There were about twenty of us at the table, and Marcelle and I were placed at one end opposite Jimmie and his wife. It began with the popping of champagne corks and was quickly followed by drunken speeches, during the course of which Marcelle and I played with each other under the table. When it came my turn to stand up and deliver a few words I had to hold the napkin in front of me. It was painful and exhilarating at the same time. I had to cut the speech very short because Marcelle was tickling me in the crotch all the while.

The dinner lasted until almost midnight. I was looking forward to spending the night with Marcelle in that beautiful home up on the cliff. But it was not to be. Collins had planned to show us about and I couldn't very well refuse. "Don't worry about her," he said "You'll have a bellyful of it before you leave. Tell her to wait here for you until we get back."

She was a bit peeved at this, Marcelle, but when we informed her that we had several days ahead of us she brightened up. When we got outdoors Fillmore very solemnly took us by the arm and said he had a little confession to make. He looked pale and worried.

"Well, what is it?" said Collins cheerfully. "Spit it out!"

Fillmore couldn't spit it out like that, all at once. He hemmed and hawed and finally he blurted out—"Well, when I went to the closet just a minute ago I noticed something. . . ."

"Then you've got it!" said Collins triumphantly, and with that he flourished the bottle of "Vénétienne." "Don't go to a doctor," he added venomously. "They'll bleed you to death, the greedy bastards. And don't stop drinking either. That's all hooey. Take this twice a day . . . shake it well before using. And nothing's worse than worry, do you understand? Come on now. I'll give you a syringe and some permanganate when we get back."

And so we started out into the night, down toward the waterfront where there was the sound of music and shouts and drunken oaths, Collins talking quietly all the while about this and that, about a boy he had fallen in love with, and the devil's time he had to get out of the scrape when the parents got wise to it. From that he switched back to the Baron de Charlus and then to Kurtz who had gone up the river and got lost. His favorite theme. I liked the way Collins moved against this background of literature continuously; it was like a millionaire who never stepped out of his Rolls Royce. There was no intermediate realm for him between reality and ideas. When we entered the whorehouse on the Quai Voltaire, after he had flung himself on the divan and rung for girls and for drinks, he was still paddling up the river with Kurtz, and only when the girls had flopped on the bed beside him and stuffed his mouth with kisses did he cease his divagations. Then, as if he had suddenly realized where he was, he turned to the old mother who ran the place and gave her an eloquent spiel about his two friends who had come down from Paris expressly to see the joint. There were about half a dozen girls in the room, all naked and all beautiful to look at, I must say. They hopped about like birds while the three of us tried to maintain a conversation with the grandmother. Finally the latter excused herself and told us to make ourselves at home. I was altogether taken in by her, so sweet and amiable she was, so thoroughly gentle and maternal. And what manners! If she had been a little younger I would have made overtures to her. Certainly you would not have thought that we were in a "den of vice," as it is called.

Anyway we stayed there an hour or so, and as I was the only one in condition to enjoy the privileges of the house, Collins and Fillmore remained downstairs chattering with the girls. When I returned I found the two of them stretched out on the bed; the girls had formed a semicircle about the bed and were singing with the most angelic voices the chorus of *Roses in Picardy*. We were sentimentally depressed when we left the house—Fillmore particularly. Collins swiftly steered us to a rough joint which was packed with drunken sailors on shore leave and there we sat awhile enjoying the homosexual rout that was in full swing. When we sallied out we had to pass through the red-light district where there were more grandmothers with shawls about their necks sitting on the doorsteps fanning themselves and nodding pleasantly to the passers-by. All such good-looking, kindly souls, as if they were keeping guard over a nursery. Little groups of sailors came swinging along and pushed their way noisily inside the gaudy joints. Sex everywhere: it was slopping over, a neap tide that swept the props from under the city. We piddled along at the edge of the basin where everything was jumbled and tangled; you had the impression that all these ships, these trawlers and yachts and schooners and barges, had been blown ashore by a violent storm.

In the space of forty-eight hours so many things had happened that it seemed as if we had been in Le Havre a month or more. We were planning to leave early Monday morning, as Fillmore had to be back on the job. We spent Sunday drinking and carousing, clap or no clap. That afternoon Collins confided to us that he was thinking of returning to his ranch in Idaho; he hadn't been home for eight years and he wanted to have a look at the mountains again before making another voyage East. We were sitting in a whorehouse at the time, waiting for a girl to appear; he had promised to slip her some cocaine. He was fed up with Le Havre, he told us. Too many vultures hanging around his neck. Besides, Jimmie's wife had fallen in love with him and she was making things hot for him with her jealous fits. There was a scene almost every night. She had been on her good behavior since we arrived, but it wouldn't last, he promised us. She was particularly jealous of a Russian girl who came to the bar now and then when she got tight. A troublemaker. On top of it all he was desperately in love with this boy whom he had told us about the first day. "A boy can break your heart," he said. "He's so damned beautiful! And so cruel!" We had to laugh at this. It sounded preposterous. But Collins was in earnest.

Around midnight Sunday Fillmore and I retired; we had been given a room upstairs over the bar. It was sultry as the devil, not a breath of air stirring. Through the open windows we could hear them shouting downstairs and the gramophone going continually. All of a sudden a storm broke—a regular cloudburst. And between the thunderclaps and the squalls that lashed the windowpanes there came to our ears the sound of another storm raging downstairs at the bar. It sounded frightfully close and sinister; the women were shrieking at the tops of their lungs, bottles were crashing, tables were upset and there was that familiar, nauseating thud that the human body makes when it crashes to the floor.

About six o'clock Collins stuck his head in the door. His face was all plastered and one arm was stuck in a sling. He had a big grin on his face.

"Just as I told you," he said. "She broke loose last night. Suppose you heard the racket?"

We got dressed quickly and went downstairs to say good-bye to Jimmie. The place was completely demolished, not a bottle left standing, not a chair that wasn't broken. The mirror and the show window were smashed to bits. Jimmie was making himself an eggnog.

On the way to the station we pieced the story together. The Russian girl had dropped in after we toddled off to bed and Yvette had insulted her promptly, without even waiting for an excuse. They had commenced to pull each other's hair and in the midst of it a big Swede had step-ped in and given the Russian girl a sound slap in the jaw —to bring her to her senses. That started the fireworks. Collins wanted to know what right this big stiff had to interfere in a private quarrel. He got a poke in the jaw for an answer, a good one that sent him flying to the other end of the bar. "Serves you right!" screamed Yvette, taking advantage of the occasion to swing a bottle at the Russian girl's head. And at that moment the thunderstorm broke loose. For a while there was a regular pandemon-ium, the women all hysterical and hungry to seize the opportunity to pay off private grudges. Nothing like a nice barroom brawl . . . so easy to stick a knife in a man's back or club him with a bottle when he's lying under a table. The poor Swede found himself in a hornet's nest; everyone in the place hated him, particularly his ship-mates. They wanted to see him done in. And so they locked the door and pushing the tables aside they made a little space in front of the bar where the two of them could have it out. And they had it out! They had to carry the poor devil to the hospital when it was over. Collins had come off rather lucky—nothing more than a sprained wrist and a couple of fingers out of joint, a bloody nose and a black eye. Just a few scratches, as he put it. But if he ever signed up with that Swede he was going to murder him. It wasn't finished yet. He promised us that.

And that wasn't the end of the fracas either. After that Yvette had to go out and get liquored up at another bar. She had been insulted and she was going to put an end to things. And so she hires a taxi and orders the driver to ride out to the edge of the cliff overlooking the water. She was going to kill herself, that's what she was going to do. But then she was so drunk that when she tumbled out of the cab she began to weep and before anyone could stop her she had begun to peel her clothes off. The driver brought her home that way, half-naked, and when Jim-mie saw the condition she was in he was so furious with her that he took his razor strop and he belted the piss out of her, and she liked it, the bitch that she was. "Do it some more!" she begged, down on her knees as she was and clutching him around the legs with her two arms. But Jimmie had enough of it. "You're a dirty old sow!" he said and with his foot he gave her a shove in the guts that took the wind out of her—and a bit of her sexy nonsense too.

It was high time we were leaving. The city looked different in the early morning light. The last thing we talked about, as we stood there waiting for the train to pull out, was Idaho. The three of us were Americans. We came from different places, each of us, but we had something in common—a whole lot, I might say. We were getting sentimental, as Americans do when it comes time to part. We were getting quite foolish about the cows and sheep and the big open spaces where men are men and all that crap. If a boat had swung along instead of the train we'd have hopped aboard and said good-bye to it all. But Collins was never to see America again, as I learned later; and Fillmore . . . well, Fillmore had to take his punishment too, in a way that none of us could have suspected then. It's best to keep America just like that, always in the background, a sort of picture post card which you look at in a weak moment. Like that, you imagine it's always there waiting for you, unchanged, unspoiled, a big patriotic open space with cows and sheep and tenderhearted men ready to bugger everything in sight, man, woman or beast. It doesn't exist, America. It's a name you give to an abstract idea. . . .

Paris is like a whore. From a distance she seems ravishing, you can't wait until you have her in your arms. And five minutes later you feel empty, disgusted with yourself. You feel tricked.

I returned to Paris with money in my pocket—a few hundred francs, which Collins had shoved in my pocket just as I was boarding the train. It was enough to pay for a room and at least a week's good rations. It was more than I had had in my hands at one time for several years. I felt elated, as though perhaps a new life was opening before me. I wanted to conserve it too, so I looked up a cheap hotel over a bakery on the Rue du Château, just off the Rue de Vanves, a place that Eugene had pointed out to me once. A few yards away was the bridge that spans the Montparnasse tracks. A familiar quarter.

I could have had a room for a hundred francs a month, a room without any conveniences to be sure—without even a window—and perhaps I would have taken it, just to be sure of a place to flop for a while, had it not been for the fact that in order to reach this room I would have been obliged to first pass through the room of a blind man. The thought of passing his bed every night had a most depressing effect upon me. I decided to look elsewhere. I went over to the Rue Cels, just behind the cemetery, and I looked at a sort of rat trap there with balconies running around the courtyard. There were birdcages suspended from the balcony too, all along the lower tier. A cheerful sight perhaps, but to me it seemed like the public ward in a hospital. The proprietor didn't seem to have all his wits either. I decided to wait for the night, to have a good look around, and then choose some attractive little joint in a quiet side street.

At dinnertime I spent fifteen francs for a meal, just about twice the amount I had planned to allot myself. That made me so wretched that I wouldn't allow myself to sit down for a coffee, even despite the fact that it had begun to drizzle. I would walk about a bit and then go quietly to bed, at a reasonable hour. I was already miserable, trying to husband my resources this way. I had never in my life done it; it wasn't in my nature.

Finally it began to come down in bucketsful. I was glad. That would give me the excuse I needed to duck somewhere and stretch my legs out. It was still too early to go to bed. I began to quicken my pace, heading back toward the Boulevard Raspail. Suddenly a woman comes up to me and stops me, right in the pouring rain. She wants to know what time it is. I told her I didn't have a watch. And then she bursts out, just like this: "Oh, my good sir, do you speak English by chance?" I nod my head. It's coming down in torrents now. "Perhaps, my dear good man, you would be so kind as to take me to a café. It is raining so and I haven't the money to sit down anywhere. You will excuse me, my dear sir, but you have such a kind face . . . I knew you were English right away." And with this she smiles at me, a strange, half-demented smile. "Perhaps you could give me a little advice, dear sir. I am all alone in the world . . . my God, it is terrible to have no money. . . ."

This "dear sir" and "kind sir" and "my good man," etc., had me on the verge of hysteria. I felt sorry for her and yet I had to laugh. I did laugh. I laughed right in her face. And then she laughed too, a weird, high-pitched laugh, off key, an altogether unexpected piece of cachin-nation. I caught her by the arm and we made a bolt for it to the nearest café. She was still giggling when we en-tered the *bistro*. "My dear good sir," she began, "per-haps you think I am not telling you the truth. I am a good girl . . . I come of a good family. Only"—and here she gave me that wan, broken smile again—"only I am so misfortunate as not to have a place to sit down." At this I began to laugh again. I couldn't help it—the phrases she used, the strange accent, the crazy hat she had on, that demented smile. . . .

"Listen," I interrupted, "what nationality are you?"

"I'm English," she replied. "That is, I was born in Poland, but my father is Irish."

"So that makes you English?"

"Yes," she said, and she began to giggle again, sheepishly, and with a pretense of being coy.

"I suppose you know a nice little hotel where you could take me?" I said this, not because I had any intention of going with her, but just to spare her the usual preliminaries.

"Oh, my dear sir," she said, as though I had made the most grievous error, "I'm sure you don't mean that! I'm not that kind of a girl. You were joking with me, I can see that. You're so good . . . you have such a kind face. I would not dare to speak to a Frenchman as I did to you. They insult you right away. . . ."

She went on in this vein for some time. I wanted to break away from her. But she didn't want to be left alone. She was afraid—her papers were not in order. Wouldn't I be good enough to walk her to her hotel? Perhaps I could "lend" her fifteen or twenty francs, to quiet the *patron*? I walked her to the hotel where she said she was stopping and I put a fifty franc bill in her hand. Either she was very clever, or very innocent—it's hard to tell sometimes—but, at any rate, she wanted me to wait until she ran to the *bistro* for change. I told her not to bother. And with that she seized my hand impulsively and raised it to her lips. I was flabbergasted. I felt like giving her every damned thing I had. That touched me, that crazy little gesture. I thought to myself, it's good to be rich once in a while, just to get a new thrill like that. Just the same, I didn't lose my head. Fifty francs! That was quite enough to squander on a rainy night. As I walked off she

waved to me with that crazy little bonnet which she
didn't know how to wear. It was as though we were old
playmates. I felt foolish and giddy. "My dear kind sir . . .
you have such a gentle face . . . you are so good, etc." I
felt like a saint.

When you feel all puffed up inside it isn't so easy to go
to bed right away. You feel as though you ought to atone
for such unexpected bursts of goodness. Passing the
"Jungle" I caught a glimpse of the dance floor; women
with bare backs and ropes of pearls choking them—or so
it looked—were wiggling their beautiful bottoms at me.
Walked right up to the bar and ordered a *coupe* of champagne. When the music stopped, a beautiful blonde—she
looked like a Norwegian—took a seat right beside me.
The place wasn't as crowded or as gay as it had appeared
from outside. There were only a half dozen couples in the
place—they must have all been dancing at once. I ordered
another *coupe* of champagne in order not to let my
courage dribble away.

When I got up to dance with the blonde there was no
one on the floor but us. Any other time I would have been
self-conscious, but the champagne and the way she clung
to me, the dimmed lights and the solid feeling of security
which the few hundred francs gave me, well. . . . We had
another dance together, a sort of private exhibition, and
then we fell into conversation. She had begun to weep—
that was how it started. I thought possibly she had had
too much to drink, so I pretended not to be concerned.
And meawhile I was looking around to see if there was
any other timber available. But the place was thoroughly
deserted.

The thing to do when you're trapped is to breeze—at
once. If you don't, you're lost. What retained me, oddly
enough, was the thought of paying for a hat check a second time. One always lets himself in for it because of a
trifle.

The reason she was weeping, I discovered soon enough,
was because she had just buried her child. She wasn't
Norwegian either, but French, and a midwife to boot. A

chic midwife, I must say, even with the tears running
down her face. I asked her if a little drink would help to
console her, whereupon she very promptly ordered a
whisky and tossed it off in the wink of an eye. "Would
you like another?" I suggested gently. She thought she
would, she felt so rotten, so terribly dejected. She thought
she would like a package of Camels too. "No, wait a minute," she said, "I think I'd rather have *les* Pall Mall."
Have what you like, I thought, but stop weeping, for
Christ's sake, it gives me the willies. I jerked her to her
feet for another dance. On her feet she seemed to be another person. Maybe grief makes one more lecherous, I
don't know. I murmured something about breaking
away. "Where to?" she said eagerly. "Oh, anywhere.
Some quiet place where we can talk."

I went to the toilet and counted the money over again.
I hid the hundred franc notes in my fob pocket and kept
a fifty franc note and the loose change in my trousers
pocket. I went back to the bar determined to talk turkey.

She made it easier for me because she herself introduced the subject. She was in difficulties. It was not only
that she had just lost her child, but her mother was home,
ill, very ill, and there was the doctor to pay and medicine
to be bought, and so on and so forth. I didn't believe a
word of it, of course. And since I had to find a hotel for
myself, I suggested that she come along with me and stay
the night. A little economy there, I thought to myself.
But she wouldn't do that. She insisted on going home,
said she had an apartment to herself—and besides she had
to look after her mother. On reflection I decided that it
would be still cheaper sleeping at her place, so I said yes
and let's go immediately. Before going, however, I decided it was best to let her know just how I stood, so that
there wouldn't be any squawking at the last minute. I
thought she was going to faint when I told her how much
I had in my pocket. "The likes of it!" she said. Highly
insulted she was. I thought there would be a scene. . . .
Undaunted, however, I stood my ground. "Very well,

then, I'll leave you," I said quietly. "Perhaps I've made a mistake."

"I should say you have!" she exclaimed, but clutching me by the sleeve at the same time. *"Ecoute, chéri . . . sois raisonnable!"* When I heard that all my confidence was restored. I knew that it would be merely a question of promising her a little extra and everything would be O.K. "All right," I said wearily, "I'll be nice to you, you'll see."

"You were lying to me, then?" she said.

"Yes," I smiled, "I was just lying. . . ."

Before I had even put my hat on she had hailed a cab. I heard her give the Boulevard de Clichy for an address. That was more than the price of room, I thought to myself. Oh well, there was time yet . . . we'd see. I don't know how it started any more but soon she was raving to me about Henry Bordeaux. I have yet to meet a whore who doesn't know of Henry Bordeaux! But this one was genuinely inspired; her language was beautiful now, so tender, so discerning, that I was debating how much to give her. It seemed to me that I had heard her say— *"quand il n'y aura plus de temps."* It sounded like that, anyway. In the state I was in, a phrase like that was worth a hundred francs. I wondered if it was her own or if she had pulled it from Henry Bordeaux. Little matter. It was Montmartre. "Good evening, mother," I was saying to myself, "daughter and I will look after you—*quand il n'y aura plus de temps!*" She was going to show me her diploma, too, I remembered that.

She was all aflutter, once the door had closed behind us. Distracted. Wringing her hands and striking Sarah Bernhardt poses, half undressed too, and pausing between times to urge me to hurry, to get undressed, to do this and do that. Finally, when she had stripped down and was poking about with a chemise in her hand, searching for her kimono, I caught hold of her and gave her a good squeeze. She had a look of anguish on her face when I released her. "My God! My God! I must go downstairs and have a look at mother!" she exclaimed. "You can take a bath if you like, *chéri*. There! I'll be back in a few minutes." At the door I embraced her again. I was in my underclothes and I had a tremendous erection. Somehow all this anguish and excitement, all the grief and histrionics, only whetted my appetite. Perhaps she was just going downstairs to quiet her *maquereau*. I had a feeling that something unusual was happening, some sort of drama which I would read about in the morning paper. I gave the place a quick inspection. There were two rooms and a bath, not badly furnished. Rather coquettish. There was her diploma on the wall—"first," as they all read. And there was the photograph of a child, a little girl with beautiful locks, on the dresser. I put the water on for a bath, and then I changed my mind. If something were to happen and I were found in the tub . . . I didn't like the idea. I paced back and forth, getting more and more uneasy as the minutes rolled by.

When she returned she was even more upset than before. "She's going to die . . . she's going to die!" she kept wailing. For a moment I was almost on the point of leaving. How the hell can you climb over a woman when her mother's dying downstairs, perhaps right beneath you? I put my arms around her, half in sympathy and half determined to get what I had come for. As we stood thus she murmured, as if in real distress, her need for the money I had promised her. It was for *"maman."* Shit, I didn't have the heart to haggle about a few francs at the moment. I walked over to the chair where my clothes were lying and I wiggled a hundred franc note out of my fob pocket, carefully keeping my back turned to her just the same. And, as a further precaution, I placed my pants on the side of the bed where I knew I was going to flop. The hundred francs wasn't altogether satisfactory to her, but I could see from the feeble way that she protested that it was quite enough. Then, with an energy that astonished me, she flung off her kimono and jumped into bed. As soon as I had put my arms around her and pulled

her to me she reached for the switch and out went the
lights. She embraced me passionately, and she groaned
as all French cunts do when they get you in bed. She was
getting me frightfully roused with her carrying on; that
business of turning out the lights was a new one to
me . . . it seemed like the real thing. But I was suspicious
too, and as soon as I could manage conveniently I put my
hands out to feel if my trousers were still there on the
chair.

I thought we were settled for the night. The bed felt
very comfortable, softer than the average hotel bed—and
the sheets were clean, I had noticed that. If only she
wouldn't squirm so! You would think she hadn't slept
with a man for a month. I wanted to stretch it out. I
wanted full value for my hundred francs. But she was
mumbling all sorts of things in the crazy bed language
which goes to your blood even more rapidly when it's in
the dark. I was putting up a stiff fight, but it was impossible with her groaning and gasping going on, and her
muttering: *"Vite chéri! Vite chéri! Oh, c'est bon! Oh,
oh! Vite, vite, chéri!"* I tried to count but it was like a
fire alarm going off. *"Vite, chéri!"* and this time she gave
such a gasping shudder that bango! I heard the stars
chiming and there was my hundred francs gone and the
fifty that I had forgotten all about and the lights were on
again and with the same alacrity that she had bounced
into bed she was bouncing out again and grunting and
squealing like an old sow. I lay back and puffed a cigarette, gazing ruefully at my pants the while; they were
terribly wrinkled. In a moment she was back again,
wrapping the kimono around her, and telling me in that
agitated way which was getting on my nerves that I
should make myself at home. "I'm going downstairs to see
mother," she said. *"Mais faites comme chez vous, chéri.
Je reviens tout de suite."*

After a quarter of an hour had passed I began to feel
thoroughly restless. I went inside and I read through a
letter that was lying on the table. It was nothing of any

account—a love letter. In the bathroom I examined all the bottles on the shelf; she had everything a woman requires to make herself smell beautiful. I was still hoping that she would came back and give me another fifty francs' worth. But time dragged on and there was no sign of her. I began to grow alarmed. Perhaps there *was* someone dying downstairs. Absent-mindedly, out of a sense of self-preservation, I suppose, I began to put my things on. As I was buckling my belt it came to me like a flash how she had stuffed the hundred franc note into her purse. In the excitement of the moment she had thrust the purse in the wardrobe, on the upper shelf. I remembered the gesture she made—standing on her tiptoes and reaching for the shelf. It didn't take me a minute to open the wardrobe and feel around for the purse. It was still there. I opened it hurriedly and saw my hundred franc note lying snugly between the silk coverlets. I put the purse back just as it was, slipped into my coat and shoes, and then I went to the landing and listened intently. I couldn't hear a sound. Where she had gone to, Christ only knows. In a jiffy I was back at the wardrobe and fumbling with her purse. I pocketed the hundred francs and all the loose change besides. Then, closing the door silently, I tiptoed down the stairs and when once I had hit the street I walked just as fast as my legs would carry me. At the Café Boudon I stopped for a bite. The whores were having a gay time pelting a fat man who had fallen asleep over his meal. He was sound asleep; snoring, in fact, and yet his jaws were working away mechanically. The place was in an uproar. There were shouts of "All aboard!" and then a concerted banging of knives and forks. He opened his eyes for a moment, blinked stupidly, and then his head rolled forward again on his chest. I put the hundred franc bill carefully away in my fob pocket and counted the change. The din around me was increasing and I had difficulty to recall exactly whether I had seen "first-class" on her diploma or not. It bothered me. About her mother I didn't give a damn. I hoped she had croaked by now. It would be strange if what she had said were true. Too good to believe. *Vite chéri . . . vite, vite!* And the other half-wit with her "my good sir" and "you have such a kind face"! I wondered if she had really taken a room in that hotel we stopped by.

It was along the close of summer when Fillmore invited me to come and live with him. He had a studio apartment overlooking the cavalry barracks just off the Place Dupleix. We had seen a lot of each other since the little trip to Le Havre. If it hadn't been for Fillmore I don't know where I should be today—dead, most likely.

"I would have asked you long before," he said, "if it hadn't been for that little bitch Jackie. I didn't know how to get her off my hands."

I had to smile. It was always like that with Fillmore. He had a genius for attracting homeless bitches. Anyway, Jackie had finally cleared out of her own accord.

The rainy season was coming on, the long, dreary stretch of grease and fog and squirts of rain that make you damp and miserable. An execrable place in the winter, Paris! A climate that eats into your soul, that leaves you bare as the Labrador coast. I noticed with some anxiety that the only means of heating the place was the little stove in the studio. However, it was still comfortable. And the view from the studio window was superb.

In the morning Fillmore would shake me roughly and leave a ten franc note on the pillow. As soon as he had gone I would settle back for a final snooze. Sometimes I would lie abed till noon. There was nothing pressing, except to finish the book, and that didn't worry me much because I was already convinced that nobody would accept it anyway. Nevertheless, Fillmore was much impressed by it. When he arrived in the evening with a bottle under his arm the first thing he did was to go to the table and see how many pages I had knocked off. At first I enjoyed this show of enthusiasm but later, when I was running dry, it made me devilishly uneasy to see him poking around, searching for the pages that were supposed to trickle out of me like water from a tap. When there was nothing to show I felt exactly like some bitch whom he had harbored. He used to say about Jackie, I remembered—"it would have been all right if only she had slipped me a piece of ass once in a while." If I had been a woman I would have been only too glad to slip him a piece of ass: it would have been much easier than to feed him the pages which he expected.

Nevertheless, he tried to make me feel at ease. There was always plenty of food and wine, and now and then he would insist that I accompany him to a *dancing*. He was fond of going to a nigger joint on the Rue d'Odessa where there was a good-looking mulatto who used to come home with us occasionally. The one thing that bothered him was that he couldn't find a French girl who liked to drink. They were all too sober to satisfy him— He liked to bring a woman back to the studio and guzzle it with her before getting down to business. He also liked to have her think that he was an artist. As the man from whom he had rented the place was a painter, it was not difficult to create an impression; the canvases which we had found in the *armoire* were soon stuck about the place and one of the unfinished ones conspicuously mounted on the easel. Unfortunately they were all of a surrealistic quality and the impression they created was usually unfavorable. Between a whore, a concierge and a cabinet minister there is not much difference in taste where pictures are concerned. It was a matter of great relief to Fillmore when Mark Swift began to visit us regularly with the intention of doing my portrait. Fillmore had a great admiration for Swift. He was a genius, he said. And though there was something ferocious about everything he tackled nevertheless when he painted a man or an object you could recognize it for what it was.

At Swift's request I had begun to grow a beard. The shape of my skull, he said, required a beard. I had to sit by the window with the Eiffel Tower in back of me because he wanted the Eiffel Tower in the picture too. He also wanted the typewriter in the picture. Kruger got the habit of dropping in too about this time; he maintained that Swift knew nothing about painting. It exasperated him to see things out of proportion. He believed in Nature's laws, implicitly. Swift didn't give a fuck about Nature; he wanted to paint what was inside his head. Anyway, there was Swift's portrait of me stuck on the easel now, and though everything was out of proportion, even a cabinet minister could see that it was a human head, a man with a beard. The concierge, indeed, began to take a great interest in the picture; she thought the likeness was striking. And she liked the idea of showing the Eiffel Tower in the background.

Things rolled along this way peacefully for about a month or more. The neighborhood appealed to me, particularly at night when the full squalor and lugubriousness of it made itself felt. The little Place, so charming and tranquil at twilight, could assume the most dismal, sinister character when darkness came on. There was that long, high wall covering one side of the barracks against which there was always a couple embracing each other furtively—often in the rain. A depressing sight to see two lovers squeezed against a prison wall under a gloomy street light: as if they had been driven right to the last bounds. What went on inside the enclosure was also depressing. On a rainy day I used to stand by the window and look down on the activity below, quite as if it were something going on on another planet. It seemed incomprehensible to me. Everything done according to schedule, but a schedule that must have been devised by a lunatic. There they were, floundering around in the mud, the bugles blowing, the horses charging—all within four walls. A sham battle. A lot of tin soldiers who hadn't the least interest in learning how to kill or how to polish their boots or currycomb the horses. Utterly ridiculous the whole thing, but part of the scheme of things. When they had nothing to do they looked even more ridiculous; they scratched themselves, they walked about with their hands in their pockets, they looked up at the sky. And when an officer came along they clicked their heels and saluted. A madhouse, it seemed to me. Even the horses looked silly. And then sometimes the artillery was dragged out and they went clattering down the street on parade and people stood and gaped and admired the fine uniforms. To me they always looked like an army corps in retreat; something shabby, bedraggled, crestfallen about them, their uniforms too big for their bodies, all the alertness, which as individuals they possess at such a remarkable degree, gone now.

When the sun came out, however, things looked different. There was a ray of hope in their eyes, they walked more elastically, they showed a little enthusiasm. Then the color of things peeped out graciously and there was that fuss and bustle so characteristic of the French; at the *bistro* on the corner they chattered gaily over their drinks and the officers seemed more human, more French, I might say. When the sun comes out, any spot in Paris can look beautiful; and if there is a *bistro* with an awning rolled down, a few tables on the sidewalk and colored drinks in the glasses, then people look altogether human. And they *are* human—the finest people in the world when the sun shines! So intelligent, so indolent, so carefree! It's a crime to herd such a people into barracks, to put them through exercises, to grade them into privates and sergeants and colonels and what not.

As I say, things were rolling along smoothly. Now and then Carl came along with a job for me, travel articles which he hated to do himself. They only paid fifty francs a piece, but they were easy to do because I had only to consult the back issues and revamp the old articles. People only read these things when they were sitting on a toilet or killing time in a waiting room. The principal thing was to keep the adjectives well furbished—the rest was a matter of dates and statistics. If it was an important article the head of the department signed it himself; he was a half-wit who couldn't speak any language well, but who knew how to find fault. If he found a paragraph that seemed to him well written he would say—"Now that's the way I want you to write! That's beautiful. You have my permission to use it in your book." These beautiful paragraphs we sometimes lifted from the encyclopaedia or an old guide book. Some of them Carl did put into his book—they had a surrealistic character.

Then one evening, after I had been out for a walk, I open the door and a woman springs out of the bedroom. "So you're the writer!" she exclaims at once, and she looks at my beard as if to corroborate her impression. "What a horrid beard!" she says. "I think you people must be crazy around here." Fillmore is trailing after her with a blanket in his hand. "She's a princess," he says, smacking his lips as if he had just tasted some rare caviar. The two of them were dressed for the street; I couldn't understand what they were doing with the bedclothes. And then it occurred to me immediately that Fillmore must have dragged her into the bedroom to show her his laundry bag. He always did that with a new woman, especially if she was a *Française*. "No tickee, no shirtee!" that's what was stitched on the laundry bag, and somehow Fillmore had an obsession for explaining this motto to every female who arrived. But this dame was not a *Française*—he made that clear to me at once. She was Russian—and a princess, no less.

He was bubbling over with excitement, like a child that has just found a new toy. "She speaks five languages!" he said, obviously overwhelmed by such an accomplishment.

"Non, *four!*" she corrected promptly.

"Well, four then. . . . Anyway, she's a damned intelligent girl. You ought to hear her speak."

The princess was nervous—she kept scratching her thigh and rubbing her nose. "Why does he want to make his bed now?" she asked me abruptly. "Does he think he will get me that way? He's a big child. He behaves disgracefully. I took him to a Russian restaurant and he danced like a nigger." She wiggled her bottom to illustrate. "And he talks too much. Too loud. He talks nonsense." She swished about the room, examining the paintings and the books, keeping her chin well up all the time but scratching herself intermittently. Now and then she wheeled around like a battleship and delivered a broadside. Fillmore kept following her about with a bottle in one hand and a glass in the other. "Stop following me like that!" she exclaimed. "And haven't you anything to drink but this? Can't you get a bottle of champagne? I must have some champagne. My nerves! My nerves!"

Fillmore tries to whisper a few words in my ear. "An actress . . . a movie star . . . some guy jilted her and she can't get over it. . . . I'm going to get her cockeyed. . . ."

"I'll clear out then," I was saying, when the princess interrupted us with a shout. "Why do you whisper like that?" she cried, stamping her foot. "Don't you know that's not polite? And *you*, I thought you were going to take me out? I must get drunk tonight, I have told you that already."

"Yes, yes," said Fillmore, "we're going in a minute. I just want another drink."

"You're a pig!" she yelled. "But you're a nice boy too. Only you're loud. You have no manners." She turned to me. "Can I trust him to behave himself? I must get drunk tonight but I don't want him to disgrace me. Maybe I will come back here afterward. I would like to talk to you. You seem more intelligent."

As they were leaving the princess shook my hand cordially and promised to come for dinner some evening— "when I will be sober," she said.

"Fine!" I said. "Bring another princess along—or a countess, at least. We change the sheets every Saturday."

About three in the morning Fillmore staggers in . . . alone. Lit up like an ocean liner, and making a noise like a blind man with his cracked cane. Tap, tap, tap, down the weary lane. . . . "Going straight to bed," he says, as he marches past me. "Tell you all about it tomorrow." He goes inside to his room and throws back the covers. I hear him groaning—"what a woman! what a woman!" In a second he's out again, with his hat on and the cracked cane in his hand. "I knew something like that was going to happen. She's crazy!"

He rummages around in the kitchen a while and then comes back to the studio with a bottle of Anjou. I have to sit up and down a glass with him.

As far as I can piece the story together the whole thing started at the Rond-Point des Champs Elysées where he had dropped off for a drink on his way home. As usual at that hour the *terrasse* was crowded with buzzards. This one was sitting right on the aisle with a pile of saucers in front of her; she was getting drunk quietly all by herself when Fillmore happened along and caught her eyes. "I'm drunk," she giggled, "won't you sit down?" And then, as though it were the most natural thing in the world to do, she began right off the bat with the yarn about her movie director, how he had given her the go-by and how she had thrown herself in the Seine and so forth and so on. She couldn't remember any more which bridge it was, only that there was a crowd around when they fished her out of the water. Besides, she didn't see what difference it made which bridge she threw herself from—why did he ask such questions? She was laughing hysterically about it, and then suddenly she had a desire to be off—she wanted to dance. Seeing him hesitate she opens her bag impulsively and pulls out a hundred franc note. The next moment, however, she decided that a hundred francs wouldn't go very far. "Haven't you any money at all?" she said. No, he hadn't very much in his pocket, but he had a checkbook at home. So they made a dash for the checkbook and then, of course, I had to happen in just as he was explaining to her the "No tickee, no shirtee" business.

On the way home they had stopped off at the Poisson d'Or for a little snack which she had washed down with a few vodkas. She was in her element there with everyone

kissing her hand and murmuring *Princesse, Princesse.*
Drunk as she was, she managed to collect her dignity.
"Don't wiggle your behind like that!" she kept saying, as
they danced.

It was Fillmore's idea, when he brought her back to the
studio, to stay there. But, since she was such an intelligent
girl and so erratic, he had decided to put up with her
whims and postpone the grand event. He had even visual-
ized the prospect of running across another princess and
bringing the two of them back. When they started out
for the evening, therefore, he was in a good humor and
prepared, if necessary, to spend a few hundred francs
on her. After all, one doesn't run across a princess every
day.

This time she dragged him to another place, a place
where she was still better known and where there would
be no trouble in cashing a check, as she said. Everybody
was in evening clothes and there was more spine-break-
ing, hand-kissing nonsense as the waiter escorted them to
a table.

In the middle of a dance she suddenly walks off the
floor, with tears in her eyes. "What's the matter?" he said,
"what did I do this time?" And instinctively he put his
hand to his backside, as though perhaps it might still be
wiggling. "It's nothing," she said. "You didn't do anything. Come, you're a nice boy," and with that she drags
him on to the floor again and begins to dance with aban-
don. "But what's the matter with you?" he murmured.
"It's nothing," she repeated. "I saw somebody, that's all."
And then, with a sudden spurt of anger—"why do you
get me drunk? Don't you know it makes me crazy?"

"Have you got a check?" she says. "We must get out
of here." She called the waiter over and whispered to him
in Russian. "Is it a good check?" she asked, when the
waiter had disappeared. And then, impulsively: "Wait
for me downstairs in the cloakroom. I must telephone
somebody."

After the waiter had brought the change Fillmore
sauntered leisurely downstairs to the cloakroom to wait

for her. He strode up and down, humming and whistling softly, and smacking his lips in anticipation of the caviar to come. Five minutes passed. Ten minutes. Still whistling softly. When twenty minutes had gone by and still no princess he at last grew suspicious. The cloakroom attendant said that she had left long ago. He dashed outside. There was a nigger in livery standing there with a big grin on his face. Did the nigger know where she had breezed to? Nigger grins. Nigger says: "Ah heerd Coupole, dassall sir!"

At the Coupole, downstairs, he finds her sitting in front of a cocktail with a dreamy, trancelike expression on her face. She smiles when she sees him.

"Was that a decent thing to do," he says, "to run away like that? You might have told me that you didn't like me. . . ."

She flared up at this, got theatrical about it. And after a lot of gushing she commenced to whine and slobber. "I'm crazy," he blubbered. "And you're crazy too. You want me to sleep with you, and I don't want to sleep with you." And then she began to rave about her lover, the movie director whom she had seen on the dance floor. That's why she had to run away from the place. That's why she took drugs and got drunk every night. That's why she threw herself in the Seine. She babbled on this way about how crazy she was and then suddenly she had an idea. "Let's go to Bricktop's!" There was a man there whom she knew . . . he had promised her a job once. She was certain he would help her.

"What's it going to cost?" asked Fillmore cautiously.

It would cost a lot, she let him know that immediately. "But listen, if you take me to Bricktop's, I promise to go home with you." She was honest enough to add that it might cost him five or six hundred francs. "But I'm worth it! You don't know what a woman I am. There isn't another woman like me in all Paris. . . ."

"That's what *you* think!" His Yankee blood was coming to the fore. "But I don't see it. I don't see that you're worth anything. You're just a poor crazy son-of-a-bitch.

Frankly, I'd rather give fifty francs to some poor French girl, at least they give you something in return."

She hit the ceiling when he mentioned the French girls. "Don't talk to me about those women! I hate them! They're stupid . . . they're ugly . . . they're mercenary. Stop it, I tell you!"

In a moment she had subsided again. She was on a new tack. "Darling," she murmured, "you don't know what I look like when I'm undressed. I'm *beautiful!*" And she held her breasts with her two hands.

But Fillmore remained unimpresesd. "You're a bitch!" he said coldly. "I wouldn't mind spending a few hundred francs on you, but you're crazy. You haven't even washed your face. Your breath stinks. I don't give a damn whether you're a princess or not . . . I don't want any of your high-assed Russian variety. You ought to get out in the street and hustle for it. You're no better than any little French girl. You're not as good. I wouldn't piss away another sou on you. You ought to go to America— that's the place for a bloodsucking leech like you. . . ."

She didn't seem to be at all put out by this speech. "I think you're just a little afraid of me," she said.

"Afraid of you? Of *you?*"

"You're just a little boy," she said. "You have no manners. When you know me better you will talk differently. . . . Why don't you try to be nice? If you don't want to go with me tonight, very well. I will be at the Rond-Point tomorrow between five and seven. I like you."

"I don't intend to be at the Rond-Point tomorrow, or any other night! I don't want to see you again . . . ever. I'm through with you. I'm going out and find myself a nice little French girl. You can go to hell!"

She looked at him and smiled wearily. "That's what you say now. But wait! Wait until you've slept with me. You don't know yet what a beautiful body I have. You think the French girls know how to make love . . . wait! I will make you crazy about me. I like you. Only you're uncivilized. You're just a boy. You talk too much. . . ."

"You're crazy," said Fillmore. "I wouldn't fall for you if you were the last woman on earth. Go home and wash your face." He walked off without paying for the drinks.

In a few days, however, the princess was installed. She's a genuine princess, of that we're pretty certain. But she has the clap. Anyway, life is far from dull here. Fillmore has bronchitis, the princess, as I was saying, has the clap, and I have the piles. Just exchanged six empty bottles at the Russian *épicerie* across the way. Not a drop went down my gullet. No meat, no wine, no rich game, no women. Only fruit and paraffin oil, arnica drops and adrenalin ointment. And not a chair in the joint that's comfortable enough. Right now, looking at the princess, I'm propped up like a pasha! That reminds me of her name: Macha. Doesn't sound so damned aristocratic to me. Reminds me of *The Living Corpse*.

At first I thought it was going to be embarrassing, a *ménage à trois*, but not at all. I thought when I saw her move in that it was all up with me again, that I should have to find another place, but Fillmore soon gave me to understand that he was only putting her up until she got on her feet. With a woman like her I don't know what an expression like that means; as far as I can see she's been standing on her head all her life. She says the revolution drove her out of Russia, but I'm sure if it hadn't been the revolution it would have been something else. She's under the impression that she's a great actress; we never contradict her in anything she says because it's time wasted. Fillmore finds her amusing. When he leaves for the office in the morning he drops ten francs on her pillow and ten francs on mine; at night the three of us go to the Russian restaurant down below. The neighborhood is full of Russians and Macha has already found a place where she can run up a little credit. Naturally ten francs a day isn't anything for a princess; she wants caviar now and then and champagne, and she needs a complete new wardrobe in order to get a job in the movies again. She has nothing to do now except to kill time. She's putting on fat.

This morning I had quite a fright. After I had washed my face I grabbed her towel by mistake. We can't seem to train her to put her towel on the right hook. And when I bawled her out for it she answered smoothly: "My dear, if one can become blind from that I would have been blind years ago."

And then there's the toilet, which we all have to use. I try speaking to her in a fatherly way about the toilet seat. "Oh zut!" she says. "If you are so afraid I'll go to a café." But it's not necessary to do that, I explain. Just use ordinary precautions. "Tut tut!" she says, "I won't sit down then . . . I'll stand up."

Everything is cockeyed with her around. First she wouldn't come across because she had the monthlies. For eight days that lasted. We were beginning to think she was faking it. But no, she wasn't faking. One day, when I was trying to put the place in order, I found some cotton batting under the bed and it was stained with blood. With her everything goes under the bed: orange peel, wadding, corks, empty bottles, scissors, used condoms, books, pillows. . . . She makes the bed only when it's time to retire. Most of the time she lies abed reading her Russian papers. "My dear," she says to me, "if it weren't for my papers I wouldn't get out of bed at all." That's it precisely! Nothing but Russian newspapers. Not a scratch of toilet paper around—nothing but Russian newspapers with which to wipe your ass.

Anyway, speaking of her idiosyncrasies, after the menstrual flow was over, after she had rested properly and put a nice layer of fat around her belt, still she wouldn't come across. Pretended that she only liked women. To take on a man she had to first be properly stimulated. Wanted us to take her to a bawdy house where they put on the dog and man act. Or better still, she said, would be Leda and the swan: the flapping of the wings excited her terribly.

One night, to test her out, we accompanied her to a place that she suggested. But before we had a chance to broach the subject to the madam, a drunken Englishman, who was sitting at the next table, fell into a conversation with us. He had already been upstairs twice but he wanted another try at it. He had only about twenty francs in his pocket, and not knowing any French, he asked us if we would help him to bargain with the girl he had his eye on. Happened she was a Negress, a powerful wench from Martinique, and beautiful as a panther. Had a lovely disposition too. In order to persuade her to accept the Englishman's remaining sous, Fillmore had to promise to go with her himself soon as she got through with the Englishman. The princess looked on, heard everything that was said, and then got on her high horse. She was insulted. "Well," said Fillmore, "you wanted some excitement—you can watch me do it!" She didn't want to watch him—she wanted to watch a drake. "Well, by Jesus," he said, "I'm as good as a drake any day . . . maybe a little better." Like that, one word led to another, and finally the only way we could appease her was to call one of the girls over and let them tickle each other . . . When Fillmore came back with the Negress her eyes were smoldering. I could see from the way Fillmore looked at her that she must have given an unusual performance and I began to feel lecherous myself. Fillmore must have sensed how I felt, and what an ordeal it was to sit and look on all night, for suddenly he pulled a hundred franc note out of his pocket and slapping it in front of me, he said: "Look here, you probably need a lay more than any of us. Take that and pick someone out for yourself." Somehow that gesture endeared him more to me than anything he had ever done for me, and he had done considerable. I accepted the money in the spirit it was given and promptly signaled to the Negress to get ready for another lay. That enraged the princess more than anything, it appeared. She wanted to know if there wasn't anyone in the place good enough for us except this Negress. I told her bluntly NO. And it was so—the Negress was the queen of the harem. You had only to look at her to get an erection. Her eyes seemed to be swimming in sperm. She was drunk with all the demands made upon her. She couldn't walk straight any more—at least, it seemed that way to me. Going up the narrow winding stairs behind her I couldn't resist the temptation to slide my hand up her crotch; we continued up the stairs that way, she looking back at me with a cheerful smile and wiggling her ass a bit when it tickled her too much.

It was a good session all around. Everyone was happy. Macha seemed to be in a good mood too. And so the next evening, after she had had her ration of champagne and caviar, after she had given us another chapter out of the history of her life, Fillmore went to work on her. It seemed as though he was going to get his reward at last. She had ceased to put up a fight any more. She lay back with her legs apart and she let him fool around and fool around and then, just as he was climbing over her, just as he was going to slip it in, she informs him nonchalantly that she has a dose of clap. He rolled off her like a log. I heard him fumbling around in the kitchen for the black soap he used on special occasions, and in a few moments he was standing by my bed with a towel in his hands and saying—"can you beat that? that son-of-a-bitch of a princess has the clap!" He seemed pretty well scared about it. The princess meanwhile was munching an apple and calling for her Russian newspapers. It was quite a joke to her. "There are worse things than that," she said, lying there in her bed and talking to us through the open door. Finally Fillmore began to see it as a joke too and opening another bottle of Anjou he poured out a drink for himself and quaffed it down. It was only about one in the morning and so he sat there talking to me for a while. He wasn't going to be put off by a thing like that, he told me. Of course, he had to be careful ... there was the old dose which had come on in Le Havre. He couldn't remember any more how that happened. Sometimes when he got drunk he forgot to wash himself. It wasn't anything very terrible, but you never knew what might develop later. He didn't want any one massaging his prostate gland. No, that he didn't relish. The first dose he ever got was at college. Didn't know whether the girl had given it to him or he to the girl; there was so much funny work going on about the campus you didn't know whom to believe. Nearly all the coeds had been knocked up some time or other. Too damned ignorant . . . even the profs were ignorant. One of the profs had himself castrated, so the rumor went. . . .

Anyway, the next night he decided to risk it—with a condom. Not much risk in that, unless it breaks. He had bought himself some of the long fish skin variety—they were the most reliable, he assured me. But then, that didn't work either. She was too tight. "Jesus, there's nothing abnormal about me," he said. "How do you make that out? Somebody got inside her all right to give her that dose. He must have been abnormally small."

So, one thing after another failing, he just gave it up altogether. They lie there now like brother and sister, with incestuous dreams. Says Macha, in her philosophic way: "In Russia it often happens that a man sleeps with a woman without touching her. They can go on that way for weeks and weeks and never think anything about it. Until paff! once he touches her . . . paff! paff! After that it's paff, paff, paff!"

All efforts are concentrated now on getting Macha into shape. Fillmore thinks if he cures her of the clap she may loosen up. A strange idea. So he's bought her a douche bag, a stock of permanganate, a whirling syringe and other little things which were recommended to him by a Hungarian doctor, a little quack of an abortionist over near the Place d'Aligre. It seems his boss had knocked up a sixteen-year-old girl once and she had introduced him to the Hungarian; and then after that the boss had a beautiful chancre and it was the Hungarian again. That's how one gets acquainted in Paris—genito-urinary friendships. Anyway, under our strict supervision, Macha is taking care of herself. The other night, though, we were in a quandary for a while. She stuck the suppository inside her and then she couldn't find the string attached to it. "My God!" she was yelling, "where is that string? My God! I can't find the string!"

"Did you look under the bed?" said Fillmore.

Finally she quieted down. But only for a few minutes. The next thing was: "My God! I'm bleeding again. I just had my period and now there are *gouttes* again. It must be that cheap champagne you buy. My God, do you want me to bleed to death?" She comes out with a kimono on and a towel stuck between her legs, trying to look dignified as usual. "My whole life is just like that," she says. "I'm a neurasthenic. The whole day running around and at night I'm drunk again. When I came to Paris I was still an innocent girl. I read only Villon and Baudelaire. But as I had then 300,000 Swiss francs in the bank I was crazy to enjoy myself, because in Russia they were always strict with me. And as I was even more beautiful then than I am now I had all the men falling at my feet." Here she hitched up the slack which had accumulated around her belt. "You mustn't think I had a stomach like that when I came here . . . that's from all the poison I was given to drink . . . those horrible *apéritifs* which the French are so crazy to drink. . . . So then I met my movie director and he wanted that I should play a part for him. He said I was the most gorgeous creature in the world and he was begging me to sleep with him every night. I was a foolish young virgin and so I permitted him to rape me one night. I wanted to be a great actress and I didn't know he was full of poison. So he gave me the clap . . . and now I want that he should have it back again. It's his fault that I committed suicide in the Seine. . . . Why are you laughing? Don't you believe that I committed suicide? I can show you the newspapers . . . there is my picture in all the papers. I will show you the Russian papers some day . . . they wrote about me wonderfully. . . . But darling, you know that first I must have a new dress. I can't vamp this man with these dirty rags I am in. Besides, I still owe my dressmaker 12,000 francs. . . ."

From here on it's a long story about the inheritance which she is trying to collect. She has a young lawyer, a Frenchman, who is rather timid, it seems, and he is trying to win back her fortune. From time to time he used to give her a hundred francs or so on account. "He's stingy, like all the French people," she says. "And I was so beautiful, too, that he couldn't keep his eyes off me. He kept begging me always to fuck him. I got so sick and tired of listening to him that one night I said yes, just to keep him quiet, and so as I wouldn't lose my hundred francs now and then." She paused a moment to laugh hysterically. "My dear," she continued, "it was too funny for words what happened to him. He calls me up on the phone one day and says: 'I must see you right away . . . it's very important.' And when I see him he shows me a paper from the doctor—and it's gonorrhea! My dear, I laughed in his face. How should I know that I still had the clap? 'You wanted to fuck me and so I fucked you!' That made him quiet. That's how it goes in life . . . you don't suspect anything, and then all of a sudden paff, paff, paff! He was such a fool that he fell in love with me all over again. Only he begged me to behave myself and not run around Montparnasse all night drinking and fucking. He said I was driving him crazy. He wanted to marry me and then his family heard about me and they persuaded him to go to Indo-China. . . ."

From this Macha calmly switches to an affair she had with a Lesbian. "It was very funny, my dear, how she picked me up one night. I was at the 'Fétiche' and I was drunk as usual. She took me from one place to the other and she made love to me under the table all night until I couldn't stand it any more. Then she took me to her apartment and for two hundred francs I let her suck me off. She wanted me to live with her but I didn't want to have her suck me off every night . . . it makes you too weak. Besides, I can tell you that I don't care so much for Lesbians as I used to. I would rather sleep with a man even though it hurts me. When I get terribly excited I can't

hold myself back any more ... three, four, five times ...
just like that! Paff, paff, paff! And then I bleed and that
is very unhealthy for me because I am inclined to be
anemic. So you see why once in a while I must let myself
be sucked by a Lesbian. ..."

When the cold weather set in the princess disappeared. It was getting uncomfortable with just a little coal stove in the studio; the bedroom was like an icebox and the kitchen was hardly any better. There was just a little space around the stove where it was actually warm. So Macha had found herself a sculptor who was castrated. She told us about him before she left. After a few days she tried coming back to us, but Fillmore wouldn't hear of it. She complained that the sculptor kept her awake all night kissing her. And then there was no hot water for her douches. But finally she decided that it was just as well she didn't come back. "I won't have that candlestick next to me any more," she said. "Always that candlestick . . . it made me nervous. If you had only been a fairy I would have stayed with you. . . ."

With Macha gone our evenings took on a different character. Often we sat by the fire drinking hot toddies and discussing the life back there in the States. We talked about it as if we never expected to go back there again. Fillmore had a map of New York City which he had tacked on the wall; we used to spend whole evenings discussing the relative virtues of Paris and New York. And inevitably there always crept into our discussions the figure of Whitman, that one lone figure which America has produced in the course of her brief life. In Whitman the whole American scene comes to life, her past and her future, her birth and her death. Whatever there is of value in America Whitman has expressed, and there is nothing more to be said. The future belongs to the machine, to the robots. He was the Poet of the Body and the Soul, Whitman. The first and the last poet. He is almost undecipherable today, a monument covered with rude hieroglyphs for which there is no key. It seems strange almost to mention his name over here. There is no equivalent in the languages of Europe for the spirit which he immortalized. Europe is saturated with art and her soil is full of dead bones and her museums are bursting with plundered treasures, but what Europe has never had is a free, healthy spirit, what you might call a MAN. Goethe was the nearest approach, but Goethe was a stuffed shirt, by comparison. Goethe was a respectable citizen, a pedant, a bore, a universal spirit, but stamped with the German trade-mark, with the double eagle. The serenity of Goethe, the calm, Olympian attitude, is nothing more than the drowsy stupor of a German burgeois deity. Goethe is an end of something, Whitman is a beginning.

After a discussion of this sort I would sometimes put on my things and go for a walk, bundled up in a sweater, a spring overcoat of Fillmore's and a cape over that. A foul, damp cold against which there is no protection except a strong spirit. They say America is a country of extremes, and it is true that the thermometer registers degrees of cold which are practically unheard of here; but the cold of a Paris winter is a cold unknown to America, it is psychological, an inner as well as an outer cold. If it never freezes here it never thaws either. Just as the people protect themselves against the invasion of their privacy, by their high walls, their bolts and shutters, their growling, evil-tongued, slatternly concierges, so they have learned to protect themselves against the cold and heat of a bracing, vigorous climate. They have fortified themselves: protection is the keyword. Protection and security. In order that they may rot in comfort. On a damp winter's night it is not necessary to look at the map to discover the latitude of Paris. It is a northern city, an outpost erected over a swamp filled in with skulls and bones. Along the boulevards there is a cold electrical imitation of heat. *Tout Va Bien* in ultraviolet rays that make the clients of the Dupont chain cafés look like gangrened cadavers. *Tout Va Bien!* That's the motto that nourishes the forlorn beggars who walk up and down all night under the drizzle of the violet rays. Wherever there are lights there is a little heat. One gets warm from watching the fat, secure bastards down their grogs, their steaming black coffees. Where the lights are there are people on the sidewalks, jostling one another, giving off a little animal heat through their dirty underwear and their foul, cursing breaths. Maybe for a stretch of eight or ten blocks there is a semblance of gaiety, and then it tumbles back into night, dismal, foul, black night like frozen fat in a soup tureen. Blocks and blocks of jagged tenements, every window closed tight, every shopfront barred and bolted. Miles and miles of stone prisons without the faintest glow of warmth; the dogs and the cats are all inside with the canary birds. The cockroaches and the bedbugs too are safely incarcerated. *Tout Va Bien.* If you haven't a sou why just take a few old newspapers and make yourself a bed on the steps of a cathedral. The doors are well bolted and there will be no draughts to disturb you. Better still is to sleep outside the Metro doors; there you will have company. Look at them on a rainy night, lying there stiff as mattresses—men, women, lice, all huddled together and protected by the newspapers against spittle and the vermin that walks without legs. Look at them under the bridges or under the market sheds. How vile they look in comparison with the clean, bright vegetables stacked up like jewels. Even the dead horses and the cows and sheep hanging from the greasy hooks look more inviting. At least we will eat these tomorrow and even the intestines will serve a purpose. But these filthy beggars lying in the rain, what purpose do they serve? What good can they do us? They make us bleed for five minutes, that's all.

Oh, well, these are night thoughts produced by walking in the rain after two thousand years of Christianity. At least now the birds are well provided for, and the cats and dogs. Every time I pass the concierge's window and catch the full icy impact of her glance I have an insane desire to throttle all the birds in creation. At the bottom of every frozen heart there is a drop or two of love—just enough to feed the birds.

Still I can't get it out of my mind what a discrepancy there is between ideas and living. A permanent dislocation, though we try to cover the two with a bright awning. And it won't go. Ideas have to be wedded to action; if there is no sex, no vitality in them, there is no action. Ideas cannot exist alone in the vacuum of the mind. Ideas are related to living: liver ideas, kidney ideas, interstitial ideas, etc. If it were only for the sake of an idea Copernicus would have smashed the existent macrocosm and Columbus would have foundered in the Sargasso Sea. The aesthetics of the idea breeds flowerpots and flowerpots you put on the window sill. But if there be no rain or sun of what use putting flowerpots outside the window?

Fillmore is full of ideas about gold. The "mythos" of gold, he calls it. I like "mythos" and I like the idea of gold, but I am not obsessed by the subject and I don't see why we should make flowerpots, even of gold. He tells me that the French are hoarding their gold away in watertight compartments deep below the surface of the earth; he tells me that there is a little locomotive which runs around in these subterranean vaults and corridors. I like the idea enormously. A profound, uninterrupted silence in which the gold softly snoozes at a temperature of 17¼ degrees Centigrade. He says an army working 46 days and 37 hours would not be sufficient to count all the gold that is sunk beneath the Bank of France, and that there is a reserve supply of false teeth, bracelets, wedding rings, etc. Enough food also to last for eighty days and a lake on top of the gold pile to resist the shock of high explosives. Gold, he says, tends to become more and more invisible, a myth, and no more defalcations. Excellent! I am wondering what will happen to the world when we go off the gold standard in ideas, dress, morals, etc. *The gold standard of love!*

Up to the present, my idea in collaborating with myself has been to get off the gold standard of literature. My idea briefly has been to present a resurrection of the emotions, to depict the conduct of a human being in the stratosphere of ideas, that is, in the grip of delirium. To paint a pre-Socratic being, a creature part goat, part Titan. In short, to erect a world on the basis of the *omphalos*, not on an abstract idea nailed to a cross. Here and there you may have come across neglected statues, oases untapped, windmills overlooked by Cervantes, rivers that run uphill, women with five and six breasts ranged longitudinally along the torso. (Writing to Gauguin, Strindberg said: "*J'ai vu des arbres que ne retrouverait aucun botaniste, des animaux que Cuvier n'a jamais soupçonnés et des hommes que vous seul avez pu créer.*")

When Rembrandt hit par he went below with the gold ingots and the pemmican and the portable beds. Gold is a night word belonging to the chthonian mind: it has dream in it and mythos. We are reverting to alchemy, to that fake Alexandrian wisdom which produced our inflated symbols. Real wisdom is being stored away in the subcellars by the misers of learning. The day is coming when they will be circling around in the middle air with magnetizers; to find a piece of ore you will have to go up ten thousand feet with a pair of instruments—in a cold latitude preferably—and establish telepathic communication with the bowels of the earth and the shades of the dead. No more Klondikes. No more bonanzas. You will have to learn to sing and caper a bit, to read the zodiac and study your entrails. All the gold that is being tucked away in the pockets of the earth will have to be re-mined; all this symbolism will have to be dragged out again from the bowels of man. But first the instruments must be perfected. First it is necessary to invent better airplanes, to distinguish *where* the noise comes from and not go daffy just because you hear an explosion under your ass. And secondly it will be necessary to get adapted to the cold layers of the stratosphere, to become a cold-blooded fish of the air. No reverence. No piety. No longing. No re-

grets. No hysteria. Above all, as Philippe Datz says—
"NO DISCOURAGEMENT!"

These are sunny thoughts inspired by a vermouth
cassis at the Place de la Trinité. A Saturday afternoon
and a "misfire" book in my hands. Everything swimming
in a divine mucopus. The drink leaves a bitter herbish
taste in my mouth, the lees of our Great Western civilization, rotting now like the toenails of the saints. Women
are passing by—regiments of them—all swinging their
asses in front of me; the chimes are ringing and the buses
are climbing the sidewalk and bussing one another. The
garçon wipes the table with a dirty rag while the *patronne*
tickles the cash register with fiendish glee. A look of
vacuity on my face, blotto, vague in acuity, biting the
asses that brush by me. In the belfry opposite the hunchback strikes with a golden mallet and the pigeons scream
alarum. I open the book—the book which Nietzsche
called "the best German book there is"—and it says:

"MEN WILL BECOME MORE CLEVER AND MORE ACUTE;
BUT NOT BETTER, HAPPIER, AND STRONGER IN ACTION—OR,
AT LEAST, ONLY AT EPOCHS. I FORESEE THE TIME WHEN GOD
WILL HAVE NO MORE JOY IN THEM, BUT WILL BREAK UP EV-
ERYTHING FOR A RENEWED CREATION. I AM CERTAIN THAT
EVERYTHING IS PLANNED TO THIS END, AND THAT THE TIME
AND HOUR IN THE DISTANT FUTURE FOR THE OCCURRENCE OF
THIS RENOVATING EPOCH ARE ALREADY FIXED. BUT A LONG
TIME WILL ELAPSE FIRST, AND WE MAY STILL FOR THOU-
SANDS AND THOUSANDS OF YEARS AMUSE OURSELVES ON THIS
DEAR OLD SURFACE."

Excellent! At least a hundred years ago there was a
man who had vision enough to see that the world was
pooped out. *Our Western world!*—When I see the figures
of men and women moving listlessly behind their prison
walls, sheltered, secluded for a few brief hours, I am ap-
palled by the potentialities for drama that are still contained in these feeble bodies. Behind the gray walls there
are human sparks, and yet never a conflagration. Are
these men and women, I ask myself, or are these shadows,
shadows of puppets dangled by invisible strings? They

move in freedom apparently, but they have nowhere to go. In one realm only are they free and there they may roam at will—but they have not yet learned how to take wing. So far there have been no dreams that have taken wing. No one man has been born light enough, *gay* enough, to leave the earth! The eagles who flapped their mighty pinions for a while came crashing heavily to earth. They made us dizzy with the flap and whir of their wings. Stay on the earth, you eagles of the future! The heavens have been explored and they are empty. And what lies under the earth is empty too, filled with bones and shadows. Stay on the earth and swim another few hundred thousand years!

And now it is three o'clock in the morning and we have a couple of trollops here who are doing somersaults on the bare floor. Fillmore is walking around naked with a goblet in his hand, and that paunch of his is drumtight, hard as a fistula. All the Pernod and champagne and cognac and Anjou which he guzzled from three in the afternoon on, is gurgling in his trap like a sewer. The girls are putting their ears to his belly as if it were a music box. Open his mouth with a buttonhook and drop a slug in the slot. When the sewer gurgles I hear the bats flying out of the belfry and the dream slides into artifice.

The girls have undressed and we are examining the floor to make sure that they won't get any splinters in their ass. They are still wearing their high-heeled shoes. But the ass! The ass is worn down, scraped, sandpapered, smooth, hard, bright, as a billiard ball or the skull of a leper. On the wall is Mona's picture: she is facing northeast on a line with Cracow written in green ink. To the left of her is the Dordogne, encircled with a red pencil. Suddenly I see a dark, hairy crack in front of me set in a bright, polished billiard ball; the legs are holding me like a pair of scissors. A glance at that dark, unstitched wound and a deep fissure in my brain opens up: all the images and memories that had been laboriously or absent-mindedly assorted, labeled, documented, filed, sealed and stamped break forth pell-mell like ants pouring out of a crack in the sidewalk; the world ceases to revolve, time stops, the very nexus of my dreams is broken and dissolved and my guts spill out in a grand schizophrenic rush, an evacuation that leaves me face to face with the Absolute. I see again the great sprawling mothers of Picasso, their breasts covered with spiders, their legend hidden deep in the labyrinth. And Molly Bloom lying on a dirty mattress for eternity. On the toilet door red chalk cocks and the madonna uttering the diapason of woe. I hear a wild, hysterical laugh, a room full of lockjaw, and the body that was black glows like phosphorus. Wild, wild, utterly uncontrollable laughter, and that crack laughing at me too, laughing through the mossy whiskers, a laugh that creases the bright, polished surface of the billiard ball. Great whore and mother of man with gin in her veins. Mother of all harlots, spider rolling us in your logarithmic grave, insatiable one, fiend whose laughter rives me! I look down into that sunken crater, world lost and without traces, and I hear the bells chiming, two nuns at the Palace Stanislas and the smell of rancid butter under their dresses, manifesto never printed because it was raining, war fought to further the cause of plastic surgery, the Prince of Wales flying around the world decorating the graves of unknown heroes. Every bat flying out of the belfry a lost cause, every whoopla a groan over the radio from the private trenches of the damned. Out of that dark, unstitched wound, that sink of abominations, that cradle of black-thronged cities where the music of ideas is drowned in cold fat, out of strangled Utopias is born a clown, a being divided between beauty and ugliness, between light and chaos, a clown who when he looks down and sidelong is Satan himself and when he looks upward sees a buttered angel, a snail with wings.

When I look down into that crack I see an equation sign, the world at balance, a world reduced to zero and no trace of remainder. Not the zero on which Van Norden turned his flashlight, not the empty crack of the prematurely disillusioned man, but an Arabian zero rather, the sign from which spring endless mathematical worlds, the fulcrum which balances the stars and the light dreams and the machines lighter than air and the lightweight limbs and the explosives that produced them. In that crack I would like to penetrate up to the eyes, make them waggle ferociously, dear, crazy, metallurgical eyes. When the eyes waggle then will I hear again Dostoevski's words, hear them rolling on page after page, with minutest observation, with maddest introspection, with all the undertones of misery now lightly, humorously touched, now swelling like an organ note until the heart bursts and there is nothing left but a blinding, scorching light, the radiant light that carries off the fecundating seeds of the stars. The story of art whose roots lie in massacre.

When I look down into this fucked-out cunt of a whore I feel the whole world beneath me, a world tottering and crumbling, a world used up and polished like a leper's skull. If there were a man who dared to say all that he thought of this world there would not be left him a square foot of ground to stand on. When a man appears the world bears down on him and breaks his back. There are always too many rotten pillars left standing, too much festering humanity for man to bloom. The superstructure is a lie and the foundation is a huge quaking fear. If at intervals of centuries there does appear a man with a desperate, hungry look in his eyes, a man who would turn the world upside down in order to create a new race, the love that he brings to the world is turned to bile and he becomes a scourge. If now and then we encounter pages that explode, pages that wound and sear, that wring groans and tears and curses, know that they come from a man with his back up, a man whose only defenses left are his words and his words are always stronger than the lying, crushing weight of the world, stronger than all the racks and wheels which the cowardly invent to crush out the miracle of personality. If any man ever dared to translate all that is in his heart, to put down what is really his experience, what is truly his truth, I think then the world would go to smash, that it would be blown to smithereens and no god, no accident, no will could ever again assemble the pieces, the atoms, the indestructible elements that have gone to make up the world.

In the four hundred years since the last devouring soul appeared, the last man to know the meaning of ecstasy, there has been a constant and steady decline of man in art, in thought, in action. The world is pooped out: there isn't a dry fart left. Who that has a desperate, hungry eye can have the slightest regard for these existent governments, laws, codes, principles, ideals, ideas, totems, and taboos? If anyone knew what it meant to read the riddle of that thing which today is called a "crack" or a "hole," if anyone had the least feeling of mystery about the phenomena which are labeled "obscene," this world would crack asunder. It is the obscene horror, the dry, fucked-out aspect of things which makes this crazy civilization look like a crater. It is this great yawning gulf of nothingness which the creative spirits and mothers of the race carry between their legs. When a hungry, desperate spirit appears and makes the guinea pigs squeal it is because he knows where to put the live wire of sex, because he knows that beneath the hard carapace of indifference there is concealed the ugly gash, the wound that never heals. And he puts the live wire right between the legs; he hits below the belt, scorches the very gizzards. It is no use putting on rubber gloves; all that can be coolly and intellectually handled belongs to the carapace and a man who is intent on creation always dives beneath, to the open wound, to the festering obscene horror. He hitches his dynamo to the tenderest parts; if only blood and pus gush forth, it is something. The dry, fucked-out crater is obscene. More obscene than anything is inertia. More blasphemous than the bloodiest oath is paralysis. If there is only a gaping wound left then it must gush forth though it produce nothing but toads and bats and homunculi.

Everything is packed into a second which is either consummated or not consummated. The earth is not an arid plateau of health and comfort, but a great sprawling female with velvet torso that swells and heaves with ocean

billows; she squirms beneath the diadem of sweat and
anguish. Naked and sexed she rolls among the clouds in
the violet light of the stars. All of her, from her generous
breasts to her gleaming thighs, blazes with furious ardor.
She moves amongst the seasons and the years with a grand
whoopla that seizes the torso with paroxysmal fury, that
shakes the cobwebs out of the sky; she subsides on her
pivotal orbits with volcanic tremors. She is like a doe at
times, a doe that has fallen into a snare and lies waiting
with beating heart for the cymbals to crash and the dogs
to bark. Love and hate, despair, pity, rage, disgust—what
are these amidst the fornications of the planets? What is
war, disease, cruelty, terror, when night presents the
ecstasy of myriad blazing suns? What is this chaff we
chew in our sleep if it is not the remembrance of fang-
whorl and star cluster.

She used to say to me, Mona, in her fits of exaltation,
"you're a great human being," and though she left me
here to perish, though she put beneath my feet a great
howling pit of emptiness, the words that lie at the bottom
of my soul leap forth and they light the shadows below
me. I am one who was lost in the crowd, whom the fizzing
lights made dizzy, a zero who saw everything about him
reduced to mockery. Passed me men and women ignited
with sulfur, porters in calcium livery opening the jaws
of hell, fame walking on crutches, dwindled by the skyscrapers, chewed to a frazzle by the spiked mouth of the
machines. I walked between the tall buildings toward the
cool of the river and I saw the lights shoot up between the
ribs of the skeletons like rockets. If I was truly a great
human being, as she said, then what was the meaning of
this slavering idiocy about me? I was a man with body
and soul, I had a heart that was not protected by a steel
vault. I had moments of ecstasy and I sang with burning
sparks. I sang of the Equator, her red-feathered legs and
the islands dropping out of sight But nobody heard. A
gun fired across the Pacific falls into space because the
earth is round and pigeons fly upside down. I saw her
looking at me across the table with eyes turned to grief;

sorrow spreading inward flattened its nose against her spine; the marrow churned to pity had turned liquid. She was light as a corpse that floats in the Dead Sea. Her fingers bled with anguish and the blood turned to drool. With the wet dawn came the tolling of bells and along the fibers of my nerves the bells played ceaselessly and their tongues pounded in my heart and clanged with iron malice. Strange that the bells should toll so, but stranger still the body bursting, this woman turned to night and her maggot words gnawing through the mattress. I moved along under the Equator, heard the hideous laughter of the green-jawed hyena, saw the jackal with silken tail and the dick-dick and the spotted leopard, all left behind in the Garden of Eden. And then her sorrow widened, like the bow of a dreadnought and the weight of her sinking flooded my ears. Slime wash and sapphires slipping, sluicing through the gay neurons, and the spectrum spliced and the gunwales dipping. Soft as lion-pad I heard the gun carriages turn, saw them vomit and drool: the firmament sagged and all the stars turned black. Black ocean bleeding and the brooding stars breeding chunks of fresh-swollen flesh while overhead the birds wheeled and out of the hallucinated sky fell the balance with mortar and pestle and the bandaged eyes of justice. All that is here related moves with imaginary feet along the parallels of dead orbs; all that is seen with the empty sockets bursts like flowering grass. Out of nothingness arises the sign of infinity; beneath the ever-rising spirals slowly sinks the gaping hole. The land and the water make numbers joined, a poem written with flesh and stronger than steel or granite. Through endless night the earth whirls toward a creation unknown. . . .

Today I awoke from a sound sleep with curses of joy on my lips, with gibberish on my tongue, repeating to myself like a litany—*"Fay ce que vouldras! . . . fay ce que vouldras!"* Do anything, but let it produce joy. Do anything, but let it yield ecstasy. So much crowds into my head when I say this to myself: images, gay ones, terrible ones, maddening ones, the wolf and the goat, the spider, the crab, syphilis with her wings outstretched and the door of the womb always on the latch, always open, ready like the tomb. Lust, crime, holiness: the lives of my adored ones, the failures of my adored ones, the words they left behind them, the words they left unfinished; the good they dragged after them and the evil, the sorrow, the discord, the rancor, the strife they created. But above all, *the ecstasy!*

Things, certain things about my old idols bring the tears to my eyes: the interruptions, the disorder, the violence, above all, the hatred they aroused. When I think of their deformities, of the monstrous styles they chose, of the flatulence and tediousness of their works, of all the chaos and confusion they wallowed in, of the obstacles they heaped up about them, I feel an exaltation. They were all mired in their own dung. All men who over-elaborated. So true is it that I am almost tempted to say: "Show me a man who over-elaborates and I will show you a great man!" What is called their "over-elaboration" is my meat: it is the sign of struggle, it is struggle itself with all the fibers clinging to it, the very aura and ambiance of the discordant spirit. And when you show me a man who expresses himself perfectly I will not say that he is not great, but I will say that I am unattracted . . . I miss the cloying qualities. When I reflect that the task which the artist implicitly sets himself is to overthrow existing values, to make of the chaos about him an order which is his own, to sow strife and ferment so that by the emotional release those who are dead may be restored to life, then it is that I run with joy to the great and imperfect ones, their confusion nourishes me, their stuttering is like divine music to my ears. I see in the beautifully bloated pages that follow the interruptions the erasure of petty intrusions, of the dirty footprints, as it were, of cowards, liars, thieves, vandals, calumniators. I see in the swollen muscles of their lyric throats the staggering effort that must be made to turn the wheel over, to pick up the pace where one has left off. I see that behind the daily annoyances and intrusions, behind the cheap, glittering malice of the feeble and inert, there stands the symbol of life's frustrating power, and that he who would create order, he who would sow strife and discord, because he is imbued with will, such a man must go again and again to the stake and the gibbet. I see that behind the nobility of his gestures there lurks the specter of the ridiculousness of it all—that he is not only sublime, but absurd.

Once I thought that to be human was the highest aim a man could have, but I see now that it was meant to destroy me. Today I am proud to say that I am *inhuman*, that I belong not to men and governments, that I have nothing to do with creeds and principles. I have nothing to do with the creaking machinery of humanity—I belong to the earth! I say that lying on my pillow and I can feel the horns sprouting from my temples. I can see about me all those cracked forebears of mine dancing around the bed, consoling me, egging me on, lashing me with their serpent tongues, grinning and leering at me with their skulking skulls. *I am inhuman!* I say it with a mad, hallucinated grin, and I will keep on saying it though it rain crocodiles. Behind my words are all those grinning, leering, skulking skulls, some dead and grinning a long time, some grinning as if they had lockjaw, some grinning with the grimace of a grin, the foretaste and aftermath of what is always going on. Clearer than all I see my own grinning skull, see the skeleton dancing in the wind, serpents issuing from the rotted tongue and the bloated pages of ecstasy slimed with excrement. And I join my slime, my excrement, my madness, my ecstasy to the great circuit which flows through the subterranean vaults of the flesh. All this unbidden, unwanted, drunken vomit will flow on endlessly through the minds of those to come in the inexhaustible vessel that contains the history of the race. Side by side with the human race there runs another race of beings, the inhuman ones, the race of artists who, goaded by known impulses, take the lifeless mass of humanity and by the fever and ferment with which they imbue it turn this soggy dough into bread and the bread into wine and the wine into song. Out of the dead compost and the inert slag they breed a song that contaminates. I see this other race of individuals ransacking the universe, turning everything upside down, their feet always moving in blood and tears, their hands always empty, always clutching and grasping for the beyond, for the god out of reach: slaying everything within reach in order to quiet the monster that gnaws at their vitals. I see that when they tear their hair with the effort to comprehend, to seize this forever unattainable, I see that when they bellow like crazed beasts and rip and gore, I see that this is right, that there is no other path to pursue. A man who belongs to this race must stand up on the high place with gibberish in his mouth and rip out his entrails. It is right and just, because he must! And anything that falls short of this frightening spectacle, anything less shuddering, less terrifying, less mad, less intoxicated, less contaminating, is not art. The rest is counterfeit. The rest is human. The rest belongs to life and lifelessness.

When I think of Stavrogin for example, I think of some divine monster standing on a high place and flinging to us his torn bowels. In *The Possessed* the earth quakes: it is not the catastrophe that befalls the imaginative individual, but a cataclysm in which a large portion of humanity is buried, wiped out forever. Stavrogin was Dostoevski and Dostoevski was the sum of all those contradictions which either paralyze a man or lead him to the heights. There was no world too low for him to enter, no place to high for him to fear to ascend. He went the whole gamut, from the abyss to the stars. It is a pity that we shall never again have the opportunity to see a man placed at the very core of mystery and, by his flashes, illuminating for us the depth and immensity of the darkness.

Today I am aware of my lineage. I have no need to consult my horoscope or my genealogical chart. What is written in the stars, or in my blood, I know nothing of. I know that I spring from the mythological founders of the race. The man who raises the holy bottle to his lips, the criminal who kneels in the marketplace, the innocent one who discovers that *all* corpses stink, the madman who dances with lightning in his hands, the friar who lifts his skirts to pee over the world, the fanatic who ransacks libraries in order to find the Word—all these are fused in me, all these make my confusion, my ecstasy. If I am inhuman it is because my world has slopped over its human bounds, because to be human seems like a poor, sorry, miserable affair, limited by the senses, restricted by moralities and codes, defined by platitudes and isms. I am pouring the juice of the grape down my gullet and I find wisdom in it, but my wisdom is not born of the grape, my intoxication owes nothing to wine. . . .

I want to make a detour of those lofty arid mountain ranges where one dies of thirst and cold, that "extra-temporal" history, that absolute of time and space where there exists neither man, beast, nor vegetation, where one goes crazy with loneliness, with language that is mere words, where everything is unhooked, ungeared, out of joint with the times. I want a world of men and women, of trees that do not talk (because there is too much talk in the world as it is!) of rivers that carry you to places, not rivers that are legends, but rivers that put you in touch with other men and women, with architecture, religion, plants, animals—rivers that have boats on them and in which men drown, drown not in myth and legend and books and dust of the past, but in time and space and history. I want rivers that make oceans such as Shakespeare and Dante, rivers which do not dry up in the void of the past. Oceans, yes! Let us have more oceans, new oceans that blot out the past, oceans that create new geological formations, new topographical vistas and strange, terrifying continents, oceans that destroy and preserve at the same time, oceans that we can sail on, take off to new discoveries, new horizons. Let us have more oceans, more upheavals, more wars, more holocausts. Let us have a world of men and women with dynamos between their legs, a world of natural fury, of passion, action, drama, dreams, madness, a world that produces ecstasy and not dry farts. I believe that today more than ever a book should be sought after even if it has only *one* great page in it: we must search for fragments, splinters, toenails, anything that has ore in it, anything that is capable of resuscitating the body and soul.

It may be that we are doomed, that there is no hope for us, *any of us,* but if that is so then let us set up a last agonizing, bloodcurdling howl, a screech of defiance, a war whoop! Away with lamentation! Away with elegies and dirges! Away with biographies and histories, and libraries and museums! Let the dead eat the dead. Let us living ones dance about the rim of the crater, a last expiring dance. But a dance!

"I love everything that flows," said the great blind Milton of our times. I was thinking of him this morning when I awoke with a great bloody shout of joy: I was thinking of his rivers and trees and all that world of night which he is exploring. Yes, I said to myself, I too love everything that flows: rivers, sewers, lava, semen, blood, bile, words, sentences. I love the amniotic fluid when it spills out of the bag. I love the kidney with its painful gallstones, its gravel and what-not; I love the urine that pours out scalding and the clap that runs endlessly; I love the words of hysterics and the sentences that flow on like dysentery and mirror all the sick images of the soul; I love the great rivers like the Amazon and the Orinoco, where crazy men like Moravagine float on through dream and legend in an open boat and drown in the blind mouths of the river. I love everything that flows, even the menstrual flow that carries away the seed unfecund. I love scripts that flow, be they hieratic, esoteric, perverse, polymorph, or unilateral. I love everything that flows, everything that has time in it and becoming, that brings us back to the beginning where there is never end: the violence of the prophets, the obscenity that is ecstasy, the wisdom of the fanatic, the priest with his rubber litany, the foul words of the whore, the spittle that floats away in the gutter, the milk of the breast and the bitter honey that pours from the womb, all that is fluid, melting, dissolute and dissolvent, all the pus and dirt that in flowing is purified, that loses its sense of origin, that makes the great circuit toward death and dissolution. The great incestuous wish is to flow on, one with time, to merge the great image of the beyond with the here and now. A fatuous, suicidal wish that is constipated by words and paralyzed by thought.

It was close to dawn on Christmas Day when we came home from the Rue d'Odessa with a couple of Negresses from the telephone company. The fire was out and we were all so tired that we climbed into bed with our clothes on. The one I had, who had been like a bounding leopard all evening, fell sound asleep as I was climbing over her. For a while I worked over her as one works over a person who has been drowned or asphyxiated. Then I gave it up and fell sound asleep myself.

All during the holidays we had champagne morning, noon and night—the cheapest and the best champagne. With the turn of the year I was to leave for Dijon where I had been offered a trivial post as exchange professor of English, one of those Franco-American amity arrangements which is supposed to promote understanding and good will between sister republics. Fillmore was more elated than I by the prospect—he had good reason to be. For me it was just a transfer from one purgatory to another. There was no future ahead of me; there wasn't even a salary attached to the job. One was supposed to consider himself fortunate to enjoy the privilege of spreading the gospel of Franco-American amity. It was a job for a rich man's son.

The night before I left we had a good time. About dawn it began to snow: we walked about from one quarter to another taking a last look at Paris. Passing through the Rue St. Dominique we suddenly fell upon a little square and there was the Eglise Ste.-Clotilde. Peo-

ple were going to mass. Fillmore, whose head was still
a little cloudy, was bent on going to mass too. "For the
fun of it!" as he put it. I felt somewhat uneasy about it;
in the first place I had never attended a mass, and in the
second place I looked seedy and felt seedy. Fillmore, too,
looked rather battered, even more disreputable than myself; his big slouch hat was on assways and his overcoat
was still full of sawdust from the last joint we had been
in. However, we marched in. The worst they could do
would be to throw us out.

I was so astounded by the sight that greeted my eyes
that I lost all uneasiness. It took me a little while to get
adjusted to the dim light. I stumbled around behind Fillmore, holding his sleeve. A weird, unearthly noise as-
sailed my ears, a sort of hollow drone that rose up out
of the cold flagging. A huge, dismal tomb it was with
mourners shuffling in and out. A sort of antechamber to
the world below. Temperature about 55 or 60 Fahrenheit.
No music except this undefinable dirge manufactured in
the subcellar—like a million heads of cauliflower wailing
in the dark. People in shrouds were chewing away with
that hopeless, dejected look of beggars who hold out their
hands in a trance and mumble an unintelligible appeal.

That this sort of thing existed I knew, but then one
also knows that there are slaughterhouses and morgues
and dissecting rooms. One instinctively avoids such
places. In the street I had often passed a priest with a
little prayer book in his hands laboriously memorizing
his lines. *Idiot*, I would say to myself, and let it go at that.
In the street one meets with all forms of dementia and
the priest is by no means the most striking. Two thousand years of it has deadened us to the idiocy of it.
However, when you are suddenly transported to the very
midst of his realm, when you see the little world in which
the priest functions like an alarm clock, you are apt to
have entirely different sensations.

For a moment all this slaver and twitching of the lips
almost began to have a meaning. Something was going
on, some kind of dumb show which, not rendering me

wholly stupefied, held me spellbound. All over the world, wherever there are these dim-lit tombs, you have this incredible spectacle—the same mean temperature, the same crepuscular glow, the same buzz and drone. All over Christendom, at certain stipulated hours, people in black are groveling before the altar where the priest stands up with a little book in one hand and a dinner bell or atomizer in the other and mumbles to them in a language which, even if it were comprehensible, no longer contains a shred of meaning. Blessing them, most likely. Blessing the country, blessing the ruler, blessing the firearms and the battleships and the ammunition and the hand grenades. Surrounding him on the altar are little boys dressed like angels of the Lord who sing alto and soprano. Innocent lambs. All in skirts, sexless, like the priest himself who is usually flat-footed and near-sighted to boot. A fine epicence caterwauling. Sex in a jockstrap, to the tune of J-mol.

I was taking it in as best I could in the dim light. Fascinating and stupefying at the same time. All over the civilized world, I thought to myself. All over the world. Marvelous. Rain or shine, hail, sleet, snow, thunder, lightning, war, famine, pestilence—makes not the slightest difference. Always the same mean temperature, the same mumbo jumbo, the same high-laced shoes and the little angels of the Lord singing soprano and alto. Near the exit a little slot-box—to carry on the heavenly work. So that God's blessing may rain down upon king and country and battleships and high explosives and tanks and airplanes, so that the worker may have more strength in his arms, strength to slaughter horses and cows and sheep, strength to punch holes in iron girders, strength to sew buttons on other people's pants, strength to sell carrots and sewing machines and automobiles, strength to exterminate insects and clean stables and unload garbage cans and scrub lavatories, strength to write headlines and chop tickets in the subway. Strength . . . strength. All that lip chewing and hornswoggling just to furnish a little strength!

We were moving about from one spot to another, surveying the scene with that clearheadedness which comes after an all-night session. We must have made ourselves pretty conspicuous shuffling about that way with our coat collars turned up and never once crossing ourselves and never once moving our lips except to whisper some callous remark. Perhaps everything would have passed off without notice if Fillmore hadn't insisted on walking past the altar in the midst of the ceremony. He was looking for the exit, and he thought while he was at it, I suppose, that he would take a good squint at the holy of holies, get a close-up on it, as it were. We had gotten safely by and were marching toward a crack of light which must have been the way out when a priest suddenly stepped out of the gloom and blocked our path. Wanted to know where we were going and what we were doing. We told him politely enough that we were looking for the exit. We said "exit" because at the moment we were so flabbergasted that we couldn't think of the French for exit. Without a word of response he took us firmly by the arm and, opening the door, a side door it was, he gave us a push and out we tumbled into the blinding light of day. It happened so suddenly and unexpectedly that when we hit the sidewalk we were in a daze. We walked a few paces, blinking our eyes, and then instinctively we both turned round; the priest was still standing on the steps, pale as a ghost and scowling like the devil himself. He must have been sore as hell. Later, thinking back on it, I couldn't blame him for it. But at that moment, seeing him with his long skirts and the little skull cap on his cranium, he looked so ridiculous that I burst out laughing. I looked at Fillmore and he began to laugh too. For a full minute we stood there laughing right in the poor bugger's face. He was so bewildered, I guess, that for a moment he didn't know what to do; suddenly, however, he started down the steps on the run, shaking his fist at us as if he were in earnest. When he swung out of the enclosure he was on the gallop. By this time some preservative instinct warned me to get a move on. I grabbed Fillmore by the coat sleeve and started to run. He was saying, like an idiot: "No, no! I won't run!"—"Come on!" I yelled, "we'd better get out of here. That guy's mad clean through." And off we ran, beating it as fast as our legs would carry us.

On the way to Dijon, still laughing about the affair, my thoughts reverted to a ludicrous incident, of a somewhat similar nature, which occurred during my brief sojourn in Florida. It was during the celebrated boom when, like thousands of others, I was caught with my pants down. Trying to extricate myself I got caught, along with a friend of mine, in the very neck of the bottle. Jacksonville, where we were marooned for about six weeks, was practically in a state of siege. Every bum on earth, and a lot of guys who had never been bums before, seemed to have drifted into Jacksonville. The YMCA, the Salvation Army, the firehouses and police stations, the hotels, the lodging houses, everything was full up. *Complet* absolutely, and signs everywhere to that effect. The residents of Jacksonville had become so hardened that it seemed to me as if they were walking around in coats of mail. It was the old business of food again. Food and a place to flop. Food was coming up from below in trainloads—oranges and grapefruit and all sorts of juicy edibles. We used to pass by the freight sheds looking for rotten fruit—but even that was scarce.

One night, in desperation, I dragged my friend Joe to a synagogue, during the service. It was a Reformed congregation, and the rabbi impressed me rather favorably. The music got me too—that piercing lamentation of the Jews. As soon as the service was over I marched to the rabbi's study and requested an interview with him. He received me decently enough—until I made clear my mission. Then he grew absolutely frightened. I had only asked him for a handout on behalf of my friend Joe and myself. You would have thought, from the way he looked at me, that I had asked to rent the synagogue as a bowling alley. To cap it all, he suddenly asked me pointblank if I was a Jew or not. When I answered no, he seemed perfectly outraged. Why, pray, had I come to a Jewish pastor for aid? I told him naively that I had always had more faith in the Jews than in the Gentiles. I said it modestly, as if it were one of my peculiar defects. It was the truth too. But he wasn't a bit flattered. No, siree. He was horrified. To get rid of me he wrote out a note to the Salvation Army people. "That's the place for you to address yourself," he said, and brusquely turned away to tend his flock.

The Salvation Army, of course, had nothing to offer us. If we had had a quarter apiece we might have rented a mattress on the floor. But we hadn't a nickel between us. We went to the park and stretched ourselves out on a bench. It was raining and so we covered ourselves with newspapers. Weren't there more than a half hour, I imagine, when a cop came along and, without a word of warning, gave us such a sound fanning that we were up and on our feet in a jiffy, and dancing a bit too, though we weren't in any mood for dancing. I felt so goddamned sore and miserable, so dejected, so lousy, after being whacked over the ass by that half-witted bastard, that I could have blown up the City Hall.

The next morning, in order to get even with these hospitable sons of bitches, we presented ourselves bright and early at the door of a Catholic priest. This time I let Joe do the talking. He was Irish and he had a bit of a brogue. He had very soft, blue eyes, too, and he could make them water a bit when he wanted to. A sister in black opened the door for us; she didn't ask us inside, however. We were to wait in the vestibule until she went and called for the good father. In a few minutes he came, the good father, puffing like a locomotive. And what was it we wanted disturbing his likes at that hour of the morning? Something to eat and a place to flop, we answered innocently. And where did we hail from, the good father wanted to know at once. From New York. From New York, eh? Then ye'd better be gettin' back there as fast as ye kin, me lads, and without another word the big, bloated turnip-faced bastard shoved the door in our face.

About an hour later, drifting around helplessly like a couple of drunken schooners, we happened to pass by the rectory again. So help me God if the big, lecherous-looking turnip wasn't backing out of the alley in a limousine! As he swung past us he blew a cloud of smoke into our eyes. As though to say—"*That* for you!" A beautiful limousine it was, with a couple of spare tires in the back, and the good father sitting at the wheel with a big cigar in his mouth. Must have been a Corona Corona, so fat and luscious it was. Sitting pretty he was, and no two ways about it. I couldn't see whether he had skirts on or not. I could only see the gravy trickling from his lips— and the big cigar with that fifty-cent aroma.

All the way to Dijon I got to reminiscing about the past. I thought of all the things I might have said and done, which I hadn't said or done, in the bitter, humiliating moments when just to ask for a crust of bread is to make yourself less than a worm. Stone sober as I was, I was still smarting from those old insults and injuries. I could still feel that whack over the ass which the cop gave me in the park—though that was a mere bagatelle, a little dancing lesson, you might say. All over the States I wandered, and into Canada and Mexico. The same story everywhere. If you want bread you've got to get in harness, get in lock step. Over all the earth a gray desert, a carpet of steel and cement. Production! More nuts and bolts, more barbed wire, more dog biscuits, more lawn mowers, more ball bearings, more high explosives, more tanks, more poison gas, more soap, more toothpaste, more newspapers, more education, more churches, more libraries, more museums. *Forward!* Time presses. The embryo is pushing through the neck of the womb, and there's not even a gob of spit to ease the passage. A dry, strangulating birth. Not a wail, not a chirp. *Salut au monde!* Salute of twenty-one guns bombinating from the rectum. "I wear my hat as I please, indoors or out," said Walt. That was a time when you could still get a hat to fit your head. But time passes. To get a hat that fits now you have to walk to the electric chair. They give you a skull cap. A tight fit, what? But no matter! It fits.

You have to be in a strange country like France, walking the meridian that separates the hemispheres of life and death, to know what incalculable vistas yawn ahead. *The body electric! The democratic soul! Flood tide!* Holy Mother of God, what does this crap mean? The earth is parched and cracked. Men and women come together like broods of vultures over a stinking carcass, to mate and fly apart again. Vultures who drop from the clouds like heavy stones. Talons and beak, that's what we are! A huge intestinal apparatus with a nose for dead meat. *Forward!* Forward without pity, without compassion, without love, without forgiveness. Ask no quarter and give none! More battleships, more poison gas, more high explosives! More gonococci! More streptococci! More bombing machines! More and more of it—until the whole fucking works is blown to smithereens, and the earth with it!

Stepping off the train I knew immediately that I had made a fatal mistake. The Lycée was a little distance from the station; I walked down the main street in the early dusk of winter, feeling my way toward my destination. A light snow was falling, the trees sparkled with frost. Passed a couple of huge, empty cafés that looked like dismal waiting rooms. Silent, empty gloom—that's how it impressed me. A hopeless, jerkwater town where mustard is turned out in carload lots, in vats and tuns and barrels and pots and cute-looking little jars.

The first glance at the Lycée sent a shudder through me. I felt so undecided that at the entrance I stopped to debate whether I would go in or not. But as I hadn't the price of a return ticket there wasn't much use debating the question. I thought for a moment of sending a wire to Fillmore, but then I was stumped to know what excuse to make. The only thing to do was to walk in with my eyes shut.

It happened that M. le Proviseur was out—his day off, so they said. A little hunchback came forward and offered to escort me to the office of M. le Censeur, second in charge. I walked a little behind him, fascinated by the grotesque way in which he hobbled along. He was a little monster, such as can be seen on the porch of any half-assed cathedral in Europe.

The office of M. le Censeur was large and bare. I sat down in a stiff chair to wait while the hunchback darted off to search for him. I almost felt at home. The atmosphere of the place reminded me vividly of certain charity bureaus back in the States where I used to sit by the hour waiting for some mealy-mouthed bastard to come and cross-examine me.

Suddenly the door opened and, with a mincing step, M. le Censeur came prancing in. It was all I could do to suppress a titter. He had on just such a frock coat as Boris used to wear, and over his forehead there hung a bang, a sort of spitcurl such as Smerdyakov might have worn. Grave and brittle, with a lynxlike eye, he wasted no words of cheer on me. At once he brought forth the sheets on which were written the names of the students, the hours, the classes, etc., all in a meticulous hand. He told me how much coal and wood I was allowed and after that he promptly informed me that I was at liberty to do as I pleased in my spare time. This last was the first good thing I had heard him say. It sounded so reassuring that I quickly said a prayer for France—for the army and for the navy, the educational system, the *bistros,* the whole *goddamned works.*

This folderol completed, he rang a little bell, whereupon the hunchback promptly appeared to escort me to the office of M. l'Econome. Here the atmosphere was somewhat different. More like a freight station, with bills of lading and rubber stamps everywhere, and pastyfaced clerks scribbling away with broken pens in huge, cumbersome ledgers. My dole of coal and wood portioned out, off we marched, the hunchback and I, with a wheelbarrow, toward the dormitory. I was to have a room on the top floor, in the same wing as the *pions.* The situation was taking on a humorous aspect. I didn't know what the hell to expect next. Perhaps a spittoon. The whole thing smacked very much of preparation for a campaign; the only things missing were a knapsack and rifle—and a brass slug.

The room assigned me was rather large, with a small stove to which was attached a crooked pipe that made an elbow just over the iron cot. A big chest for the coal and wood stood near the door. The windows gave out on a row of forlorn little houses all made of stone in which lived the grocer, the baker, the shoemaker, the butcher, etc.—all imbecilic-looking clodhoppers. I glanced over the rooftops toward the bare hills where a train was clattering. The whistle of the locomotive screamed mournfully and hysterically.

After the hunchback had made the fire for me I inquired about the grub. It was not quite time for dinner. I flopped on the bed, with my overcoat on, and pulled the covers over me. Beside me was the eternal rickety night table in which the piss pot is hidden away. I stood the alarm on the table and watched the minutes ticking off. Into the well of the room a bluish light filtered in from the street. I listened to the trucks rattling by as I gazed vacantly at the stove pipe, at the elbow where it was held together with bits of wire. The coal chest intrigued me. Never in my life had I occupied a room with a coal chest. And never in my life had I built a fire or taught children. Nor, for that matter, never in my life had I worked without pay. I felt free and chained at the same time—like one feels just before election, when all the crooks have been nominated and you are beseeched to vote for the right man. I felt like a hired man, like a jack-of-all-trades, like a hunter, like a rover, like a galley slave, like a pedagogue, like a worm and a louse. I was free, but my limbs were shackled. A democratic soul with a free meal ticket, but no power of locomotion, no voice. I felt like a jellyfish nailed to a plank. Above all, I felt hungry. The hands were moving slowly. Still ten more minutes to kill before the fire alarm would go off. The shadows in the room deepened. It grew frightfully

silent, a tense stillness that tautened my nerves. Little
dabs of snow clung to the windowpanes. Far away a
locomotive gave out a shrill scream. Then a dead silence
again. The stove had commenced to glow, but there was
no heat coming from it. I began to fear that I might doze
off and miss the dinner. That would mean lying awake
on an empty belly all night. I got panic-stricken.

Just a moment before the gong went off I jumped out
of bed and, locking the door behind me, I bolted downstairs to the courtyard. There I got lost. One quadrangle
after another, one staircase after another. I wandered in
and out of the buildings searching frantically for the
refectory. Passed a long line of youngsters marching in
a column to God knows where; they moved along like
a chain gang, with a slave driver at the head of the column. Finally I saw an energetic-looking individual, with
a derby, heading toward me. I stopped him to ask the
way to the refectory. Happened I stopped the right man.
It was M. le Proviseur, and he seemed delighted to have
stumbled on me. Wanted to know right away if I were
comfortably settled, if there was anything more he could
do for me. I told him everything was O.K. Only it was
a bit chilly, I ventured to add. He assured me that it was
rather unusual, this weather. Now and then the fogs
came on and a bit of snow, and then it became unpleas-
ant for a while, and so on and so forth. All the while he
had me by the arm, guiding me toward the refectory. He
seemed like a very decent chap. A regular guy, I thought
to myself. I even went so far as to imagine that I might
get chummy with him later on, that he'd invite me to
his room on a bitter cold night and make a hot grog for
me. I imagined all sorts of friendly things in the few moments it required to reach the door of the refectory.
Here, my mind racing on at a mile a minute, he suddenly
shook hands with me and, doffing his hat, bade me good
night. I was so bewildered that I tipped my hat also.
It was the regular thing to do, I soon found out. Whenever you pass a prof, or even M. l'Econome, you doff
the hat. Might pass the same guy a dozen times a day.

Makes no difference. You've got to give the salute, even though your hat is worn out. It's the polite thing to do.

Anyway, I had found the refectory. Like an East Side clinic it was, with tiled walls, bare light, and marble-topped tables. And of course a big stove with an elbow pipe. The dinner wasn't served yet. A cripple was running in and out with dishes and knives and forks and bottles of wine. In a corner several young men conversing animatedly. I went up to them and introduced myself. They gave me a most cordial reception. Almost too cordial, in fact. I couldn't quite make it out. In a jiffy the room began to fill up; I was presented from one to the other quickly. Then they formed a circle about me and, filling the glasses, they began to sing. . . .

> L'autre soir l'idée m'est venue
> Cré nom de Zeus d'enculer un pendu;
> Le vent se lève sur la potence,
> Voilà mon pendu qui se balance,
> J'ai dû l'enculer en sautant,
> Cré nom de Zeus, on est jamais content.

> Baiser dans un con trop petit,
> Cré nom de Zeus, on s'écorche le vit;
> Baiser dans un con trop large,
> On ne sait pas ou l'on décharge;
> Se branler étant bien emmerdant,
> Cré nom de Zeus, on est jamais content.

With this, Quasimodo announced the dinner.

They were a cheerful group, *les surveillants*. There was Kroa who belched like a pig and always let off a loud fart when he sat down to table. He could fart thirteen times in succession, they informed me. He held the record. Then there was Monsieur le Prince, an athlete who was fond of wearing a tuxedo in the evening when he went to town; he had a beautiful complexion, just like a girl, and never touched the wine nor read anything that might tax his brain. Next to him sat Petit Paul, from the

Midi, who thought of nothing but cunt all the time; he used to say every day—"*à partir de jeudi je ne parlerai plus de femmes.*" He and Monsieur le Prince were inseparable. Then there was Passeleau, a veritable young scallywag who was studying medicine and who borrowed right and left; he talked incessantly of Ronsard, Villon and Rabelais. Opposite me sat Mollesse, agitator and organizer of the *pions,* who insisted on weighing the meat to see if it wasn't short a few grams. He occupied a little room in the infirmary. His supreme enemy was Monsieur l'Econome, which was nothing particularly to his credit since everybody hated this individual. For companion Mollesse had one called Le Pénible, a dour-looking chap with a hawklike profile who practiced the strictest economy and acted as moneylender. He was like an engraving by Albrecht Dürer—a composite of all the dour, sour, morose, bitter, unfortunate, unlucky and introspective devils who compose the pantheon of Germany's medieval knights. A Jew, no doubt. At any rate, he was killed in an automobile accident shortly after my arrival, a circumstance which left me twenty-three francs to the good. With the exception of Renaud who sat beside me, the others have faded out of my memory; they belonged to that category of colorless individuals who make up the world of engineers, architects, dentists, pharmacists, teachers, etc. There was nothing to distinguish them from the clods whom they would later wipe their boots on. They were zeros in every sense of the word, ciphers who form the nucleus of a respectable and lamentable citizenry. They ate with their heads down and were always the first to clamor for a second helping. They slept soundly and never complained; they were neither gay nor miserable. The indifferent ones whom Dante consigned to the vestibule of Hell. The uppercrusters.

It was the custom after dinner to go immediately to town, unless one was on duty in the dormitories. In the center of town were the cafés—huge, dreary halls where the somnolent merchants of Dijon gathered to play cards and listen to the music. It was warm in the cafés, that is the best I can say for them. The seats were fairly comfortable, too. And there were always a few whores about who, for a glass of beer or a cup of coffee, would sit and chew the fat with you. The music, on the other hand, was atrocious. Such music! On a winter's night, in a dirty hole like Dijon, nothing can be more harassing, more nerve-racking, than the sound of a French orchestra. Particularly one of those lugubrious female orchestras with everything coming in squeaks and farts, with a dry, algebraic rhythm and the hygienic consistency of toothpaste. A wheezing and scraping performed at so many francs the hour—and the devil take the hindmost! The melancholy of it! As if old Euclid had stood up on his hind legs and swallowed prussic acid. The whole realm of Idea so thoroughly exploited by the reason that there is nothing left of which to make music except the empty slats of the accordion, through which the wind whistles and tears the ether to tatters. However, to speak of music in connection with this outpost is like dreaming of champagne when you are in the death cell. Music was the least of my worries. I didn't even think of cunt, so dismal, so chill, so barren, so gray was it all. On the way home the first night I noticed on the door of a café an inscription from the *Gargantua*. Inside the café it was like a morgue. However, *forward!*

I had plenty of time on my hands and not a sou to spend. Two or three hours of conversational lessons a day, and that was all. And what use was it, teaching these poor bastards English? I felt sorry as hell for them. All morning plugging away on *John Gilpin's Ride*, and in the afternoon coming to me to practice a dead language. I thought of the good time I had wasted reading Virgil or wading through such incomprehensible nonsense as *Hermann und Dorothea*. The insanity of it! Learning, the empty breadbasket! I thought of Carl who can recite *Faust* backwards, who never writes a book without praising the shit out of his immortal, incorruptible Goethe. And yet he hadn't sense enough to take on a rich cunt and get himself a change of underwear. There's something obscene in this love of the past which ends in breadlines and dugouts. Something obscene about this spiritual racket which permits an idiot to sprinkle holy water over Big Berthas and dreadnoughts and high explosives. Every man with a bellyful of the classics is an enemy to the human race.

Here was I, supposedly to spread the gospel of Franco-American amity—the emissary of a corpse who, after he had plundered right and left, after he had caused untold suffering and misery, dreamed of establishing universal peace. Ffui! What did they expect me to talk about, I wonder? About *Leaves of Grass*, about the tariff walls, about the Declaration of Independence, about the latest gang war? What? Just what, I'd like to know. Well, I'll tell you—I never mentioned these things. I started right off the bat with a lesson in the physiology of love. How the elephants make love—that was it! It caught like wildfire. After the first day there were no more empty benches. After that first lesson in English they were standing at the door waiting for me. We got along swell together. They asked all sorts of questions, as though they had never learned a damned thing. I let them fire away. I taught them to ask still more ticklish questions. *Ask anything!*—that was my motto. I'm here as a plenipotentiary from the realm of free spirits. I'm here to create a fever and a ferment. "In some ways," says an eminent astronomer, "the material universe appears to be passing away like a tale that is told, dissolving into nothingness like a vision." That seems to be the general feeling underlying the empty breadbasket of learning. Myself, I don't believe it. I don't believe a fucking thing these bastards try to shove down our throats.

Between sessions, if I had no book to read, I would go upstairs to the dormitory and chat with the *pions*. They were delightfully ignorant of all that was going on —especially in the world of art. Almost as ignorant as the students themselves. It was as if I had gotten into a private little madhouse with no exit signs. Sometimes I snooped around under the arcades, watching the kids marching along with huge hunks of bread stuck in their dirty mugs. I was always hungry myself, since it was impossible for me to go to breakfast which was handed out at some ungodly hour of the morning, just when the bed was getting toasty. Huge bowls of blue coffee with chunks of white bread and no butter to go with it. For lunch, beans or lentils with bits of meat thrown in to make it look appetizing. Food fit for a chain gang, for rock breakers. Even the wine was lousy. Things were either diluted or bloated. There were calories, but no cuisine. M. l'Econome was responsible for it all. So they said. I don't believe that, either. He was paid to keep our heads just above the water line. He didn't ask if we were suffering from piles or carbuncles; he didn't inquire if we had delicate palates or the intestines of wolves. Why should he? He was hired at so many grams the plate to produce so many kilowatts of energy. Everything in terms of horse power. It was all carefully reckoned in the fat ledgers which the pasty-faced clerks scribbled in morning, noon and night. Debit and credit, with a red line down the middle of the page.

Roaming around the quadrangle with an empty belly most of the time I got to feel slightly mad. Like Charles the Silly, poor devil—only I had no Odette Champdivers with whom to play stinkfinger. Half the time I had to grub cigarettes from the students, and during the lessons sometimes I munched a bit of dry bread with them. As the fire was always going out on me I soon used up my allotment of wood. It was the devil's own time coaxing a little wood out of the ledger clerks. Finally I got so riled up about it that I would go out in the street and hunt for firewood, like an Arab. Astonishing how little firewood you could pick up in the streets of Dijon. However, these little foraging expeditions brought me into strange precincts. Got to know the little street named after a M. Philibert Papillon—a dead musician, I believe—where there was a cluster of whorehouses. It was always more cheerful hereabouts; there was the

smell of cooking, and wash hanging out to dry. Once in a
while I caught a glimpse of the poor half-wits who
lounged about inside. They were better off than the poor
devils in the center of town whom I used to bump into
whenever I walked through a department store. I did
that frequently in order to get warm. They were doing
it for the same reason, I suppose. Looking for someone
to buy them a coffee. They looked a little crazy, with the
cold and the loneliness. The whole town looked a bit
crazy when the blue of evening settled over it. You could
walk up and down the main drive any Thursday in the
week till doomsday and never meet an expansive soul.
Sixty or seventy thousand people—perhaps more—
wrapped in woolen underwear and nowhere to go and
nothing to do. Turning out mustard by the carload.
Female orchestras grinding out *The Merry Widow*. Silver service in the big hotels. The ducal palace rotting
away, stone by stone, limb by limb. The trees screeching
with frost. A ceaseless clatter of wooden shoes. The Uni-
versity celebrating the death of Goethe, or the birth, I
don't remember which. (Usually it's the deaths that are
celebrated.) Idiotic affair, anyway. Everybody yawning
and stretching.

Coming through the high driveway into the quadrangle a sense of abysmal futility always came over me.
Outside bleak and empty; inside, bleak and empty. A
scummy sterility hanging over the town, a fog of book-
learning. Slag and cinders of the past. Around the interior courts were ranged the classrooms, little shacks
such as you might see in the North woods, where the
pedagogues gave free rein to their voices. On the black-
board the futile abracadabra which the future citizens of
the republic would have to spend their lives forgetting.
Once in a while the parents were received in the big
reception room just off the driveway, where there were
busts of the heroes of antiquity, such as Molière, Racine,
Corneille, Voltaire, etc., all the scarecrows whom the
cabinet ministers mention with moist lips whenever an
immortal is added to the waxworks. (No bust of Villon,

no bust of Rabelais, no bust of Rimbaud.) Anyway, they met here in solemn conclave, the parents and the stuffed shirts whom the State hires to bend the minds of the young. Always this bending process, this landscape gardening to make the mind more attractive. And the youngsters came too, occasionally—the little sunflowers who would soon be transplanted from the nursery in order to decorate the municipal grassplots. Some of them were just rubber plants easily dusted with a torn chemise. All of them jerking away for dear life in the dormitories as soon as night came on. The dormitories! where the red lights glowed, where the bell rang like a fire alarm, where the treads were hollowed out in the scramble to reach the educational cells.

Then there were the profs! During the first few days I got so far as to shake hands with a few of them, and of course there was always the salute with the hat when we passed under the arcades. But as for a heart-to-heart talk, as for walking to the corner and having a drink together, nothing doing. It was simply unimaginable. Most of them looked as though they had had the shit scared out of them. Anyway, I belonged to another hierarchy. They wouldn't even share a louse with the likes of me. They made me so damned irritated, just to look at them, that I used to curse them under my breath when I saw them coming. I used to stand there, leaning against a pillar, with a cigarette in the corner of my mouth and my hat down over my eyes, and when they got within hailing distance I would let squirt a good gob and up with the hat. I didn't even bother to open my trap and bid them the time of the day. Under my breath I simply said: "Fuck you, Jack!" and let it go at that.

After a week it seemed as if I had been here all my life. It was like a bloody, fucking nightmare that you can't throw off. Used to fall into a coma thinking about it. Just a few days ago I had arrived. Nightfall. People scurrying home like rats under the foggy lights. The trees glittering with diamond-pointed malice. I thought it all out, a thousand times or more. From the station to the

Lycée it was like a promenade through the Danzig Corridor, all deckle-edged, crannied, nerve-ridden. A lane of dead bones, of crooked, cringing figures buried in shrouds. Spines made of sardine bones. The Lycée itself seemed to rise up out of a lake of thin snow, an inverted mountain that pointed down toward the center of the earth where God or the Devil works always in a straitjacket grinding grist for that paradise which is always a wet dream. If the sun ever shone I don't remember it. I remember nothing but the cold greasy fogs that blew in from the frozen marshes over yonder where the railroad tracks burrowed into the lurid hills. Down near the station was a canal, or perhaps it was a river, hidden away under a yellow sky, with little shacks pasted slap up against the rising ledge of the banks. There was a barracks too somewhere, it struck me, because every now and then I met little yellow men from Cochin-China—squirmy, opium-faced runts peeping out of their baggy uniforms like dyed skeletons packed in excelsior. The whole goddamned medievalism of the place was infernally ticklish and restive, rocking back and forth with low moans, jumping out at you from the eaves, hanging like broken-necked criminals from the gargoyles. I kept looking back all the time, kept walking like a crab that you prong with a dirty fork. All those fat little monsters, those slablike effigies pasted on the façade of the Eglise St. Michel, they were following me down the crooked lanes and around corners. The whole façade of St. Michel seemed to open up like an album at night, leaving you face to face with the horrors of the printed page. When the lights went out and the characters faded away flat, dead as words, then it was quite magnificent, the façade; in every crevice of the old gnarled front there was the hollow chant of the nightwind and over the lacy rubble of cold stiff vestments there was a cloudy absinthe-like drool of fog and frost.

Here, where the church stood, everything seemed turned hind side front. The church itself must have been twisted off its base by centuries of progress in the rain and snow. It lay in the Place Edgar-Quinet, squat against the wind, like a dead mule. Through the Rue de la Monnaie the wind rushed like white hair streaming wild: it whirled around the white hitching posts which obstructed the free passage of omnibuses and twenty-mule teams. Swinging through this exit in the early morning hours I sometimes stumbled upon Monsieur Renaud who, wrapped in his cowl like a gluttonous monk, made overtures to me in the language of the sixteenth century. Falling in step with Monsieur Renaud, the moon busting through the greasy sky like a punctured balloon, I fell immediately into the realm of the transcendental. M. Renaud had a precise speech, dry as apricoats, with a heavy Brandenburger base. Used to come at me full tilt from Goethe or Fichte, with deep base notes that rumbled in the windy corners of the Place like claps of last year's thunder. Men of Yucatan, men of Zanzibar, men of Tierra del Fuego, save me from this glaucous hog rind! The North piles up about me, the glacial fjords, the blue-tipped spines, the crazy lights, the obscene Christian chant that spread like an avalanche from Etna to the Aegean. Everything frozen tight as scum, the mind locked and rimed with frost, and through the melancholy bales of chitter-wit the choking gargle of louse-eaten saints. White I am and wrapped in wool, swaddled, fettered, hamstrung, but in this I have no part. White to the bone, but with a cold alkali base, with saffron-tipped fingers. White, aye, but no brother of learning, no Catholic heart. White and ruthless, as the men before me who sailed out of the Elbe. I look to the sea, to the sky, to what is unintelligible and distantly near.

The snow under foot scurries before the wind, blows, tickles, stings, lisps away, whirls aloft, showers, splinters, sprays down. No sun, no roar of surf, no breaker's surge. The cold north wind pointed with barbed shafts, icy, malevolent, greedy, blighting, paralyzing. The streets turn away on their crooked elbows; they break from the hurried sight, the stern glance. They hobble away down the drifting lattice work, wheeling the church hind side front, mowing down the statues, flattening the monuments, uprooting the trees, stiffening the grass, sucking the fragrance out of the earth. Leaves dull as cement: leaves no dew can bring to glisten again. No moon will ever silver their listless plight. The seasons are come to a stagnant stop, the trees blench and wither, the wagons roll in the mica ruts with slithering harplike thuds. In the hollow of the white-tipped hills, lurid and boneless Dijon slumbers. No man alive and walking through the night except the restless spirits moving southward toward the sapphire grids. Yet I am up and about, a walking ghost, a white man terrorized by the cold sanity of this slaughterhouse geometry. Who am I? What am I doing here? I fall between the cold walls of human malevolence, a white figure fluttering, sinking down through the cold lake, a mountain of skulls above me. I settle down to the cold latitudes, the chalk steps washed with indigo. The earth in its dark corridors knows my step, feels a foot abroad, a wing stirring, a gasp and a shudder. I hear the learning chaffed and chuzzled, the figures mounting upward, bat slime dripping aloft and clanging with pasteboard golden wings; I hear the trains collide, the chains rattle, the locomotive chugging, snorting, sniffing, steaming and pissing. All things come to me through the clear fog with the odor of repetition, with yellow hangovers and Gadzooks and whettikins. In the dead center, far below Dijon, far below the hyperborean regions, stands God Ajax, his shoulders strapped to the mill wheel, the olives crunching, the green marsh water alive with croaking frogs.

The fog and snow, the cold latitude, the heavy learning, the blue coffee, the unbuttered bread, the soup and lentils, the heavy pork-packer beans, the stale cheese, the soggy chow, the lousy wine have put the whole penitentiary into a state of constipation. And just when everyone has become shit-tight the toilet pipes freeze. The shit piles up like ant hills; one has to move down from the little pedestals and leave it on the floor. It lies there stiff and frozen, waiting for the thaw. On Thursday the hunchback comes with his little wheelbarrow, shovels the cold, stiff turds with a broom and pan, and trundles off dragging his withered leg. The corridors are littered with toilet paper; it sticks to your feet like flypaper. When the weather moderates the odor gets ripe; you can smell it in Winchester forty miles away. Standing over that ripe dung in the morning, with a toothbrush, the stench is so powerful that it makes your head spin. We stand around in red flannel shirts, waiting to spit down the hole; it is like an aria from one of Verdi's great operas—an anvil chorus with pulleys and syringes. In the night, when I am taken short, I rush down to the private toilet of M. le Censeur, just off the driveway. My stool is always full of blood. His toilet doesn't flush either but at least there is the pleasure of sitting down. I leave my little bundle for him as a token of esteem.

Toward the end of the meal each evening the *veilleur de nuit* drops in for his bit of cheer. This is the only human being in the whole institution with whom I feel a kinship. He is a nobody. He carries a lantern and a bunch of keys. He makes the rounds through the night, stiff as an automaton. About the time the stale cheese is being passed around in he pops for his glass of wine. He stands there, with paw outstretched, his hair stiff and wiry, like a mastiff's, his cheeks ruddy, his mustache gleaming with snow. He mumbles a word or two and Quasimodo brings him the bottle. Then, with feet stolidly planted, he throws back his head and down it goes, slowly in one long draught. To me it's like he's pouring rubies down his gullet. Something about this gesture which seizes me by the hair. It's almost as if he were drinking down the dregs of human sympathy, as if all the love and compassion in the world could be tossed off like that, in one gulp—as if that were all that could be squeezed together day after day. A little less than a rabbit they have made him. In the scheme of things he's not worth the brine to pickle a herring. He's just a piece of live manure. And he knows it. When he looks around after his drink and smiles at us, the world seems to be falling to pieces. It's a smile thrown across an abyss. The whole stinking civilized world lies like a quagmire at the bottom of the pit, and over it, like a mirage, hovers this wavering smile.

It was the same smile which greeted me at night when I returned from my rambles. I remember one such night when, standing at the door waiting for the old fellow to finish his rounds, I had such a sense of well-being that I could have waited thus forever. I had to wait perhaps half an hour before he opened the door. I looked about me calmly and leisurely, drank everything in, the dead tree in front of the school with its twisted rope branches, the houses across the street which had changed color during the night, which curved now more noticeably, the sound of a train rolling through the Siberian wastes, the railings painted by Utrillo, the sky, the deep wagon ruts. Suddenly, out of nowhere, two lovers appeared; every few yards they stopped and embraced, and when I could no longer follow them with my eyes I followed the sound of their steps, heard the abrupt stop, and then the slow, meandering gait. I could feel the sag and slump of their bodies when they leaned against a rail, heard their shoes creak as the muscles tightened for the embrace. Through the town they wandered, through the crooked streets, toward the glassy canal where the water lay black as coal. There was something phenomenal about it. In all Dijon not two like them.

Meanwhile the old fellow was making the rounds; I could hear the jingle of his keys, the crunching of his boots, the steady, automatic tread. Finally I heard him coming through the driveway to open the big door, a monstrous, arched portal without a moat in front of it. I heard him fumbling at the lock, his hands stiff, his mind numbed. As the door swung open I saw over his head a brilliant constellation crowning the chapel. Every door was locked, every cell bolted. The books were closed. The night hung close, dagger-pointed, drunk as a maniac. There it was, the infinitude of emptiness. Over the chapel, like a bishop's miter, hung the constellation, every night, during the winter months, it hung there low over the chapel. Low and bright, a handful of dagger points, a dazzle of pure emptiness. The old fellow followed me to the turn of the drive. The door closed silently. As I bade him good night I caught that desperate, hopeless smile again, like a meteoric flash over the rim of a lost world. And again I saw him standing in the refectory, his head thrown back and the rubies pouring down his gullet. The whole Mediterranean seemed to be buried inside him—the orange groves, the cypress trees, the winged statues, the wooden temples, the blue sea, the stiff masks, the mystic numbers, the mythological birds, the sapphire skies, the eaglets, the sunny coves, the blind bards, the bearded heroes. Gone all that. Sunk beneath the avalanche from the North. Buried, dead forever. A memory. A wild hope.

For just a moment I linger at the carriageway. The shroud, the pall, the unspeakable, clutching emptiness of it all. Then I walk quickly along the gravel path near the wall, past the arches and columns, the iron staircases, from one quadrangle to the other. Everything is locked tight. Locked for the winter. I find the arcade leading to the dormitory. A sickish light spills down over the stairs from the grimy, frosted windows. Everywhere the paint is peeling off. The stones are hollowed out, the banister creaks; a damp sweat oozes from the flagging and forms a pale, fuzzy aura pierced by the feeble red light at the head of the stairs. I mount the last flight, the turret, in a sweat and terror. In pitch darkness I grope my way through the deserted corridor, every room empty, locked, molding away. My hand slides along the wall seeking the keyhole. A panic comes over me as I grasp the doorknob. Always a hand at my collar ready to yank me back. Once inside the room I bolt the door. It's a miracle which I perform each night, the miracle of getting inside without being strangled, without being struck down by an ax. I can hear the rats scurrying through the corridor, gnawing away over my head between the thick

rafters. The light glares like burning sulfur and there is
the sweet, sickish stench of a room which is never ven-
tilated. In the corner stands the coal box, just as I left it.
The fire is out. A silence so intense that it sounds like
Niagara Falls in my ears.

Alone, with a tremendous empty longing and dread.
The whole room for my thoughts. Nothing but myself
and what I think, what I fear. Could think the most fantastic thoughts, could dance, spit, grimace, curse, wail—
nobody would ever know, nobody would ever hear. The
thought of such absolute privacy is enough to drive me
mad. It's like a clean birth. Everything cut away. Separate, naked, alone. Bliss and agony simultaneously. Time
on your hands. Each second weighing on you like a
mountain. You drown in it. Deserts, seas, lakes, oceans.
Time beating away like a meat ax. Nothingness. The
world. The me and the not-me. *Oomaharumooma.* Everything has to have a name. Everything has to be learned,
tested, experienced. *Faites comme chez vous, chéri.*

The silence descends in volcanic chutes. Yonder, in the
barren hills, rolling onward toward the great metallurgical regions, the locomotives are pulling their merchant
products. Over steel and iron beds they roll, the ground
sown with slag and cinders and purple ore. In the baggage car, kelps, fishplate, rolled iron, sleepers, wire rods,
plates and sheets, laminated articles, hot rolled hoops,
splints and mortar carriages, and Zorès ore. The wheels
U-80 millimeters or over. Pass splendid specimens of
Anglo-Norman architecture, pass pedestrians and pederasts, open hearth furnaces, basic Bessemer mills, dynamos and transformers, pig iron castings and steel ingots.
The public at large, pedestrians and pederasts, goldfish
and spun-glass palm trees, donkeys sobbing, all circulat-
ing freely through quincuncial alleys. At the Place du
Brésil a lavender eye.

Going back in a flash over the women I've known. It's
like a chain which I've forged out of my own misery.
Each one bound to the other. A fear of living separate,
of staying born. The door of the womb always on the

latch. Dread and longing. Deep in the blood the pull of paradise. The beyond. Always the beyond. It must have all started with the navel. They cut the umbilical cord, give you a slap on the ass, and presto! you're out in the world, adrift, a ship without a rudder. You look at the stars and then you look at your navel. You grow eyes everywhere—in the armpits, between the lips, in the roots of your hair, on the soles of your feet. What is distant becomes near, what is near becomes distant. Inner-outer, a constant flux, a shedding of skins, a turning inside out. You drift around like that for years and years, until you find yourself in the dead center, and there you slowly rot, slowly crumble to pieces, get dispersed again. Only your name remains.

It was spring before I managed to escape from the penitentiary, and then only by a stroke of fortune. A telegram from Carl informed me one day that there was a vacancy "upstairs"; he said he would send me the fare back if I decided to accept. I telegraphed back at once and as soon as the dough arrived I beat it to the station. Not a word to M. le Proviseur or anyone. French leave, as they say.

I went immediately to the hotel at 1 *bis*, where Carl was staying. He came to the door stark naked. It was his night off and there was a cunt in the bed as usual. "Don't mind her," he says, "she's asleep. If you need a lay you can take her on. She's not bad." He pulls the covers back to show me what she looks like. However, I wasn't thinking about a lay right away. I was too excited. I was like a man who has just escaped from jail. I just wanted to see and hear things. Coming from the station it was like a long dream. I felt as though I had been away for years.

It was not until I had sat down and taken a good look at the room that I realized I was back again in Paris. It was Carl's room and no mistake about it. Like a squirrel cage and shithouse combined. There was hardly room on the table for the portable machine he used. It was always like that, whether he had a cunt with him or not. Always a dictionary lying open on a gilt-edged volume of *Faust*, always a tobacco pouch, a beret, a bottle of *vin rouge*, letters, manuscripts, old newspapers, water colors, teapot, dirty socks, toothpicks, Kruschen Salts, condoms,

260

etc. In the *bidet* were orange peels and the remnants of a ham sandwich.

"There's some food in the closet," he said. "Help yourself! I was just going to give myself an injection."

I found the sandwich he was talking about and a piece of cheese that he had nibbled at beside it. While he sat on the edge of the bed, dosing himself with his argyrol, I put away the sandwich and cheese with the aid of a little wine.

"I liked that letter you sent me about Goethe," he said, wiping his prick with a dirty pair of drawers.

"I'll show you the answer to it in a minute—I'm putting it in my book. The trouble with you is that you're not a German. You have to be German to understand Goethe. Shit, I'm not going to explain it to you now. I've put it all in the book. . . . By the way, I've got a new cunt now—not this one—this one's a half-wit. At least, I had her until a few days ago. I'm not sure whether she'll come back or not. She was living with me all the time you were away. The other day her parents came and took her away. They said she was only fifteen. Can you beat that? They scared the shit out of me too. . . ."

I began to laugh. It was like Carl to get himself into a mess like that.

"What are you laughing for?" he said. "I may go to prison for it. Luckily, I didn't knock her up. And that's funny, too, because she never took care of herself properly. But do you know what saved me? So I think, at least. It was *Faust*. Yeah! Her old man happened to see it lying on the table. He asked me if I understood German. One thing led to another and before I knew it he was looking through my books. Fortunately I happened to have the Shakespeare open too. That impressed him like hell. He said I was evidently a very serious guy."

"What about the girl—what did *she* have to say?"

"She was frightened to death. You see, she had a little watch with her when she came; in the excitement we couldn't find the watch, and her mother insisted that the watch be found or she'd call the police. You see how things are here. I turned the whole place upside down—but I couldn't find the goddamned watch. The mother was furious. I liked her too, in spite of everything. She was even better-looking than the daughter. Here—I'll show you a letter I started to write her. I'm in love with her. . . ."

"With the *mother?*"

"Sure. Why not? If I had seen the mother first I'd never have looked at the daughter. How did I know she was only fifteen? You don't ask a cunt how old she is before you lay her, do you?"

"Joe, there's something funny about this. You're not shitting me, are you?"

"Am I shitting you? Here—look at this!" And he shows me the water colors the girl had made—cute little things—a knife and a loaf of bread, the table and teapot, everything running uphill. "She was in love with me," he said. "She was just like a child. I had to tell her when to brush her teeth and how to put her hat on. Here—look at the lollypops! I used to buy her a few lollypops every day—she liked them."

"Well, what did she do when her parents came to take her away? Didn't she put up a row?"

"She cried a little, that's all. What *could* she do? She's under age. . . . I had to promise never to see her again, never to write her either. That's what I'm waiting to see now—whether she'll stay away or not. She was a virgin when she came here. The thing is, how long will she be able to go without a lay? She couldn't get enough of it when she was here. She almost wore me out."

By this time the one in bed had come to and was rubbing her eyes. She looked pretty young to me, too. Not bad looking, but dumb as hell. Wanted to know right away what we were talking about.

"She lives here in the hotel," said Carl. "On the third floor. Do you want to go to her room? I'll fix it up for you."

I didn't know whether I wanted to or not, but when I saw Carl mushing it up with her again I decided I did want to. I asked her first if she was too tired. Useless question. A whore is never too tired to open her legs. Some of them can fall asleep while you diddle them. Anyway, it was decided we would go down to her room. Like that I wouldn't have to pay the *patron* for the night.

In the morning I rented a room overlooking the little park down below where the sandwich-board men always came to eat their lunch. At noon I called for Carl to have breakfast with him. He and Van Norden had developed a new habit in my absence—they went to the Coupole for breakfast every day. "Why the Coupole?" I asked. "Why the Coupole?" says Carl. "Because the Coupole serves porridge at all hours and porridge makes you shit." —"I see," said I.

So it's just like it used to be again. The three of us walking back and forth to work. Petty dissensions, petty rivalries. Van Norden still bellyaching about his cunts and about washing the dirt out of his belly. Only now he's found a new diversion. He's found that it's less annoying to masturbate. I was amazed when he broke the news to me. I didn't think it possible for a guy like that to find any pleasure in jerking himself off. I was still more amazed when he explained to me how he goes about it. He had "invented" a new stunt, so he put it. "You take an apple," he says, "and you bore out the core. Then you rub some cold cream on the inside so as it doesn't melt too fast. Try it some time! It'll drive you crazy at first. Anyway, it's cheap and you don't have to waste much time."

"By the way," he says, switching the subject, "that friend of yours, Fillmore, he's in the hospital. I think he's nuts. Anyway, that's what his girl told me. He took on a French girl, you know, while you were away. They used to fight like hell. She's a big, healthy bitch—wild like. I wouldn't mind giving her a tumble, but I'm afraid she'd claw the eyes out of me. He was always going around with his face and hands scratched up. She looks bunged up too once in a while—or she used to. You know how these French cunts are—when they love they lose their minds."

Evidently things had happened while I was away. I was sorry to hear about Fillmore. He had been damned good to me. When I left Van Norden I jumped a bus and went straight to the hospital.

They hadn't decided yet whether he was completely off his base or not, I suppose, for I found him upstairs in a private room, enjoying all the liberties of the regular patients. He had just come from the bath when I arrived. When he caught sight of me he burst into tears. "It's all over," he says immediately. "They say I'm crazy—and I may have syphilis too. They say I have delusions of grandeur." He fell over onto the bed and wept quietly. After he had wept a while he lifted his head up and smiled—just like a bird coming out of a snooze. "Why do they put me in such an expensive room?" he said. "Why don't they put me in the ward—or in the bughouse? I can't afford to pay for this. I'm down to my last five hundred dollars."

"That's why they're keeping you here," I said. "They'll transfer you quickly enough when your money runs out. Don't worry."

My words must have impressed him, for I had no sooner finished than he handed me his watch and chain, his wallet, his fraternity pin, etc. "Hold on to them," he said. "These bastards'll rob me of everything I've got." And then suddenly he began to laugh, one of those weird, mirthless laughs which makes you believe a guy's goofy whether he is or not. "I know you'll think I'm crazy," he said, "but I want to atone for what I did. I want to get married. You see, I didn't know I had the clap. I gave her the clap and then I knocked her up. I told the doctor I don't care what happens to me, but I want him to let me get married first. He keeps telling me to wait until I get better—but I know I'm never going to get better. This is the end."

I couldn't help laughing myself, hearing him talk that way. I couldn't understand what had come over him.

Anyway, I had to promise him to see the girl and explain things to her. He wanted me to stick by her, comfort her. Said he could trust me, etc. I said yes to everything in order to soothe him. He didn't seem exactly nuts to me—just caved-in like. Typical Anglo-Saxon crisis. An eruption of morals. I was rather curious to see the girl, to get the lowdown on the whole thing.

The next day I looked her up. She was living in the Latin Quarter. As soon as she realized who I was she became exceedingly cordial. Ginette she called herself. Rather big, rawboned, healthy, peasant type with a front tooth half eaten away. Full of vitality and a kind of crazy fire in her eyes. The first thing she did was to weep. Then, seeing that I was an old friend of her Jo-Jo—that was how she called him—she ran downstairs and brought back a couple of bottles of white wine. I was to stay and have dinner with her—she insisted on it. As she drank she became by turns gay and maudlin. I didn't have to ask her any questions—she went on like a self-winding machine. The thing that worried her principally was—would he get his job back when he was released from the hospital? She said her parents were well off, but they were displeased with her. They didn't approve of her wild ways. They didn't approve of him particularly—he had no manners, and he was an American. She begged me to assure her that he would get his job back, which I did without hesitancy. And then she begged me to know if she could believe what he said—that he was going to marry her. Because now, with a child under her belt, and a dose of clap besides, she was in no position to strike a match—with a Frenchman anyway. That was clear, wasn't it? Of course, I assured her. It was all clear as hell to me—except how in Christ's name Fillmore had ever fallen for her. However, one thing at a time. It was my duty now to comfort her, and so I just filled her up with a lot of baloney, told her everything would turn out all right and that I would stand godfather to the child, etc. Then suddenly it struck me as strange that she should have the child at all—especially as it was likely to be born blind. I told her that as tactfully as I could. "It doesn't make any difference," she said, "I want a child by him."

"Even if it's blind?" I asked.

"*Mon Dieu, ne dites pas ça!*" she groaned. "*Ne dites pas ça!*"

Just the same, I felt it was my duty to say it. She got hysterical and began to weep like a walrus, poured out more wine. In a few moments she was laughing boisterously. She was laughing to think how they used to fight when they got in bed. "He liked me to fight with him," she said. "He was a brute."

As we sat down to eat, a friend of hers walked in—a little tart who lived at the end of the hall. Ginette immediately sent me down to get some more wine. When I came back they had evidently had a good talk. Her friend, Yvette, worked in the police department. A sort of stool pigeon, as far as I could gather. At least that was what she was trying to make me believe. It was fairly obvious that she was just a little whore. But she had an obsession about the police and their doings. Throughout the meal they were urging me to accompany them to a *bal musette*. They wanted to have a gay time—it was so lonely for Ginette with Jo-Jo in the hospital. I told them I had to work, but that on my night off I'd come back and take them out. I made it clear too that I had no dough to spend on them. Ginette, who was really thunderstruck to hear this, pretended that that didn't matter in the least. In fact, just to show what a good sport she was, she insisted on driving me to work in a cab. She was doing it because I was a friend of Jo-Jo's. And therefore I was a friend of hers. "And also," thought I to myself, "if anything goes wrong with your Jo-Jo you'll come to me on the double-quick. Then you'll see what a friend I can be!" I was as nice as pie to her. In fact, when we got out of the cab in front of the office, I permitted them to persuade me into having a final Pernod together. Yvette wanted to know if she couldn't call for me after work. She had a lot of things to tell me in confidence, she said. But I managed to refuse without hurting her feelings. Unfortunately I did unbend sufficiently to give her my address.

Unfortunately, I say. As a matter of fact, I'm rather glad of it when I think back on it. Because the very next day things began to happen. The very next day, before I had even gotten out of bed, the two of them called on me. Jo-Jo had been removed from the hospital—they had incarcerated him in a little château in the country, just a few miles out of Paris. The *château,* they called it. A polite way of saying "the bughouse." They wanted me to get dressed immediately and go with them. They were in a panic.

Perhaps I might have gone alone—but I just couldn't make up my mind to go with these two. I asked them to wait for me downstairs while I got dressed, thinking that it would give me time to invent some excuse for not going. But they wouldn't leave the room. They sat there and watched me wash and dress, just as if it were an everyday affair. In the midst of it, Carl popped in. I gave him the situation briefly, in English, and then we hatched up an excuse that I had some important work to do. However, to smooth things over, we got some wine in and we began to amuse them by showing them a book of dirty drawings. Yvette had already lost all desire to go to the château. She and Carl were getting along famously. When it came time to go Carl decided to accompany them to the château. He thought it would be funny to see Fillmore walking around with a lot of nuts. He wanted to see what it was like in the nuthouse. So off they went, somewhat pickled, and in the best of humor.

All the time that Fillmore was at the château I never once went to see him. It wasn't necessary, because Ginette visited him regularly and gave me all the news. They had hopes of bringing him around in a few months, so she said. They thought it was alcoholic poisoning—nothing more. Of course, he had a dose—but that wasn't difficult to remedy. So far as they could see, he didn't have syphilis. That was something. So, to begin with, they used the stomach pump on him. They cleaned his system out thoroughly. He was so weak for a while that he couldn't get out of bed. He was depressed, too. He said he didn't want to be cured—he wanted to die. And he kept repeating this nonsense so insistently that finally they grew alarmed. I suppose it wouldn't have been a very good recommendation if he had committed suicide. Anyway, they began to give him mental treatment. And in between times they pulled out his teeth, more and more of them, until he didn't have a tooth left in his head. He was supposed to feel fine after that, yet strangely he didn't. He became more despondent than ever. And then his hair began to fall out. Finally he developed a paranoid streak—began to accuse them of all sorts of things, demanded to know by what right he was being detained, what he had done to warrant being locked up, etc. After a terrible fit of despondency he would suddenly become energetic and threaten to blow up the place if they didn't release him. And to make it worse, as far as Ginette was concerned, he had gotten all over his notion of marrying her. He told her straight up and down that he had no intention of marrying her, and that if she was crazy enough to go and have a child then she could support it herself.

The doctors interpreted all this as a good sign. They said he was coming round. Ginette, of course, thought he was crazier than ever, but she was praying for him to be released so that she could take him to the country where it would be quiet and peaceful and where he would come to his right senses. Meanwhile her parents had come to Paris on a visit and had even gone so far as to visit the future son-in-law at the château. In their canny way they had probably figured it out that it would be better for their daughter to have a crazy husband than no husband at all. The father thought he could find something for Fillmore to do on the farm. He said that Fillmore wasn't such a bad chap at all. When he learned from Ginette that Fillmore's parents had money he became even more indulgent, more understanding.

The thing was working itself out nicely all around.

Ginette returned to the provinces for a while with her parents. Yvette was coming regularly to the hotel to see Carl. She thought he was the editor of the paper. And little by little she became more confidential. When she got good and tight one day, she informed us that Ginette had never been anything but a whore, that Ginette was a bloodsucker, that Ginette never had been pregnant and was not pregnant now. About the other accusations we hadn't much doubt, Carl and I, but about not being pregnant, that we weren't so sure of.

"How did she get such a big stomach, then?" asked Carl.

Yvette laughed. "Maybe she uses a bicycle pump," she said. "No, seriously," she added, "the stomach comes from drink. She drinks like a fish, Ginette. When she comes back from the country, you will see, she will be blown up still more. Her father is a drunkard. Ginette is a drunkard. Maybe she had the clap, yes—but she is not pregnant."

"But why does she want to marry him? Is she really in love with him?"

"*Love?* Pfooh! She has no heart, Ginette. She wants someone to look after her. No Frenchman would ever marry her—she has a police record. No, she wants him because he's too stupid to find out about her. Her parents don't want her any more—she's a disgrace to them. But if she can get married to a rich American, then everything will be all right. . . . You think maybe she loves him a little, eh? You don't know her. When they were living together at the hotel, she had men coming to her room while he was at work. She said he didn't give her enough spending money. He was stingy. That fur she wore—she told him her parents had given it to her, didn't she? Innocent fool! Why, I've seen her bring a man back to the hotel right while he was there. She brought the man to the floor below. I saw it with my own eyes. And what a man! An old derelict. He couldn't get an erection!"

If Fillmore, when he was released from the château, had returned to Paris, perhaps I might have tipped him off about his Ginette. While he was still under observation I didn't think it well to upset him by poisoning his mind with Yvette's slanders. As thing turned out, he went directly from the château to the home of Ginette's parents. There, despite himself, he was inveigled into making public his engagement. The banns were published in the local papers and a reception was given to the friends of the family. Fillmore took advantage of the situation to indulge in all sorts of escapades. Though he knew quite well what he was doing he pretended to be still a little daffy. He would borrow his father-in-law's car, for example, and tear about the countryside all by himself; if he saw a town that he liked he would plank himself down and have a good time until Ginette came searching for him. Sometimes the father-in-law and he would go off together—on a fishing trip, presumably—and nothing would be heard of them for days. He became exasperatingly capricious and exacting. I suppose he figured he might as well get what he could out of it.

When he returned to Paris with Ginette he had a complete new wardrobe and a pocketful of dough. He looked cheerful and healthy, and had a fine coat of tan. He looked sound as a berry to me. But as soon as we had gotten away from Ginette he opened up. His job was gone and his money had all run out. In a month or so they were to be married. Meanwhile the parents were supplying the dough. "Once they've got me properly in their clutches," he said, "I'll be nothing but a slave to them. The father thinks he's going to open up a stationery store for me. Ginette will handle the customers, take in the money, etc., while I sit in the back of the store and write—or something. Can you picture me sitting in the back of a stationery store for the rest of my life? Ginette thinks it's an excellent idea. She likes to handle money. I'd rather go back to the château than submit to such a scheme."

For the time being, of course, he was pretending that everything was hunky-dory. I tried to persuade him to go back to America but he wouldn't hear of that. He said he wasn't going to be driven out of France by a lot of ignorant peasants. He had an idea that he would slip out of sight for a while and then take up quarters in some outlying section of the city where he'd not be likely to stumble upon her. But we soon decided that that was impossible: you can't hide away in France as you can in America.

"You could go to Belgium for a while," I suggested.

"But what'll I do for money?" he said promptly. "You can't get a job in these goddamned countries."

"Why don't you marry her and get a divorce, then?" I asked.

"And meanwhile she'll be dropping a kid. Who's going to take care of the kid, eh?"

"How do you know she's going to have a kid?" I said, determined now that the moment had come to spill the beans.

"How do I know?" he said. He didn't quite seem to know what I was insinuating.

I gave him an inkling of what Yvette had said. He listened to me in complete bewilderment. Finally he interrupted me. "It's no use going on with that," he said. "I know she's going to have a kid, all right. I've felt it kicking around inside. Yvette's a dirty little slut. You see, I didn't want to tell you, but up until the time I went to the hospital I was shelling out for Yvette too. Then when the crash came I couldn't do any more for her. I figured out that I had done enough for the both of them. . . . I made up my mind to look after myself first. That made Yvette sore. She told Ginette that she was going to get even with me. . . . No, I wish it were true, what she said. Then I could get out of this thing more easily. Now I'm in a trap. I've promised to marry her and I'll have to go through with it. After that I don't know what'll happen to me. They've got me by the balls now."

Since he had taken a room in the same hotel with me I was obliged to see them frequently, whether I wanted to or not. Almost every evening I had dinner with them, preceded, of course, by a few Pernods. All through the meal they quarreled noisily. It was embarrassing because

I had sometimes to take one side and sometimes the other. One Sunday afternoon, for example, after we had had lunch together, we repaired to a café on the corner of the Boulevard Edgar-Quinet. Things had gone unusually well this time. We were sitting inside at a little table, one alongside the other, our back to a mirror. Ginette must have been passionate or something for she had suddenly gotten into a sentimental mood and was fondling him and kissing him in front of everybody, as the French do so naturally. They had just come out of a long embrace when Fillmore said something about her parents which she interpreted as an insult. Immediately her cheeks flushed with anger. We tried to mollify her by telling her that she had misunderstood the remark and then, under his breath, Fillmore said something to me in English—something about giving her a little soft soap. That was enough to set her completely off the handle. She said we were making fun of her. I said something sharp to her which angered her still more and then Fillmore tried to put in a word. "You're too quick-tempered," he said, and he tried to pat her on the cheek. But she, thinking that he had raised his hand to slap her face, she gave him a sound crack in the jaw with that big peasant hand of hers. For a moment he was stunned. He hadn't expected a wallop like that, and it stung. I saw his face go white and the next moment he raised himself from the bench and with the palm of his hand he gave her such a crack that she almost fell off her seat. "There! that'll teach you how to behave!" he said—in his broken French. For a moment there was a dead silence. Then, like a storm breaking, she picked up the cognac glass in front of her and hurled it at him with all her might. It smashed against the mirror behind us. Fillmore had already grabbed her by the arm, but with her free hand she grabbed the coffee glass and smashed it on the floor. She was squirming around like a maniac. It was all we could do to hold her. Meanwhile, of course, the *patron* had come running in and ordered us to beat it. "Loafers!" he called us. "Yes, loafers; that's it!" screamed Ginette. "Dirty foreigners! Thugs! Gangsters! Striking a pregnant woman!" We were getting black looks all around. A poor Frenchwoman with two American toughs. Gangsters. I was wondering how the hell we'd ever get out of the place without a fight. Fillmore, by this time, was as silent as a clam. Ginette was bolting it through the door, leaving us to face the music. As she sailed out she turned back with fist upraised and shouted; "I'll pay you back for this, you brute! You'll see! No foreigner can treat a decent Frenchwoman like that! Ah, no! Not like that?"

Hearing this the *patron*, who had now been paid for his drinks and his broken glasses, felt it incumbent to show his gallantry toward a splendid representative of French motherhood such as Ginette, and so, without more ado, he spat at our feet and shoved us out of the door. "Shit on you, you dirty loafers!" he said, or some such pleasantry.

Once in the street and nobody throwing things after us, I began to see the funny side of it. It would be an excellent idea, I thought to myself, if the whole thing were properly aired in court. *The whole thing!* With Yvette's little stories as a side dish. After all, the French have a sense of humor. Perhaps the judge, when he heard Fillmore's side of the story, would absolve him from marriage.

Meanwhile Ginette was standing across the street brandishing her fist and yelling at the top of her lungs. People were stopping to listen in, to take sides, as they do in street brawls. Fillmore didn't know what to do—whether to walk away from her, or to go over to her and try to pacify her. He was standing in the middle of the street with his arms outstretched, trying to get a word in edgewise. And Ginette still yelling: *"Gangster! Brutes! Tu verras, salaud!"* and other complimentary things. Finally Fillmore made a move toward her and she, probably thinking that he was going to give her another good cuff, took it on a trot down the street. Fillmore came back to where I was standing and said: "Come on, let's follow her quietly." We started off with a thin crowd of stragglers behind us. Every once in a while she turned back toward us and brandished her fist. We made no attempt to catch up with her, just followed her leisurely down the street to see what she would do. Finally she slowed up her pace and we crossed over to the other side of the street. She was quiet now. We kept walking behind her, getting closer and closer. There were only about a dozen people behind us now—the others had lost interest. When we got near the corner she suddenly stopped and waited for us to approach. "Let me do the talking," said Fillmore, "I know how to handle her."

The tears were streaming down her face as we came up to her. Myself, I didn't know what to expect of her. I was somewhat surprised therefore when Fillmore walked up to her and said in an aggrieved voice: "Was that a nice thing to do? Why did you act that way?" Whereupon she threw her arms around his neck and began to weep like a child, calling him her little this and her little that. Then she turned to me imploringly. "You saw how he struck me," she said. "Is that the way to behave toward a woman?" I was on the point of saying yes when Fillmore took her by the arm and started leading her off. "No more of that," he said. "If you start again I'll crack you right here in the street."

I thought it was going to start up all over again. She had fire in her eyes. But evidently she was a bit cowed, too, for it subsided quickly. However, as she sat down at the café she said quietly and grimly that he needn't think it was going to be forgotten so quickly; he'd hear more about it later on . . . perhaps tonight.

And sure enough she kept her word. When I met him the next day his face and hands were all scratched up. Seems she had waited until he got to bed and then, without a word, she had gone to the wardrobe and, dumping all his things out on the floor, she took them one by one and tore them to ribbons. As this had happened a number of times before, and as she had always sewn them up afterward, he hadn't protested very much. And that made her angrier than ever. What she wanted was to get her nails into him, and she did, to the best of her ability. Being pregnant she had a certain advantage over him.

Poor Fillmore! It was no laughing matter. She had him terrorized. If he threatened to run away she retorted by a threat to kill him. And she said it as if she meant it. "If you go to America," she said, "I'll follow you! You won't get away from me. A French girl always knows how to get vengeance." And the next moment she would be coaxing him to be "reasonable," to be "*sage*," etc. Life would be so nice once they had the stationery store. He wouldn't have to do a stroke of work. She would do everything. He could stay in back of the store and write —or whatever he wanted to do.

It went on like this, back and forth, a seesaw, for a few weeks or so. I was avoiding them as much as possible, sick of the affair and disgusted with the both of them. Then one fine summer's day, just as I was passing the Credit Lyonnais, who comes marching down the steps but Fillmore. I greeted him warmly, feeling rather guilty because I had dodged him for so long. I asked him, with more than ordinary curiosity, how things were going. He answered me rather vaguely and with a note of despair in his voice.

"I've just gotten permission to go to the bank," he said, in a peculiar, broken, abject sort of way. "I've got about half an hour, no more. She keeps tabs on me." And he grasped my arm as if to hurry me away from the spot.

We were walking down toward the Rue de Rivoli. It was a beautiful day, warm, clear, sunny—one of those days when Paris is at its best. A mild pleasant breeze blowing, just enough to take that stagnant odor out of your nostrils. Fillmore was without a hat. Outwardly he looked the picture of health—like the average American tourist who slouches along with money jingling in his pockets.

"I don't know what to do any more," he said quietly. "You've got to do something for me. I'm helpless. I can't get a grip on myself. If I could only get away from her for a little while perhaps I'd come round all right. But she won't let me out of her sight. I just got permission to run to the bank—I had to draw some money. I'll walk around with you a bit and then I must hurry back—she'll have lunch waiting for me."

I listened to him quietly, thinking to myself that he certainly did need someone to pull him out of the hole he was in. He had completely caved in, there wasn't a speck of courage left in him. He was just like a child—like a child who is beaten every day and doesn't know any more how to behave, except to cower and cringe. As we turned under the colonnade of the Rue de Rivoli he burst into a long diatribe against France. He was fed up with the French. "I used to rave about them," he said, "but that was all literature. I know them now. . . . I know what they're really like. They're cruel and mercenary. At first it seems wonderful, because you have a feeling of being free. After a while it palls on you. Underneath it's all dead; there's no feeling, no sympathy, no friendship. They're selfish to the core. The most selfish people on earth! They think of nothing but money, money, money. And so goddamned respectable, so bourgeois! That's what drives me nuts. When I see her mending my shirts I could club her. Always mending, mending. Saving, saving. *Faut faire des économies!* That's all I hear her say all day long. You hear it everywhere. *Sois raisonnable, mon chéri! Sois raisonnable!* I don't want to be reasonable and logical. I hate it! I want to bust loose, I want to enjoy myself. I want to *do* something. I don't want to sit in a café and talk all day long. Jesus, we've got our faults—but we've got enthusiasm. It's better to make mistakes than not do anything. I'd rather be a bum in America than to be sitting pretty here. Maybe it's because I'm a Yankee. I was born in New England and I belong there, I guess. You can't become a European overnight. There's something in your blood that makes you different. It's the climate—and everything. We see things with different eyes. We can't make ourselves over, however much we admire the French. We're Americans and we've got to remain Americans. Sure, I hate those puritanical buggers back home—I hate 'em with all my guts. But I'm one of them myself. I don't belong here. I'm sick of it."

All along the arcade he went on like this. I wasn't saying a word. I let him spill it all out—it was good for him to get it off his chest. Just the same, I was thinking how strange it was that this same guy, had it been a year ago, would have been beating his chest like a gorilla and saying: "What a marvelous day! What a country! What a people!" And if an American had happened along and said one word against France Fillmore would have flattened his nose. He would have died for France—a year ago. I never saw a man who was so infatuated with a country, who was so happy under a foreign sky. It wasn't natural. When he said *France* it meant wine, women, money in the pocket, easy come, easy go. It meant being a bad boy, being on a holiday. And then, when he had had his fling, when the tent top blew off and he had a good look at the sky, he saw that it wasn't just a circus, but an arena, just like everywhere. And a damned grim one. I often used to think, when I heard him rave about glorious France, about liberty and all that crap, what it would have sounded like to a French workman, could he have understood Fillmore's words. No wonder they think we're all crazy. We *are* crazy to them. We're just a pack of children. Senile idiots. What we call life is a five-and-ten-cent store romance. That enthusiasm underneath—what is it? That cheap optimism which turns the stomach of any ordinary European? It's illusion. No, illusion's too good a word for it. Illusion means something. No, it's not that— it's *delusion*. It's sheer delusion, that's what. We're like a herd of wild horses with blinders over our eyes. On the rampage. Stampede. Over the precipice. Bango! Anything that nourishes violence and confusion. On! On! No matter where. And foaming at the lips all the while. Shouting Hallelujah! *Hallelujah!* Why? God knows. It's in the blood. It's the climate. It's a lot of things. It's the end, too. We're pulling the whole world down about our ears. We don't know why. It's our destiny. The rest is plain shit. . . .

At the Palais Royal I suggested that we stop and have a drink. He hesitated a moment. I saw that he was worrying about her, about the lunch, about the bawling out he'd get.

"For Christ's sake," I said, "forget about her for a while. I'm going to order something to drink and I want you to drink it. Don't worry, I'm going to get you out of this fucking mess." I ordered two stiff whiskies.

When he saw the whiskies coming he smiled at me just like a child again.

"Down it!" I said "and let's have another. This is going to do you good. I don't care what the doctor says—this time it'll be all right. Come on, down with it!"

He put it down all right and while the *garçon* disappeared to fetch another round he looked at me with brimming eyes, as though I were the last friend in the world. His lips were twitching a bit, too. There was something he wanted to say to me and he didn't quite know how to begin. I looked at him easily, as though ignoring the appeal and, shoving the saucers aside, I leaned over on my elbow and I said to him earnestly: "Look here, Fillmore, what is it you'd *really* like to do? Tell me!"

With that the tears gushed up and he blurted out: "I'd like to be home with my people. I'd like to hear English spoken." The tears were streaming down his face. He made no effort to brush them away. He just let everything gush forth. Jesus, I thought to myself, that's fine to have a release like that. Fine to be a complete coward at least once in your life. To let go that way. Great! Great! It did me so much good to see him break down that way that I felt as though I could solve any problem. I felt courageous and resolute. I had a thousand ideas in my head at once.

"Listen," I said, bending still closer to him, "if you mean what you said why don't you do it . . . why don't you go? Do you know what I would do, if I were in your shoes? I'd go today. Yes, by Jesus, I mean it . . . I'd go right away, without even saying good-bye to her. As a matter of fact that's the only way you can go—she'd never let you say good-bye. You know that."

The *garçon* came with the whiskies. I saw him reach forward with a desperate eagerness and raise the glass to his lips. I saw a glint of hope in his eyes—far-off, wild, desperate. He probably saw himself swimming across the Atlantic. To me it looked easy, simple as rolling off a log. The whole thing was working itself out rapidly in my mind. I knew just what each step would be. Clear as a bell, I was.

"Whose money is that in the bank?" I asked. "Is it her father's or is it yours?"

"It's mine!" he exclaimed. "My mother sent it to me. I don't want any of her goddamned money."

"That's swell!" I said. "Listen, suppose we hop a cab and go back there. Draw out every cent. Then we'll go to the British Consulate and get a visa. You're going to hop the train this afternoon for London. From London you'll take the first boat to America. I'm saying that because then you won't be worried about her trailing you. She'll never suspect that you went via London. If she goes searching for you she'll naturally go to Le Havre first, or Cherbourg. . . . And here's another thing—you're not going back to get your things. You're going to leave everything here. Let her keep them. With that French mind of hers she'll never dream that you scooted off without bag or baggage. It's incredible. A Frenchman would never dream of doing a thing like that . . . unless he was as cracked as you are."

"You're right!" he exclaimed. "I never thought of that. Besides, you might send them to me later on—if she'll surrender them! But that doesn't matter now. Jesus, though, I haven't even got a hat!"

"What do you need a hat for? When you get to London you can buy everything you need. All you need now is to hurry. We've got to find out when the train leaves."

"Listen," he said, reaching for his wallet, "I'm going to leave everything to you. Here, take this and do whatever's necessary. I'm too weak. . . . I'm dizzy."

I took the wallet and emptied it of the bills he had just drawn from the bank. A cab was standing at the curb. We hopped in. There was a train leaving the Gare du Nord at four o'clock, or thereabouts. I was figuring it out— the bank, the Consulate, the American Express, the station. Fine! Just about make it.

"Now buck up!" I said, "and keep your shirt on! Shit, in a few hours you'll be crossing the Channel. Tonight you'll be walking around in London and you'll get a good bellyful of English. Tomorrow you'll be on the open sea—and then, by Jesus, you're a free man and you needn't give a fuck what happens. By the time you get to New York this'll be nothing more than a bad dream."

This got him so excited that his feet were moving convulsively, as if he were trying to run inside the cab. At the bank his hand was trembling so that he could hardly sign his name. That was one thing I couldn't do for him— sign his name. But I think, had it been necessary, I could have sat him on the toilet and wiped his ass. I was determined to ship him off, even if I had to fold him up and put him in a valise.

It was lunch hour when we got to the British Consulate, and the place was closed. That meant waiting until two o'clock. I couldn't think of anything better to do, by way of killing time, than to eat. Fillmore, of course, wasn't hungry. He was for eating a sandwich. "Fuck that!" I said. "You're going to blow me to a good lunch. It's the last square meal you're going to have over here—maybe for a long while." I steered him to a cosy little restaurant and ordered a good spread. I ordered the best wine on the menu, regardless of price or taste. I had all his money in my pocket—oodles of it, it seemed to me. Certainly never before had I had so much in my fist at one time. It was a treat to break a thousand franc note. I held it up to the light first to look at the beautiful watermark. Beautiful money! One of the few things the French make on a grand scale. Artistically done, too, as if they cherished a deep affection even for the symbol.

The meal over, we went to a café. I ordered Chartreuse

with the coffee. Why not? And I broke another bill—a five-hundred franc note this time. It was a clean, new, crisp bill. A pleasure to handle such money. The waiter handed me back a lot of dirty old bills that had been patched up with strips of gummed paper; I had a stack of five and ten franc notes and a bagful of chicken feed. Chinese money, with holes in it. I didn't know in which pocket to stuff the money any more. My trousers were bursting with coins and bills. It made me slightly uncomfortable also, hauling all that dough out in public. I was afraid we might be taken for a couple of crooks.

When we got to the American Express there wasn't a devil of a lot of time left. The British, in their usual fumbling farting way, had kept us on pins and needles. Here everybody was sliding around on castors. They were so speedy that everything had to be done twice. After all the checks were signed and clipped in a neat little holder, it was discovered that he had signed in the wrong place. Nothing to do but start all over again. I stood over him, with one eye on the clock, and watched every stroke of the pen. It hurt to hand over the dough. Not all of it, thank God—but a good part of it. I had roughly about 2,500 francs in my pocket. Roughly, I say. I wasn't counting by francs any more. A hundred, or two hundred, more or less—it didn't mean a goddamned thing to me. As for him, he was going through the whole transaction in a daze. He didn't know how much money he had. All he knew was that he had to keep something aside for Ginette. He wasn't certain yet how much—we were going to figure that out on the way to the station.

In the excitement we had forgotten to change all the money. We were already in the cab, however, and there wasn't any time to be lost. The thing was to find out how we stood. We emptied our pockets quickly and began to whack it up. Some of it was lying on the floor, some of it was on the seat. It was bewildering. There was French, American and English money. And all that chicken feed besides. I felt like picking up the coins and chucking them out of the window—just to simplify matters. Finally we sifted it all out; he held on to the English and American money, and I held on to the French money.

We had to decide quickly now what to do about Ginette—how much to give her, what to tell her, etc. He was trying to fix up a yarn for me to hand her—didn't want her to break her heart and so forth. I had to cut him short.

"Never mind what to tell her," I said. "Leave that to me. How much are you going to *give* her, that's the thing? Why give her anything?"

That was like setting a bomb under his ass. He burst into tears. Such tears! It was worse than before. I thought he was going to collapse on my hands. Without stopping to think, I said: "All right, let's give her all this French money. That ought to last her for a while."

"How much is it?" he asked feebly.

"I don't know—about 2,000 francs or so. More than she deserves anyway."

"Christ! Don't say that!" he begged. "After all, it's a rotten break I'm giving her. Her folks'll never take her back now. No, give it to her. Give her the whole damned business. . . . I don't care what it is."

He pulled a handkerchief out to wipe the tears away. "I can't help it," he said. "It's too much for me." I said nothing. Suddenly he sprawled himself out full length—I thought he was taking a fit or something—and he said: "Jesus, I think I ought to go back. I ought to go back and face the music. If anything should happen to her I'd never forgive myself."

That was a rude jolt for me. "Christ!" I shouted, "you can't do that! Not now. It's too late. You're going to take the train and I'm going to tend to her myself. I'll go see her just as soon as I leave you. Why, you poor boob, if she ever thought you had tried to run away from her she'd murder you, don't you realize that? You can't go back any more. It's settled."

Anyway, what *could* go wrong? I asked myself. Kill herself? *Tant mieux.*

When we rolled up to the station we had still about

twelve minutes to kill. I didn't dare to say good-bye to him yet. At the last minute, rattled as he was, I could see him jumping off the train and scooting back to her. Anything might swerve him. A straw. So I dragged him across the street to a bar and I said: "Now you're going to have a Pernod—your *last* Pernod and I'm going to pay for it . . . with *your* dough."

Something about this remark made him look at me uneasily. He took a big gulp of the Pernod and then, turning to me like an injured dog, he said: "I know I oughtn't to trust you with all that money, but . . . but. . . . Oh, well, do what you think best. I don't want her to kill herself, that's all."

"*Kill herself?*" I said. "Not her! You must think a hell of a lot of yourself if you can believe a thing like that. As for the money, though I hate to give it to her, I promise you I'll go straight to the post office and telegraph it to her. I wouldn't trust myself with it a minute longer than is necessary." As I said this I spied a bunch of post cards in a revolving rack. I grabbed one off—a picture of the Eiffel Tower it was—and made him write a few words. "Tell her you're sailing now. Tell her you love her and that you'll send for her as soon as you arrive. . . . I'll send it by *pneumatique* when I go to the post office. And tonight I'll see her. Everything'll be Jake, you'll see."

With that we walked across the street to the station. Only two minutes to go. I felt it was safe now. At the gate I gave him a slap on the back and pointed to the train. I didn't shake hands with him—he would have slobbered all over me. I just said: "Hurry! She's going in a minute." And with that I turned on my heel and marched off. I didn't even look round to see if he was boarding the train. I was afraid to.

I hadn't thought, all the while I was bundling him off, what I'd do once I was free of him. I had promised a lot of things—but that was only to keep him quiet. As for facing Ginette, I had about as little courage for it as he had. I was getting panicky myself. Everything had happened so quickly that it was impossible to grasp the nature of the situation in full. I walked away from the station in a kind of delicious stupor—with the post card in my hand. I stood against a lamppost and read it over. It sounded preposterous. I read it again, to make sure that I wasn't dreaming, and then I tore it up and threw it in the gutter.

I looked around uneasily, half expecting to see Ginette coming after me with a tomahawk. Nobody was following me. I started walking leisurely toward the Place Lafayette. It was a beautiful day, as I had observed earlier. Light, puffy clouds above, sailing with the wind. The awnings flapping. Paris had never looked so good to me; I almost felt sorry that I had shipped the poor bugger off. At the Place Lafayette I sat down facing the church and stared at the clock tower; it's not such a wonderful piece of architecture, but that blue in the dial face always fascinated me. It was bluer than ever today. I couldn't take my eyes off it.

Unless he were crazy enough to write her a letter, explaining everything, Ginette need never know what had happened. And even if she did learn that he had left her 2,500 francs or so she couldn't prove it. I could always say that he imagined it. A guy who was crazy enough to walk off without even a hat was crazy enough to invent the 2,500 francs, or whatever it was. How much was it, anyhow?, I wondered. My pockets were sagging with the weight of it. I hauled it all out and counted it carefully. There was exactly 2,875 francs and 35 centimes. More than I had thought. The 75 francs and 35 centimes had to be gotten rid of. I wanted an even sum—a clean 2,800 francs. Just then I saw a cab pulling up to the curb. A woman stepped out with a white poodle dog in her hands; the dog was peeing over her silk dress. The idea of taking a dog for a ride got me sore. I'm as good as her dog, I said to myself, and with that I gave the driver a sign and told him to drive me through the Bois. He wanted to know where exactly. "Anywhere," I said. "Go through the Bois, go all around it—and take your time, I'm in no hurry." I sank back and let the houses whizz by, the jagged roofs, the chimney pots, the colored walls, the urinals, the dizzy *carrefours*. Passing the Rond-Point I thought I'd go downstairs and take a leak. No telling what might happen down there. I told the driver to wait. It was the first time in my life I had let a cab wait while I took a leak. How much can you waste that way? Not very much. With what I had in my pocket I could afford to have two taxis waiting for me.

I took a good look around but I didn't see anything worth while. What I wanted was something fresh and unused—something from Alaska or the Virgin Islands. A clean fresh pelt with a natural fragrance to it. Needless to say, there wasn't anything like that walking about. I wasn't terribly disappointed. I didn't give a fuck whether I found anything or not. The thing is, never to be too anxious. Everything comes in due time.

We drove on past the Arc de Triomphe. A few sight-seers were loitering around the remains of the Unknown Soldier. Going through the Bois I looked at all the rich cunts promenading in their limousines. They were whizzing by as if they had some destination. Do that, no doubt, to look important—to show the world how smooth run their Rolls Royces and their Hispano Suizas. Inside me things were running smoother than any Rolls Royce ever ran. It was just like velvet inside. Velvet cortex and velvet vertebrae. And velvet axle grease, what! It's a wonderful thing, for half an hour, to have money in your pocket and piss it away like a drunken sailor. You feel as though the world is yours. And the best part of it is, you don't know what to do with it. You can sit back and let the meter run wild, you can let the wind blow through your hair, you can stop and have a drink, you can give a big tip, and you can swagger off as though it were an everyday occurrence. But you can't create a revolution. You can't wash *all* the dirt out of your belly.

When we got to the Porte d'Auteuil I made him head for the Seine. At the Pont de Sèvres I got out and started walking along the river, toward the Auteuil Viaduct. It's about the size of a creek along here and the trees come right down to the river's bank. The water was green and glassy, especially near the other side. Now and then a scow chugged by. Bathers in tights were standing in the grass sunning themselves. Everything was close and palpitant, and vibrant with the strong light.

Passing a beer garden I saw a group of cyclists sitting at a table. I took a seat nearby and ordered a *demi*. Hearing them jabber away I thought for a moment of Ginette. I saw her stamping up and down the room, tearing her hair, and sobbing and bleating, in that beastlike way of hers. I saw his hat on the rack. I wondered if his clothes would fit me. He had a raglan that I particularly liked. Well, by now he was on his way. In a little while the boat would be rocking under him. English! He wanted to hear English spoken. What an idea!

Suddenly it occurred to me that if I wanted I could go to America myself. It was the first time the opportunity had ever presented itself. I asked myself—"do you want to go?" There was no answer. My thoughts drifted out, toward the sea, toward the other side where, taking a last look back, I had seen the skyscrapers fading out in a flurry of snowflakes. I saw them looming up again, in that same ghostly way as when I left. Saw the lights creeping through their ribs. I saw the whole city spread out, from Harlem to the Battery, the streets choked with ants, the elevated rushing by, the theaters emptying. I wondered in a vague way what ever happened to my wife.

After everything had quietly sifted through my head a great peace came over me. Here, where the river gently winds through the girdle of hills, lies a soil so saturated with the past that however far back the mind roams one can never detach it from its human background. Christ, before my eyes there shimmered such a golden peace that only a neurotic could dream of turning his head away. So quietly flows the Seine that one hardly notices its presence. It is always there, quiet and unobstrusive, like a great artery running through the human body. In the wonderful peace that fell over me it seemed as if I had climbed to the top of a high mountain; for a little while I would be able to look around me, to take in the meaning of the landscape.

Human beings make a strange fauna and flora. From a distance they appear negligible; close up they are apt to appear ugly and malicious. More than anything they need to be surrounded with sufficient space—space even more than time.

The sun is setting. I feel this river flowing through me —its past, its ancient soil, the changing climate. The hills gently girdle it about: its course is fixed.